HIGHLAND JEWEL

CELESTE BARCLAY

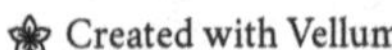 Created with Vellum

THE CLAN SINCLAIR LEGACY

Highland Lion

Highland Bear

Highland Jewel

SUBSCRIBE TO CELESTE'S NEWSLETTER

Subscribe to Celeste's bimonthly newsletter to receive exclusive insider perks.

Have you read *The Highland Ladies Guide*? This FREE first in series is available to all new subscribers to Celeste's monthly newsletter. Subscribe on her website. Subscribe Now

SINCLAIR FAMILY

Liam Sinclair m. Kyla Sutherland

    b. **Callum Sinclair** *m. Siùsan Mackenzie* (SH-IY-oo-san)

        b. Thormud Seamus Magnus Sinclair (TOR-mood SHAY-mus)
        b. Rose Kyla Sinclair
        b. Shona Mary Sinclair

    b. **Alexander Sinclair** *m. Brighde Kerr* (BREE-ju KAIR)

        b. Saoirse Sinead Sinclair (SEER-sha shi-NAYD)
        b. Nessa Elise Sinclair
        b. Mirren Louise Sinclair

    b. **Tavish Sinclair** *m. Ceit Eithne Comyn* (KAIT-ch En-ya CUM-in)

        b. Ailish Elizabeth Sinclair (A-lish)
        b. Tate Henry Sinclair
        b. William "Wiley" Matthew Sinclair

    b. **Magnus Sinclair** *m. Deirdre Fraser* (DEER-dreh FRA-zer)

        b. Blake Magnus Sinclair m. Cerys Kerr (CARE-is KAIR)
        b. Torquil Lachlan Sinclair
        b. Maisie Blair Sinclair

b. ***Mairghread Sinclair*** (Mah-GAID) *m.* *Tristan Mackay*

b. "Wee" Liam Brodie Mackay m. Elene Isbister
b. Alec Daniel Sinclair
b. Hamish Kincaid Sinclair
b. Ainsley Maude Sinclair

PREFACE

Welcome to *The Clan Sinclair Legacy*, a spinoff from my *The Clan Sinclair* series. As you join the second generation of this remarkable family, you may recognize heroes and heroines from the first series. For some of you, it may be a chance to become reacquainted with old friends. For those who haven't read *The Clan Sinclair*, take heart: all of my books can be read as standalones, so you don't have to read the earlier series to enjoy this one. Many readers of the original books wondered what would become of the couples from my *The Highland Ladies* series. Fear not. The children of several of those couples will have their chance to find love with the younger Sinclairs and their Sutherland relatives over the course of my next twenty books.

The Clan Sinclair Legacy takes place roughly twenty years after *The Clan Sinclair* ended and about ten years after the final installment of *The Highland Ladies*. In my first series, I never explicitly stated who ruled Scotland at the time; however, King Robert the Bruce and Queen Elizabeth de Burgh appear throughout *The Highland Ladies*. By the time this new series would take place, the Bruce is dead, and his son, David II, is on the throne.

You will discover more about King David's complicated reign in later books in this new series.

Highland Jewel tells the tale of Brighde and Alex's (*His Highland Prize*) daughter, Saoirse (SEER-sha), and Siùsan's (SH-IY-oo-san) younger brother, Magnus. When I wrote Siùsan and Callum's story (*His Bonnie Highland* Temptation), I didn't know that four years later I would write her younger brother's tale. I thought it was endearing to have two Magnuses toward the end of the book. Then a few months ago, the idea struck me to bring Magnus Mackenzie back as an adult and write an age gap story with one of the second generation Sinclairs.

As I've done in previous books where there are two characters by the same name, usually father and son, the elder is referred to as Mòr, which means greater or bigger, and the younger is referred to as Óg, which means lesser or smaller. In this book, I use the same differentiation. In scenes where both Magnuses appear, I use Mòr and Óg to make it clear. Magnus, our hero, is also referred to as Óg in much of the dialogue, as the characters would have done that if they spoke in real life.

As I often do, I tried to keep the alliances and events true to history. The Mackenzies and the MacLeods of Assynt and of Lewis were enemies. If you've read *His Bonnie Highland Temptation* or *A Devil at the Highland Court*, you've encountered their enmity before. In *Temptation*, I set the Mackenzies and the MacLeods of Assynt against one another through an accident that took Siùsan's mother's life. It also set the stage for the true hostility between Clan Gunn and its surrounding neighbors.

As was the case in real life, the Mackenzies were allied with the Clans Sutherland, Macrae, Matheson, and Mackintosh. Clan Mackenzie and Clan Matheson are believed to have descended from Gilleoin of the Aird, a Gaelic dynast, from the 12th century. This sparked the idea for Magnus's failed betrothal.

If you've read any of my Highlander books, you know the Sinclairs and the Sutherlands are inextricably bound through Liam and Kyla's marriage (*Their Highland Beginning*). This enabled me to include well-loved Sutherland characters in this story. You'll encounter Hamish and Amelia (their story coming in 2023), Lachlan and Arabella (*A Beauty at the Highland Court*), and you'll briefly meet Lachlan and Arabella's sons.

The Mackenzies and Rosses were rival for decades. As I sometimes do, I took creative license with the dates. In 1452, tribes allied with the Mackenzies of Kintail kidnapped the Earl of Ross's relative, which resulted in the Battle of Bealach nam Broig, near the mountain Ben Wyvis. Thirty years later, in 1488, the Mackenzies were defeated by the king's forces and returned to Ross-shire, where they attacked and claimed land from Clan Rose, who were allied with Clan Ross. I mention both clans in this story, and Monty and Donan (*A Hellion at the Highland Court*) have cameos in this story.

Many of you will recognize Eilean Donan, arguably one of the most famous castles in not just Scotland but all of the British Isles. It was the Mackenzies' ancestral home for centuries. They'd settled there by 1297 and remained the protectors and residents until their involvement in the Jacobite rebellions and government ships destroyed much of it in 1719. It has long been claimed that Robert the Bruce sheltered there during the winter of 1306 to 1307; however, contemporary research calls that into question. The keep and its surrounding land were the focus of several encounters between the Mackenzies and Rosses, with the Mackenzies often suffering defeat to the Earls of Ross.

I know that having such a large cast of characters can cause confusion when you join a spinoff series or if it's been a while since you've read the previous series. I'm including a family tree on the next page as a reference. A list of family members and name pronunciations is provided just before this Prologue.

I hope this preface places you in good stead for the story you're about to read. It's been wonderful to revisit the characters from the series that launched my career. I'm thoroughly enjoying introducing readers to the next generation of Highlanders. And for those who had a special place in their hearts for *His Bonnie Highland Temptation*, Callum and Siùsan's daughter, Rose Kyla, will have her story told next, in *His Highland Rose*.

Happy reading,
Celeste

Clan
Sinclair

Liam m. Kyla Sutherland
(*Their Highland Beginning*)

Callum m. Siùsan Mackenzie (*His Bonnie Highland Temptation*)	**Alexander m. Brighde Kerr** (***His Highland Prize***)	Tavish m. Catherine (Ceit) Comyn (*His Highland Surprise*)	Magnus m. Deirdre Fraser (*His Highland Pledge*)	Mairghred m. Tristan Mackay (*His Highland Lass*)
Thormud, Rose Kyla, Shona	**Saoirse, Nessa, Mirren**	Ailish, Tate, William (Wiley)	Blake, Torquil, Maisie	"Wee" Liam, Alec, Hamish, Ainsley

CHAPTER 1

$\mathcal{M}$agnus Mackenzie breathed a sigh of relief as Castle Dunbeath came into view. His second home during the years he fostered with Clan Sinclair, seeing the brick structure on the cliffside felt like slipping on his favorite leine. Three years had passed since he last visited, but it felt like a lifetime. He was eager to see his half-sister, Siùsan, and to visit with the rest of the extended family.

As his gaze swept the surrounding land, a head with white-blonde hair popped out of a heather patch. The hue and waves made him assume it was Brighde, his half-sister's sister-by-marriage. But as he drew closer to the woman picking flowers, he realized it was Saoirse, Brighde and Alexander's daughter. The last time he'd seen her, she was emerging as a young woman, still a bit more gangly than curvy. But the lady who stood before him was breathtaking.

"Magnus?"

Her melodic voice carried on the sea breeze, sending a heated shiver along his spine. She shielded her brown eyes and waved as she recognized him. She said something to her guard, who stood ten feet from her. She lifted her skirts and made her way back to the path. She waited for him with a basket over her bent arm.

"Lady Saoirse, hello."

"We've been expecting ye, but nae until this evening."

"I was impatient to arrive. I'm certain ma men wished I'd developed that virtue."

Magnus glanced back at the three Mackenzie warriors who rode with him and would remain during his visit. The journey forced Magnus to travel across Clan Gunn territory. His family's complicated history with that clan, paired with the ongoing strife between the Sinclairs and them, necessitated him traveling with guards.

Saoirse's tinkling laughter made Magnus want to shift in his saddle. It was doing things to him that hadn't happened since he was a green lad. It had been years since a woman's laughter aroused him so instantaneously.

Control yerself, mon. She's nae more than a lass. A lass ye used to watch over when ye took her and the other weans fishing and swimming. Aye, but she didna look like that. Ye're closer to her da's age than hers, even if ye're more than a decade younger than him.

"What're ye doing outside the gates, ma lady?"

"Ma lady? I'm Saoirse to ye, Magnus."

Something in her tone pricked at Magnus. Was she insulted by his formality? No. She looked hurt. That made his mind spin as he wondered why it affected her so.

"What're ye doing outside the gates, Saoirse?"

When she beamed at him, the heavens opened, and a choir of angels danced upon his shoulders. She was the most beautiful creature he'd ever spied. It was clear she much preferred him using her given name.

"Gathering flowers for ma medicinals."

Magnus's brow furrowed. She looked healthy.

"Yer medicinals? Do ye ail?"

Her tinkling laughter once again made him want to shift in his saddle. The weight of his sporran against his arousal was uncomfortable, but it was all that kept the world from seeing his reaction to the young woman.

"Nay. I'm the clan's healer." Her smile faded as she looked past Magnus and his men, as though she could see something in the distance that no one else could. "Aileen passed last year from an ague that swept the clan. She exhausted herself tending to those who needed us, and in the end, she hadn't the strength to fight the illness. Since then, I've been the one tending to those who are poorly or injured."

Magnus recalled Saoirse had always been interested in the healing arts and apprenticed with Aileen. But he hadn't imagined she would take on that role. As Laird Liam Sinclair's granddaughter, he supposed he'd assumed she would marry and leave Dunbeath. As he watched her walk to his horse's head and pat the beast's neck, he realized how grateful he was that she was still here.

He swung down from his horse and drew the reins over his steed's head. When he stood next to Saoirse, he reached out his free hand.

"May I carry that for ye?"

"It's nae heavy, but thank ye."

He watched her cheeks pinken as she passed the basket to him. Freckles from being outside smattered her fair skin. He studied them, finding patterns. When they moved along the path toward the village and keep, it dawned on Magnus that he'd assumed she was through with her task.

"Saoirse, would ye allow me to accompany ye if ye arenae done?"

"Ye dinna need to ask, Magnus. I ken ye havenae been here in three years, but yer formality feels—odd."

Her cheeks darkened further as she looked toward the castle's barmekin. He knew she regretted being so forward, but three years ago, there wouldn't have been a hesitation on his part. He'd been a man by then, but she'd still seemed more like a child than someone who needed a chaperone with him.

Magnus turned back to his men and gave them instructions to tend to his horse and present themselves to Alexander, Saoirse's father and captain of the clan's guard. Callum, Alex's older brother and the oldest of his generation, was the clan's tánaiste and Laird Liam Sinclair's heir. Callum was also Magnus's brother-by-marriage. He figured Callum was likely meeting with Liam since it was mid-afternoon. Magnus nodded to Saoirse's guard as they made their way back into the heather field. As the prickly flowers jabbed at the bare section of skin above the top of his boots and below the hem of his plaid, he reconsidered the wisdom of his offer. But he couldn't stop himself from asking to join her.

"Mayhap this wasna such a good idea, Magnus. These must poke ye something dreadful. It's why Albert stays on the path when I come out here. Ma skirts protect me."

"Dinna fash. As long as they arenae nettles, then I'm fine."

They may as bluidy well be nettles. They bluidy hurt.

Saoirse watched him as though she waited for him to reconsider. Instead, he pulled a *sgian dubh* from his boot and bent to cut a stalk low to the ground. He held it up before putting it in the basket he still carried.

"I dinna ken if ye need the stems this long."

Saoirse cursed her fair skin because she knew she must look like a summer apple the way she blushed.

She shook her head as she gathered her tongue-tied ideas. She found it difficult to concentrate on her flower gathering, with Magnus standing so close.

"I dinna need them quite that long. Aboot half that much stem will work. Thank ye."

She looked back down at the patch within which she stood. If she didn't focus on her task, she was liable to slice her fingers off with her own *sgian dubh*. She recalled thinking Magnus was a handsome man with his light brown hair, but never had her body betrayed her by reacting so viscerally. Recalling why he visited was a bucket of cold water. He was family, even if not by blood. He was her aunt's younger brother, and not a man to make doe-eyes at.

She opted to put some distance between them as she walked a few feet away and turned her back to him. She nearly jumped out of her skin five minutes later when he stepped behind her and reached around to present the basket to her. She'd held the blooms she collected in her skirt. She dropped all of them as she twisted to find Magnus close enough for her nose to rest against his chest. She tilted her head back, his height blocking the sun from her whisky-brown eyes. Their gazes locked, and they stared until a throat clearing reminded them that they stood in Albert's full view, along with anyone standing on the wall walk. Saoirse glanced at Albert, but he was looking at the battlements.

Magnus and Saoirse turned to follow Albert's gaze, and Saoirse fought the urge to cringe. Her father stood with his arms crossed, staring down at them. She was certain he'd planted his feet hip-width apart, since all the men in her family adopted that stance whenever they—breathed. It was as natural to them as standing upright, but they did it purposely to intimidate. People knew Highlanders for their height and physique, but the Sinclair men were mighty oaks, while every other man was a sapling. Except for Magnus, who Saoirse realized rivaled her father in size.

"Welcome, Magnus." Alex's voice boomed from above. The tone sounded welcoming, but his expression didn't share that sentiment.

"Hello, Alex." Magnus nodded before looking back at Saoirse. "I didna mean to startle Lady Saoirse. I'll pick up what ma lady dropped and walk back with her."

Alex merely nodded, but his attention remained riveted on his daughter and his clan's guest. He'd known Magnus since he was a lad of two-and-ten. He'd arrived at Castle Dunbeath twenty-three years earlier, when Saoirse hadn't even been born. He and Brighde had only been married a few weeks.

Magnus was quick to gather the scattered plant cuttings before they turned toward the gate. Albert trailed behind them, and Magnus felt the man's silent disapproval. He'd known Albert since he arrived two decades ago. They were the same age at five-and-thirty. He had done nothing wrong, but the temptation had been far too strong. It unsettled him that he'd been so ready to kiss the young woman who he should still think of as more a child than an adult. But nothing about Saoirse's appearance or demeanor made him think of a child. A shy young woman, yes. A child in need of sheltering, no. Then again, perhaps she was a woman in need of sheltering from him. He would have to curb his interest lest he cause a rift between the Sinclairs and him.

"Óg!"

A wave of strawberry-blonde hair flew behind his sister as she raced down the front steps. Siùsan opened her arms and launched herself at her younger brother once she was within arms' reach. She kissed his cheek as he lifted her off her feet.

"It's good to see ye, Siùsan. Seamus and I miss ye fiercely. Ye ken I would have come sooner if I could have."

He placed her back on her feet as Callum and Liam emerged from the keep. Callum wrapped his arm around his wife's waist and kissed her temple. She placed her hands over his and looked back, beaming.

"It's good to see ye, Óg. We've missed ye and Seamus." Liam extended his arm, which Magnus clasped around the older man's forearm in a warrior handshake.

"Ma brother wishes he could come, but ye ken things havenae been easy lately. It wouldnae be wise for us both to travel so far afield." As the younger of the two brothers, Magnus served as Clan Mackenzie's tánaiste, while Seamus was their laird. Magnus's older nephew was only five, so he was far too young to assume the duties of the heir and the clan's second-in-command.

Magnus looked toward Liam, Callum, and Siùsan, but he knew the moment Saoirse moved away from the group. He wanted to watch where she went and what she did, but he knew it would be far too obvious. He didn't doubt Alex was still observing him. He was certain when a heavy hand landed on his shoulder and squeezed. To others, it appeared a warm welcome, but Magnus felt it for what it was. A warning.

"It's good to see ye, Óg. Ye dinna look any different from ye did when ye left here five-and-ten years ago at a ripe auld age of twenty." Alex grinned, but there was little humor in his dark eyes. It was a not-so-subtle reminder to Magnus that he'd been barely younger than Saoirse was now when he finished his fostering and was considered man enough to help run the clan.

"I canna believe it's been that long, yet nae seeing ye in three years has been an eternity." Siùsan wrapped her arm around her brother's arm, playfully batting away Callum's when he pretended not to let her go. They'd been married two and a half decades, but they were still as attached to one another as when they fell in love. All the married couples in the Sinclair family were the same, including Saoirse's parents. Magnus watched Brighde and Saoirse join the group. Alex wrapped his arm around Brighde's shoulders as she smiled up to her husband. Magnus looked between mother and daughter, and if he hadn't known better, he would have thought them to be twins and Saoirse's age.

"Óg!"

Magnus turned and grinned. He stepped around Callum and Liam, holding out his arm. The bear of a man who greeted him, ignored the proffered arm, and pulled Magnus in for an embrace.

"Mòr, it's good to see ye."

Both men shared the same given name, so when Seamus and the younger Magnus moved to Dunbeath to foster, both Magnuses adopted nicknames to keep them separate. The older Magnus went by Mòr, which translated to greater or bigger, and the younger Magnus adopted Óg, which meant lesser. The youngest of four brothers and the fourth of five children, Mòr volunteered himself as his foster brothers' mentor. Everyone teased that he was happy to no longer be the youngest male in the family. He never denied the claim's truth.

"It's been too long. I'm glad ye've finally come to visit."

"It hasnae been an easy three years."

Saoirse watched her family, and she wondered what Magnus meant. She knew from her aunt that the Mackenzies suffered a wave of illnesses that claimed many lives, and there'd been ongoing strife with the Sinclairs' distant relatives-by-marriage, the Rosses. But

Magnus seemed to mean more, even if he said nothing else.

"Come inside. I'll have a bath brought up for ye." Siùsan served as the chatelaine, even though she didn't carry the title of Lady Sinclair yet. With Liam still alive, Siùsan wouldn't adopt the title until Callum became laird. But Liam's beloved wife, Kyla, died while Callum, Alex, Tavish, Magnus Mòr, and Mairghread were still young. "Saoirse can show ye yer chamber. It isnae the one ye're used to. Now that Blake and Cerys are married, we had to make some changes."

"I look forward to meeting Cerys. Yer family tree is —complicated." Magnus grinned as he looked at Mòr, then Brighde. Magnus Mòr and Deirdre's son married Brighde's half-niece the summer before. There was no blood relation, but there was a blood feud between the Sinclairs and the Kerrs because of Brighde's marriage to Alex. From everyone's expression, there'd been no resolution. He suspected a second marriage between the Kerrs and Sinclairs only antagonized the Kerrs more.

"Aye. Complicated." Alex gestured toward the stairs while everyone else went their separate ways. "Saoirse, help your mama. I'll show Óg the way."

"Thank ye. I look forward to seeing Dedric. Are he and Lady Isabella here?" Dedric Hartley and his wife, Isabella, joined the Clan Sinclair twenty years ago. They'd left their lives near the border and moved to the Highlands to avoid the ever-ongoing conflict between Scotland and England.

"Aye."

Óg expected little more from Alex, since he was the most reserved of the four Sinclair brothers. But Óg planned to do most of the talking, so Alex couldn't admonish him for paying Saoirse attention.

"Where are Thormud and Tate? I look forward to

seeing them in the lists tomorrow." Thormud was Callum's heir, and Tate was Tavish and Ceit's older son. When Blake and Torquil, Mòr and Deirdre's sons, joined the other two cousins, there was always trouble. Tor and Thor loved living up to their mythological namesake. Óg enjoyed watching the four boys when they were weans. They'd been lively since they were born. He'd been at Dunbeath for Thormud's, Tate's, and Blake's births. He'd already returned home when Torquil was born. But he'd visited often enough to know the young men well.

"They're in the lists. Ye'll see them at the evening meal."

"The laird looks well. How is he keeping?"

"Fitter than most of us."

In his sixth decade, Liam could still be confused for his sons, especially Tavish, since they shared the same barrel-chested build. He continued to train daily and rode into battle last summer in France to aid Blake and Cerys.

"I'm as excited to see Siùsan as she is to see me. I miss ma sister despite how long we've lived apart."

"Aye. It has been more than a score since ye left here a mon."

Magnus nearly swallowed his tongue at that pointed comment. Fortunately, they reached the chamber on the third story, and they could hear servants coming up the back stairway. They remained quiet while two men rolled the enormous wood and copper tub into the chamber. Since all the Sinclair men stood nearly six-and-a-half feet tall and were as broad at Ben Nevis, they needed tubs large enough to fit them. That they liked to share baths with their wives was a bonus. Magnus appreciated the size, since he wasn't a small man, either. Women filled it with hot water, leaving two more buckets within reach and on the hearth. Magnus looked forward to a long soak.

"Thank ye." Magnus smiled graciously at the servants, and two of the women offered coy smiles he understood. He paid no attention. The last thing he needed was for Alex to imagine he would accept any offer after he'd just seen Magnus with his daughter. "I'll see ye at the evening meal, Alex."

Alex nodded before he turned away. Magnus thought the older man may have thawed—slightly—after seeing Magnus ignore the maids. He didn't want Alex to believe he chased any skirt that swished past him. The moment the door closed behind Alex, Magnus stripped and stepped into the tub. The steam wafted around him as he curled enough to slide his shoulders beneath the surface. It felt like the first time in nearly two years since he'd had a moment of peace. No one hounded him. No one guilted him. No one expected anything of him. When he tipped his head back to rest against the rim, he nearly fell asleep. A knock at the door roused him.

"Aye?"

"It's me." Siùsan stood on the other side of the portal.

"Give me a minute. I dozed off. Let me get clean and put on some clothes." Magnus hurried to wash his hair and pour fresh water over it before he scrubbed the grime from his journey from his skin. He was out of the tub and wrapping a clean plaid around his waist in two minutes. He walked to the door and opened it for his sister.

"Weary? Would ye prefer a tray in here and an early night?"

"Nay. I wish to see everyone. It's been a nice respite to have an hour to maself, but I'm ready to visit our family." Family. Saoirse was already family. He needed to remind himself of that before he found himself at the end of Alex's, or any of the Sinclair men's, sword.

"It was nice of ye to walk Saoirse back. She's convinced Alex that one guard is enough, but ma sisters and I worry." Magnus knew the women who married the Sinclair brothers considered themselves sisters with no qualifier. In turn, it felt like he'd gained three other sisters, plus Mairghread Mackay, who was the fifth of the older generation's Sinclair siblings. That meant Saoirse was more a niece than a woman to ogle.

"Is there reason to fear her going outside the wall with only one guard?"

"Ye saw her. She's more than just bonnie. Her blonde hair is too recognizable as one of the laird's granddaughters. She could easily be a target."

"Does Shona go out with more guards?" Shona was the youngest of Siùsan's three children, the twins Thormud and Rose Kyla being barely a year older than Shona. She shared the strawberry-blonde hair she inherited from Siùsan's MacLeod family.

"That lass shall be the death of me. She's more Mairghread's child than mine. She inherited a wild streak from her aunt. She and Maisie are a right pair. They can still keep up with the lads. I dinna ken what Deirdre and Mòr are going to do with her because I havenae a clue how to tame Shona."

From the smile on Siùsan's face, he knew no one intended to tame either of the lasses. His niece was a spitfire, despite how she'd been a quiet child. She'd grown into her personality. Magnus looked forward to his nephew and two nieces. He wondered if Thormud was as large as Callum now that he'd entered true manhood. At four-and-twenty, Magnus figured his nephew had likely stopped growing.

"They're all waiting belowstairs. Everyone's eager to see ye. We thought ye might have drowned."

"Nay. Just too comfortable in the hot water. Give me another minute, and I'll be down." Siùsan stretched to kiss her brother's cheek before leaving so he could dress. He joined her in the passageway.

As Magnus reached the last three steps to the Great Hall, he looked across the enormous gathering hall and spied the four Sinclair brothers and their father. All five men stood in the Sinclair stance—feet hip-width apart and arms crossed—and watched Magnus approach.

What the bluidy hell did Alex already say to them?

CHAPTER 2

Saoirse observed the wave flow through the men in her family. Some of her male cousins noticed their father's stance, and it was the catalyst for them to broaden their legs and cross their arms. It was like telepathy. Half of them weren't even facing their father or uncles. She scanned the gathering clan members to see what prompted the intimidating response. She noticed Magnus immediately. It was like a magnet drew her to him. She glanced back at her father, grandfather, and uncles. They all watched Magnus descend the stairs with her aunt Siùsan.

"Saoirse, stop staring." Rose Kyla whispered. She was only a few months older than Saoirse, so they'd always felt more like sisters than cousins.

"I'm nae."

"Ye are. And ye're practically drooling. If yer da sees ye, Óg'll be dead before morning."

"He saw us in the heather field. I was picking flowers when Óg arrived, and he offered to help. Da noticed us standing too close, but it was an accident. He came to gather the flowers I needed to put in the basket he carried. It startled both of us when I turned around."

"Yer da isnae a daft mon, Saoirse. Watch yerself."

"It's naught. It just surprised me to see how different he is from three years ago."

"There's naught different aboot him. Ye're the one who's different. Ye werenae thinking aboot men three years ago. Ye were too busy learning all ye could from Aileen."

Saoirse turned her attention away from Magnus and to her cousin. She considered Rose's observation and realized Rose was right. It was only within the last few months that she wondered who and when she would marry. The older generation promised all the second-generation love matches rather than arranged marriages. The first generation were all devoted to their spouses and as in love as they were the day they married—likely even more. They wished the same for their children. But no one sparked Saoirse's interest. At least, not before Magnus helped her pick heather that afternoon.

She made her way to the dais, which carpenters had expanded four times over the years to accommodate the laird's ever-expanding family. Many of the cousins sat among their friends at meals, but when guests arrived, they crowded the table. There were nearly forty people seated at the rectangle formed by four tables. Saoirse sat between Rose and Ailish, Tavish and Ceit's daughter. It placed her across from Magnus Óg. Saoirse smiled to their guest before she turned to listen to Ailish.

Magnus observed Saoirse as she laughed with her cousins seated on either side of her. It jarred Magnus to realize so many of the children he'd known were now adults. No longer would anyone ask him to supervise them at the loch or beach. He wouldn't teach any of the lads how to fish or shoot a slinger while hunting. It was a bittersweet moment as he suddenly felt more like a guest than family. He shifted his gaze to his sister, who watched him intently. She'd raised him until she left home to marry Callum. Theirs was the only arranged marriage since Liam married Kyla Sutherland and began their dynasty.

Siùsan had protected Seamus and him from their parents' discord and ambivalence toward their sons. His parents barely recognized Siùsan as the old Laird Mackenzie's daughter, despite her legitimacy. Their father hadn't even watched Siùsan ride away from their keep when she left for Castle Dunbeath. Within two months, she and Callum returned under less than auspicious circumstances, but they departed for Dunbeath with Seamus and him as foster-children. They were there under the guise of training to be warriors and leaders, but the Sinclairs adopted them. He and Seamus dragged their feet about returning to Clan Mackenzie and their father. If they hadn't been the laird's sons, they would have asked to join Clan Sinclair.

"Óg, how goes yer betrothal? Have ye set a date?" Magnus watched as Saoirse's gaze darted to him, even though she was turned to Rose. He didn't want to answer Ceit's question, but he had no choice.

"I'm nae betrothed anymore. It fell through." He suddenly felt like he needed to explain to Saoirse before he did anyone else. He didn't owe anyone an explanation, but it embarrassed him that Ceit brought it up in front of everyone.

"That's a pity," Brighde said with a sympathetic smile.

"Nay, it wasna. It was a blessing." Magnus offered a tight smile before he turned to speak to Torquil. Luckily, the man was too eager to regale him with the story of how his brother, Blake, met his bride at court. Magnus tried to follow the tale, but he sat with an even heavier heart than when the meal began. As soon as it was over, he hastened to his chamber and locked the door. Once in bed, he stared at the ceiling. Two questions shattered the sense of respite. He had told no one since it happened a moon ago. He'd figured he'd have a little more time before he had to discuss it. He should have prepared himself for it to be among the first pieces of news his extended family would want.

By the time he drifted to sleep, he wondered if he'd erred in coming here. He felt unsettled and slept worse than the nights spent on the ground. He felt like he'd nodded off only minutes before the sun rose for all the rest he'd gotten. He dragged himself belowstairs for a bowl of porridge before venturing to the lists.

"Óg!"

Magnus turned to find Kirk Hartley and Blake waving to him. Kirk was Dedric and Isabella's son He shared his mother's white-blonde hair, while his twin sister, Keira, and their younger sister, Sarah, inherited Ric's darker locks. Before Kirk was born, the only two people he'd ever met with such fair hair were Brighde and Isabella, and they weren't related. The thatch of light-colored locks made him think of Saoirse, who'd avoided him that morning. He'd received a perfunctory nod and smile before she hurried from the Great Hall. He'd returned the barely there greeting and wondered if he'd imagined everything from yesterday, but he realized she was being discreet. There were too many people at the morning meal for him to appear like a lovesick pup. Once he joined the men at the hearth the night before, he realized they'd adopted their intimidating stance in jest. At least, most of them. He wasn't certain about Alex.

"I challenge ye first." Blake was the second largest man in the clan after his father, Magnus Mòr. It was only by a hair's breadth that Mòr and Blake outsized the others, but they had legs like tree trunks and appeared as unmovable as the Cairngorm Mountains. Blake's younger brother, Torquil, was nearly the same size at two years Blake's junior.

Kirk followed his father's warrior build, but he wasn't as tall or broad as the Sinclairs. He was one of the quieter young men, but he was a keen observer. Magnus often wondered what Kirk thought about everyone. He suspected Kirk would share insights that no one else noticed.

"Ye sure ye wish to start yer morning on yer arse? Yer bonnie bride might pass by." Magnus elbowed the younger man.

"She likes ma arse just fine, so I dinna mind." Blake grinned, then flushed, his whisky-brown eyes closing for a protracted blink. Magnus looked toward the lists' entrance, which Blake faced. His bride scowled at him before laughing. She walked away, shaking her head.

"Ye should think before ye speak one of these days." Kirk clapped his friend on the back. "Why she married ye is anyone's guess."

"Oh?" Magnus learned some of the story last night, but he didn't recall hearing anything about Blake miss-peaking.

"Aye. I spotted her in Stirling Caste's bailey just after we arrived. I may have made an inopportune comment that she heard while I watched her walking by."

"Inopportune?" Kirk howled. It was his turn to shake his head. "That's nae how Torquil tells it."

"Tor has a big mouth." Blake frowned, but mirth danced in his eyes.

"Now I must ken what ye said."

"I might have said, 'All I want is an ale and a willing wench' while ma family and I were in the stables. Then I might have also said, 'I wouldnae mind that one' as Cerys walked by. I didna think she would hear me."

"Ye didna?"

"Aye, Óg. She wasna too impressed with me at first. As handsome as she kenned I was, she thought me a wee bossy when I took issue with her leaving the keep at night without a guard. I understood she was helping someone, but I might have been a wee heavy-handed."

"She must have liked ye well enough to talk to ye more than once." Magnus waggled his eyebrows.

"That she does." Magnus watched Blake's gaze soften as it followed Cerys across the bailey until she was out of sight. A pang of envy surged through him. He wondered if he would ever find someone who softened his warrior heart as much as Cerys had Blake's. He'd escaped a marriage destined to fail, so he'd known it wouldn't have happened if he'd followed that path.

Magnus Mòr walked over to the trio. "Are ye going to stand around clishmaclavering, or are ye going to train? Blake, ye're with me."

"I already challenged Óg, Da."

Mòr's eyebrows rose as he fought to suppress his smile. His son was battle tested and skilled, but he didn't have Óg's years of experience. Mòr nodded and stepped back. The two men took their positions as they studied one another. They went on the attack, their swords clashing and the sound of steel ringing in their ears. Óg knew Mòr watched him as much as he did his son. While Óg trained with all the Sinclair warriors when he'd fostered there, Mòr had been his mentor. He could see the same training coming through Blake's strategy. It soon became a battle of strength, since they could read each other's intentions like they were their own.

Sweat poured from both men's foreheads, and their leines soon stuck to their chests and backs, the sleeves strained over the bulging muscles. Each time the swords met, the force from Blake's swing reverberated through Óg's arms and down his spine. He hadn't expected how much strength he would need to wield to hold his own against the younger man. This wasn't the boy he remembered. It ended in a draw when both men wound up on their arses, the force of their swords pushing against their opponent sending them sailing.

"I told ye, ye would wind up on yer arse."

"Aye, and I have a bonnie wife to tend to ma bruises. Ye have—a salve?" Blake came to his feet as Óg rose to his. Both men walked to the water barrel, each grabbing a ladle. First drinking from it, then pouring water over their heads.

"Ye still talk as much shite as ye did when ye barely came to ma chest." Magnus bumped his shoulder against Blake's. The sense of alienation Magnus felt the night before slipped away. He felt at home on the training field. He'd spent countless hours on the grassy expanse. He knew every dip and rut, every worn patch of dirt. There were still times when the Mackenzie keep felt more like a place to lay his head, but the Sinclair keep felt like home.

"Ye remembered everything I taught ye." Mòr joined the pair.

"He isnae that auld that his memory fails him. He's still younger than ye, Da." Blake teased. Both Magnuses filled a ladle and dumped it over Blake. "It's something aboot the name."

The trio returned to the sparring warriors and found new partners. It still fascinated Magnus to watch the Sinclair brothers partner while Liam called out instructions. Even in their forties, the four men listened to their father's corrections. It began with the same partners as always: Callum and Alex, and Tavish and the older Magnus. It was a choreographed battle that was never quite the same. Intuition seemed to tell the men when to switch. Callum and Mòr paired, while

Tavish and Alex dueled. A few minutes later, it shifted again. Callum and Tavish, while Alex and Mòr battled. It was awe-inspiring when Liam joined the mix, rotating between the pairs as an opponent while the brothers defended together.

"It never gets auld, does it?" Blake watched while standing beside Magnus Óg.

"Nay, it doesnae. But I think ye, Torquil, Thormud, and Tate will soon be like that."

Alex was the only one to have no sons. But he doted on his daughters Saoirse, Mirren, and Nessa. A man couldn't be prouder of his children, and the entire clan valued women as much as they did any man. Thinking about that made Magnus wonder where Saoirse was.

Ye need to be rid of those thoughts. Naught will come of it except disappointment and trouble.

The men took their midday meal in the lists and didn't return to the keep until the evening meal. Magnus found himself seated among the male cousins as they teased one another about the day's training and planned a hunting party the next day.

Saoirse spent the day tending to four sick village children. They'd all eaten berries they shouldn't have, and their bellies punished them worse than their mothers. She'd ministered to them as she gave them medicinals to flush their systems from both ends. It wasn't a part of her job that she relished. But, the families were grateful by evening when their children appeared no worse for wear.

When she returned to the keep, she felt filthy and exhausted. Two of the four were worse than the others, and she'd feared for their lives since they were the smallest and had eaten the most. She retired to the chamber she shared with her sisters and welcomed the bath her mother ordered. She was washing her hair when her sisters entered.

"Did ye hear aboot Óg and Blake today?"

Saoirse looked over her shoulder as Nessa spoke, but she realized her sister spoke to Mirren.

"Aye. Apparently, a lot of the men stopped to watch. From what I heard, Uncle Magnus watched them like a new father, beaming at them both. At least until they knocked each other down. Tate said Uncle Magnus was grinning one moment, the next, back to being the surly warrior Da and our uncles always are."

"They're nae surly," Saoirse said as she rose from the tub. She giggled as Mirren handed her a towel. "They're foreboding." She deepened her voice for the last word. Her sisters joined in her giggles. Nessa was four years younger than Saoirse, and Mirren was seven years younger than her. At eighteen and fifteen, Saoirse knew the girls still had a tendency toward silliness, but she also knew they noticed the lads. She waited to see if either of them commented on Magnus.

"I dinna remember Óg being so handsome," Mirren observed. And there it was. Saoirse kept her whisky-hued eyes down while she dried herself. She knew every single woman in the clan over the age of two-and-ten noticed him last night. It embarrassed her how jealous she was, and it disappointed her when she thought he was betrothed. She wanted to know why he sounded so relieved that it fell through. She wondered if he had a sweetheart at home that he preferred. She knew he'd watched her as he answered her aunt's questions.

"What do ye think, Saoirse?" Nessa handed her a comb to run through her tresses.

"Auntie Siùsan and her brothers are all good looking. It runs in their family." She hoped it would be evasive enough.

"But Auntie Siùsan and Óg arenae the same kind of good looking, dinna ye think?"

"I suppose." Saoirse shrugged as she turned her back to fetch a gown from the armoire. She remained facing the tall piece of furniture as she waited for the heat to leave her cheeks. She didn't want her sisters to see. They weren't as fair as her, and they shared their father's deep chestnut colored hair. If they blushed, few people could tell. Everyone knew when Saoirse felt flushed.

By the time she and her sisters arrived in the Great Hall, she felt calmer. But the moment she noticed Magnus, her heart fluttered. He seemed more attractive every time she saw him. She chalked it up to a young woman's infatuation. She kept herself occupied during the meal, telling herself that she wanted to hear her cousins' and sisters' chatter, but it was to keep from glancing down the table. She and Magnus sat at opposite ends, but once more, they faced each other. Was her aunt tormenting her with the seating arrangements? Or did Magnus choose to sit far from her? She chided herself as she realized that her family had naturally separated themselves by gender, mostly because the men wanted to chat with Magnus. The meal felt interminable.

CHAPTER 3

"*L*ady Saoirse?" Magnus approached her four days after he arrived. He'd spied her heave an overflowing basket onto her bent arm. "May I help ye?"

They hadn't approached each other in the days since his arrival, and it frustrated him. With each passing day, Saoirse seemed less inclined to even say hello. He wondered if she believed him disinterested, or if he'd imagined any interest at all. He still knew it was a horrible idea, but he couldn't help himself.

"Thank ye, Óg." Saoirse looked around before nodding. She hated that she grew nervous being seen with Magnus. It should be ridiculous for her to worry, but things had settled down in the past three days since his arrival. She didn't want to cause a further stir. "I'm taking them to ma workroom."

Saoirse hadn't moved into Aileen's croft when the older woman died, so Siùsan offered her a storage building to serve as her apothecary and place to see the poorly or injured. She enjoyed having a quiet space to herself. There were few within the keep or bailey. She could shut the door to the outside world as she worked.

Magnus followed her once he lifted the basket from her arm. She noticed the weight didn't register with

Magnus while it practically pulled her off balance. She pushed open the door and drew back the small window covering. It allowed plenty of light into the small building, but the hanging rabbit hides also offered privacy for patients. She pointed to a table in the center of the single room. It served as both an examining table and a workstation. He recognized the lingering scent of lavender and heather when he saw the plants hanging from a rafter. It was the same scent Saoirse wore. He identified only a handful of the plants, so he was curious to learn more.

"When did ye start training with Aileen? I never realized ye spent so much time with her."

"I was aboot four-and-ten when I realized how much the healing arts interest me. It wasna until I was seven-and-ten that ma parents felt I was ready to assist Aileen with more than a simple cough or minor wound. Once they allowed me to do more, I spent every day with her. I learned quickly because it fascinated me, and I enjoy helping people. It makes me feel good to ken I helped them feel good."

"What's the worst thing ye've treated?" Magnus sat on a stool while Saoirse moved around the room, putting away dried flowers she removed from the rafter's hanging strings.

"I had to stitch a lad's leg after a dog bit nearly clean through. I could see the bone. I feared he would lose it. Even if he kept it, I worried he would forever have a limp. His father's a guard, and that's what he wished to become. It took weeks of tending to it, keeping any infection from setting in. Then it took weeks for him to learn how to walk again properly. But he kept the leg and chases around with the other weans."

"That must have been vera hard. I dinna ken that I could watch a child in such pain and still pay attention to ma work."

"It's never easy to see anyone in pain, but it breaks ma heart when it's a wean. He hadnae done aught but surprise the hound while it was eating. Thormud had to put the animal down, since none of the parents trusted it around their children. I think that pained Thor as much as the stitching pained the wean. But Thor volunteered. He was the one to pry the dog from the lad."

"Ye have a generous heart, Saoirse."

"I try." Saoirse focused on the chamomile she ground with a pestle and mortar. She knew her face grew red.

As much as Magnus didn't want to leave, he knew he shouldn't linger. He rose from his stool, and Saoirse looked up, surprised. "I should leave ye to yer work."

"Ye dinna have to." Saoirse's cheeks glowed brighter, embarrassed at her own forthrightness. But she enjoyed their conversation. Magnus hesitated before returning to the stool. "Do ye have a healer on yer lands?"

"We have several, but they all live in the villages far from the keep. Our healer died during one of the early waves of sickness. It's likely why so many others did. Nay one kenned how to treat the poorly. Caroline did as best she could with the knowledge she had, but it wasna nearly enough."

"There was nay one who could help?"

"Nay. We needed them among their neighbors. And we did what we could to keep people from leaving their homes. It only got worse when clan members visited loved ones in other places."

"That must have been vera hard to enforce."

"It was. Our chiefs saved hundreds of lives by ensuring the rule was followed. But there were always a few who disregarded it. I ken they felt they didna have any choice but to help their family or friends. However, it only made the contagion spread."

Magnus aged before Saoirse's eyes as he recalled his hellacious past two and a half years. He forced his smile, and she scrambled to think of another topic.

"Do ye remember when Tate was seven and thought it was a fine idea to tie a rope to the branch over the rocks at the loch's edge? He was brave enough to swing out from it, but once he was over the water, he couldnae let go."

"Aye. I remember. I heard everyone's cheers and taunts from the lists."

"It was a good thing ye came to investigate."

"Aye. I caught him when he swung back over the rocks. But before I could do aught to cut down the rope, Ainsley stuck out her tongue and leaped. She didna hesitate to drop into the water. Shona was right behind her."

"Ye had to convince the lads nae to torment Tate."

"I understood why he froze."

"Do ye really have a fear of heights?"

"I did as a lad. I outgrew it, but I kenned how Tate felt. Blessedly, he wasna the same size back then. I dinna ken if I could catch him now without him knocking us both into the loch." Magnus grinned.

He'd been visiting with Seamus the day the misadventure at the loch had happened. It was during the same visit that they learned what their father had done to the MacLeods of Assynt. Siùsan's cousin from her mother's side, Michail MacLeod, was there. He and Seamus created a truce, but it was also the visit that signaled the end of his father's lairdship. Condemned for the deadly raid, the clan council ousted the old laird and initiated Seamus into his place. His father died within days.

"That wasna an easy visit after that day, was it?"

"Nay, it wasna. I thought Aidan was going to slay me in the bailey when he arrived. His news shocked

Seamus and me to the core. It felt like the ultimate betrayal by our father. He'd sent us here, so he could send that raiding party without us kenning. He kenned we would have stopped him." Magnus shook his head. He had no fond memories of his parents. That was a source of great hurt when he'd fostered among the Sinclairs. Everywhere he turned, there were doting parents, and none were his. Even at his age now, he knew that wound hadn't completely healed.

"Yer father must have been a hard mon to live with." Saoirse kept her voice soft. She knew her aunt's history with her clan of birth. Siùsan rarely spoke of her life before she arrived at Dunbeath to marry Callum. She only did when she spoke about her brothers.

"He was an example of what I will never be. I would never lead like him, and I would never be the father he was."

Saoirse kept her gaze on the work in front of her. "Do ye wish to be a father?"

Magnus wanted nothing more than to spin Saoirse around, lift her onto the table, push back her skirts, and sink into her so they could start trying for a family of their own. "Aye. It wasna the right time before. The right woman wasna in ma life."

Saoirse glanced up and found Magnus watching her intently. Their eyes met, and heat sparked between them. When she caught her finger between the pestle and mortar, she grimaced. She brought it to her mouth and sucked. She witnessed Magnus swallow as he fisted his hands at his side. She hadn't thought her action was sexual, but it was clear he found it arousing. That only made her more aroused.

"I'm distracting ye. I will take ma leave. Let me ken when ye have another basket to carry." Magnus flashed her a smile and practically sprinted to the door. He looked back to find Saoirse appearing curious, but she merely nodded. Once he was outside, he made his way to the loch. He stripped and plunged into the water. When he surfaced, he looked around to ensure no one could spy him. He took himself in hand as he pictured Saoirse's mouth around his cock instead of around her finger.

Saoirse listened to one of the village children speaking to his father. "Óg said he would take us fishing."

The man nodded, and the boy ran to join the others at the postern gate. It was two days after their conversation in her workroom. They'd danced together the night before, but only when the partner changes put them together. They chatted when they could. Magnus regaled her with a story about Kirk finally knocking his father, Dedric, from his feet in the lists. He suspected Dedric hadn't put up as much resistance as he might, but he'd been proud of his son's accomplishment. They kept being interrupted, so Magnus could only tell the story in spurts, but Saoirse hung on every word.

"Lady Saoirse, will ye come?" Saoirse found Timmy, the milliner's son, pulling on her hand. "Ye make the fish jump into the basket."

"I dinna quite do that." Saoirse laughed. She enjoyed fishing because of the solitude most of the time. It wasn't a pastime encouraged among women in most clans, but Liam couldn't deny his granddaughters what he'd allowed Mairghread to do. If any of the lasses took interest in fishing, hunting, climbing trees, and swimming, the family encouraged it. The clan's children enjoyed when Magnus and Seamus used to visit because they would always take a gaggle with them. Seeing the children gathering around Magnus at the postern gate reminded her of childhood memories when she was in the group who followed him.

Magnus grinned as Timmy pulled her through the portal. "Are ye still the best fisherwoman in the clan?"

"Best fisher of all." Saoirse grinned while stepping past Magnus. When he returned her smile, she nearly tripped over Timmy. The heat in his gaze was enough to make her break out in a sweat.

"We shall see. Mary claims she's better than ye now that she's eight." Magnus's gaze moved to a curly-haired blonde girl leading the charge to the loch.

"She doesnae ken all ma tricks. Only the ones I taught her." Saoirse waggled her brows as she hurried to keep up with Timmy, whose short legs moved surprisingly fast at a walk.

"I recall teaching ye how to fish." Magnus nudged Saoirse with his elbow.

"Aye. And ye dinna ken all ma tricks, either. Only the ones ye taught me."

When they reached the loch's shore, they helped the youngest children tie strings around the bait. Once everyone settled, Saoirse and Magnus tended to their own tackle. They remained with the youngest children, not willing to let them wander.

"Do ye fish often?" Magnus noticed Saoirse still prepared the fishing lines with ease.

"Aye. Sometimes I come down with others to catch things for Cook. But sometimes, I come here just for the quiet. It's usually after a trying healing. People ken I like the peace. It lets me get over the suffering I saw. What aboot ye?"

"Lately, it's only been to catch food while on patrol. But usually I was the one who volunteered. It gave me time to think—or nae think—when I was always with at least two other guards."

"Ye dinna think it odd that I still enjoy it? It's nae something most lasses do."

"I would never think it odd. If ye like it for the same reasons as me, how could I?"

"Most lasses—"

"I'm glad ye arenae like most lasses, Saoirse." Magnus stepped closer, so he could whisper to her. "Being who ye are isnae a bad thing. It's what draws people to ye."

She canted her head to look up at him since he stood so close. The rest of the world disappeared as Magnus made her feel like she was all that existed to him. She nodded, but she didn't know what to say. Fortunately, her fishing line bobbed. She drew it out of the water, hand over hand, until she held up a shimmering fish.

"Lady Saoirse is Queen of the Fishers!" Magnus bowed to her, his fanfare exaggerated with a twirling arm before he bent forward. "She caught the first. What say ye? Does she keep it or toss it back?"

"Keep it!" A chorus of young voices cheered. Saoirse giggled as she looked at Magnus, who grinned.

"Queen of the Fishers?" Saoirse shook her head as she withdrew her dirk and cut the head from the fish. She tossed it back into the water before placing the rest of the fish on the grass.

"Ye canna be king." Magnus shrugged as his line bobbed next. He withdrew his line to find a much smaller fish at the end. He called out, "Keep it or toss it?"

"Toss!" The kids laughed at the fish that was barely the length of Magnus's hand.

"But ye can still be the King of the Fishers," Mary assured Magnus with an assertive nod. "Óg is king, and Lady Saoirse is queen. They're king and queen together."

Magnus enjoyed the sound of them being anything together. He leaned over once more when Saoirse came to stand beside him. "Shall I make ye a flower crown?"

"Do ye ken how?" Saoirse couldn't stop smiling. Between more time with Magnus and the children's jests, she felt a lightness she rarely experienced now that pain and death surrounded her.

"Mayhap ye could teach me."

Saoirse's lips pulled between her teeth before she nodded. They remained at the loch for more than an hour. They sent the children back to the keep with their catches. Meanwhile, Saoirse and Magnus walked toward the meadow. Cows grazed in the tall grass, swishing their tails periodically, their deep brown eyes following the visitors. When they arrived at a flower patch, Saoirse kneeled and pulled at stems. Magnus sat facing her, his long legs stretched in front of him and beside her.

"When's the last time ye made a flower crown, Saoirse?"

"May Day."

Magnus felt his cock twitch as he thought about the ancient holiday. The Church renounced its pagan history, but it was still an excuse for festivities. He could picture Saoirse's hair flying around her back as she twirled around a May pole with the other maidens. He wondered what types of flowers she wore. He also thought about the traditional fertility ideas and how many bairns were born nearly nine months to the day. He swept his gaze over the field and imagined stripping her bare and laying her on the soft bed of grass. He would worship every inch of her as she watched him.

"Magnus?"

"Hmm?"

"Is there something else ye need to do?"

"Nay. Why?"

"Ye're distracted and seem to be thinking of something else. I dinna wish to keep ye."

"I'm exactly where I want to be. Ma mind wandered to this blonde wood nymph I met as I rode into Castle Dunbeath last sennight. She drives me to distraction."

"Do ye think that nymph thinks aboot ye?"

"I hope so. I pray so."

"I think she does." Saoirse handed Magnus the flower crown she made. She covered her mouth with her hand to stifle her laughter when he placed it on his head.

"Will ye teach me to make yers?"

Saoirse realized he was in earnest. She nodded, and they spent the next five minutes making hers. They returned to the keep nearly two hours later, having spent the time talking and getting to know one another more. People stared, and some pointed to Magnus as they laughed. Timmy was the one to announce the King and Queen of the Fishers had arrived at their royal court. People nodded their approval as Magnus carried their miniature town crier on his shoulder. Saoirse imagined Timmy was a son she shared with Magnus. She wished any of the children who went with them to the loch could be theirs. She hoped one day they would have their own family.

After their fishing adventure, they found time to talk every day for a fortnight. Sometimes they captured minutes here and there, and at other times, they spoke at length. It was usually when she worked in her storage building, and he accompanied her. They always kept the door open and a safe distance between them. If asked, they would have said it was for propriety. But it was to keep them from indulging in their growing feelings.

CHAPTER 4

"Óg, have ye been avoiding me?"

Magnus turned toward his sister as he made his way to the Great Hall two and a half weeks after he arrived. His chamber was on the third floor, but most of the family ones were on the second. He waited as Siùsan approached.

"Nay. Nae at all. What makes ye think that?"

"Because we havenae talked once since ye arrived. Ye've been with the men practically every minute ye've been awake."

Magnus couldn't tell her he was spending time with Saoirse or doing his best to distract himself from a blonde beauty who danced through his mind at the most inconvenient times.

"Are ye busy now? Would ye walk with me to the village? I was going to browse the market." Magnus wanted to buy Siùsan a gift for her upcoming saint's day.

"I was headed there too. Ye can carry ma baskets." Siùsan winked before they went to the kitchens. She gathered two large baskets that Magnus took from her before they stepped outside. They walked in silence until they left the gates. Three guards trailed them since Callum had a fit whenever Siùsan or his daughters left with less than that. Shona had a skill at evading more than one guard. "I ken it's been a difficult three years, but I've missed ye and Seamus tremendously. It's wonderful when Michail and Blythe visit, but it isnae quite the same as having ma brothers."

Magnus remained quiet. It wasn't only Brighde and Cerys who had a complicated family tree with branches tangling with the Sinclair family's. Siùsan's mother was a MacLeod of Assynt before she met their shared father. Rose MacLeod died on the way to marry their father after handfasting. Magnus and Seamus's mother contributed to her death, and Siùsan's unexpected birth when Rose fell from her horse. Elizabeth Gunn was on her way to marry their father in an alliance arranged by their grandfather. After Rose's death, their father lied to the MacLeods and said Siùsan died along with Rose.

It wasn't until after Siùsan and Callum married that the MacLeods learned Siùsan was not only alive but more than twenty-years-old. That discovery only reignited a simmering feud between the Mackenzies and the MacLeods of Assynt. Once Seamus became laird, and Magnus took over as tánaiste, they made peace with the MacLeods. But it was still uncomfortable to be in the same room as Michail MacLeod, Siùsan's cousin. The only thing the Mackenzies, MacLeods, and Sinclairs shared was animosity with the Gunns. After their father died, Seamus and Magnus's mother—Siùsan's stepmother—returned to her clan of birth. She did it out of spite and to encourage the ongoing strife. The Gunns were the bane of several northern clans' lives.

"I ken. I've missed ma big sister. Ye give sage advice."

"I do ma best. Ye and Seamus are ma only direct blood relatives besides ma children. That still means a great deal to me. What's happened since we last saw each other? I ken aboot the sickness and the floods."

"Aye. It's been one thing after another. The floods destroyed our crops two and a half years ago. Leaking roofs meant much of our stored foods spoiled. The roofs would have been fine throughout a normal winter or even a heavy rainy season, but they werenae a match to our weather. It chucked it down for days, and it felt as though the Lord was punishing us. The Chisholms fared as badly as we did, but the Frasers and Mathesons barely had a drop. We're a large clan with more land than nearly any other clan in Scotland, but it also means Seamus and I are responsible for many people's wellbeing. He and I took turns riding our territory to check on our farmers and villages. We were each gone for sennights at a time. I kept waiting for Noah to offer me safe passage."

Magnus smiled, but Siùsan noticed the strain and sadness in her younger brother's eyes. The Sinclairs sent what they could, including men, to help rebuild villages on the lands that bordered the Sutherlands. The Sinclairs and Sutherlands were bound by marriage when Liam married Kyla, and they remained the closest allies over the decades by choice. Laird Hamish Sutherland, Liam's brother-by-marriage, sent men and supplies too. But everyone knew nothing they sent would be enough.

"The foul weather led to sickness sweeping through the clan time and time again. One village seemed to recover when another fell victim. We tried to keep people from traveling, but our holdings are too vast to control that. People wanted to help their families in other villages. Traveling merchants likely spread it too. We lost hundreds from it. I never imagined I could attend so many funerals that werenae caused by a battle."

"But I thought things improved."

Magnus looked toward the cliffs that overlooked the North Sea. The sea breeze lifted his hair from his forehead and neck, a comfortable reprieve from the oppressive weight that bore down upon him with unceasing heaviness.

"It was supposed to. Since Seamus already married one of Deirdre's cousins, we have an alliance with the Frasers. Despite being away so much, Seamus and I agreed after a year that it was time for me to marry, or at least become betrothed. With the way things stood, we needed an alliance with a clan nearby. It left the Chisholms, who were in the same boat as us, and the Mathesons. The laird only has sons, but he has a niece."

"Aye, I ken. I remember Louisa from when we were weans. It shocked me that ye agreed to marry her."

"I never wanted to. But it was what was best for the clan. She is nae an easy woman to be around."

"Is she still as manipulative as she was when we were younger?"

"Worse. She's had years of practice to hone her skills. She has a vindictive and malicious streak that runs from the roots of her hair to the end of her toenails. She hides it well, but when ye see it, ye canna unsee it."

"Was she horrible to ye?"

"Nae in the beginning. She kept it hidden, but Seamus and I have devoted ourselves to repairing the relationships with our people that Father destroyed. Our clansmen trust us, and so they talk to us. The women in the village told their husbands how Louisa treated them. The men came with their pitchforks. I had to arrange a hunting party to get them away from the keep to tell me what happened. I long suspected Louisa had spies, and at the end, I discovered I was right. She'd paid nearly a score of people working within the keep and living in the village to report to her."

"What did the men have to say?"

"Louisa is an attractive woman, and when she smiles, ye believe she means it. She beguiles ye until ye think ye've made the closest friend ye'll ever find. Or at least, that's what the women thought. Thinking her a close friend, they were always eager to see her when she and her uncle visited. They came nearly every moon, and her uncle pushed a wedding date each time. But everyone kenned, it wasna the right time for me to take a bride once the illnesses started. I was away from home too often."

"Did they visit even when ye werenae there?"

"Aye. That's how the trouble started. Louisa appeared flighty and oblivious half the time. She knew Caroline was Lady Mackenzie, so she had no reason to appear like she could be an effective chatelaine. She began sharing things the women told her in confidence or blatantly making up lies. She riled the women, pitting them against each other, but positioning herself as the only one who could solve the problems. It took a few moons before the women deduced what she'd done. After Louisa's seventh visit, they talked when she returned home and compared the things Louisa told them. Louisa's meddling caused strife within families' homes and in the village. But she kept it away from the keep's servants, so Seamus, Caroline, and I were none the wiser until the husbands came to me. They held naught back."

"That's horrible."

"If only that were the worst of it."

"There's more?"

"Tons upon tons." Magnus looked at the market and had second thoughts about sharing his tale of woe where others could hear. "I ken ye need to go to the market, but could we walk to the loch instead?"

"Of course."

The brother and sister walked in silence again as Magnus reflected on a miserable and wasted eighteen months.

"She stirred trouble among the women, but it spilled over to the men. Part of what she did was make the women competitive and envious aboot their husbands' prowess in and out of their beds. The men grew combative outside of the lists, and more accidents started happening in the lists. Seamus and I couldnae reason why until the men talked to me. Things returned to normal once everyone realized what happened, but it meant many were hostile to Louisa the next time she visited. Women snubbed her, so she turned her attention to the maids. She would threaten them if they didna tell her any gossip they knew. She forced one maid to steal from Caroline, then turned her over to Seamus and Caroline. She stood witness against the poor lass. It was Henry who saved the lass. He'd been playing by the hearth while Seamus and Caroline heard the case against Mary. Henry climbed onto Seamus's lap and whispered in his ear. Then Seamus conferred with Caroline. Turns out, Henry heard Louisa ordering Mary to go into the lady's chamber. He'd watched, too scared to let Louisa ken he could see from the narrow crack of his open door. Louisa held a knife to Mary."

"But why?"

"Because she could. Louisa is nae a well woman. In fact, she's barmy, a complete bampot. But it took time for people to believe what others already knew. I was away from the keep for the incident with Mary. I missed most of what happened in the village, hearing aboot it secondhand from the men."

"Using Mary so ill is still so extreme. There had to be a better reason for Louisa's plotting than that."

"She thought it made her indispensable. Rather than be of use in the keep and help Caroline, she thought manipulating everyone into depending on her was better."

"What were Caroline and Seamus doing aboot it? Ye must have discussed breaking the betrothal."

"We did. But I was away from the keep more often than I was home for nearly a year. We were nearly at eight-and-ten months since the floods began. Most of the illnesses had cleared, but it decimated our crops that year. We had people near starving since the weather drove much of the wildlife away. There was naught to harvest and naught to hunt. Once the crofts were repaired and people had clothes and the things they needed for their day-to-day lives, I worked in the fields. I went from village to village, helping to dig drainage ditches to push the water out of the fields. But it took months before the sun was enough to dry the water-logged earth. We had infestations of bugs from the sitting water. We had people filling buckets and carting it off to the Minch to dump there or into lochs. But that wasna ideal since they'd all swollen their banks too."

"Why didna ye tell us it was this bad, Magnus? We could have helped more. It hurts to ken ye've waited this long to tell me. Did ye think we wouldnae help?"

"Nay. It wasna that. When Seamus negotiated the betrothal contract, things were horrible. But we never expected it would carry on for so long. One term Laird Matheson insisted upon was we honor their alliances with the Macraes, Donalds and Mackintoshes. He insisted we strengthen those alliances by asking them for help first. The last thing Seamus and I wanted was for us to be indebted to those three. Ye and the Sutherlands had already offered help, but he pushed for us to nae look to ye or the Mackays for help unless we used his alliances first."

"But the Mathesons are allied with the Sutherlands. Ye never asked for more from Hamish."

"If we had, it would have gotten ye involved, which is what Matheson didna want."

"Why did ye and Seamus allow Matheson to rule ye?"

"Because they had the men to help us defend against the Rosses and Roses. Ye ken with the Rosses come the Campbells."

"Ye dinna have trouble with the Campbells."

"We would if things got worse with the Rosses. Monty and Brodie are as close as Brodie is with his real brother, Dominic. I wouldnae put it past Laurel to ride into battle between Brodie and Dominic. The woman both fascinates me and terrifies me. I havenae ever met someone so quick thinking and sharp tongued. If she hadnae married Brodie, I might have fallen in love with her maself."

"Can ye imagine the red hair yer bairns would have? With her strawberry-blonde hair, it would have looked like a fire riding toward ye."

"Aye. Our trouble with the Rosses brought the Roses in. The Rosses seized the opportunity to en-croach on our land because they kenned eventually it would be good arable land again, but we were strug-gling to defend it. Seamus and I could defend our land with just the Mathesons at our backs. We didna have to involve any of their allies."

"Was Louisa's dowry that big?"

"Aye."

Siùsan fell silent as she and Magnus stood at the loch's banks. She leaned toward him and rested her head against his shoulder as she wrapped her arm around his.

"I still wish ye'd told us. We would have helped. Mayhap ye could have broken the betrothal sooner. What was the last straw?"

"She tried to force me."

"Force ye? She was pressuring ye to set a wedding date?"

"Nay. Nae that kind of force. That would have been fine."

Siùsan pulled away and stepped in front of Magnus to look at him.

"What did she do?"

Magnus recognized the simmering anger in Siùsan's hardened gaze. He might be more than a foot taller than her and riddled with battle scars, but he almost took a step back. As renowned as the Sinclair men were for their military prowess, the women were known for their familial protectiveness. It was a fool who ran afoul of the five Sinclair women. Mairghread was doubly so since she was a Sinclair by birth and a Mackay by marriage.

"She slipped a sleeping draught into ma ale at the evening meal. I still dinna ken how she did it. It took Seamus and her uncle to get me up to ma chamber. She must have waited an hour, but it was a powerful brew. I didna hear her or feel when she lifted ma arms. She tied them to the headboard."

"Ye said she tried to force ye. Did she force ye?"

Magnus looked away. He still battled the shame he felt for how that scene ended.

"Nay. But she was vera close. I woke to her stroking me. She was aboot to mount me when I realized what was happening. I'd thought I was dreaming. I roared with rage and twisted, sending her flying off the bed. When I realized she'd tied me to the bed, I was even more enraged. I broke the headboard when I pulled it from the frame. Fool woman didna think I slept with a dirk under ma pillow. What warrior doesnae? She obviously wasna a virgin, so she'd shared at least one mon's bed."

"Ye broke the headboard? What did ye do with the knife?"

"It was a *sgian dubh*. I keep it wickedly sharp. I nearly shredded ma arms and slit ma wrists, but I got one hand free. I got hold of a handful of her hair and pushed her to the door, which she'd locked and bared. The headboard dragged behind me and made a horrific noise. I still dinna ken how I did it. When we got to the door, I maneuvered her against the wall and nearly crushed her as I opened it. Once again, I had a handful of her hair. I pushed her into the passageway and bellowed for her uncle, Laird Matheson. People were already gathering. It gave me the chance to cut ma other hand free, but enough people had candles to see what I was doing."

"St. Columba's bones!"

Magnus hung his head.

"I'm nae proud of what happened next."

"What did she do?"

"Nae her. Me. I pushed her against the wall, pulled her head back, and was ready to slit her throat. She spat in ma face. I was beyond reason. Ma elbow went to her face. It broke her nose and cracked a cheekbone. Matheson came out and started blaming me. Mind ye, it was early spring. We werenae building fires anymore because we needed to conserve the wood. I slept in ma leine. She was naked. The moment Matheson accused me of defiling his niece, I launched maself at him. All the anger from that night, along with everything I'd learned aboot her, came pouring out. It only took one punch to knock him out. Seamus was trying to reason with me. I'm telling ye, Siùsan. I didna hear aught. Nae that I ignored him. I heard none of it. I dragged Louisa down the stairs, uncaring that she was falling down most of them. I slung her into a cell in the dungeon and took the key to a garderobe and tossed it."

"Bluidy hell."

"How we arenae at war with the Mathesons and all their allies is beyond me."

"What happened to her?"

"It took a few hours for the blacksmith to get the cell open. By then, I'd calmed slightly. I was pacing Seamus's solar, though. Plenty of servants spied the broken headboard. The pillowcase she'd used to bind my wrists remained tied to the headboard. Ma plaid was hanging on a peg with ma boots beneath it. Ma belt was on the peg next to it. But she'd strewn her clothes from the door to the side I'd been sleeping on. It was clear it wasna a moment of passion soured."

"I'm so sorry that happened."

"Thank ye. A search of her belongings found more things Caroline didna ken had been stolen, along with the sleeping draught. All I could think aboot as I paced was how different things would have been if I werenae the stronger of the two of us. How easy it is for men to molest women if a mon ma size nearly had it happen to him. I couldnae stop thinking aboot what nearly happened to ye. Hearing yer screams came flooding back to me. It started when I realized what she was trying to do. It was like I was seeing what I imagined happened to ye in that tower chamber when I was two-and-ten, but I was living it at four-and-thirty."

Siùsan wrapped her arms around her younger brother and drew him in for the same embrace she'd given him thirty years ago when he would hurt himself climbing trees. Magnus found the same comfort as he had all those years ago. His mother never hugged him.

He had not a single memory of any affection from her. It had always been Siùsan once she moved into the keep who cared for Seamus and him.

"Is she dead?"

"Nay." Magnus felt Siùsan stiffen before she pulled away. "Ye canna do aught, Siùsan. Dinna think aboot it."

"I ken I canna do aught, but I can think aboot it all I want. She'd better keep her distance at the next Highland Gathering, otherwise, she will breathe her last."

Magnus didn't doubt Siùsan was making a pledge. She was not a woman prone to violence. She had the patience of an archangel and a capacity to forgive much. But there was no redeeming oneself if they crossed Siùsan's family.

"What happened once she was free of the dungeon?"

"Seamus had to lock me into the solar to keep me from dropping her in the oubliette. Ma mind was stuck replaying that night we met Callum and the others. I couldnae stop hearing yer screams or how Callum roared as he ran up those stairs to ye. He got to ye before ye were forced, but I still have nightmares. Seamus kenned without me saying aught. He told me later that he experienced the same thing, but obviously, nae as extreme as I did. They gave her clothes before she came out, and I had to stand before Seamus and the clan for assaulting a woman."

"What?"

"It wasna Seamus's fault. He kenned it had to be done, so we could lay the matter to rest. It was humiliating to admit that I'd been drugged and molested. I was so ashamed that a mon ma size—a warrior who wakes to a fly sneezing—could have been so taken advantage of. We learned from Louisa's maid that she was to wait in the passageway until Louisa was through. That would have been after I planted ma seed in her. Then the maid was to come in and scream. The tale they planned to tell was, I woke from ma ale stupor and dragged Louisa back to ma chamber through seduction. Bedding her and spilling ma seed would have forced a marriage within days."

"Ye being dressed, the sleeping draught, and the pillowcase tied to the headboard, and ye dragging it to the door exonerated ye."

"It did, but I still had to recount what happened. I feared the men would think me weak, and the women would think me a liar and a threat."

"Did they?"

"Some did. Mostly that I was weak. The women didna believe me a threat, but most believed me a liar. They still blamed me despite the maid confessing and admitting she did Louisa's bidding because she had a bastard infant Louisa threatened to drown. Kenning Louisa, I believe she would have done it."

"What happened to that lass?"

"As best I ken, her mother's people were MacDonalds, so she fled to them once they returned to their land."

"And the betrothal?"

"Seamus severed it. They had already paid half the dowry. He demanded Matheson pay it in full or he would invoke our alliances with ye, the Sutherlands, the Mackays, and through ye, the extended alliances with the MacLeods of Lewis and of Assynt."

"Matheson kenned he wouldnae stand a chance."

"Aye. And drawing in the Sutherlands is the only way to ensure the Rosses would leave us alone. Amelia is still Monty's aunt. He wouldnae dare fight against his uncle and Lachlan. It wouldnae happen."

"Ye said this happened while ye were four-and-thirty. Yer saint's day was only two sennights ago. We celebrated here."

"Aye. It happened a moon and a half ago. Bluidy

wonderful gift. We've been sorting everything out since the Mathesons left and took their men with them, but I left as soon as I could. I spent a sennight meeting with Monty to repair the damage Father did. Seamus rode out to talk to Torrian at our border. Michail rode with his father. The Gunns bided their time while the land at our northern border was so undesirable, but they're making incursions again. It doesnae matter that ma mother lives there. I think it's because of her. Mother doesnae care that her cousin is Lady MacLeod of Assynt, either. They're causing trouble with the MacLeods again. Ye ken, *amicus meus, inimicus inimici mei.*" My friend, the enemy of my enemy.

"May I tell Callum?"

"Aye. I would never ask ye to keep aught from yer husband. Besides, he'll be laird one day. He must ken what occurs with yer enemies and yer allies. I would tell Liam, though. Once I have, then the others may as well ken."

"Nay one else has to, Magnus. We dinna usually keep secrets, but this is nae mine nor Liam's nor Callum's secret to tell."

"It's hardly a secret after two hundred people watched me stand before ma brother and tell how a woman half ma size nearly raped me."

A sound to Magnus's right made him turn. He squinted, but he saw naught but a couple leaves on a bush move. He watched, but nothing else happened. He assumed it was a rabbit or a squirrel. He prayed it wasn't someone listening. He didn't want the story spread throughout the clan. He'd come to escape the incident, not relive it every time someone saw him.

"Magnus, is the shame that she nearly assaulted ye worse than the shame of how ye reacted?"

"Aboot the same. Seamus and I were basically raised here. Sinclair men dinna harm women. We dinna use our size to threaten or hurt them. I did that from the moment I woke until the moment they rode through the gates."

Siùsan tilted her head as she rubbed between her eyebrows. She closed her eyes and exhaled before she looked up at her brother. She didn't see a warrior. She saw a little boy whose parents ignored him. Parents who spent more time yelling at one another than remembering they had two sons to raise. She saw a boy whose father told him he was never good enough despite his years training with the Sinclairs. She saw the toddler who climbed into her lap for her to mother when she was only two-and-twelve.

"I'm glad ye came, Magnus. I ken ye canna stay forever, but I wish ye could. I wish Seamus, Caroline, and the weans could all move here."

"I ken ye would protect us just as ye did when we were all weans, but ye canna. Other than foul memories, I didna suffer any lasting damage."

Siùsan was slow to nod, but she wouldn't argue with him. She wrapped her arm around his as they turned back to the village. The moment they entered the market, a pit formed in his stomach. He knew it wasn't a rabbit or squirrel that was behind the bush.

CHAPTER 5

agnus entered the market with Siùsan, but she soon recognized a group of women, so she took her baskets and joined them. Before their talk, Magnus planned to find Siùsan a gift. Now he considered turning on his heel and running from the village. But he couldn't. He needed the gift, and he couldn't avoid Saoirse since she was watching him.

"Ye heard." It wasn't fully an accusation, but it definitely wasn't a question.

"I did. I'm sorry."

"Did ye hear all of it?"

"Aye."

"And ye didna think to leave? That mayhap I wouldnae appreciate ye hearing aboot such a shameful event?" Magnus couldn't meet Saoirse's gaze. He looked over her head, scanning the crowd for anyone who might watch them.

"Will ye walk with me?"

"Where are yer guards?" Magnus frowned as he realized he didn't see anyone assigned to her.

"Da says I can come to the market without any, but

if I intend to leave the path between the village and the keep, then I must have someone accompany me. I'm never to walk alone anywhere but between the keep and village."

Magnus nodded. Saoirse left the stall where she browsed dried flowers. She'd been curious rather than an intent shopper. She led Magnus to the far side of the market, which ended at the northern outskirts of the village.

"Magnus, the only shame is on her. Ye did naught wrong." Saoirse had rattled the leaves when she'd fisted her hands and shifted in anger. She'd forced herself to remain still until she heard the part about Magnus blaming himself.

"It doesnae make it any less humiliating."

"I understand that. Women are blamed when this happens to them. They're seductresses who asked for it. Ye're blamed because ye should have been too strong for her to force ye. Neither case makes it right to blame the victim. She drugged ye."

"I'm also ashamed of how I reacted."

"That ye made sure she couldnae assault ye? She shouldnae have tried to take what wasna hers. Dinna feel guilty for having the strength to defend yerself."

"I didna need to throw ma elbow into her face, and I didna need to drag her down the stairs to the dungeon."

"Ye didna kill her, which is what I would try to do to any mon who intended to take advantage of me. I'd say ye showed restraint."

"But—"

"Nay, Magnus. Ye arenae going to convince me that ye should shoulder the blame here. I willna encourage ye to carry more shame." Saoirse placed her hand on his, which rested on his belt. She slid her fingers into his palm and squeezed. "Ye are nae a weak mon, nor are ye one who abuses women. She put ye in a position where ye had to defend yerself just as ye would defend yerself if attacked at night on patrol. She may nae have held a sword to ye, but she was prepared to have her uncle hold one to ye if ye refused to marry her after she'd bedded ye. And as for weak, honestly, I dinna ken any mon outside ma family who could rip a headboard from a bed."

"I can think of a few, but aye, it took strength."

Saoirse squeezed his hand again before she pulled away, but he captured her fingers and brought the back of her hand to his lips. She felt heat course through her as his lips brushed her skin. She knew she was blushing again. Would that ever cease around Magnus?

"Magnus, I will keep yer secret. It's nae mine to repeat. But ye must ken nay one in our family would blame ye. I heard ye sent Blake arse over heels again yesterday. He's enormous. Nay one will think ye're weak."

"I feel foolish for allowing her to keep returning to ma keep after learning how she'd treated the women."

"Ye arenae Laird Mackenzie. Seamus made the contract, so it wasna yer decision to break it. I'm just glad that he did." Saoirse's ears were on fire once she realized what she said. She'd meant it innocently, but she knew how it sounded. Magnus said nothing. She withdrew her hand and held her basket with both while she looked at their feet. "I—"

"Will ye help me pick a gift for Siùsan? I'd like to get her something nice for her saint's day. I'm a wee auld for just picking hair ribbons. I'd like something more thoughtful."

"I'd like that."

Magnus followed Saoirse throughout the market as they examined different booths. He settled on a set of four scented candles and a brooch for her arisaid. The candles were too long to fit in his sporran, so Saoirse hid them in the bottom of her basket. Before returning to the keep, Magnus bought them each a meat pie. They found a table at which to sit and watch people while they ate.

"What do ye enjoy most aboot being a healer?" Magnus wanted to learn more about the woman who sat across from him. He'd observed her for the past fortnight and a half, and he discovered she wasn't much like the girl he'd once known. She was still shy, even around people she knew well, but she moved with more self-assurance than the last time he'd visited. She radiated a sense of calm and compassion, which hadn't been there years ago.

"I suppose I should say helping people. I enjoy that vera much. But I enjoy solving the puzzles."

"Puzzles?"

"Aye. Figuring out what ails someone, then figuring out the best cure. Most often, it's simple. But some-times it's nae, and I love those challenges. I dinna want anyone to suffer for ma entertainment, but I like ken-ning I bested the mystery."

"Ye sound like me when I think aboot dealing with the flooded land. I dinna want anyone to suffer for it, and I loathe that it's caused endless hardship. But I enjoy conquering each obstacle. I like planning and testing ma ideas, seeing which solutions work."

"Aye. If I could study people's illnesses without them actually being ill, it would be perfect."

Magnus nodded as he watched Saoirse take another bite of meat pie. Her fine boned fingers led to dainty looking hands, but he'd felt the calluses at the base of her fingers. Her full pink lips were bow shaped. Her neck was swanlike, and her movements were graceful.

He forced his eyes to remain on her face, but he'd noticed her figure every day since he arrived. However, sitting this close to her allowed him a view of her full bust beneath her kirtle. It was warm, so she wore no arisaid. The gown hugged her figure without being indecent. But every thought running through his mind was very indecent. For at least the hundredth time since arriving, he appreciated his sporran hiding the evidence of his arousal.

"Magnus?"

"Aye?"

"Ye seem to have drifted far away."

"Och, I didna mean to woolgather."

"What're ye thinking aboot?"

Now there was a question he couldn't answer honestly.

"That this has been an unexpected morning, but it's turned out well."

"I'm glad ye found yer gifts, too."

"That wasna what I meant, Saoirse." Magnus waited for her reaction. He wondered if he'd gone too far. The pink blooming beneath her freckles made him wonder what she'd look like flushed with pleasure.

"I enjoyed ma morning too, Magnus. I'm still sorry for eavesdropping, but I'm glad we're spending the time together."

"And when yer da finds out? I dinna ken why he hasnae said aught yet. Mayhap he doesnae ken since we havenae been anywhere as public as the market."

"Finds out what? That I spoke to someone I've kenned ma entire life." Saoirse arched a brow. "If he finds fault in that, then someone's been telling him tales. We've done naught wrong."

"Saoirse."

"Magnus, we have done naught wrong."

"Ye are nay longer a lass I was told to mind."

Saoirse's lips curled in as she tried not to grin. She looked away as she tried to compose herself. When she focused back on Magnus, she gave up trying to fight her smile. She hoped he wouldn't ask why she tried to hide her amusement.

"What're ye thinking aboot, Saoirse?"

"Do I really have to tell ye?"

"Of course nae. I wouldnae insist on ye sharing yer private thoughts."

Saoirse nodded, appreciating what he said. "I wouldnae refuse if they sent ye to mind me."

Magnus blinked several times as he stared at Saoirse. He didn't know what to say to the brazen comment, and he realized his failure to respond embarrassed her. He watched her retreat. He suspected it was the most flirtatious thing she'd ever said.

"Is that what ye want, Saoirse? I ken what I want."

"What is that?"

"To get to ken ye as a woman and see if we suit. I want ye to get to ken me as the mon I am now, nae the lad ye probably remember."

"Ye've been a mon a long time, Magnus. I remember ye as such. But I have a different—appreciation—for ye now." Saoirse knew they were treading dangerous ground, speaking so openly about their attraction and where anyone might hear.

"I dinna think yer da will take to the idea."

"Probably nae. But I dinna think it would be aboot ye. I dinna think he'd take well to anyone showing an interest in me or ma sisters. But he kens it's bound to happen."

"I dinna think he'll approve of me. I'm closer to his age than yers."

"Ye make yerself sound auld. Ye are exactly between us. Three-and-ten years each way."

"Aye, but at a certain point, the years between yer father and me feel like they shrank. He willna approve, Saoirse. Ye saw how he reacted to seeing us in the heather field."

"Because everyone thought ye were still betrothed. He likely thought that made it inappropriate."

"What do ye want, Saoirse?"

"To find out if we suit. I think we both ken that's what we've been doing for the past two sennights." Saoirse didn't have to think twice about her answer. She'd been thinking about it incessantly since Magnus arrived. "I dinna believe in hiding things from ma parents, but mayhap we could be discreet for a while. Mayhap we'll discover we arenae a good match. If we arenae, then there's nay point in making a fuss for naught."

"Vera well. But if yer da, yer grandda, or any of yer uncles ask, I willna lie. I will state ma intentions."

"What are those intentions, Magnus?"

"To marry ye."

"Ye sound vera certain."

"I'm certain that I want to get to ken ye, so we both ken marrying is what we want. I am nae here to toy with ye or play ye for a fool. I willna make ye think I'm interested only to ride away. I hope we suit. I want to find out if we do. I'm already yer friend. I hope to one day be more."

"I hope so too."

Magnus's long legs bracketed Saoirse's under the table. She rested her hand on his knee for a moment before pulling it away. She was more brazen that morning than she'd ever been. She couldn't imagine doing that to any other man, but it felt right with Magnus.

"I should head back. I ken they'll wonder why I

didna go to the lists. I havenae seen Siùsan, so she probably already returned to the keep."

"Aye. I have herbs to hang to dry and a few people to check on. Will ye walk with me?"

"I'd like that."

They made their way back to the gate, but as they approached, they spied Callum, Alex, Tavish, and Mòr leaving the lists. Magnus and Saoirse glanced at each other before Saoirse went through the gate ahead of him. He hung back a minute before making his way to the men.

"Where'd ye disappear to?" Callum asked.

"I chatted with ma sister then found her gifts for her saint's day." Magnus realized Saoirse still had the candles. He knew the moment she remembered because he could see her behind Callum and Alex. Her hand went into her basket as she turned back toward him. But she decided it was better not to approach him. She dipped her chin, then hurried toward a storage building.

"Dinna outdo me, lad. I willna appreciate ma wife liking yer gift better than mine."

Tavish rolled his eyes. "We all ken she likes yer gifts the best. How ye dinna have ten weans is beyond me."

"Ye're one to talk." Mòr elbowed Tavish.

"We dinna have any more children than the rest of ye. Mairghread's the one with the most at four. We each have three." Tavish stood with his hands on his hips.

"That isnae what I meant. Everyone kens when Ceit loves ye and when ye irritate her. Ye're nae discreet either."

"I irritate her because she loves it when I make it up to her." Tavish waggled his eyebrows. Óg listened to the brothers banter with one another. Riding into battle for the first time hadn't made him feel as much like a man as when the four brothers allowed him to listen to their teasing about each other's prowess with their wives. He realized he would never join in if he married Saoirse. The four of them were more likely to murder him. It made him wonder what other strains it might put on his relationships with the men he most admired.

"Callum, I got ma sister some candles and a brooch. I dinna want to do aught to get in the way of the gifts ye—the ones we can ken aboot." He pretended to look disgusted since it was his sister Callum jested about.

"She'll like that. But I think the best gift is ye being here. She's worried aboot ye and Seamus. If it werenae for the sicknesses going around, she would have visited ye."

"I ken. But I was rarely at the keep, anyway. I've missed her too." Óg watched as Siùsan left the kitchens and spotted the men. She approached and slipped her arm around Callum's waist.

"Ma bonnie temptation." Callum leaned over to kiss Siùsan, and Óg wondered if one day he would greet Saoirse the same way, and if she would one day greet him by sliding her arm around him.

"Óg, Liam's in the solar if ye wish to talk to him."

"Thank ye. I will." Óg nodded to Siùsan and was about to turn toward the keep. "Ye may as well all come. I've already explained this once today. I dinna want to do it thrice."

"Explain what?" Callum looked between Óg and Siùsan.

"How I pulled a noose from around ma neck." Óg led the way to Liam's solar. As they passed the men's wives, he invited them to come. He just wanted this conversation over with. Fifteen minutes later it was. He slipped away as everyone stood in stunned silence.

Saoirse waited by the postern gate two days after sharing meat pies with Magnus in the market. They'd danced together that night and the last, but they'd had little chance to do more than chat between partners. She'd asked a maid to give Magnus the candles he bought for Siùsan. He was due to leave with several of her cousins for a sennight-long hunting trip, so when she mentioned she needed to go to the sea caves to collect algae, he offered to go with her. It would be their only chance to talk without hundreds of ears near enough to overhear.

"Torquil doesnae come up for a breath when he starts a story."

"I ken." Saoirse grinned as Magnus pushed the gate open. He nodded to the guard posted at the portal and looked back for Albert, or whoever would accompany them.

"I didna request a guard, Magnus."

"Saoirse, yer da—"

"Kens ye're a trained warrior. If he thought ye'd do aught to disgrace any woman in this clan, ye'd be dead or already back at yer family's keep."

"It's aboot appearances."

"It's aboot being able to spend time together, Magnus. Ye're leaving for a sennight. Then ye're bound to head back to Mackenzie territory soon. You've been here nearly three sennights."

"Nay. Seamus kens I came here for an extended visit. At least two moons, if nae longer. He encouraged it. Saoirse, someone might send me away, but this is yer home. I dinna want to leave ye here in disgrace. It was one thing to leave the walls with the children as our chaperones, but we've pushed our luck talking as often as we did in your workroom. Straying away from the market risks much for ye." Magnus wouldn't hesitate to defend Saoirse's honor and slay anyone mad enough to question it. But what would he do if it was their own family who doubted it?

They made their way along the path to the cliffs. As they passed the loch, Saoirse pointed to the far side.

"Do ye remember when Tate and Wee Liam raced each other across, certain they were the fastest swimmers in the clan?" Mairghread's son and the oldest grandchild, Wee Liam bore the moniker, so people wouldn't confuse him for his grandfather and namesake.

"Aye. I remember how ye and Rose and Shona dove in after them and stayed under water so long I thought I would have to tell yer mothers a fish swallowed ye."

"Tate and Wee Liam were livid when they reached the shore, and the three of us were already sitting there." Saoirse giggled as she recalled her oldest cousin, Liam, visiting from Castle Varrich, where he lived with his parents, Mairghread and Tristan Mackay. "If Wee Liam had listened to his mama, he might have won. Only Rose, Shona, and I listened to Auntie Mairghread's strategy. It worked."

"Wars would be won with yer aunt's strategies."

Magnus watched Saoirse as she laughed, her entire face radiating her amusement. She seemed completely at ease with him, so it made him wonder if she wasn't as shy as he recalled. Perhaps she was like her father and merely reserved.

"Saoirse!"

They stopped as two young men rode toward them from the woods. Magnus squinted into the sun, trying to identify the pair. He didn't recognize either of them. They weren't part of the laird's family, but they appeared close to Saoirse's age. When she shifted, he looked down and saw her body language change from a moment ago. She seemed to shrink. No longer did she appear confident or jovial. This was the shy woman he thought of when Saoirse used to come to mind.

"Hello, Nicholas, Conan."

"What're ye doing outside the gates without a guard?"

Saoirse stared before she tilted her head to meet Magnus's gaze.

"Last I checked, a clan tánaiste is qualified to be a guard." Magnus inhaled, his chest broadening. Both men were clearly warriors, but their smugness irritated Magnus as they looked down at him—literally and figuratively.

"Ye're nae a Sinclair guard."

"Nicholas!" Saoirse's eyes were wide as saucers. "He was for years."

She didn't look at the offensive young man, instead watching Magnus. He wished to ease her fears that he would retaliate. He loathed seeing her worry how he might react. He never wanted her to fear being near him.

"Laird Sinclair gifted me ma sword when I became a member of his guard. I didna have a grandda or da to do it, so he and Callum presented it to me as a fosterling within their clan and keep. It's kept me alive for more than a score of years because it was the Sinclairs who taught me to wield it. Do ye nae think me capable?"

"Saoirse, does yer da ken ye're out here without a guard?"

This time it was Conan who spoke. It mortified Saoirse. She wished to hide behind Magnus's back and pretend they'd never stopped. Or better yet, she wished they could be on the beach instead of on the path. The young men's behavior embarrassed her, and she disliked conflict.

"Nicholas, Conan, ye owe Óg yer apologies. Ye

canna speak to a tánaiste, a guest, or the laird's family like that. Óg is all three. I will speak to ma da aboot this. Go back to the keep."

"And leave ye alone with—"

"Conan, go." Saoirse infused all the authority her petite frame could muster into her command.

"Straight to yer da, Saoirse. Alex will want to ken." Nicholas smirked.

"*Lady* Saoirse and I are going to the beach, so ma lady can gather the algae she needs." Among the many things that irked Magnus about this conversation, he didn't care for the informality with which these young men addressed Saoirse. They may have known each other since they were weans, but as an adult, she was due her title. That was at the very least. He didn't care for how they asserted themselves and attempted to dictate to her. She was well above their station.

"Alone?"

"Conan, how would it be any different from when Albert accompanies me? Óg and Albert are the same age and trained together when they were lads. Da has nay objection to me leaving the keep with just Albert."

"He's a Sinclair."

Saoirse didn't know what to say. They were going around in circles. All she wanted was time with Magnus to talk and enjoy each other's company.

"Then run and tittle-tattle to ma da or anyone else who wants to listen to yer clishmaclaver. If Da or Grandda or any of ma uncles take issue, then they can send one of ma cousins to fetch me."

Magnus watched the men stare agog at Saoirse. From the way her shoulders just rounded and how she leaned away from them, along with their reaction, he figured she rarely asserted herself like this.

"We need to make our way to the beach, Lady Saoirse, or we'll miss the tide." Magnus gestured for

Saoirse to go ahead of him on the path. He turned toward the cliffs, but before he followed her, he looked over his shoulder at the young men. "Just remember that if ye speak out against me just to be arses, ye risk ruining Lady Saoirse. She's done naught wrong. If ye take issue with me, see me in the lists tomorrow. If we return, and there's even a hint of a rumor or gossip aboot our lady, I will challenge ye. Then I will kill ye."

CHAPTER 6

Magnus's long legs easily caught up to Saoirse, his plaid swishing against the back of his thighs. He took several deep breaths to calm his irritation before he came alongside her. She kept her eyes straight ahead, even though he was certain she knew he was looking at her. Once they were far enough along the descent to the beach that no one could see them, Magnus stopped and put his hand on her arm.

"Saoirse?"

"Ye're right. The tide will change while I'm in the cave if we dinna hurry."

"First of all, ye're nae going in the cave alone. Yer da would really kill me if I allowed that. Look at me, Saoirse."

She shook her head and looked at her feet. He stepped in front of her, using his forefinger to ease her chin up until he could see her face. She still wouldn't meet his gaze, but he saw the tears in her eyes.

"Dinna fash."

"I'm so sorry they behaved that way. I'm so embarrassed. I will talk to Da and Grandda aboot that. It's nae acceptable."

"Wheest, wee one. How they behaved isnae accept-able, but it isnae yer shame to carry."

"It reflects poorly on the clan. I dinna want ye to think—"

"Saoirse, they are their own men. They arenae a re-flection of anyone but themselves. Mayhap it would be different if I were a stranger, but I ken the Sinclairs. And even if they were rude, at least they take guarding the laird's family seriously. They take guarding their clanswomen seriously."

"Nay. I mean, they do. But they've always bullied me. Even as weans. They still like to tell me what to do. They wouldnae do it to Rose or Shona, or even ma sis-ters. They definitely wouldnae dare do it to Maisie. Nae because Blake and Torquil would get upset, but be-cause she would castrate them."

"Why ye?"

"Because until today, I've never stood up for maself. I've either avoided them, or someone else has defended me."

"And today?"

Saoirse looked straight ahead, which placed her gaze squarely on his chest. She would much rather con-template Magnus's physique than why she stood up for herself. But he deserved an answer.

"Because I felt confident with ye beside me."

"Do ye fear them doing something to ye if ye arenae with someone big enough to defend ye?"

"Nay. They've been like that in front of ma boy cousins. Ma cousins have defended me, but I've never felt confident enough to stand up for maself before."

"Were ye worried that if ye didna, I would get in a fight with them?"

"Nay. Ye arenae a lad like them. Ye ken ye dinna need to prove yerself. They think they do."

"Shall we get yer algae?"

"Aye."

Magnus offered Saoirse his arm and took the basket in his other hand while she gathered her skirts with her free hand. He didn't want to press her further and ruin the little time they had together. They made their way to the beach and across to the sea caves. Magnus remembered exploring the area with Seamus. They weren't allowed to go inside when they first arrived without Mòr or one of the other Sinclair brothers to go with them.

"The light inside has always fascinated me." Magnus pulled his boots off and rolled down his stockings.

"Aye. The way it comes in through the hole in the top but looks like it shines up from the bottom is incredible. It fascinates me, too." Saoirse pulled the back of her skirts between her legs and up to her belt, where she tucked them in. She pulled off her stockings and tucked them into her boots.

"How long do ye think it'll take ye to gather what ye need?"

If they missed the tide changing, they would be stuck in the cave and inevitably drown. It was why Liam and the adults allowed no one to go in alone. As children, Callum, Alex, Tavish, Magnus, and Mairghread would go together. There was always someone to stay outside in case someone became trapped, and at least two people to run for help.

"Nae long. Mayhap a quarter of an hour. Well before the tide changes." Saoirse waded into the low surf and picked her way to the slippery rocks. Magnus took her hand when she raised it to keep her balance. His sure-footedness made it look easy, but Saoirse knew to take her time lest she slip. Water swirled around their ankles, and the wind gusted around the cave's entrance. Magnus's solid frame buffeted the wind and allowed her to move faster than usual. Normally, she would inch along the mossy boulders until she could slip inside the cavernous space.

Saoirse inched along the ledge that the low tide exposed. She slipped her dirk from her belt and squatted to shave the algae from the rocks that the waves would submerge once they came in. Magnus remained out of the way, careful not to block the dim light. He remained close in case Saoirse should stumble or lose her balance. But he was content to watch her work, her concentration on her task absolute. He knew nothing about the plants she gathered, but Saoirse appeared purposeful and certain.

"I'm going to move further inside, Magnus. I wish to collect more from the pool."

"Can ye see that far back? The clouds are shifting. There willna be much light back there."

"I'll be quick."

"Ye dinna need to rush. I just—" Magnus stopped himself before he said too much.

Saoirse came to stand in front of him. "Ye just what?"

"Worry."

Magnus gazed into her earnest brown eyes. He didn't catch himself until after he tucked a loose lock of hair behind her ear. She leaned her cheek into his hand and closed her eyes. His other hand took the basket from hers and placed it on the ground. He dropped her dirk into it. He cupped her jaw with both hands until her eyes met his. He waited to see if she would pull away, but she lifted her chin instead. This moment had been building for weeks. Her eyes fluttered closed again as he drew closer. His lips brushed against hers. He paused to see if she would regret it. Her body swayed toward his. He eased his right hand to her waist, and she took a step closer.

"Saoirse, I wish to kiss ye, lass."

She nodded, her eyes still closed. But they opened when he did nothing to further their embrace.

"Please?" Saoirse felt the heat creeping into her cheeks. It embarrassed her to ask. She was tired of questioning herself, but she would have regretted it if Magnus didn't pull her against his body and press his lips to hers. He kept the pressure light, not forcing her to give more. Her hands rested on his biceps, but when the muscles bunched beneath her palms, she tightened her grip. She lifted her chin higher. Magnus slid the tip of his tongue along the seam of her lips. Her lips parted, but her teeth were still together. He flicked his tongue between her lips until she opened her mouth. He eased it into hers. He went slowly, ensuring he didn't scare her.

Her hands slid up his arms, over his shoulders, and around his neck. She was unprepared for how silky his hair would feel. The dark locks slid through her fingers as she tunneled them into his hair. She went up on her toes, trying to make it easier to kiss him. His arms tightened around her as her hands cupped his jaw. When they pulled apart, breathless, their foreheads pressed together. Magnus laid gentle kisses to her cheeks before brushing his thumbs over her freckles.

"Saoirse, I dinna want to push ye too fast."

"One kiss isnae too fast, Magnus. Can I let ye ken if we're moving too fast after our sixth or mayhap hundredth kiss?"

"Ye'd like more than just the one?" Magnus regretted his question the moment she withdrew. He didn't understand what went wrong. "Saoirse?"

"I would like more than one." Saoirse's voice was so low that he could barely hear over the crash of the sea outside the cave.

"Why'd ye just retreat from me? Ye said we werenae

going too fast, but ye're uncomfortable telling me ye want more."

Saoirse shrugged. She suddenly felt overwhelmed, uncertain how to handle her attraction to a man with so much more experience than her. She didn't know what he expected or how she should act.

"Saoirse, are ye embarrassed that ye wish to share more than one kiss?" Magnus waited until she nodded. "Did I scare ye?"

"Nay. I just dinna ken what to do."

"Lass, I dinna understand. Do ye mean ye dinna ken what to do now that we've kissed? Or what to do when we kiss?"

"Aye."

Magnus smiled at her shy response. It reminded him of her youth and inexperience. It should have warned him away, but he wished to see her reemerge as the confident woman he'd spent time with earlier.

"If ye wish for me to kiss ye again, I will. If once is all ye wish, then I willna press ye."

"I want ye to kiss me again. But I dinna ken how to do it properly."

"Wee one," Magnus whispered before he kissed her forehead. "Ye did it properly. Are ye worried that ye dinna have the experience I do?"

She nodded.

"Saoirse, we dinna need to rush aught."

"But I dinna ken what—how—"

"I dinna expect aught from ye, Saoirse. I dinna expect ye to ken what to do or to ken what ye want. If ye're curious, ask me, wee one. If ye dinna like something, tell me. I ken I'm aulder than ye, and I have more experience than ye. But that doesnae mean there is aught wrong with ye nae kenning what I do. I dinna want ye to be nervous around me."

"I dinna want to disappoint ye because I dinna ken what to do."

"Ye willna disappoint me."

"I'm sure ye're used to—"

"I've been as good as a monk for the past three years. There's been too much to deal with to consider ma own pleasure. And before that, I had arrangements that suited me and the women I was with. But never have I kept a leman, and I never will. The experience I have isnae the kind a mon wishes to share with a wife."

When Saoirse appeared morose, it confounded Magnus why the conversation was deteriorating further when he hoped to ease her worries.

"Why does that upset ye?"

She shook her head, miserable.

"Saoirse, dinna hide from me. It pains me that ye feel ye canna trust me."

"I trust ye completely, Magnus."

"I willna push ye to share yer inner thoughts. They're yers alone, but I wish ye to share them. We canna tell if we suit if we hide things from one another."

"This is a lot for one day. It's a lot for a few sennights."

Magnus nodded and withdrew his arms from around her waist. He was unprepared for her to grasp his leine and pull him toward her. She rested her head against his chest, her arms caught between their bodies. He wrapped his arms around her again.

"Are ye one of those men who thinks he canna enjoy pleasure with his lady wife? Would ye seek it elsewhere?"

Magnus froze. What he said a moment ago came back to him, and he realized how she'd interpreted it. He should have remembered that the Sinclair women would be honest with their daughters about what a loving marriage should involve in and out of the bedroom.

"When I said ma experience isnae what a mon wants with his wife, I didna mean I want less with a wife. I meant there is a type of intimacy a mon should only share with his wife, a woman he cares for deeply. Things he wishes to only share with a partner, someone he holds more dearly than anyone else. They may be the same acts, but they're special with a wife."

"Are there things ye wouldnae do with a wife that ye would with other women?" Saoirse continued to lean against him. She found more of her wavering confidence by not having to look at Magnus while they talked.

"How much has yer mother talked to ye aboot what happens between men and women?"

"I havenae done any of it, but I dinna think there is much I dinna ken aboot what can happen."

"Is there something in particular ye think I wouldnae want with ye? That I would seek elsewhere?"

"I can think of a few."

It was Magnus's turn to blush. It only made his mind run wild with images of them stripped naked in his chamber at home. When he looked toward the cave's entrance, he pictured them coupling on the beach and even in the almost always frigid North Sea. He thought about the tub that awaited him here at the keep. He prayed his sporran kept her from feeling the poleaxe beneath his plaid.

"If we marry, I wish to explore all those things with ye. But I will never force ye to accept aught ye dinna want or enjoy."

"I dinna think ye're the type of mon to insist that it's yer right to do as ye wish with ma body."

"Never."

"And if what I wish to learn scandalizes ye?"

"Then I'm a vera lucky mon to have a wife who desires me so."

"Ye dinna think me wanton to speak so brazenly?"

"I'm thinking many things right now, but none of it is negative. I'm grateful ye can talk to me openly aboot this."

"Is it wrong that we're discussing this without even being betrothed?" Saoirse squeezed her eyes shut.

"Nay. What we talk aboot in private is our business, just like what we do once we marry is only our business."

"Once? Nae if?" Her eyes flew open.

"I wouldnae have this conversation with a maiden if I didna plan to make her ma wife. I wish to give ye time to decide if I'm the mon ye wish to marry. But I ken what I want."

"Is it because ye desire me, Magnus?"

"Partly. Ye're the bonniest woman I've ever seen. But ye're intelligent, kind, and I love hearing ye laugh. Ye're easy to trust. I didna think I would ever trust a woman again without reservations first. Something felt wrong aboot Louisa from the beginning, but I forced maself to set aside ma concerns. I shouldnae have. Mayhap it's because I've kenned ye yer entire life, but I dinna think that's it. I remember ye as a child, but it's as though ye're a different person to me now."

Saoirse leaned back. Neither loosened their hold, but they could now see each other's face.

"I feel the same way. I remember ye as someone who was always patient with the weans and fun when ye'd take us on adventures. But the mon before me could be a stranger I've met for the first time. It's so different, how I felt aboot that lad and how I feel aboot ye now."

"How do ye feel, Saoirse?"

"Like I can finally be maself without worrying what

others think. That I can be confident aboot what I want and what I wish to say. I dinna have a reason for being so shy. Naught happened to make me so. I just get overwhelmed when there are so many people around. And there always are in such a large family. I enjoy time by maself. But for once, I've found someone who I wish to share that time with. I even wish for time away from Rose, and I'm closer to her than I am ma own sisters."

"I'm nae shy, but I understand enjoying time without all the effort that goes in to being around others. It's why I didna mind riding patrols so often. Aye, I was with other guards, but it was so much quieter than being at the keep or in the villages."

"Since Grandda and Uncle Callum have sworn none of us will ever have to marry for an alliance, I thought I might make a home with a husband in a croft. But ye're a tánaiste, so I suppose ye must live in yer keep."

"Nay. It's a luxury afforded the laird's family, but it isnae a requirement. If we marry, and ye wish for a croft, then that's what we shall have. It would be wise to live within the walls, but if ye truly prefer living in a village, then I will see to it."

"Ye'd give up living with yer family in yer home for a croft that would be smaller than yer Great Hall?"

"If it made ye happy, then aye. If ye come to the Mackenzie clan as ma bride, then I will provide for ye always. That doesnae just mean fine clothes and wine. It means whatever ye need to make ye happy, so ye dinna regret yer choice."

"Magnus, living in a keep wouldnae make me regret marrying ye. I may prefer a croft, but where I live isnae as important as the mon I marry. If we canna have a croft, it's nae what would make me say nay. It's if we dinna suit."

Their gazes locked, and heat surged between them. Magnus leaned forward as Saoirse went on her toes again. Their mouths collided this time. Saoirse didn't hesitate to open to him as his tongue slid along hers. She matched his movements as her hands roamed over his massive shoulders and broad chest. She'd seen naked men because of her time spent as a healer. She'd seen men training without their leines. But never had she seen or felt a man's body that made her wish to climb him like a tree and hang on.

Magnus's left arm slid between her shoulder blades until his hand cupped her nape. The other rested at the small of her back. When she shifted restlessly and pressed his sporran against his cock, he inhaled sharply. Need coursed through him as he fought to recall that she was a virgin. She was the most desirable woman he'd ever met, and he'd never had to exercise restraint before. His past partners were experienced and there for their mutual pleasure. But what he wanted with Saoirse wasn't a quick tumble to satisfy an urge.

He kissed along her jaw to her neck, nipping at the crook of her neck before kissing behind her ear. Each shuddering breath she took spurred him on to discover her next reaction. When she reached between them to push his sporran out of the way with a disgruntled huff, he caught her wrist.

"Saoirse, kenning what lies beneath a mon's plaid and feeling it are two different things. Even if ye are a healer." Magnus realized he found it unpleasant knowing his wasn't the first and only male body she would see. But he named himself a hypocrite in the same instant. He doubted Saoirse wanted any reminders that she would be neither the first nor the only woman to see him bare.

"Do ye nae want me closer?"

"I'd share a body to have ye close enough, but I dinna want to make ye uncomfortable and ruin this."

"It willna ruin it, Magnus. It's what I want."

Magnus hesitated for a moment before spinning his sporran toward his back. His hands rested in the dip at the small of her back, just above her backside. His fingers pressed against the top of the plush flesh. Saoirse arched her back, her hips touching Magnus's. She felt his arousal against her mons, and she wanted to rub herself against it like a contented kitten. Magnus wished to lift her and wrap her legs around his waist before thrusting his cock into her.

The ledge upon which they stood was barely wide enough for them to stand facing one another. One step backward had Saoirse's back brushing against the wall. She moaned her satisfaction at the feel of being sandwiched between two unmovable objects. She thought he'd aroused her as much as she could get a moment ago, but being pressed against the wall with Magnus's body pinning her there was more exciting than she imagined. Their kisses grew wild, both insatiable.

"Saoirse! Saoirse!"

"Bluidy hell, it's Thormud." Saoirse looked toward the cave entrance as Magnus stepped away, careful not to fall backward into the pool within the cave. She scrambled to grab her basket and knife. She moved to a spot where she hadn't yet collected the algae. "We're in the cave, Thor."

Thormud appeared in the entrance and stared at the pair. Magnus leaned against a wall with one shoulder pressing against the surface, his arms crossed, and his sporran back in place. Saoirse was several feet away, bent over a rock but looking toward Thormud.

"Ye're collecting algae?"

"Aye. Ye didna think I came for a swim, did ye?"

"Nay. But—"

Magnus pushed away from the wall. "Saoirse, move back, please." He walked to Thormud and pointed outside. He kept his voice low. "What the hell did those two arses say to ye?"

"That ye were coming down here to tryst with ma cousin."

Thormud wasn't wrong. But Magnus had only hoped to do that on the way down here. He hadn't planned to make it happen.

"Who'd they crow that to?"

"Uncle Alex and Da."

"Did anyone else hear them?"

"Mayhap."

Magnus's hands fisted. He'd warned Nicholas and Conan. It mattered not that they'd assumed rightly. He would make good on his pledge if there was even a hint of gossip that besmirched Saoirse's reputation.

"Saoirse, gather yer things. We're headed back with Thormud." Magnus didn't take his eyes off Thormud until he turned to offer Saoirse his hand as they walked over the slippery rocks. Once Magnus and Saoirse had their stockings and boots back on, they made their way up the cliffside path. Saoirse kept the conversation going among them, so Thormud wouldn't think they were guilty and hiding anything. Both men played their part, but the tension was nearly palpable. When they stepped through the postern gate, Magnus's patience snapped.

CHAPTER 7

lenty of eyes turned toward the trio as they passed through the gate. Saoirse wondered what happened. She glanced up at Thormud, who looked angry. But when she looked up at Magnus, she almost shrank away. She followed his gaze until she spied Nicholas and Conan.

"Magnus, dinna."

"Go aboot yer business, Saoirse. I will go aboot mine."

"Dinna do this, Magnus. Please."

"I willna—canna—let it stand, Saoirse. It'll make us look guilty, like we're accepting fault." As far as Magnus was concerned, he was courting Saoirse. They'd done nothing wrong discussing what they wished for in a marriage. He'd done nothing dishonorable kissing her, even if they'd toed a fine line.

"Magnus—"

"Saoirse, I'll find ye after I settle this. Please trust me aboot this."

"Listen to him, Saoirse. He's right. Whatever was said after I left to find ye was far worse than what they told Da and Uncle Alex. We were in Grandda's solar, but the door was open. Mayhap someone overheard, but there shouldnae be this many people staring. Go inside."

Saoirse knew it was pointless to argue. She trusted Magnus to know what to do among the men. She prayed her mother and aunts could repair the damage done among the women. She felt no regret for what transpired in the cave, and she resented anyone ruining her memories. She hurried into the keep through the kitchens. But she looked back as Magnus stalked toward Nicholas and Conan. She disappeared inside, not wanting to watch. She almost felt bad for the young men.

Magnus's instinct to protect Saoirse was to draw his sword and lop off both heads. But he would give Nicholas and Conan the chance to defend themselves. Then he would decapitate them.

"What the bluidy hell did ye say?" Magnus demanded as he came to stand in front of the pair of smirking faces.

"We told ye we would tell Alex."

"And I told ye I would kill ye if there was even a whisper of gossip. Go to the lists."

"Ye dinna command us."

"But I do." Thormud stepped beside Magnus. "Do as he says."

Magnus watched a moment of trepidation flash across their faces. The moment they were all within the lists, he drew his sword. He poked both in the back. They spun around as they drew their own swords. Magnus went on the offensive, forcing the other two to walk backwards until they were far enough into the training ground that people away from the area couldn't see what was happening.

"I told ye I would challenge ye. I told ye I would kill ye. Mayhap I should let ye say yer goodbyes to yer mamas." Magnus's sword crashed against Conan's, leaving a dent. Surprise gave Magnus an opening as Conan glanced down at his sword. Magnus plowed his fist into his opponent's nose. Blood squirted in every direction.

Nicholas swore and launched his own attack. Magnus knocked the sword from the younger man's hands with one block. His leg kicked out and swept Nicholas's feet out from under him. Magnus kicked him in the gut. He stepped back from both opponents. He wanted to silence them permanently, but he knew he didn't have the right. He couldn't justify it without knowing what they said or how bad the damage was.

"Óg!"

Magnus knew the voice, but he didn't turn toward Alex. He wouldn't take his hazel eyes off the two men whose loose lips would likely have him banished from Dunbeath and made an enemy to the Sinclairs.

He sheathed his sword as he took another step back. He waited for Alex to come to his side before he shifted his focus. His heart sank at the anger he witnessed in Alex's mien. But the older warrior wasn't looking at him. He glared at the two men on the ground.

"Callum and I explicitly told ye nae to tell tales. Ye arenae laird, tánaiste, or the lass's father. Ye dinna decide who can and canna guard ma daughter. Ye insulted our guest and slighted ma daughter's honor."

"We didna do aught wrong. We didna insult him."

"Now ye'd call ma daughter a liar? Get up." Alex reached forward and yanked Conan to his feet. Magnus could tell Alex barely held his temper in check. He was a wiser man than Magnus had been. He wondered if Alex directed some of his rage toward him and if it would be his turn next. "I just spoke to Lady Saoirse. I ken how ye acted. Ye're lucky Óg didna beat ye senseless then. Óg has been part of this clan since before either of ye shites were born. Go clean yerselves up. Ye've just earned yerselves a fortnight of evening watch. I expect ye in the lists at sunrise. Find yer own time to sleep. The rest of it is mine."

Alex adopted the Sinclair Stance, and both men hurried out of the lists. Alex waited until Thormud realized he was unwelcome, too. His nephew hurried out of the training area, leaving Alex and Magnus to talk.

"I didna think I would ever have to warn ye nae to dally with one of our lasses."

"I am nae dallying with anyone, Alex."

"Ye were alone in that cave with Saoirse for a long time."

"Any guard would have been. It would be unacceptable to send anyone inside alone."

"Nay other guard is pining over ma daughter, imagining things he has nay business doing."

"Ye arenae inside ma head, Alex. I'm nae pining for anyone."

"Bullshite. Ye think I dinna recognize how ye look at Saoirse? She's the bluidy image of her mother. I look at Brighde the same way. I ken what yer look means."

"I havenae done whatever those two claimed. I havenae dishonored Lady Saoirse, and I never would."

"Lady?" Alex mocked. "I doubt that's how ye see her."

Magnus took a step forward until he was nearly nose-to-nose with Alex. "Dinna question ma integrity or ma intentions toward Lady Saoirse. Dinna make her sound as though I think her a whore. I dinna care if ye are her father. I willna stand for anyone slighting her like that. Ye might think it's only directed to me, but it dishonors her too."

"Ye think ye can fight me, lad? Ye still needed yer sister to wipe yer nose when ye arrived here."

"Better than being so auld now that someone needs to wipe ma arse."

"Ye little fucker." Alex reached back for his claymore, and so did Magnus. "Stay away from ma daughter, ye lecher."

"Da!"

Both men looked toward Saoirse, who had her skirts lifted to her knees as she ran across the field. It surprised both men to see how fast she could run. Callum, Mòr, Tavish, and Liam were behind her. When she reached the livid men, she pushed Óg a step away, then slid between them. She looked up at Óg, beseeching him to stop. He returned his sword to the sheath across his back. She spun to look up at her father.

"Go inside, Saoirse. I ken Óg already told ye to. Ye dinna have to listen to him, but ye have to listen to me."

"Nay. I'm nae leaving if ye're going to fight."

"Yer *uncle* has nae business lusting after ye."

"Da!"

"I'm nae her uncle, and well ye ken it. Dinna make this sound incestuous on top of yer accusations. I willna tolerate it."

"Ye will tolerate whatever I bluidy well say, or yer arse can be on yer horse in the next two minutes." Alex's hands were on his waist as he leaned forward. Óg snarled, as he gripped Saoirse's arm lightly but pulled her from between them.

"Dinna ever trap yer daughter between us. Dinna make her choose, and dinna put her in danger. I willna forgive ye, Alex."

Alex glanced at Saoirse before narrowing his deep brown eyes at Magnus. "I'm nae the one who'd harm her. I'm nae the one she needs protecting from."

"Dinna put her in the middle, Alex. I willna hit ye, but ye dinna put a lass between two men able to kill each other. I dinna care if ye are her da."

Callum wrapped his arm around Saoirse's shoulders and moved her to stand among him, Tavish, and Mòr. Liam stepped up to the two enraged men, putting a hand on each chest and pushing hard. It was enough to make them each move.

"Ye're causing a scene. The laird's family doesnae argue in public."

"Ye've been a foster brother to me as much as Callum has. I've felt like part of this family since the moment I left home to come here. But I'm nae anyone's uncle but Thormud's, Rose's, and Shona's. Dinna sully ma reputation or imply I'm a monster. I dinna prey on the innocent or abuse ma relationship with this family."

"Alexander, Óg, we'll discuss this in ma solar."

"Nay." All eyes swung to Saoirse. "At least, ye arenae discussing it without me. Ye willna talk aboot me as though I'm a child who doesnae understand what's happening, nor will ye talk aboot me as though I'm some object two weans fight over."

Everyone but Óg stared at Saoirse, flabbergasted by her strident tone. Óg's smile encouraged her to stand up for herself. She was furious at both men, but Óg's support emboldened her, and she appreciated it. She spread her feet hip-width apart and crossed her arms. She appeared like a lamb among bulls, but none of her family ever recalled her seeming so mature. They sensed her iron will, and it matched their wives'. Óg continued to watch Saoirse while everyone else's gaze swung to Alex, who appeared defeated.

"Find yer mama, lass." Liam continued to block Óg and Alex from each other, not convinced it wouldn't come to blows.

"Da, they're all here already." Tavish pointed to the entrance to the lists. Siùsan, Brighde, Ceit, and Deirdre stood fanned out, making it impossible for anyone else to enter the lists. They faced inward, watching the men and Saoirse, and there was no doubt they were guarding them.

Liam led the way, dreading the conversation about

to be had. He knew there was no way everyone would leave pleased. He hoped to keep it from erupting again, but he doubted today was the only battle in this war. Each of the husbands wrapped his arm around his wife's waist, separating Saoirse and Óg. She walked between her grandfather and her family, and Óg followed them all. When they stepped outside of the lists, Saoirse stopped. She looked back at Óg and waited.

"Saoirse, dinna hold us up." Brighde was more successful hiding her anger than her husband, but she struggled not to snap at her daughter.

"Nay. We arenae walking through the bailey with Óg trailing behind like a kicked puppy. Everyone is behaving disgracefully. Ye should be ashamed."

"Dinna speak to—"

"Alex, cease. The lass is right. Óg, walk beside me." Liam didn't relish this moment as laird or patriarch. Óg squeezed between Callum and Mòr, the latter appearing entirely disappointed in Óg. The younger of the two Magnuses felt most demoralized at disappointing the elder of that name. He glanced at Siùsan, who looked conflicted and nearly in tears. It wouldn't be the first time Mackenzies and the rest of her family caught her in the middle.

They filed into Liam's solar, and Alex pushed the door shut with a bang. He elbowed his way forward, his brothers barely trying to slow him. Once again, Saoirse stepped between Magnus Óg and Alex.

"Hiding behind a lass again?"

"Saoirse, please stand with yer mama."

"Nay. I'm standing just where this situation has put me. Da, dinna make me choose. Óg wouldnae ask it of me, but I ken ye will."

"Then let him walk away." Alex crossed his arms.

"I dinna want him to."

The declaration hung in the air.

"Ye dinna ken what ye want, *leannan*." Brighde came to stand beside her daughter.

"Ye were ma age when ye married Da. Did ye nae ken what ye wanted?"

"I wasna sure at first. It wasna a simple decision made in just a few days of kenning him."

"I've kenned Óg ma entire life. Ye act as though I dinna ken him at all. Ye act as though none of ye ken him."

"This is aboot our ages, Saoirse. They think me a lecher who's corrupting ye."

"Corrupting me? Mayhap if I didna ken what happens between a mon and a woman, I'd be easily led. But ye havenae done aught to corrupt me. Just the opposite. Nay one else has ever made me feel like they respect ma wishes as much as ye do."

"He's too auld, Saoirse." It was Callum's turn to speak up. "He has experience a husband for a lass like ye shouldnae have."

Saoirse narrowed her whisky-colored eyes at Callum before she darted them to Siùsan. She cocked an eyebrow at her aunt. Siùsan rested a hand on Callum's chest, hoping to deter him, but he clearly wouldn't back down.

"I believe it was yer experience, Uncle Callum, that led ye to meet Óg and Seamus."

Callum jerked back. Callum's past was a lesson to the lads on not dallying or keeping a mistress. It was a harsh memory for any of them to recall because it was his past that endangered Siùsan's life when they were newly married. It was that threat that haunted Óg's memories.

"Mayhap ye shouldnae have had that experience as a husband for a lass like Auntie Siùsan."

"Saoirse, ye dinna have to hurt them to defend me." Óg kept his voice low.

"I willna have any of them be hypocrites aboot this. Ye think I dinna ken why our family handfasts before the kirking. Ye canna act the way ye do, then explain marriage as ye have with all of us, then think we dinna understand why none of ye waited to stand before a church. All of ye were impatient, and every mon in here had more experience than his bride. Except for Uncle Mòr and Auntie Deirdre, years more experience."

"What did he do to ye that ye think ye can speak this way?" Brighde demanded.

"Óg didna do aught! Stop speaking as though Óg isnae here. Ye must have thought me an eejit without a thought of ma own if it surprises ye that I have them now."

"Saoirse—"

"Nay. Dinna make excuses for them, Óg. I ken ye're trying to keep the peace, and this is why I usually dinna speak up. I dinna like arguing, but this matters enough to me to stand up for maself."

"I forbid it," Alex growled.

A resolve came into Saoirse's eyes that made everyone in the chamber realize that, not only did she have an iron will they didn't expect, she would be more stubborn than they realized.

"Good thing ye have experience chasing runaway brides, Da. Ye might need to catch me one of these days. Dinna push too hard."

"Enough." Óg turned Saoirse to face him. "I wish to speak to Saoirse alone. Leave the door open and listen if ye want, but we dinna need anyone hovering."

"Nay," Alex snapped.

"Out." No one could argue with Liam, so Óg and Saoirse waited until they were alone. He pulled out a chair at the oblong table in the center of the chamber.

He waited until she sat before turning a chair toward her and taking her hands in his.

"Saoirse, throwing past mistakes back in yer family's face isnae going to move them to our side. I understand ye're hurt and frustrated. I am too. But this isnae the way to go aboot it. I'm nae backing down, and I'm nae walking away, so dinna think for a moment I'll give up without a fight. I just dinna want ye to leave with me one day and feel like ye can never come back. I dinna want us to ruin our relationships with our family. I didna understand how important family is until I lived here. *Familia prima.*"

"*Semper familia.*"

Family first. Always family. It was the laird's family motto. It was what the Sinclairs lived and breathed by. It was what made them undefeatable on the battlefield and what made them an indivisible family.

"Give them time, and while we wait, we dinna do aught to make them uncomfortable."

"Are ye so wise since ye're ancient?"

"Mayhap. I told ye, I willna give up. I willna give in either. We have a lifetime ahead of us together. It doesnae matter if it takes a while to convince everyone else."

"We could handfast." Saoirse laughed, only partly serious. She could imagine how agitated that idea must make everyone eavesdropping in the passageway.

"Let's be sure we suit first. Mayhap ye'll realize they're right, and I am nae the right choice for ye."

Saoirse's gaze rested on his lips before darting up to his blue-hazel eyes. She mouthed, "Ye are."

Magnus willed his rod to ignore Saoirse's implications. Holding her hands was enough to bring it to life. Any implication that she wished to kiss him again was enough to make him as hard as a post. He squeezed her hands before he rose. Once he pushed their chairs in, he took a place beside the fireplace.

"We're done talking." He knew the others heard the entire conversation, but he would announce it without asking them to return. Everyone but Brighde and Alex appeared mollified by what they heard. Saoirse's parents looked no more convinced than they had before they waited in the passageway. He'd hope Brighde might be on their side. He should have known she would react the same way as Alex. They were too in sync after so many years of marriage not to agree that they disagreed with their daughter's choice. He steeled himself for an uphill battle. He just hoped it wouldn't be a war of attrition.

CHAPTER 8

"Jt's just as well that ye get away from the keep for a few days." Thormud rode beside Magnus as they left the keep for their sennight-long hunting party. Tate, Kirk, Torquil, and Wiley, who was Ceit and Tavish's other son, accompanied them. Wiley and Torquil were the same age, and three years younger than Tate and Kirk. Magnus realized Saoirse was older than all but Thormud. Tate and Kirk were a year her junior. Even Blake, who'd married nearly a year ago, was two years younger than Saoirse. She was only a couple months younger than Thormud, and he'd been training to be Callum's heir for years. Once Callum became laird, he would be tánaiste.

Everyone trusted these young men to take part in leading the clan and to provide for them. No one complained that, at twenty-years-old, Blake was too young to marry. No one had even objected that Saoirse was too young. It was all about the gap in their ages.

"Why do ye think our ages bother them so much? I'm nae auld enough to be her father. Some siblings are that far apart in age."

"She's always been one of the quietest of the cousins. Mayhap it makes her seem younger to them than she is. Mayhap they canna reconcile kenning how long ago it was that ye left here a young mon with Saoirse being auld enough to choose ye as a husband."

"Is there nay hope of them coming around?"

"There's always hope." Torquil nudged his horse forward to ride alongside Magnus's left while Thormud remained to his right. "It wouldnae be a Sinclair marriage if it were easy."

"That doesnae reassure me."

"I merely mean that the Sinclairs fight for the ones they love, and they arenae deterred when things arenae easy from the start." Torquil shrugged.

"I shall remind ye of that when yer turn comes. Let's see how eager ye are for whatever battle lies ahead for ye." Magnus sighed. He wondered what Saoirse did that day. They'd had no opportunity to talk that morning. For the sake of appearances, they'd only danced together last night when changing partners put them together. People watched them, and he knew they whispered. But no one was as blatant as when they'd arrived in the bailey.

Magnus was lost in thought for the next three hours before they reached their first camping spot. The six men jested as they fished for their evening meal. Wiley and Torquil entered a friendly grappling match, and both wound up in the river. By the time they settled for the night, Magnus's heart felt lighter, but he wondered how Saoirse fared.

"Stop whittling, Óg." Thormud moved his bedroll next to Magnus's after setting up the night watch. He lifted his sword from his back and laid it next to his right arm before drawing the extra length of plaid over his shoulders and head. "They willna do aught to her."

"I didna think they would. I was wondering aboot her day."

"I can tell ye aboot that."

Magnus cocked an eyebrow. He hadn't been at Dunbeath long enough to know Saoirse's routines. They'd spent as much time together as they could, but he doubted she usually hid in her workroom for as many hours as they had. He realized he wanted to know exactly how she spent her day. He wanted her to share how it went, who she helped. He hoped they would one day sit before a fire in their own croft or lie beside each other in their bed. He wanted to ask her questions and listen to her answers, so she knew he valued her.

"She will have gone into the village to visit anyone who's ailed in the past moon. She'll have checked on the elderly to ensure they're eating and keeping well. She will have spent some time with the children, telling them stories aboot which berries or toadstools they canna eat. She'll have come back for the midday meal, then Auntie Brighde would have sent her to help wherever they needed her in the keep. In the late afternoon, she probably went with Albert to pick medicinals."

"Is that what she does every day?"

"Mostly, unless someone is ailing or giving birth. Then she'll tend them as long as they need her. How do ye nay ken this?"

"I've clearly interrupted her routine."

Magnus had so many more questions, but he wanted to ask Saoirse, not learn about her from her cousin. But he wondered if he would have the opportunity to speak to her. Alex and Brighde made it clear they wanted them apart. Magnus didn't relish the idea of causing strife with the Sinclairs. Doubt nipped at him, making him wonder if pursuing Saoirse was worth the risk of alienating himself. But the more he thought about it, the more convinced he became that he would risk everything short of endangering his clan to see if they suited.

"Ye didna hear me, did ye?"

Magnus turned to Thormud, realizing he'd forgotten the younger man was still talking. "I'm sorry. I didna."

"Saoirse is the first of the lasses to wish to wed. Nay one kens what to do. Yer age difference complicates things, but I suspect ye wouldnae have an easy time, even if ye were closer in age. If ye dinna have to rush home, then give it time. Remind everyone of the mon they ken ye to be. Let them see they couldnae ask for better mon than ye for any of the lasses."

"Thank ye." Magnus smiled for the first time in what seemed like an eternity, but the last time was only the day before in the cave. He wondered if Thormud's advice would make the week move any faster. He doubted it, but he told himself it would.

"Mama, why is Magnus's age such an issue? Do ye think he would toy with me, then walk away? That would speak to his character, nae his age."

"Ye're a lass. A mon that age has nae business looking in such a young woman's direction."

"Blake's younger than I am, and he's married."

"And Cerys is close to his age."

"But ye said I'm such a young woman. I'm aulder than him. I'm a year younger than Wee Liam, and he's married. Nay one said he was too young. Wouldnae it be better if someone in the marriage had some wisdom and had learned the way of the world? Laird Campbell is more than a decade aulder than Lady Campbell, and Dominic is aulder than Lady Emelie."

"They arenae our family." Brighde snapped.

Saoirse couldn't understand why her parents were so adamantly opposed to Magnus. They'd relented over the past four days, saying that he was family, but not exactly. They admitted that the lack of blood relation between Saoirse and him meant the argument about familial ties was moot. But they hadn't capitulated about their ages.

"How auld should the mon I marry be?"

Brighde stared at her daughter. She knew Magnus's age was a sliver of her objection, but she didn't wish to voice aloud the deeper reason—that she couldn't imagine her daughter moving away from Dunbeath, that they would go many moons between seeing each other. She'd assumed Saoirse and her other daughters would marry Sinclair clansmen and live near their family. It pained her to imagine not seeing Saoirse every day. But she didn't dare say that since it was far too smothering, so she clung to the age argument.

"Younger than Óg. He shouldnae be nearly auld enough to be yer da."

"I canna think of any mon who was two-and-ten when he became a father. Óg is nay where near auld enough to be ma father. An aulder brother, aye. Da, nay."

"I'm nae arguing with ye, Saoirse. The answer is nay."

"We arenae arguing. I want to understand. So far, I havenae heard aught that makes sense. Only ye and Da are holding our ages against us. Everyone else seems reconciled to it."

"None of them birthed ye or were there when we made ye." Brighde felt her temper growing shorter by the word. Where was the submissive daughter she knew? What had Óg done in the space of a couple weeks to make Saoirse so obstinate and assertive?

The voice inside Brighde's head continued to grow louder that reminded her she'd run away from her family, then stubbornly hid her identity from Alex when she collapsed outside the keep's gates. She knew where her daughter's stubbornness and determination came from. After all, Brighde traveled the length of Scotland almost entirely on foot to pursue what she wanted—her freedom. She didn't want to imagine what Saoirse would do to pursue her freedom to marry who she wanted.

"What is it aboot Óg that appeals to ye?"

Saoirse stared at her mother before her eyes narrowed. "Do ye think it's only because he's braw?"

Brighde smiled but shook her head. "Nay. Yer da is the handsomest mon I've ever seen. But that isnae what's made us love each other for so long."

Saoirse returned her mother's smile. Each wife claimed her Sinclair brother was the handsomest husband. They were so much alike in appearance that people confused them into their forties.

"I dinna deny he's braw, Mama. But after I got over ma surprise that I find him so after kenning him ma entire life, I realized I feel like I can talk to him aboot aught. And more than that, I ken he listens. He encourages me to speak ma mind and nay hide what I think or feel. As much as it frustrates me, I admire that he considers everyone else's feelings and understands. Mayhap it's his age that gives him the wisdom to remind me patience and forgiveness will prevail over bitterness. He's steadfast. There's naught that makes me fear he'll change his mind, or his interest will fade. After what happened with that dreadful woman, I ken he's cautious aboot who he'll bring into his clan. That he wishes it to be me means he's already given this serious consideration. He kens his duty to the Mackenzies."

"What do ye think he sees in ye beyond yer bonnie face?"

Saoirse's lips pursed as she tried not to take offense. She understood what her mother meant. "It's nae ma being young enough to bear him plenty of bairns. He says he kens I'm intelligent, kind, and he likes ma laugh. He's interested in what I say, and it feels like I'm all that he sees and hears when we talk. There's always so many people around that it's always felt like it distracts people when they talk to me."

"Do ye feel yer da and I dinna give ye our full attention?"

Saoirse's shoulders slumped before she nodded. "Mama, we're sitting together in the orchard and doing naught but talking, but I ken ye're thinking aboot all that ye still need to do. Every time someone walks by, ye glance to see who it is. Da dotes on Mirren, Nessa, and me, but I ken he's always aware that he needs to be ready in case someone calls him away. He's thinking aboot what he still needs to do, or what he needs to tell other people to do. It's nae always. But a lot of times it feels like people are thinking aboot all the things they could be doing besides being with me. With Óg, I ken he's aware of every single thing happening around him. I could ask him who's behind him and what they're doing, and he would ken without looking. He always guards against any threat that might harm me. But I feel like I'm the only thing in the world when we're together." She shrugged. "He makes me feel special."

"Ye are special."

"I ken, but it doesnae feel like that in a family this large. There are others who could do what I can. With Óg, it's like nay one else can be as important to him as I am."

"And ye ken all this after a few days?"

"Aye. I ken ye say that ye didna agree to marry Da the first time he asked. But ye never deny that ye loved him from the beginning or that he loved ye immediately. Yer objection was aboot circumstances and danger, nae aboot Da as a mon. Yer objections aboot Óg are aboot circumstances, nae the mon Óg is."

Brighde nodded. She fought back tears that her daughter ever felt less than special or valued. It made her wonder if Mirren and Nessa felt the same.

"Mama, I didna say what I did because ye havenae been the best mother. I only wanted ye to understand how Óg makes me feel." Saoirse felt wretched that she made her mother feel guilty. It only made her miss Magnus more. She wished to turn to him for consolation.

"I ken. I willna say that understanding means I'll change ma mind, but thank ye for explaining."

"The only thing that could change yer mind is Óg somehow changing his age."

Brighde rose from the bench upon which they sat. There was little point in denying the sentiment. When Saoirse stood, the two women embraced. Saoirse's sigh was one of someone bone weary but not defeated. She would give it more time to ensure it wasn't infatuation for either Magnus or her, but if it grew into love, then she would do whatever she had to.

Magnus dismounted in the Dunbeath bailey. He was filthy and tired, but the hunting excursion was a success. He and the young Sinclair men returned with two bucks, a doe, a boar, and various grouse. The women would dry and preserve the deer, then cut it into strips for the men to eat while on patrol. They would likely have the grouse that night and the boar soon.

"Welcome back."

Magnus turned to find Alex standing behind him as he drew the reins over his horse's ears. He wasn't in the mood to deal with Alex until after he bathed and ate a proper meal. He forced a neutral expression before he turned around.

"Thank ye. I trust all was well while we were away."

Alex narrowed his eyes. Magnus shook his head and walked his horse to a stableboy. He sighed before turning back to Alex.

"I didna mean aught than what I said, Alex. But I see nae all is well. Ye're even more suspicious of me than ye were a sennight ago."

"I want to ken just what ye did to make ma daughter feel so *special*."

Magnus's brow furrowed. He knew Saoirse would never reveal the kisses they shared or even their frank conversation about intimacy. He wondered what someone else told Alex. "I dinna do aught but listen when Saoirse talks to me. I admire her sincerity, gentleness, and how she enjoys solving puzzles."

"She doesnae do puzzles." Alex's disgust dripped from his words.

"She considers finding the right cure for her patients to be like a puzzle. She enjoys looking at what she kens and finding what to do to heal the person."

Alex continued to glower. Realizing Magnus knew things about his daughter that Alex didn't, placed Magnus at an even greater disadvantage.

"Ye think she looks at healing like a game."

"Alex, ye are purposely twisting ma words. Ye ken I didna say that. I've heard ye say planning battles is like putting together a puzzle. There is naught entertaining aboot trying nae to die."

"Óg, Mama says the tub is going up to yer chamber first." Thormud joined the two men. He'd felt the anger pulsing from his uncle from yards away. He watched Óg nod to Alex before his long legs carried him across the bailey. "Uncle Alex, all ye will do is make Saoirse miserable. Óg will protect her and do whatever he must to make her happy. She'll want to leave, and he'll take her. Dinna make her wish to never look back."

"It's nae her decision to make."

"Then ye and everyone else have lied our entire lives. Ye've always said it's our choice. She's making hers. Since she may nae ken for certain, Óg said he really wants them to take the time to get to ken each other. He never wants her to regret choosing him. He'd rather they find out they dinna suit before they exchange vows that canna be broken. It's nae as though they wish to marry today. If ye make her miserable, then ye'll only hasten the inevitable. I'm telling ye, he willna stop if he feels he must protect her."

"How is he so damn certain?"

Thormud shrugged. "I dinna ken because I've never felt this for a woman. But how did ye ken aboot Auntie Brighde? How'd ma da ken aboot ma mama? Ye and Da and the others will do aught to protect yer wives, and nae just to keep their bodies safe. Ye'd do aught to make them happy. Ye raised Óg to be the same. Ye canna fault him when he lives by what ye and the others taught him. Ye ken the mon he is because ye helped make him that way. I dinna think this is aboot age. I think ye dinna want Saoirse to leave. I think ye arenae ready to say goodbye."

"And ye think it's inevitable that we will, and it will only happen faster if we keep refusing." The truth Thormud spoke didn't surprise Alex because he knew it for what it was. But hearing it from someone else— someone half his age—forced him to accept what he wished to deny: his feelings and that his daughter was no longer his wee lass.

"Aye. He's been miserable for the past sennight. He hasnae said aught, and he worked as hard as the rest of us. But I could tell he was getting more anxious by the day. He worried that ye and Auntie Brighde would be at odds even more with Saoirse by the time we returned. He doesnae want that, and it really bothered him to think she'd be upset. He feels guilty that he's the cause."

"Then he should—"

"Uncle Alex, ye shouldnae have married Auntie Brighde."

The older man glowered at his nephew. "Tread carefully."

"Auntie Brighde felt guilty and thought she shouldnae stay. It bothered ye that she thought that. But ye didna relent, so dinna tell me that Óg should stay away. We all ken our family's love stories. Yer daughter may look like her mama, but dinna underestimate that she'll be as defensive of Óg as ye were of Auntie Brighde, or that she'll be as determined as ye were."

"But she isnae the same lass. He's already changed her."

"Nay. He's the first person to really see her. Dinna ye want yer daughters to marry men who make them feel safe and appreciated for being them? Óg isnae interested in an alliance because it already exists. He isnae interested in a dowry because, despite what's happened lately, the Mackenzies dinna need one. He just wants Saoirse for who she is."

"He doesnae ken—"

Thormud sighed and shook his head. Alex's lips hardened into a line.

"Uncle Alex, ye dinna want to accept that she's auld enough to have a husband or that she might leave us. Those are nae the right reasons to keep her from Óg. He's a good mon. If he were interested in one of yer nieces, ye wouldnae object like ye are. I hope ye think aboot what I've said. I dinna want a rift in the family, but I think the cousins will side with Saoirse. I think

Grandda has come around, but he willna gainsay ye as her father. But I think others will soon side with them too. Just watch for a while longer, Uncle. See how he is with her rather than assuming the worst."

"When did ye become so wise?"

"I always have been. I listen to ma da, ma uncles, and Grandda."

Alex nodded with a sigh. He'd talked to Brighde the night before. They'd both admitted why they didn't want Saoirse to marry, and it was for the reasons Thormud said. They weren't ready to relent, but they were ready to observe.

CHAPTER 9

"How was the hunting?" Saoirse kept her voice low as she and Magnus stood behind a storage building. Neither of them enjoyed the guilt that went along with meeting in secret. The illicitness didn't build excitement. It built dread. But they'd had no opportunity to speak that day. After Alex's greeting, which Saoirse heard about from Wiley, it seemed ill-advised to meet in the open.

It was now well past sundown, and most of the clan had already retired. Saoirse slipped from her chamber and crept outside through the kitchens. Magnus remained belowstairs in the Great Hall, nursing a mug of ale and looking into the fire. He'd heard someone slip past the Great Hall, despite the sounds from the people bedded down on the floor. He'd looked behind him and spied Saoirse. She'd canted her head.

He waited a minute before leaving his seat. He scanned the sleeping clan members, praying no one was awake and noticing. He followed Saoirse to the back of the small building set at the far end of the bailey. He'd watched the guards on the wall walk, but most faced outward. He hid in the shadows whenever a guard looking down at the bailey turned in his direction. He opened his arms to Saoirse once the building hid them, and she remained there as he spoke.

"Successful. We brought home plenty of meat, but it was one of the longest sennights of ma life, wee one."

"Oh? It wasna one of ma better sennights either."

"What happened?"

"Ye first, Magnus."

"But I worry aboot ye."

She leaned away. "And ye think I dinna worry aboot ye? I asked ye first."

Saoirse's soft smile melted Magnus. He inhaled the fresh scent of lavender and heather. Everything felt right in the world now that she was in his arms again. He kissed her forehead, and she leaned against his chest again.

"I missed ye, and I worried aboot how things were between ye and yer parents. I didna like leaving ye alone to fend off anyone's naysaying. It made the days between seeing ye agonizing. I felt like I abandoned ye."

"Ye didna abandon me, Magnus. Ye have duties, and I willna break because ye canna be at ma side always. It wasna enjoyable, but I survived. I missed ye too. I spoke to ma mama, and I think she understands better. But that doesnae mean either of ma parents is more likely to approve than they were before ye left."

"Did ye feel better for talking to her?"

"I did, but she didna. I didna mean to hurt her, but she asked what draws me to ye. I told her I feel special when I'm with ye. As though naught else matters, even when I ken ye're aware of everything around us. I told her I ken she and Da are usually distracted when they pay me attention. Ye dinna seem that way."

"Ye ken they arenae like that on purpose."

"I do. That's why I feel guilty that I said aught to her. But I wanted her to understand it isnae just lust. I'm certain that's what everyone believes it is. I want an aulder mon with experience, and ye wish for a young virgin. I'd want ye even if ye were the virgin." Saoirse winked at Magnus, who tilted her head back. His lips descended to hers, and she opened to him. Neither rushed since neither knew when they might have another opportunity to enjoy the luxury of privacy. She opened to him without prompting, gladly accepting his tongue as it slid along hers. Her hands cupped his neck as she pressed her hips forward. Once more, his sporran presented a barrier to what she wanted. She reached between them and spun it out of the way.

Magnus inched Saoirse farther into the shadows until there wasn't even a hint of their presence. His large hands, with his fingers spread wide, covered her backside as she sucked on his tongue. He didn't know how she learned that trick, but he nearly climaxed on the spot. He struggled when his cock twitched, and his bollocks ached. He squeezed her backside before drawing up the back of her skirts. He brought his lips to her ear.

"If ye dinna want aught that I do, tell me."

"I canna imagine ye doing aught I wouldnae want." Saoirse kissed Magnus as his hands gathered the fabric, bunching it high enough for his hands to slide beneath. He stifled his groan as his rough palms landed against the smooth skin.

"I want to touch ye too, Magnus."

"Nae tonight. If ye do, ye'll have me roaring ma release, and there willna be anyone this side of Edinburgh who doesnae ken ye pleasured me."

Saoirse playfully pouted. Magnus caught her bottom lip and pretended to tug. She flicked her tongue at him as his left hand meandered between her thighs. He could feel the heat emanating from her, like a cheery fire he wished to enjoy in the middle of a winter day. She was a respite from a stormy life. When the tip of his middle finger slipped between her netherlips, she buried her face against his chest. No one could know what they were about.

"Ye ken which part of me would rather be inside ye, Saoirse. But I will content maself with watching ye climax. I will have to save tasting ye for another day."

A shiver passed along Saoirse's spine and fanned across her arms. His words were nearly as tantalizing as his touch. He pressed his fingertip into her entrance, moving slowly to allow her to grow accustomed to the feel. She reached behind her and pressed his hand to her more firmly. His deep chuckle puffed air against her ear, sending that delicious shiver through her once more.

"Magnus—" Saoirse's mind blanked. She couldn't remember her name if anyone asked. His thumb brushed against her pearl, and she feared her legs might collapse beneath her. An ache built within her core, and she feared she might expire from the need to feel him within her. She had no experience to know that was the only solution, but it was like her soul spoke to her. Joining with Magnus was the only way she would ever feel complete.

"Aye?" Magnus's teeth tugged at her earlobe before his tongue skimmed along her neck. "What were ye going to say?"

"I dinna ken." Her answer came out on an exhalation.

"I wish to hold ye in ma arms every night. I dreamed aboot ye while I was away. Some were sinful and lurid, but they werenae ma favorites. The ones I liked best were us together with white hair, watching our bairns with their bairns. We both had lines around our eyes and mouths from smiling. It told me we'd had many years of happiness together."

"Did ye dream we walked together in a field when

we were auld, but there were weans around us?" Saoirse pressed kisses to Magnus's chest and collarbones, exposed by the unlaced ties of his leine, savoring the woodsy scent from his soap. She punctuated every couple words with a peck.

"I did, Saoirse."

They looked at each other, the uncanniness distracting them for a moment. Their mouths fused as his thumb continued to work her nub until she writhed against him. He felt her body growing impatient as he inched her toward climax. His fingers dipped within her as he rubbed circles against her pearl. She stiffened, arched, and he swallowed her moan, keeping anyone from hearing her as she climaxed.

She melted against him, her breath ragged. "Magnus, that—I dinna ken if I'm supposed to say thank ye. I feel as though I've lost all ma bones, but ma limbs feel heavy. I'm wide awake, yet I could fall asleep at any moment."

"Was that the first time ye've ever experienced yer release?"

Saoirse's brow furrowed, horror flooding her expression. "Of course, it was. Did I make ye think I would ken? Did I enjoy it too much?"

"That isnae what I meant. Nae even what I thought. Did ye ken that ye can bring yerself that feeling of bliss?"

Saoirse's eyes widened as she nodded. "I suppose so. I just never have. I thought only men really did that." She glanced down to his plaid.

"Aye. I will do just that when I get to ma chamber. Again. But a woman can pleasure herself."

"Isnae that a sin?"

"If it were, God wouldnae have made it possible. He gave mon free will, but He didna do it just for us to fail Him. It's mon who's decided it's a sin. It's as natural as breathing to wish to experience pleasure. But we canna always be with the one we want."

"I assumed men went to whores when they wanted it."

Magnus's ears were on fire. "That is an option. But they arenae always available. Or they arenae who a mon wants."

"A moment ago, ye said again."

"Aye. I thought of ye constantly, Saoirse, but I never had the time alone while away hunting. I saw ye in the Great Hall when I returned. Ye were leaning over a table. I barely made it to ma chamber before I exploded. I eased ma lust maself even before the hunting trip."

"If I did what ye did, would I be able to do it maself?"

"Aye."

"Would ye think me wrong if I did it when ye canna?" Saoirse wondered if she shouldn't have asked.

"Nay. Would ye think of me?"

"I can barely think aboot aught but ye. I wish I could bring ye pleasure tonight. Why canna I?"

"Because tonight wasna aboot me. I wanted to give ye a hint of what we can share. I wanted ye to enjoy a taste of passion without having to reciprocate."

"Vera well. I dinna have to. But what aboot how much I want to?" She didn't want their brief time together to be one sided. Taking without giving went against her nature, and she especially disliked it with Magnus.

"We shouldnae linger much longer. We're tempting fate, and it willna be on our side."

"I ken that's true. But I want to learn what will make ye feel the way ye made me feel."

"Another time, wee one. We must get ye back into the keep."

"Do ye think we could spend time together tomorrow? Mayhap a game of chess. Anyone could see us and ken we arenae doing aught scandalous."

"I would like that. Let's see what the day brings." Magnus wanted to promise they would have the time together, but he doubted anyone would allow them such a luxury. Things hadn't improved while being away. He would have to satisfy himself with secret trysts, even though they didn't sit well with his conscience.

He guided her to walk ahead of him, and he fell into step behind her, blocking any of the guards from seeing her. When they reached the Great Hall, he stepped into a recessed area and watched her walk up the stairs alone. When she was out of sight, he drew in a fortifying breath, dreading another night alone. Once he barred his door, he stripped and stood before the window embrasure. He stared at the constellations as he wrapped his hand around his length. He thought he would be in a hurry, since his desire threatened to steal his good sense. But as he pictured Saoirse, her hair fanned out around them, and her core hungry for him, he stroked slowly. It was sweet, tantalizing agony. By the time he spent himself in a linen washing square, he was exhausted. He fell into his first dreamless sleep in weeks.

Magnus wiped the profusive sweat from his brow. It was warm, and he'd already stripped off his leine. But he could feel the sea breeze with a chill to it. However, it did nothing to cool him. His throat felt parched, and even his tongue felt too large. He'd felt off the evening after he returned from hunting. It was a mild discomfort then, and it hadn't gotten worse during the past two days. But now, he feared he would be ill or that he would keel over.

"Ye dinna look good." Callum came to stand beside Magnus as he sipped from the ladle at the water bucket.

"I dinna feel right. Something is off."

"A summer ague?"

"Mayhap." Magnus drew his leine, which he held, across the back of his neck, hoping it would absorb as much as wipe away his perspiration. "I dinna have a cough, though. I'm certain it'll right itself in a day or two."

Callum looked unconvinced, but he didn't argue. As they left the lists, Magnus's chest began to ache. It was the same pain he sometimes developed after eating too much, but it was behind his ribs, high to the left. It tempted him to rub his fist over it, but he didn't want anyone else to notice that he wasn't hale. A few more steps had his stomach twisting in a knot that threatened to double him over.

"Ye dinna look well, Óg. Go to yer chamber and rest."

Any other time, and Magnus might have felt like a chastised child, but he saw the merit in the older man's instructions. He nodded before Callum went to join his brothers. He struggled to lift his arms over his head to don his leine. He didn't bother to tuck it into his belt and plaid. He was panting too hard to raise his arm again to place his sword in the sheath across his back. He forced one foot in front of the other until he left the lists. As he entered the bailey, he looked toward Saoirse's workroom. He loathed looking weak in front of her until he reminded himself only a weak man didn't ask for help. He trudged his way there, but he heard Brighde's voice before he reached the door. He almost turned around. He knocked before walking through the door.

"Óg?" Saoirse dropped the bowl she held on to the table and rushed around it, wiping her hands on her kirtle as she walked.

"Hello." Each sound took a monumental effort to produce.

"What's wrong?" Saoirse was almost to his side when her mother stepped between them. Her eyes narrowed.

"Ye could at least refresh yerself before coming into such a tight space." It surprised Brighde to find Magnus so unkempt. It displeased her that he wished to see Saoirse so much that he couldn't bother to get clean. She wondered if he thought to sneak a tryst with her daughter. "Go back to the keep, Óg. Saoirse and I are working. Ye can see her at the evening meal. I'm certain ye'll find ways to dance together."

"Mama—"

Brighde shot her daughter a warning glare, but Saoirse ignored it.

"Magnus, what's the matter?" She made to move around her mother when she glimpsed Magnus waver, then lean against the door jamb. He shook his head and stepped back from the doorway. She looked back at Brighde. "Da, saved yer life when ye ailed for weeks after arriving here. Nay one turned ye away."

She hurried past her mother. There was something extremely wrong. Magnus squinted as the bright sunlight dazzled his eyes. He leaned a forearm against the building and retched twice before emptying his stomach. He heard Saoirse and felt her hand on his back, but it was as though he were in a jar. The sound and her touch were distorted. The touch distant, but the sound amplified. He took four steps before the ground rose unexpectedly and crashed into his face. The impact hurt, but it felt good to close his eyes and allow the ground to bear his weight.

"Da!" Saoirse assumed her father was somewhere nearby, since she saw other men returning from the lists. She gathered her skirts and stepped over Magnus before kneeling. He was unconscious, so his weight was too much for her to push. She stepped back over him and tried to pull him onto his back. But it was to no avail. She glanced around. "Da! Grandda! Help me."

Alex heard his daughter's cry the first time and ran toward her. He was nearly there when she called for him again. Liam came running from the keep's steps. Alex searched for his daughter, finding her kneeling beside Magnus, trying to pull him onto his back. Brighde stepped beside their daughter and helped. They'd just rolled him over when Alex and Liam reached their side.

"Ye shouldnae have sent him away, Mama." Saoirse brushed the hair back from Magnus's forehead. He had no fever, which worried her more. There was no easy explanation for why sweat drenched him. She shook the veritable giant's shoulder. Somehow, having him lying before her made her realize how large he was. "Magnus? Magnus?"

"I didna think he was sick." Brighde felt horrible that she'd assumed the reason for his visit. Now that she took the time to look, she could see all the telltale signs. His pallor was nearly gray, his eyes were glazed when Saoirse peeled his lids open, and his body trembled. "Alex, Da, help us get him inside."

All of Liam's daughters-by-marriage called him Da and had since nearly the day they wed. He might be one of the most intimidating warriors on the British Isles, but he was a father-figure to most people younger than him. He and Alex grasped an arm each and heaved. They got Magnus to his feet as his eyes flew open. He jerked free, stumbled, then emptied his belly again. His legs crumpled, and Saoirse barely caught him in time to keep him from landing in his own vomit. Alex caught her when Magnus's weight forced her backward.

"Mòr! Callum!" Tavish was running toward them as he bellowed for his other brothers. "What happened?"

"We dinna ken. He came to see me, but he left before I could do aught." Saoirse glowered at her mother. "He fell and passed out before he landed. He roused long enough to empty his belly a second time."

"I sent him to his chamber because he didna look well. Why'd he leave ye if he sought yer help?" Callum grabbed a leg while Mòr grabbed the other. Liam, Callum, Alex, and Mòr hoisted Óg into the air while Saoirse supported his head. The four men carried the supine warrior with ease. Tavish ran ahead to open the keep's doors.

"I sent him away," Brighde confessed. "I thought he wished to sneak a visit with Saoirse and hadn't bothered to get cleaned up first."

"Can ye carry him up the three flights? It's going to be tight." Saoirse considered how narrow the stairway would be with three abreast. She was unconvinced they could get Magnus to his chamber. She had to let go of his head and walk behind the others.

"We'll take him to Wiley and Tate's," Tavish suggested. They would only have to maneuver Magnus up one flight of stairs.

"Óg?" Siùsan rushed from the kitchens. Someone must have told her that the men carried her brother inside. Tavish took the leg Callum held as the oldest Sinclair brother wrapped his arm around his wife.

"We dinna ken what's wrong yet, Auntie Siùsan. He was ill outside and collapsed. I'll see to him. Can ye send a bath up?"

"I'll take care of it," Brighde offered. She turned toward the kitchens while everyone else began taking the stairs.

"Saoir…" Magnus croaked.

"I'm here."

"Saoir…"

"I'm right here, Magnus." It was awkward, but she reached through Mòr's arm to grasp Óg's hand.

"Saoir…"

It was clear he didn't know what happened around him or who was there. He was calling to her in his delirium. Saoirse squeezed his hand, then let go. It made climbing the stairs too hard, and she knew Magnus wouldn't know the difference.

"Saoir!"

Maybe he did. His hand reached into space, as though he might catch Saoirse's retreating one. She wrapped her fingers around his and squeezed.

"I'm here, Magnus."

Despite the awkwardness, they moved him to Tavish's sons' chamber while Saoirse held his hand. They'd barely entered and hadn't yet laid him on the bed when a line of servants rushed in with the tub. They brought buckets of water that they took to the fireplace.

"Dump it in. It doesnae need warming." Saoirse's voice held an air of command since she was in her element. "Elizabeth and Catriona, get a stack of fresh linens for the bed and for his bath. Kirsten, go to ma healing room and fetch ma bag. We need to get him undressed."

"Nay. Ye arenae tending to him while he's undressed." Alex shook his head. His daughter, whose nose came to the center of his chest, came to stand in front of her mountainous father.

"Aye, I am. If he dies because ye canna get past him being five-and-thirty, I promise yer problems will be far greater than our ages. Either ye help, or ye move out of ma way, Da. He's sick. Ye wouldnae stop me from tending anyone else this ill. Ye should be ashamed that ye'd deny him help."

"I didna say nay one would tend to him. Siùsan can do it."

"Nay, I canna," Siùsan protested. "I dinna ken what's wrong. He looks far worse than I ken how to heal. Why's he sweating so much if he doesnae have a fever?"

"There's something in him that his body is trying to expel, but it canna." Saoirse spoke as she dumped a bucket of cool water into the tub. "Da, let Auntie Siùsan help me. Ye can go."

Alex blinked as he stared at his daughter. Never had she dared to command him before. He was uncertain what to make of it. Part of him was proud of the command she held over the situation. Part of him wanted to spin her around and march her out of the chamber. Part of him was too dumbfounded to do anything. When his thoughts finally coalesced, he reached forward and unpinned the length of wool from Magnus's shoulder and placed the brooch on the bedside table. He tugged Magnus's arm, and Tavish did the same until they sat him up enough for Siùsan to lift the soaked leine from his body. Saoirse worked to get his boots and stockings off. In the meantime, the two maids returned with the linens Saoirse requested, and Brighde entered the chamber with Saoirse's bag. She'd passed the other maid and offered to bring it up.

Saoirse had the sense to allow her aunt to unfasten Magnus's belt and unwrap his plaid. She had a moment of disappointment that she wasn't alone with him, and this wasn't a romantic encounter. But his groan as he pitched sideways, vomiting on the floor, brought her back to her senses. She snatched her bag from her mother and rummaged in it as she continued to give orders.

"Get him in the tub, all the way under. His feet can

stick out, but ye need to submerge his shoulders." She watched from beneath her lashes, impressed with the physique on display as the men lifted Magnus from the bed. Muscles seemed to grow upon muscle as his body shifted with each movement. His torso was sun-kissed, but his waist down was a stark white in comparison. It wasn't the first time she'd noticed such a contrast on a man, but it drew her eyes to his cock. She tried not to stare when she realized he was a well-endowed man. She'd seen a variety of men's cocks during her years as a healer. None made her curious anymore, but Magnus's made her wish for his speedy recovery, and not just for his sake.

As they lowered Magnus into the cool water, he groaned and winced. Saoirse pulled a sachet from the bag and moved toward the fire, grabbing a mug her mother brought. She scooped water from a bucket on the hearth and placed the mug on the stones. It wouldn't take long for it to heat, even without being over the direct flames. She gathered other things from her bag as Magnus soaked.

"What was he doing in the lists? Anything unusual?" Saoirse looked at her father and uncles.

"Nay. He trained like usual and looked fine, except he started sweating and couldnae stop," Callum explained. "I thought he looked peaky, so I sent him to his chamber. He must have decided he was poorly enough to seek yer help. I dinna think he wanted to at first."

Saoirse glanced at Magnus, whose head hung back over the tub's rim. Siùsan has placed a folder towel beneath it to pad the lip. "Did he eat aught while he was out there?"

"Nae aught anyone else didna eat," Mòr explained. "I shared an apple with him, and I stood beside him when he grabbed the dried beef sticks Blake offered him. He drank from the same waterskin as Torquil. In fact, it was Torquil's waterskin. I saw Torquil leave the lists after Óg. He didna look any worse for wear." Mòr hovered over the younger man. He'd been concerned, but he had said nothing when he noticed Óg didn't look well. Now he regretted not sending for Saoirse or telling Óg to see her.

Saoirse nodded as she watched Siùsan run a soapy linen square over Magnus's body. A pang of possessiveness unlike anything she'd ever felt crashed over her. She had no reason to feel territorial when it was Magnus's sister who tended him. But she wished it were her. Not just because she wished to explore his body, but because she wanted it to be her right. She waited as Siùsan washed his hair. Once he was clean, the men hoisted him from the tub. Siùsan and Brighde hurried to dry him while Saoirse prepared a tea.

"What did he eat to break his fast?" Saoirse had already been away from the keep. A pregnant woman's husband was certain she was in labor and came, insisting Saoirse attend to her. The poor woman was flustered and embarrassed when Saoirse arrived. She'd tried to convince her husband that she wasn't going to deliver yet. She pointed out that with five children already, her husband should have known it wasn't time. Saoirse reassured the village woman that it was fine, and that she respected the man's wish to care for his wife.

"Porridge, just like us." Alex watched Saoirse's every move. He knew she was a competent healer. He'd turned to her more than once over the years. But he saw her through new eyes as she moved around the chamber, setting up her supplies and monitoring Magnus.

Once they settled him on the bed with the covers drawn over him, she sat beside him to spoon tea into him. He grimaced several times, but he swallowed. His gray skin worried Saoirse. She couldn't think of an easy diagnosis yet. She didn't know enough to put all the puzzle pieces in place.

"There's naught much to do right this minute. I need to finish getting this tincture in him, then I'll observe. Da, will ye stay and help? This tea will force out whatever else is in his belly. He's too heavy for me to move him to the chamber pot when he needs it."

Alex nodded, surprised she asked for his help. He shot Brighde a glance, but she only shrugged. Saoirse asked for no one else to stay, so the rest of the family filed out. When Liam closed the door behind him, Saoirse turned toward Alex, who now stood by the window embrasure.

"Da, I dinna ken what's wrong with him. I'm scared. He shouldnae be so pale without a fever. I didna lie aboot needing yer help when it's time for him to use the chamber pot. But I really need ma da right now." She stood, blinking back tears, before she rushed into Alex's embrace. "What if I canna cure him?"

Alex held his daughter against his chest, unsure what to say. He didn't want to give her false platitudes. As the healer, she best understood the risks. If she feared Magnus's death, then the situation was grave.

"Ye'll do the best ye can. He kens ye're here, even if he hasnae woken. The way he calmed when ye held his hand makes it clear he trusts ye. Trust yerself. He said ye like healing partly because it's a puzzle. Ye're still sorting through the pieces right now. Ye'll put him back together soon enough."

"Da, what am I supposed to do if I lose him?"

That was an even harder question to answer. He and Brighde knew they'd met each day before the hunting trip. They'd allowed it because the couple remained within the walls, where anyone could walk in on them in her workstation. But he'd been livid when he learned they'd gone to the beach together. It was only Callum's insistence that kept him from dragging Magnus's corpse from the cave. He witnessed how Saoirse retreated into herself while he was away. She seemed back to her usual self, but after seeing her stand up to everyone, he'd realized that she'd lost the confidence she'd gained from Magnus. He'd seen how she glanced toward the gate the last two days before the men returned.

"*Nighean.*" Daughter. "Dinna assume the worst, even if ye ken we must prepare for it. But I understand yer fear. I've sat beside yer mama while she nursed ye and yer sisters. I've worried over Da and ma brothers while they've healed from battle wounds. I was beside maself with yer sisters' and yer births. Yer mama didna have an easy go with any of them. It was me who insisted that we have nay more bairns because I couldnae face losing her. I ken I canna rid ye of yer fear, but I'll stay and help as long as ye want me."

"Thank ye, Da. Dinna let go yet, please." Saoirse squeezed her father's waist as Alex continued to embrace her. She'd always felt safe from everything when she was in Alex's arms. Even at her age now, the world seemed less daunting with him protecting her. But she wanted nothing more than for Magnus to be awake and holding her. She'd never imagined she could feel safer than with Alex, but she knew now that Magnus offered her a sense of calm her father never could. For now, she would accept her father's support because it was all she had. She drew strength from his love, in no hurry to pull away. They stood together for a long time before Magnus's groan drew their attention.

CHAPTER 10

Saoirse and Alex remained with Magnus throughout the night and into the following morning. The tincture she gave him worked, and Alex maneuvered him to the chamber pot. He insisted Saoirse allow him to do it alone. He knew it would humiliate Magnus once he woke if he learned Saoirse helped. He'd been hard enough on the man already. He didn't need to kick him at his lowest moment.

"He's nae sweating anymore, and I dinna think there is aught left for his body to pass." Saoirse straightened the covers around Magnus's chest after running a cool, wet linen over his arms and chest. She didn't dare push the sheets lower. Her father had been an angel of mercy, so she wouldn't summon the devil.

"Saoirse?"

"Magnus? I'm here." Saoirse ran the cloth over his brow as his eyes fluttered open. She breathed a silent sigh of relief. But his glassy eyes still concerned her. She would wait to see if they cleared once he came around more.

"What happened?"

"Ye were ill. Ye vomited twice outside and once in here."

"Why? I didna eat aught that others didna."

"I dinna ken. When did ye start to feel poorly?"

"The day after I returned from the hunting trip. I was uncomfortable, but I didna think it was aught serious. But today I couldnae stop sweating, and ma chest hurt."

"That was yesterday," Alex chimed in as he came to stand behind Saoirse. Magnus's gaze jumped to Alex. Saoirse didn't care for the wariness that entered them. Magnus no longer trusted Alex.

"Magnus, ye collapsed outside ma healing room. Da and the others carried ye up here. He's been helping me since yesterday afternoon."

Magnus once more looked up at Alex. He nodded his appreciation when Alex cocked an eyebrow and darted his eyes to the chamber pot that sat near the bed, then looked down at Saoirse and shook his head.

"How do ye feel now?"

"Thirsty. Is there aught I can drink?"

Saoirse handed him a mug of cool water. "Sip."

Magnus managed six sips before he covered his mouth. Saoirse snatched the chamber pot from the floor and barely placed it under his chin in time. The water came back up along with bile. Magnus slumped back against the pillows and shut his eyes.

"Magnus?" Saoirse handed the pot to her father and touched Magnus's shoulder. When he didn't rouse, she shook his shoulder. "Magnus?"

There was no response. The pattern continued throughout the day and through the next. He would rouse and try to sip water, but it wouldn't stay down. He remained awake long enough to say he wished to sleep. Saoirse understood, but she felt a pang of hurt when he rolled away and adjusted his pillows.

"Da, I dinna ken what else to do. If he canna keep water in his belly, I canna give him aught else. His belly is empty, yet bile keeps coming up. It must burn his throat badly. He needs something to eat, or he'll grow too weak to get better."

"How much longer do ye think he can carry on if he doesnae start eating and drinking?"

"A couple more days." It frustrated Saoirse that she couldn't figure out a diagnosis, and it pained her to see the man she was falling in love with suffer so much. She'd returned to Alex's embrace countless times during their hours of nursing Magnus. Most of the time, they didn't speak. She drew strength from Alex's companionable silence. He observed his daughter's every move, concerned that she appeared exhausted too. He knew he was tired, but he had experience remaining awake for more than a day at a time.

"I'll stay awake, Saoirse. Why dinna ye try to rest for a few hours in the chair?" He knew he would never convince her to leave. She hesitated, then nodded. She felt ready to drop. She dozed but never settled into a deep sleep.

Another night passed, as did a morning. By the fourth afternoon, Saoirse felt desperate. She tried spooning bone broth into him, hoping his stomach would accept something different. It stayed down longer than water, but it inevitably came up.

"Magnus, I dinna have any other solutions." Saoirse murmured as she leaned forward to check on him. Her father rested in the chair, his breathing deep and regular. But she knew he would be awake in a flash if something disturbed him. She didn't know any man who was a deep sleeper, which made Magnus's condition so grave.

"Ye're doing just what I need."

Saoirse's eyes widened. Magnus's gaze met hers, and his eyes were clear. His stomach picked that moment to growl. It had gurgled angrily the first day, but then it had been silent until now. He shifted his gaze to Alex, who he could tell was awake, even if he kept his eyes closed.

"How do ye feel?"

"Much recovered. I'm starving." Magnus mouthed, "For ye."

"Do ye think ye could keep some broth down?"

"I'd rather have a hearty bowl of potage, but I'll accept broth." Magnus's grin eased the tightness that had settled around Saoirse's heart. She watched Magnus sit up with ease, as though he hadn't spent the better part of four days unresponsive. "Whatever it was has sorted itself out. I'm ready to return to the land of the living."

Saoirse prepared to spoon feed him more bone broth, but he took the bowl from her. He brought it to his mouth and sipped. "Ye're exhausted, *leannan*." Sweetheart. It was the first time he'd ever used an endearment. She beamed. "Ye need rest more than I do now."

"I can sleep now that I ken ye're on the mend."

"Ye and yer da both deserve a good night's sleep. Ye should both retire. I dinna want ye to be the next one to fall ill."

Saoirse hesitated. She wasn't certain he was ready to be left alone. Plus, she didn't want to leave. She wanted more time with him now that he was awake. But she knew her father would soon agree with Magnus and shoo her from the chamber.

"Vera well. I'll go, but I'm sending Auntie Siùsan to check on ye. I'm nae convinced ye should be alone yet."

"I'm certain she worried. I'd like her company."

"She did. Whenever her duties didna keep her away, she came to check on ye."

"Thank ye, Saoirse." He brought her hand to his lips and kissed her fingertips. He'd known she never left his side. He'd been too miserable to talk or do more than breathe, but he'd heard her talk to him while he dozed. He'd heard Alex comfort her when she expressed her mounting fears. He loathed that he'd upset her so, but he hadn't the energy to do more than sleep. But now he felt rested and almost back to his usual vim and vigor.

She leaned forward and dropped a peck on his cheek. She rose before her father could object. She was certain now that he was awake. She tidied the room, leaving the ingredients for her tinctures out in case she had to try them again.

"I'm glad ye're well. We all worried greatly." Alex gave Magnus a pointed look before he smiled. He'd seen how distrusting the younger man was when he woke. It pained him that he'd caused the rift by being so obstinate. Watching Saoirse's reactions and sensing her distress made him accept her feelings were far more than superficial. Magnus called out to her the few times she moved away from the bed to nap in the chair. He'd sensed her absence. A man who merely lusted for a woman wouldn't seek her in his darkest hours of illness.

"Thank ye."

"We shall talk soon. I've changed ma mind." Alex squeezed Magnus's shoulder before moving away from the bed. Magnus watched him, struck silent at the unexpected change. Saoirse continued to tidy the chamber, but she heard Alex.

As her father waited at the door, she looked at Magnus and mouthed, "Later."

"Could ye hand me a sprig of mint before ye go, please?"

Saoirse couldn't blame him for wanting to refresh his mouth. She grabbed some fresh leaves. They appeared on each tray sent up for Magnus, but they'd gone to waste until now. He gladly chewed on it, letting it sit in the gap between his teeth and cheek for a moment. He spat it out and watched Saoirse and Alex leave.

The door hadn't been closed a minute when the stomach cramping began again. He threw back the covers, threw on a leine from the foot of the bed, wobbled on his feet, then dived for the chamber pot. The broth, mixed with mint, made him heave even more.

"Saoirse!"

He gripped the pot as the door flew open. Saoirse ran back inside, Siùsan and Alex following her.

"What happened?"

"I dinna ken. One moment I was right as rain, the next I was racing to the chamber pot."

Saoirse helped him back onto the bed. "How do ye feel?"

"Better. It was vera odd. Naught aboot the broth made me feel ill until I had the mint."

Saoirse's brow furrowed. She grabbed the remaining mint and carried it to the window embrasure. She pushed aside the hide covering and held the plant to the light. She ran her finger over the leaves and stem before putting the tip to her tongue. There was a residue that shouldn't have been on the plant. She could taste nothing, but she was certain someone tampered with the mint. She recalled how Magnus's breath always smelled of mint. She'd not given it much consideration until now.

"Do ye chew mint throughout the day?"

"Aye. I noticed I dinna grow as hungry if I chew on it from time to time."

Saoirse looked at her aunt, then at her father, before she spoke. "Who's been cutting the mint that comes with Magnus's trays?"

"I dinna ken." Siùsan approached her niece and looked over her shoulder at the mint. "Is something wrong with it?"

"I think so. There's something on it that shouldnae be. The leaves arenae the right texture. But whatever it is has nay taste or smell. I canna tell what it is."

"Ye think someone is poisoning me?" Magnus spoke in disbelief.

Saoirse looked at him for a long time before she nodded. She looked at Alex, but there was no accusation in her gaze. He knew she was asking for his help to discover who would do this.

"Ye canna have any more mint unless I cut it for ye and bring it." Saoirse trusted Siùsan, but she feared trusting anyone else with the gravity of the situation. She feared asking one of her relatives and them passing the chore to someone else. They would never hurt Magnus intentionally, but neither did she want to broadcast the threat. She wanted Alex to investigate.

"I'll talk to Da and Callum. Siùsan, can ye ask who's been bringing in the sprigs? I dinna recall it being the same maid each time who brought up the broth."

"It wasna. That's what confuses and alarms me most." Saoirse almost dropped the plant in the chamber pot, but she thought better of it. She wanted to be certain the mint was the culprit before ruling out everything else. "Auntie Siùsan, please make sure only ye or I bring Magnus aught to eat or drink, including water."

"I will." Siùsan drew the chair closer to the bed and sat. Magnus noticed the strain around her eyes. He took her hand in his and squeezed.

"I'll be all right. Ye've seen me sick before. I already feel better than a moment ago." He hated causing her to worry. She'd spent more years like his mother than his sister. She'd sacrificed much during her childhood to help raise Seamus and him. Tending her younger brothers often forced aside the few joys of childhood their father allowed her. She nodded but remained quiet.

Saoirse and Alex left and headed to the bailey. They didn't speak while passing through the keep. Once they were outside, Saoirse pointed to the storage building where she worked. Alex followed her inside.

"Da, I'm certain now that someone is poisoning Magnus. But I'll check before I say it to anyone else. Did ye mean what ye said?"

"Aye. It's pointless to pretend any longer that either of ye will abandon yer feelings. I dinna want ye even more miserable than ye've been. And I witnessed the sincerity of yer feelings for one another. I canna ignore that."

"What aboot Mama?"

"I think she already kens. Saoirse, ye mama and I struggle with kenning Magnus will leave with ye. We never imagined ye'd marry someone outside of the clan, so we didna prepare ourselves for ye leaving. Neither of us is ready, but we ken we must make ourselves. That's been our true objection. We fear missing ye."

"Och, Da." Saoirse embraced Alex once more. His affection and steadfastness had bolstered her while she ministered to Magnus. She wasn't certain how she would have coped without him. They'd shared more hugs in the past three days than they had in years. It righted the strain that was developing in their relationship.

"Saoirse?"

She and Alex turned to the door as Brighde entered. Alex opened an arm, inviting her to join them. She wrapped her arms around her husband and daughter and sighed. All was right in Brighde's world when she was with the family she and Alex built.

"*Mo ghràidh.*" My darling. "I explained to Saoirse why we've objected to Magnus."

Brighde leaned back as tears glistened in her eyes. She could only nod.

"Mama, I'm sorry this hurts ye. That's nae what I want. It's nae what Magnus wants, either." Saoirse's lip trembled as she spoke, and her heart broke. "Since he canna remain here, he'll return home without me."

"Nay!" Alex and Brighde shook their heads as they spoke at once.

"Nay, Saoirse. That's nae what Da and I want for ye. Ye're a grown woman, and ye deserve the love I share with yer da. We canna take that chance from ye. Yer da fought a battle to ensure I remained by his side. I dinna doubt Magnus would do the same. I nearly ruined ma chances to be with a mon who's loved me unconditionally since the vera beginning. I clung to the reasons I thought I shouldnae and couldnae be with him. I dinna want ye to live with the regret that threatened to consume me."

"But—"

"Nay, Saoirse," Alex interrupted. "If ye wish to marry Magnus, then we willna stand in yer way. I hope ye will take longer to get to ken each other before ye commit, but I can see yer connection. It canna be denied. He called for ye and reached out when ye slept. His sleep was only peaceful when he sensed ye were near. I saw the relief in yer eyes each time he woke, then the agony each time he was ill. I've never seen it when ye've cured others. I dinna want to live with regret either."

Saoirse sighed. "I wish it hadnae taken something so grave to make ye see this. I understand yer reasons now, but it hurts me that ye didna tell me the truth. Ye treated Magnus horribly and embarrassed me. Ye made me feel guilty for ma attraction to him and for how much I care aboot him. If he hadnae nearly died, I dinna believe ye would have accepted this. It shouldnae take nearly losing someone we've welcomed into our family for decades for ye to acknowledge it was yer shortcomings, nae his, that made ye say nay."

"I'm sorry, Saoirse, that I hurt ye. But I canna apologize for how much I love ye." Brighde swiped at the tears on her cheek.

"Ye'll understand one day, *nighean*. It'll be hard enough each time yer bairns leave yer home to marry. Ye canna imagine how frightening and painful it is when they intend to move so far away. We've loved ye since the moment we conceived ye. It's nae easy to let go of something so precious, such a jewel, when ye've spent all these years protecting and nurturing it. But it's yer time to be brilliant, and ye're at yer brightest when ye're with Magnus."

"Thank ye." Saoirse leaned against her parents again. She made herself consider their feelings by imagining saying goodbye to a child she and Magnus conceived. She knew she had barely scratched the surface of the deep emotions. "Ye ken we'll visit as often as we can, and I'd like ye to visit whenever ye wish."

"We love ye." Brighde and Alex spoke at the same time again. They'd done that for nearly twenty-four years. Saoirse listened and hoped one day she and Magnus would be so attuned to one another.

CHAPTER 11

"*W*iley," Saoirse waved to her cousin as she stepped out of her workroom. Her parents left, and she felt better for talking to them, but she was still trying to determine what caused Magnus's ailment. She had a suspicion, but she needed to test it.

"How's Óg?"

"Improving. Do ye have a rabbit I could borrow? I may kill it, but that isnae ma intention."

"That wasna a question I expected ye to ask. Aye. I have one. What're ye going to do with it?"

"I'd like it to eat a couple pieces of mint."

"Why? Ye ken they like it."

"I need it to eat a couple pieces that I have. I need to see what happens. I canna explain more yet, but it's important, Wiley. Please."

"Aye. Come with me."

Saoirse walked alongside Wiley as they moved across the bailey. They came to the animal enclosures. There were chicken coops, a falconry, and a rabbit hutch. Wiley opened the hatch and drew out a medium sized animal. It hung limply in Wiley's hand. Saoirse wondered if it was already weak. But its nose twitched and ears wiggled when it looked up at Wiley. She realized the animal was content and trusted her cousin. He had a knack with animals. He was practically the Pied Piper.

"Is there part of the chicken coop ye could put him that's away from the other animals? I want to observe him, and I dinna want any of the other animals to bother him."

"Her. And I'll make space here." Wiley shooed four chicks to a different end of the coop and dropped a divider in place. He pressed the rabbit into the enclosure and reached for the mint Saoirse held.

"Nay. I dinna want people to handle it. I must scrub ma hands afterwards." She broke off two leaves and stepped in front of Wiley. She fed them to the rabbit and closed the door. "I dinna ken how long we'll have to wait."

It took less than five minutes before the animal heaved and threw up. It was a bubbly pool with traces of the leaves, but Saoirse could tell most of what it ingested remained in its belly. Two minutes later, and the rabbit passed more from its other end.

"Is she going to die?"

Saoirse heard the genuine concern in Wiley's voice. He bred and raised rabbits for food, but she supposed he used more humane ways to kill them than watching them spew from both ends. After another minute of observing, the rabbit shook itself and hopped toward the coop's door. It looked no worse for wear than before Wiley put it inside.

Saoirse waited for Wiley to retrieve the animal before she poured the water she'd fetched into the coop. It washed away the remnants of her experiment as the dirty water dribbled from the open slats. She ground the leaves beneath her boots until nothing was left of them.

"Thank ye. I need to see Grandda and Uncle Callum. Are they in the lists?"

"Nay. They went to Grandda's solar."

Saoirse nodded and made her way back into the keep. She went to the kitchens and scrubbed her hands until they were nearly raw. She knocked on her grandfather's door and waited to be bade entry. She stuck her head around the door as she opened it.

"Grandda, do ye have a moment?"

"Of course." Liam got up from the chair behind his desk and walked toward the door. Callum stood by his chair and moved aside when Saoirse approached.

"I ken what caused Óg's illness. At least, I ken part of it. Someone's been putting a drug on his mint. I ken he chews it often, so that's how he got sick. He felt better this morning and swore he was healed. He'd had none in days. The moment he chewed some, he was violently ill again. I examined the sprig and found something on it, but I still dinna ken what it is. But I ken it made Wiley's rabbit ill when I fed it two leaves. It's the mint, nae Óg."

"Do ye ken who's responsible? Any suspicions?" Callum glanced toward the door, as though he might see through it and spy the culprit.

"Nay. None. Siùsan's going to investigate who's been cutting the mint and preparing Óg's trays. I dinna remember which maids came up. I wasna paying attention to them."

"Before Óg arrived, did any of the men favor ye?" Liam didn't like his suspicions, but it was the first explanation that came to mind.

"I dinna think so. Conan asked me to walk with him twice, but I made it clear I wasna interested. I havenae been interested in anyone before Óg."

"Anyone else? Even if they didna approach ye. Mayhap just paid attention to ye," Liam pressed.

"A couple, but Da scared them all away a couple years ago."

"Saoirse, that was nearly six years ago," Callum corrected.

"It's been that long?" Callum's comment shocked her. He nodded. "I've seen a few men watch me now and again, but none seemed keen."

"Anyone overly grateful when ye healed them?" Liam returned to questioning her.

That made Saoirse stop short. She shifted uncomfortably as she recalled one such patient. "Nicholas brought me flowers twice and bought me a meat pie in the village four moons ago after I tended to his broken nose. I had to tell him I felt appreciated enough when he arranged to be ma guard three or four times."

"Does yer da ken aboot this?" Liam watched his granddaughter. She was the mirror of her mother. He recalled the stormy night Alex carried Brighde into the keep after she collapsed outside their gates. He'd taken her to his chamber without thought and had hovered while she was unconscious for days. Liam knew something destined Alex and her to be together within a sennight once Brighde was well enough to leave her bed. He could imagine how the clan's young men felt about Saoirse. She was as beautiful as her mother at the same age, and he'd had to warn away several men when Brighde arrived, lest Alex kill them all.

"I think he kens Nicholas offered me a few gifts, but I dinna think he fashed over aught."

"He did." Callum shook his head and frowned. "He warned Nicholas away from ye. He kenned the mon made ye uncomfortable, and he was livid that Nicholas altered the guard schedule for ye."

"Anyone else?" Liam was certain there were, but he doubted she'd noticed. She was as oblivious to her beauty as Brighde had been. She shook her head.

"Have ye shared yer suspicions with anyone else?" Callum looked toward the door again.

"Nay one but Wiley, and that was only because I needed his rabbit. I was vague. Da and Mama ken there's something wrong with the mint, but I came straight here, so they dinna ken aboot the animal."

"We'd do well to remain quiet and watch," Liam advised. "If whoever is responsible realizes we've learned aboot the mint, they're likely to try a different approach."

"I told Auntie Siùsan that nay one is to handle Óg's trays, except for her and me. Óg kens I dinna want him to accept any mint that I didna cut maself." She looked between her grandfather and uncle. "Does Óg need a guard?"

"Nay. But I want a member of our family with him at all times. He's only to be alone when he's in his chamber." Liam directed his instructions to Callum, who would see them through. "Ye've done vera well, Saoirse. I'm proud of ye, lass."

"Thank ye, Grandda." She beamed, and heat suffused her. She'd seen her grandfather in the lists countless times, and she'd heard him angry. But to her, he was still the man who let her ride on his back and told stories that made her giggle so hard she nearly wet herself. She remembered how he used to carry her and Rose in each arm. He'd play chase with his grandchildren and took them out riding and fishing when their parents needed a reprieve. She adored him. "There's something else. I spoke to Da and Mama before I found Wiley. They've given their consent."

Liam walked around the desk and enveloped her in his arms. If she married Magnus, she would miss all of her family, but she would miss her grandfather as much as she would her parents and sisters.

"I kenned he would. It was a matter of patience. It

tore at me when we took Mairghread to Varrich. I thought I was leaving a piece of ma soul behind. Besides losing yer grandmama, it's the hardest thing I've ever done. But I kenned it was right once I saw how much Mairghread and Tristan love each other. Yer parents just needed time like I did. I refused to leave Varrich for sennights because I wasna ready."

Saoirse nodded against his chest. When she released him, she turned and found Callum standing with his arms open. She accepted her uncle's hug.

"If he hadnae come around soon, I would have beaten it into him," Callum assured. She almost wished to see that. In their fourth decade, her father and uncles terrified most of the young men in the lists. When they scrimmaged and grappled together, it always drew a crowd. Invariably, it would come out a draw or very close. Saoirse doubted Callum could beat anything into or out of her father. At least, not without receiving the same beating in return.

"I shall go up to see Óg now and discuss what ye shared." Liam dropped a kiss on her forehead.

"Grandda, either dinna tell him aboot Conan and Nicholas, or let me come with ye. He was ready to kill them the last time he was near them. He willna be pleased to ken they made me uncomfortable even before the day at the cave."

Liam nodded. He knew the young couple needed opportunities to work through problems and learn to communicate. It would do them well to practice before they married in case they discovered they couldn't come to accords. He led Saoirse from his solar while Callum went to find his brothers. Callum would ask them, his son, and his nephews if they knew anyone who fancied Saoirse. He'd also organize them, so Magnus wasn't alone outside his chamber.

"Magnus." Saoirse hurried toward the stairs as she watched Magnus descend. "What're ye doing?"

"Siùsan arranged for a bath, and I feel worlds better. But what I need most is sunshine and fresh air." Magnus looked over Saoirse's head to find Liam watching him. He'd scrubbed his soapy finger over his teeth and tongue to rid himself of any lingering mint taste.

"We can talk outside." Liam turned toward the massive iron studded wood doors, knowing Saoirse wished to argue. He wouldn't give her the chance. He knew Magnus was likely crawling out of his skin to be away from his sickbed. The warrior wasn't accustomed to spending so much time abed. He agreed with Magnus's observation that he needed sunshine and fresh air. He led the couple to the garden, passing the vegetables and herbs. He didn't stop until he reached the Lady's Garden. He'd spent countless hours with Kyla in the secluded spot. It had been one of her favorite places from the moment she arrived at Dunbeath.

"Have ye learned something? Did something else happen?" Magnus waited until they were far from anyone else.

"I gave one of Wiley's rabbits two leaves of that mint. Within minutes, the animal was ill. It survived, but it proved someone tainted the mint."

"Have I caused such an uproar with ma arrival that someone wants me dead?" Magnus's grin slipped as he watched Saoirse and Liam exchange a brief glance. "Saoirse?"

"Before ye arrived—quite some time before—both Nicholas and Conan showed interest in me. I refused them both and thought naught of it. Ye ken why I dinna like them. I dinna think it's them, but it might be. Da probably kens if anyone else was interested, but I was oblivious to it. I didna notice anyone before ye."

Saoirse's fair skin once again betrayed her. Her cheeks were nearly scalding when Magnus slipped his hand into hers in front of Liam. Her grandda only nodded.

"Is there anyone else who might wish me ill? Anyone who harbors animosity to the Mackenzies?"

"Nay one I ken." Liam appeared thoughtful. "The clan's kenned ye since ye were a lad, and everyone kens how close ye are to Siùsan. Hurting ye would hurt her. She's too well-loved and well-respected for that."

"Apparently, nae." Saoirse frowned. Someone held an aversion to Magnus, and his relation to Siùsan wasn't protecting him. She thought aloud. "Poison is a woman's weapon. Wouldnae a mon use a blade? Is there a woman here ye slighted once?"

Magnus looked down at Saoirse and shook his head. He'd bedded his first woman while he lived among the Sinclairs. He'd gone to the village tavern with Seamus and a few other lads when he turned six-and-ten. He went back occasionally before returning home, and he'd spent time with women there during his visits. But he hadn't the last three times he visited, and that was more than three years ago. He couldn't imagine any woman carrying a flame for him.

"I dinna believe so."

"Any of the women ye've bedded here?"

Magnus's eyes widened, and he held his breath. He couldn't believe Saoirse asked so bluntly in front of Liam. He felt like a lad again brought before Liam for sneaking fruit tarts before the evening meal. He shook his head.

"It's been years, Saoirse. Even before ma time away from here."

She nodded, and he sensed his answer reassured her. He wished they were alone, so he could hold her and remind her he wanted no one but her.

"Saoirse is right, though. Poison is a woman's choice

most of the time. Siùsan needs to learn which of the servants has been near yer food and toiletries." Liam kissed Saoirse's cheek before embracing Magnus. "I'm glad to see ye hale. Ye gave me an awful fright. I shall skelp ye if ye do it again."

Magnus and Saoirse watched Liam leave the garden without them. They were alone for the first time since their tryst behind a storage building. Magnus cupped her face and gazed into her brown eyes. It was the one trait she inherited from Alex. Her hands rested at his waist.

"I've missed ye, wee one."

"Ye were asleep."

"And I dreamed of ye the entire time. Too many of them involved a gust of wind sweeping ye away from me. It made me want to hold on all the tighter. Thank ye for taking care of me."

"Always." Saoirse lifted her chin. His lips brushed against hers before she opened to him. The moment their tongues collided, passion exploded. Magnus guided her into a dark corner of the garden and pressed her against the wall.

"I wish to have ye as ma first meal." Magnus whispered, his warm breath spiking her arousal. He trailed his lips along her neck and down to the crook of her shoulder. He kissed along her collarbone until he came back up her throat and found her lips once more. Saoirse could taste his hunger as it fueled hers. He gathered her skirts in the back as he slid his muscular thigh between hers. Instinct told her to move against it.

The feeling of his solid leg against her pearl set her ablaze. It was her turn to smatter kisses along his neck and jaw. When his finger slipped along the seam of her netherlips, she fisted his leine and tugged him closer. Their bodies were already pressed together, unable to get any closer with clothes as a barrier. Between his finger working her entrance and his leg against her mons, she stood no chance at keeping her ecstasy at bay. She didn't want to, and from how Magnus encouraged her to move, she didn't think he wanted her to cease.

"Magnus, I want more."

"Ye shall have it, *mo ghaol.*" Both froze when he called her "my love." Saoirse eased back as her whisky-hued orbs met his hazel ones. "I mean it, Saoirse."

"How can ye be sure so soon?"

"Because even in ma delirium, I kenned when ye were near. It was the only time I felt at peace. I enjoy every minute we share, and ma admiration grows by the day. I love what I've learned aboot ye and the time we've spent together. I love watching ye with the people in yer clan and kenning ye'll bring strength and kindness to mine. I love the feel of ye in ma arms, and there is nay where I want to be but in yers. I long to find ye at the end of each day and hear what ye did, share stories from mine. I want to make a family with ye and grow auld with ye. Mayhap it is because I'm aulder than ye. Mayhap it's because of ma failed betrothal. Mayhap it's God's guidance. I dinna have an answer other than I ken I love ye."

"I love ye, Magnus. Everything ye said is how I would describe ma feelings for ye. All I wanted was to turn to ye and have ye promise all would be right again, but ye couldnae console me while I feared losing ye. We ken more aboot each other than most couples do when they wed. But mayhap it isnae truly that soon. I've kenned ye ma whole life. I ken the person ye are and always have been. I appreciate it differently now."

"We arenae strangers, Saoirse. Ye arenae the young lass I once knew, but yer spirit is still the same. Now ye're the woman I wish to marry."

"I talked to Mama and Da earlier. They've agreed to give us their blessing."

"They have?" Magnus recalled what Alex said before leaving his chamber.

"Aye." Saoirse grinned at the wonderment that filled Magnus's eyes. Their kiss drew out, neither in a hurry to end this poignant moment. She moved against his leg as her fingers tunneled into his hair, and her other hand cupped the side of his neck. He leaned forward and nibbled on her earlobe.

As her core tightened, she recognized the sensation. He sensed her eagerness and guided her to move faster. His hand slid over her hip and thigh until his thumb found her button. His fingers bit into her hip, controlling her speed as he rubbed tantalizingly slow circles until he sensed she was on the verge of frustration. Then he gave her what she sought. Her moan was more of a whisper, but it made his cock pulse beneath his plaid. Before he knew what she was about, Saoirse's hand dove beneath his plaid and wrapped around his length.

"Tell me what to do, Magnus."

"Stroke." His voice cracked mid-word. His forehead rested against her shoulder, no longer able to focus on anything but the feel of her hand working his engorged cock. If he weren't so engulfed by his pounding emotions, it might have embarrassed him that she only had to stroke him five times before he erupted. He shuddered as Saoirse tilted her head and snagged his mouth in a passionate kiss that ended in affection. Once they settled their clothes, they walked out of the garden with Magnus's arm around her waist. As far as Saoirse was concerned, they were as good as betrothed. From how he smiled, she knew he felt the same.

"Saoirse, I want to speak to yer parents tonight. I dinna want to wait in case—"

"Dinna ye dare tempt fate, Magnus. We can find them now. It's almost time for the evening meal."

"Saoirse, nay matter what, I love ye. I willna walk away if they turn me down."

"If ye go anywhere, I'm coming along. I love ye."

CHAPTER 12

Saoirse spotted her parents first. They stood near the barracks talking, but Alex turned to go up the wall walk.

"Da!" Saoirse hurried, and Magnus's long legs easily carried him at her speed. Alex turned back and came to stand beside Brighde.

"I'm happy to see ye recovered, Óg. Ye worried all of us." Brighde stepped forward and offered Magnus a warm embrace. It was the first one he'd received since he arrived, which was unusual, since Brighde had always been much like an older sister.

"Thank ye. I'm much improved. A bath and a fresh cup of bone broth that Siùsan brought helped."

Saoirse wasn't sure she liked that Siùsan brought Magnus food without her knowledge, but she'd said that he should only take food that came from her aunt or her. It still made her anxious. He must have sensed it because he slipped his arm around her, and his fingers squeezed her waist.

"Alex, Saoirse says ye and Brighde changed yer minds." Magnus addressed Alex directly as Saoirse's father, but his attention was on both of her parents.

"We have." Alex wrapped his arm around his wife's

138

waist, and she leaned her head against his chest. Saoirse wished to do the same with Magnus, but she wouldn't press her luck. It was already scandalous that he had his arm around her.

"Ye can see Saoirse's already accepted ma suit. I would ask ye and Brighde for Saoirse's hand in marriage. May I marry yer daughter?"

"Aye." Alex and Brighde answered together. There was a moment's pause as they realized the significance of their answer, but they soon offered the couple bright smiles and warm embraces. For the first time in weeks, things felt normal among the four of them. Confessing their true reservations had cleared the air, and everyone's heart felt lighter.

"Thank ye, Da. Thank ye, Mama." Saoirse radiated joy, and her smile blinded Magnus as she looked up at him. They wrapped their arms around each other, their gazes focused only on one another.

"I suppose ye wish to marry soon." Alex brought them back to Earth. "I dinna want ye handfasting, Magnus. It's a proper kirking for ma daughter."

"We can wait three sennights." Magnus conceded, but he nearly laughed at the look of vehement annoyance in Saoirse's gaze. Apparently, they were not in agreement.

"Alex, I think ye'd better reconsider," Brighde whispered.

"What? Nay. Absolutely nae. Ma daughter isnae—"

"Alex." Brighde canted her head and gave her husband a pointed look. She knew he struggled with the idea that another man would lay claim as protector of their oldest daughter. And she knew he struggled with the notion that Saoirse would engage in the same intimate acts she and Alex shared. She wasn't so eager to accept that, either. But it was pointless to deny the couple. They were likely to do it, anyway.

"Fine," Alex huffed. "Ye're still marrying in a bluidy church."

"We ken, Da." Saoirse pulled away and wrapped her arms around her father's waist. She whispered to him. "I love Magnus, but that doesnae mean I love ye any less. Ye'll always be ma da."

"Ye'll always be *mo leannan*." My sweetheart.

"Thank ye, Da. We saw Grandda, and he kens ye've changed yer minds. I believe we have his blessing too, but I'd like to ask him, nonetheless."

"He'll appreciate that, Saoirse. Ye're the first lass to marry here in twenty-five years. I ken how special it will be to him. He's going to miss ye."

"I'm going to miss him, Da. We can ask him at the evening meal. I ken he'll give his blessing, too." Saoirse glanced toward the keep. "I'd like a bath and a fresh kirtle before then."

"I'll send maids up with the tub and water," Brighde offered.

"I'd speak to Callum aboot rejoining the guard rotation," Magnus said.

Saoirse stared at Magnus, her cheeks pinkening. She didn't want to speak her thoughts aloud, but she wasn't pleased with his suggestion if they were handfasting soon.

"In a sennight or so." Magnus read Saoirse's expression, and he knew it embarrassed her in front of her parents. Alluding to them coupling or having a week of seclusion didn't thrill him. He should have thought better before speaking. Alex and Brighde merely nodded.

Alex and Magnus walked toward the battlements, while Saoirse and Brighde turned toward the keep. Brighde led the way into the kitchens, shooing her daughter abovestairs, assuring her that she'd arrange the bath.

Saoirse sensed someone watching her as she entered the keep. She glanced around, but nothing seemed out of the ordinary. She wished to bathe after only using a wet linen square behind the wood screen in Magnus's chamber for four days, but something told her not to go abovestairs yet. She didn't want to be in the passageway alone. Instead, she slipped into Liam's solar. She didn't knock, but she knew she didn't have to. Her grandfather's only rule was to knock if he was meeting with the clan council. Since she knew he wasn't, she knew she could enter unannounced. It was rare that she would. However, she needed to hurry. It relieved her to find the chamber empty. She shut the door all but a crack.

A maid walked past with a ewer of water and a basin. Saoirse's eyes narrowed when she spied something leafy in the bowl. When the woman reached halfway up the servants' stairs, which Saoirse could see from the laird's solar, she followed. She kept to the shadows, avoiding the steps she knew squeaked or wobbled. When she reached the second landing, she witnessed the woman enter Magnus's original chamber, just as she suspected. The woman left the door open, so Saoirse crept into an alcove across from the doorway. She could see clearly into Magnus's chamber.

The woman set the basin and ewer on a table and lifted the mint from the bowl. She laid it next to the pottery before looking around. Saoirse supposed she could be assessing whether anything else needed straightening, but she wanted to know why the woman brought the mint. Had Siùsan not told the maids to cease bringing it? What if Magnus entered before her and thought she'd left it for him? Was all the mint that came to Magnus contaminated?

The young maid went to the bedside and peeled back the bedcovers before fluffing the pillows.

Someone had changed the bedding since he'd last slept there. There was no need for the woman to do anything with the bed right now. Saoirse grew more suspicious by the moment. The servant looked around again, seeming unsure what to do next.

Leave. That's what ye bluidy well do next. Get out of ma betrothed's chamber and take yer bleedin' weed with ye.

"Who are we spying on?" Magnus had hurried inside and up the stairs to the chamber he would soon share with Saoirse. He'd stopped short when he spied a hint of her hair within an alcove near his chamber door. He'd wondered why she was hiding.

Saoirse nearly jumped out of her skin when Magnus eased into the alcove and wrapped his arm around her waist. She'd turned when her peripheral vision caught his movement, but he was far closer than she expected.

"Shh." Saoirse pointed toward the chamber. Magnus squeezed behind her and leaned forward to peer over her shoulder, their heads next to each other. They watched as the woman walked to Magnus's leines hanging on a peg. She lifted one down and sniffed. It was clear she relished the scent, even though they were freshly laundered and likely didn't smell like Magnus yet. Saoirse's hands fisted. This woman coveted Magnus. Why would she poison him?

"I want her out of our chamber, Saoirse. She has nay business near our belongings."

Magnus knew it would be at least a day before it was truly theirs, and none of Saoirse's things were in the chamber yet, but he cared not. The space was now theirs in his mind, and he disliked the maid—a woman he didn't know—encroaching upon what would be their love nest and sanctuary for the rest of their time at Dunbeath. Watching her sniff his leines felt beyond intrusive.

Saoirse nodded and stepped out of the alcove. She

walked across the passageway and stood in the doorway. She arched an eyebrow and adopted an imperious expression she'd never directed at a servant before.

"That belongs to ma betrothed."

The woman's head jerked up as she noticed Saoirse standing with her arms crossed, her feet hip-width apart. The stance alone wouldn't have been as intimidating as it would have been if it were one of the men, but Saoirse's expression made the woman want to shrivel into the floor.

"I'm sorry, ma lady. I—Yer betrothed?" The servant blinked several times, her attention no longer on Saoirse but riveted to Magnus.

"Lady Saoirse and I agreed today. The wedding is in three sennights. What are ye doing in our chamber and touching our belongings?" Magnus didn't care for how the woman looked at him. He didn't know who she was, and he didn't wish to. But it was clear she was overly aware of him. He would ensure she understood his commitment to Saoirse and how he already saw them as good as married.

"I was told to bring up the water and basin."

"Who gave ye the mint?" Saoirse entered the chamber and stalked toward the table. She picked up the sprig with the end of her kirtle and held it to the light. She rounded on the woman and shoved it into her face. "Who?"

"I dinna ken. It was beside the ewer and bowl when Lady Siùsan told me to deliver it. I assumed she put it there."

"Out." Magnus pointed to the passageway. He wouldn't indulge the woman a moment longer. He loathed that she'd trespassed in what was now Saoirse's space and made her interest in him so obvious, even if she hadn't realized someone watched. They waited until the woman closed the door behind her. Saoirse dropped the herb onto the table.

"Auntie Siùsan did nae set this out for ye. Whatever was on the mint that made ye ill is on this, too. I can see it, even if I already ken it has nay taste or scent."

"I wouldnae have chewed it, Saoirse. Ye told me nae to take mint ye didna give me." He rested his hands on her shoulders as she tilted her chin up to look at him.

"I ken. But it terrifies me. Someone thinks ye'd still accept it, which means they still believe they're poisoning ye. I dinna ken that lass well, but she's a Sinclair."

"Do ye have any guess what might be on the leaves?"

"Nay. But there are poisons that arenae that difficult to get. Some of them are deadly in the smallest amount and dinna have much taste or smell. Someone meant to weaken ye slowly. Mayhap to nae make it obvious that they're poisoning ye."

"Saoirse?" Brighde spoke from the doorway. The couple hadn't heard her open the door. "I heard yer voices. I ken ye're betrothed, but this isnae appropriate."

"Mama." Saoirse picked up the mint with her skirts covering her hand again and held it out to her mother. "Bessy just delivered this with the water and basin. She said it was with the ewer and bowl when she gathered them. She said Auntie Siùsan told her to bring the pottery up here. She assumed the mint was to come, too. She lingered in here, and we found her."

"What do ye mean lingered?" Brighde stepped farther into the chamber and reached for the sprig, but Saoirse shook her head.

"Dinna touch it. I'm certain it has the poison on it again. Bessy looked around the chamber, rearranged the pillows, then sniffed Óg's leine."

"Sniffed?" Brighde's expression grew serious. She

sensed her daughter's building annoyance, and it concerned her that the maid intruded upon Magnus's privacy. "I'll speak to her."

"Thank ye, Mama. Is ma bath ready?"

Brighde nodded. Saoirse looked at the mint still in her hand, her skirts protecting her skin. She wished to keep this one to see if she could learn any more from it. She looked up at Magnus. "I'll see ye at the evening meal."

"I look forward to it." Magnus winked. He struggled not to shift uncomfortably as his sporran pressed against his arousal. The thought of Saoirse in a bath, naked, caught his attention while they were outside. It's why he'd decided not to follow her into the keep and trail after temptation incarnate. Now, he wished the tub was coming to this chamber, and that it was theirs. He wished to soak with her after making love to her for the first time.

Brighde shot him a reproving glare before shaking her head in mock disgust. Saoirse was already walking to the door, so she didn't see her mother. Magnus was certain it was his turn to blush. He glanced down, but his sporran hid the evidence of his arousal. Brighde simply knew because she'd been in love and eager at Saoirse's age.

"A toast to the betrothed!" Liam held up his mug of whisky as he smiled at Saoirse and Magnus. They sat beside each other at the massive table. Much like the night he arrived, the entire family gathered on the dais. The couple found the celebratory air a reprieve from their ongoing worries. A few rounds of cheers and ale wouldn't negate the lingering threat, but it was a chance for them to make merry and look toward a bright future.

Musicians began playing, and Magnus escorted Saoirse to the floor once servants cleared the tables and benches. He swung her through two reels before they came together for a slower dance that would keep them together.

"Are ye happy, *mo ghaol*?" Magnus enjoyed having the excuse to keep his arm around Saoirse while in public, but not yet wed.

"Vera. Ye?"

"Beyond imagination. When do ye wish to handfast?"

"Tomorrow?" Saoirse grinned.

"I suppose I can wait one more night before I'm yers."

"Ye're mine? Ye're nae claiming me?"

"Ye are yer own person, Saoirse, and ye always will be. But I gladly give maself to ye, in thought, word, and deed. I have nay reservations."

"Neither do I."

The music increased pace, and they moved with the other couples until they were breathless and laughing. It was the best evening since Magnus arrived. He accepted too many mugs of ale and whisky from the men, but he appreciated the comradery after the rocky start to his visit. When the festivities wound down, Magnus stole a kiss before Saoirse went abovestairs with Nessa and Mirren. Magnus made his way to his chamber, suddenly exhausted. He'd felt fully recovered until now. He supposed four days with no food or drink had to catch up to him, eventually. He barred his door and stripped before climbing into bed. It was only moments later that slumber claimed him.

A storm the night Magnus and Saoirse celebrated their betrothal caused flooding in villages half a day's ride. It forced Alex, Tavish, Mòr, and their sons, along with a dozen guardsmen, to ride out. Saoirse and Magnus agreed their handfasting could wait until her family returned. But the days drew out. They soon worried the priest would read the banns a third time, allowing them to marry in the church, before they could handfast. It made the less formal arrangement seem moot.

"Magnus?" Saoirse approached him while he stood in the bailey.

"Aye? Good morning, *mo chridhe*." My heart. Magnus stooped to kiss Saoirse's cheek. "Did ye sleep well?"

"Aye. What are ye doing?"

"I came out here to do something, but I canna remember what. Memories of a wee wood nymph keep distracting me."

Saoirse nodded. She'd noticed over the past sennight that Magnus often lost his train of thought or forgot what he was about to do. It was unusual and disconcerting.

"Were ye going to the lists?" It was still early morning, and that was where most of the men were.

"Nay…Mayhap…Nay. There was something else I wished to do. It'll come to me."

"I'm going to the market. Do ye wish to come with me?"

Like a lightning bolt, Magnus remembered what he'd been about to do. It was frustrating him that his thoughts kept wandering. He'd never been flighty or forgetful, but over the past week, he found it hard to concentrate, and his mind often felt fuzzy.

"I canna join ye, *mo chridhe*. I need to get ma horse reshod."

Saoirse nodded. It seemed like a flimsy excuse, but she said nothing. She strained to kiss him as his arms engulfed her. He lifted her off her feet and offered her a kiss. They weren't as brazen as the married couples in her family, but they no longer pretended not to be in love.

Magnus watched Saoirse leave through the postern gate. He shook his head as he headed to the stables. He made his way to his horse's stall, but rather than bringing the animal outside, he waited.

"Óg?"

"Aye, Albert. I'm here." Magnus waved to the guard as the man drew closer. They'd been close friends growing up. Albert was one of the first lads to accept Seamus and Magnus into the circle of boys beginning their training. They'd grown apart over the years after Magnus returned home, but he still trusted him implicitly. And it reassured him that Albert had been Saoirse's guard.

"Why are ye hiding in here?" Albert looked around. They were no longer adolescents sneaking whisky and hiding behind haystacks.

"I'm nae hiding. But I wanted to be discreet while I talked to ye." Magnus talked to Alex briefly about any young men who'd been overly interested in Saoirse, but his soon-to-be father-by-marriage hadn't much luck when he asked around. Magnus suspected no one wanted to say anything to the laird's son. "Other than Conan and Nicholas, has anyone shown an interest in Saoirse? Anyone who might be angry that she's chosen me?"

"She chose ye?" Albert chuckled. "I dinna ken that it's that way around, but nay, there isnae anyone specific I can think of. There are a few who are disappointed. I think a handful of lads hoped they'd catch her eye soon. I think they figured within the next year or so, Alex and Brighde would start encouraging her to marry. They wanted to be in line when she chose."

"Do any of them resent me enough to kill me?"

Albert's eyebrows shot up under his bangs. He shook his head. "Nay. Do ye think someone is?"

"Aye. When I was ill, Saoirse discovered someone tampered with the mint brought to ma chamber. Now I chew only what she brings me, and I am nae ill anymore."

"St. Columba's bones!"

"Dinna go repeating that. I'm trusting ye, Albert."

"I willna say aught. I dinna want Lady Saoirse in danger, so I willna say aught that endangers ye."

"Thank ye. If ye think of anyone, will ye tell me?"

"Of course. Just be careful, Óg. It's clear the lass loves ye. It'll devastate her if aught happens to ye."

"I love her, and I plan to have a long life by her side."

Albert nodded, and they walked out of the stables together. Neither noticed who watched, curious why neither entered with a horse nor came out with one.

CHAPTER 13

Saoirse entered the market with two guards a handful of steps behind her. It surprised her to find men other than Albert assigned to her, but Callum said Albert was busy. She'd already told David and Samuel that she wished to visit some fabric vendors since she had time to make a wedding gown. She wound through the stalls until she spied the merchant she wanted. She had to walk past the village tavern on her way.

"I wish he were still warming ma bed. There's naught little aboot Óg."

Saoirse's heart pinched as she looked at the blonde woman standing outside the tavern. She followed the woman's gaze and noticed Magnus walking toward her.

"It's a shame he isnae still coming by." A brunette replied to the blonde. "He was so much fun when he was younger. I dinna ken what he wants with a lass when he kens what he can have with a woman."

"Do ye remember the night we both had him?"

Saoirse froze. She thought she might be ill. She looked around, mortified to realize David and Samuel heard. They hurried forward, but she shook her head. She didn't want either woman to know she heard. But when she looked back, she knew they'd seen her.

"How could I forget? He was insatiable. I bet he's only gotten better with age."

"He kenned plenty the last time he was in ma bed."

Saoirse didn't know what to do. She wanted to bolt, but she refused to do anything so undignified. She reminded herself that with such a large age difference came the acceptance that Magnus had a life before she was even born, and she was barely toddling when he probably bedded his first woman. But it didn't make it any easier to hear.

"I doubt it'd take much to get him back here." The blonde wrapped her arm around the brunette's before they strolled past Saoirse. She watched in horror as they approached Magnus. He made to step around them, barely taking note. He raised his hand to wave to Saoirse, but the women stopped in front of him.

"Hello, Óg," the brunette purred.

"Excuse me." Magnus nodded and shifted in the opposite direction, but the women wouldn't budge. Saoirse noticed the annoyance on his face which mollified her.

"Dinna ye remember us?"

Magnus's brow furrowed before he shook his head. "Nay. Excuse me, ma betrothed is waiting for me."

"Betrothed." The blonde veritably cackled. "She's naught more than a little girl. A mon of yer appetites needs more to sink his teeth into. Besides, the laird already considers ye family. Marrying the lass willna endear ye. But I ken I can do plenty that ye thought endearing before."

"Endearing? I dinna think ye ken what that means. If I tupped ye, then it was years ago, and I dinna remember. I'm sorry, but I simply dinna recall. But I willna keep Lady Saoirse waiting." Magnus's scowl made the women step aside.

"Ye should be nicer to us, Óg. We ken things. Things that could hurt yer bonnie wee bride." The brunette stared at Saoirse as she taunted Magnus, so she was unprepared for him to step so close she swayed backwards.

"I'm a mon of five-and-thirty. Ma betrothed kens I'm nay innocent. I dinna have secrets from her either. But if ye say aught aboot whatever past we might have had just so ye can hurt her, I will make yer life so bluidy miserable ye'll run away without me having to chase ye off. Stay away from Lady Saoirse."

Magnus moved so quickly his plaid swished across the back of his thighs. He glanced at Samuel and David, who stood beside Saoirse as the trio starred at the two tavern wenches and Magnus. He opened his arms to Saoirse when he stood before her. He canted his head back to the keep, and the two guards beat a hasty retreat. Magnus guided Saoirse away from the crowds.

"I'm so sorry."

"Do ye really nae remember them?"

"Nay, I dinna. I havenae been with a woman at that tavern in nigh on six years, Saoirse. I told ye, I've been a monk for the past three. Even if I hadnae been on patrol, I wouldnae have bedded anyone because I was betrothed."

Saoirse nodded. "What did they mean they ken things?"

"I dinna ken. Mayhap things they remember that I dinna. Things that would hurt ye and embarrass ye."

"Or mayhap they ken something aboot the mint and who tried to hurt ye."

"I doubt it."

"But they might. I want to ask."

"Saoirse, stay away from them. Naught good will come of it. They'll be spiteful and cruel."

"I dinna care. If there's a chance they ken why someone tried to kill ye, then I want to hear it." Saoirse stuck out her hand. Magnus didn't hesitate to take it, but he was in no hurry to walk back to the tavern. "Leslie, Amy, I want to talk to ye."

"Hello, Lady Saoirse." The two women dipped into pathetic pantomimes of curtsies. Magnus glowered at them over Saoirse's head, making the women show a more appropriate level of respect.

"What did ye mean that ye ken things? What things? Were ye talking aboot how ye tupped ma betrothed? Or was it something more important?" Saoirse kept her voice light, pretending that the notion of Magnus bedding either of the women didn't bother her.

"We remember plenty aboot Óg. If things dinna work out, ye ken where to find us." Leslie, the blonde, winked. But she shrank back at Magnus's withering glare. Amy, the brunette, opted to be more circumspect.

"One vendor said that ye were chasing Lady Saoirse's skirts because the Mackenzies canna scrape two coins together. And since yer betrothal fell apart, ye need a Sinclair dowry. He said ye're marrying Lady Saoirse for her money."

Saoirse laughed. Magnus didn't expect that reaction. She looked up at Magnus over her shoulder before looking at the women. "Óg doesnae need to marry me or any other Sinclair to get money if that's what he needed. The laird would give it freely, and we all ken it."

"Then why else would he marry ye?" Leslie appeared genuinely baffled.

"Enough. Since ye like to nashgab with whomever

will listen, ye can share this piece of gossip. I love Lady Saoirse. I dinna need her dowry, nor do I want it. I'm marrying ma bride because there is nay one bonnier or better than Lady Saoirse. The next person who has an opinion aboot ma marriage can come straight to me."

"Wait." Saoirse shook her head as Magnus tried to guide her away. "Who told ye that?"

Leslie pointed across her chest and to the right. "That one. The one selling the ribbons. He said he'd just come from Clan Macrae, and people were talking aboot it."

Saoirse and Magnus looked at each other before Saoirse handed a coin to each woman. "Thank ye for telling us. Dinna make me regret ma generosity. And dinna think me the weakling most do. Just because I'm nae the loudest of the cousins doesnae mean I'm nae the stubbornest. Stay away from Óg. I dinna share ma mon with anyone. He will never stray, but I dinna trust ye nae to touch. Come near ma betrothed again, and I will tell every woman in this clan to keep their sons and brothers from darkening yer doorstep."

Saoirse took Magnus's hand as they walked toward the vendor who'd arrived from the Macraes.

"How could he ken aboot us? They're several days' ride from here." Magnus was having a tough time making sense of what he'd heard. At first, he'd thought it was his annoyance that distracted him. But his thoughts felt jumbled.

"Óg, ye were ill for four days. That was after ye were away hunting for a sennight and had already been here a fortnight. It's been a moon since ye arrived. If anyone saw us the first few days ye were here, they would have enough gossip to spread."

"I suppose."

The couple stopped at the merchant's stand. The man turned toward them, but his smile dropped when he recognized Magnus. "Hello, ma lady. What interests ye today?"

"The gossip ye've been spreading. What did ye hear aboot Óg and me while ye were with the Macraes?"

"Naught much, ma lady. I just ken Mackenzie broke his betrothal with the Matheson lass and was trailing after yer skirts—pardon me, that's just what I heard—as soon as he arrived. That he'd found a bonnier and wealthier bride. Some said it was incestuous, but most thought that a hideous accusation. Everyone kens the only Sinclairs Mackenzie is related to are his sister and her weans. Ye two arenae related by blood."

"Is this something many people are clish-maclavering over?" Saoirse couldn't understand why anyone would take an interest in Óg or her.

"Enough for me to hear aboot it. But I was at Ding-wall, so nae far from the laird's home."

"What of the Mathesons? What have they to say?" Magnus wondered.

"Dinna ken. Nay one mentioned them. People seemed more curious than aught else. From what I heard, ye were a lucky mon to get away from that witch. She'd have shriveled yer bollocks from what I've heard."

"Thank ye." Magnus paid the man for his informa-tion before he and Saoirse turned toward the keep. As they walked, Saoirse's foot slid over a stone, and she tipped sideways. Magnus caught her with a grunt. She looked up at him, surprised. She wasn't the lightest woman she knew, but neither did she weigh enough for him to notice. She watched him scratch his waist, his fingers slipping beneath his belt.

"What's wrong?" Saoirse steered Magnus to her healing room as they entered the bailey.

"Naught. I think I've been wearing ma belt too tight for the weather."

"Magnus, I've seen yer belt. There is only one hole that's worn. Ye've been wearing it the same way for years from the looks of the leather. If aught, ye've lost weight since ye've been here. Let me see, please."

They entered the storage building Saoirse used, and she drew back the rabbit hides from the window. She gestured for him to step into the light. She eased his leine from beneath his belt and pushed down the plaid. There was a red welt that wrapped around his waist, just below where his belt rested. She pulled up his leine and walked around him, noticing the red patches covered nearly all of his waist.

"When did this start?"

"A few days ago. I dinna remember exactly. It itches and is tender, but only when I touch it."

"Ye didna think to tell me?" Saoirse shot him a disapproving glance as she pushed down on the material, but his belt was in the way. "Take off yer belt and let me see properly."

"Saoirse—"

"Nay as yer betrothed, as yer healer. Come on, Magnus. Someone's already tried to kill ye by poisoning ye. Ye canna keep aught like this from me."

"I dinna want ye to fash."

"I'll be a sight angrier if ye die." Saoirse crossed her arms and tapped her toes. Magnus sighed. His forefinger and thumb caught her chin as he kissed her. He drew back and laid his belt over the table before coming to stand in the light again. He folded the plaid in at his waist to keep it in place and to reveal more for Saoirse to examine. She peered at his skin, leaning closer as she gently twisted him in different directions. "I need to see yer hip better."

She ran her cool fingers over the angry welts, but she stopped when she reached a patch of scaly skin on his left hip, near his buttocks. She pushed the fabric down farther and frowned.

"Magnus, ye havenae been out in the sun without yer plaid, have ye?"

"Nay. I havenae been prancing around in the altogether."

"Nae prancing. But have ye been in the sun, mayhap at the loch? I dinna ken why yer skin is darker here and here than anywhere else." Saoirse pointed to two places. She moved around to his other side, but she found nothing there. "Lift yer plaid, so I can see yer thighs."

Magnus didn't bother arguing. The places Saoirse touched were sensitive, almost like a sunburn, but he hadn't been uncovered enough to get one. She pulled a stool over and gestured for him to sit. She sat on one facing him. She pushed back his plaid, letting it gather between his legs. She ran her hands over the outside and inside, then top and bottom of his thigh.

"Look here. This skin shouldnae be so dark, either. When did this happen?"

Magnus stared where she pointed. He had no idea. "I dinna remember seeing that before."

"Magnus, ye've said that a lot lately. Callum and Siùsan mentioned ye saying ye forgot things they told ye. I've seen ye think aboot things far longer than ye needed to before answering a question."

"I ken. Ma mind grows fuzzy at times. I dinna ken why. I've slept plenty." Magnus offered her a sardonic smile.

Saoirse went back to examining his legs. She noticed spots with yellowy-white patches of scaly skin. She was growing more alarmed by the moment. She stood but motioned for him to remain seated.

"Take off yer leine. I want to see the rest of ye."

Magnus followed her instructions, but he worried if

anyone walked in. They'd left the door open, but it still wouldn't appear appropriate. Even though they were betrothed—or rather because they were betrothed—he could imagine what people would say.

"I dinna see aught unusual aboot yer chest or back. Ye arms dinna have any discoloration either." Saoirse was growing fed up with only seeing Magnus unclothed when she had to examine him. She wished to enjoy his physique without worrying about him dying. She turned away but thought better of it. She moved behind him and combed her fingers through his hair. His light brown hair was thick, so it wasn't easy to see his scalp, but she noticed patches of discolored skin similar to what she found on his thighs. "Something isnae right, Magnus. Do ye feel out of sorts?"

"I've had a headache for three days, but naught I canna manage."

"Why didna ye ask me for a tincture?"

"Because I can manage, Saoirse. It's just a dull ache."

Saoirse didn't agree that it was "just" anything, but she wouldn't nag him. She went to a shelf and reached for a jar. She gasped when Magnus reached over her shoulder and lifted it down. She hadn't heard him approach. He went to wrap his arm around her waist but thought better of it.

"Could ye catch what this is? Are ye at risk being near me?"

She turned to look at him. "I dinna ken. I dinna think so. Nay one else has complained of aught similar. I dinna think it's catching."

"What do ye think it is?"

"I really dinna ken, *mo ghaol*. But I think this salve will help. Slather it on. Be generous and use it everywhere that I found dark spots and around yer waist."

"I love ye, Saoirse. Thank ye for taking care of me."

Saoirse assumed Siùsan was the only other person

he'd ever said that to. She cupped his cheeks and smiled. "I love ye. I'll always take care of ye."

They moved into the room's shadows, knowing they risked discovery. But this time the illicitness only added to the excitement of once more being in one another's arms. Saoirse was careful where she rested her hands, avoiding his waist. She glided them over his ribs, then over his chest, before draping her arms around his neck. Without the same need to be careful where he touched, Magnus's hands roamed her body. He squeezed her backside as she pushed his sporran out of the way. The feel of his rod against her mons overheated her. His kisses along her neck made her breasts feel heavy. When his hand kneaded her right one, she arched into it. His thumb swept over her nipple until it hardened. His other hand slipped her left sleeve over her shoulder until he could free her breast. As he massaged the right one, he suckled from the left.

Saoirse constantly glanced toward the door. She feared someone noticing, but she longed for Magnus's touch more. Their physical need grew alongside their emotional connection. She wouldn't have minded being caught if it meant they could marry immediately. She wondered if they could slip away like they had to the cave, or if they could have a late-night tryst again.

Magnus's continued to lick and suck her nipple as he gathered her skirts. She felt the cooler air on her left leg, and she knew Magnus's destination. Her core ached for his attention, and when it finally received it, she melted against him. He slid his finger along her entrance before dipping between her netherlips. She rubbed her mound against his rod, unsatisfied with their clothes keeping her from what she desired. She drew her skirts higher and bared her left hip. Magnus's fingers bit into her buttocks while his other hand worked her sheath. She reached between them and drew up his plaid.

When she wrapped her hand around his cock, Magnus thought he would come undone without a single stroke. But when her damp folds touched his turgid length, he clung to his fading control. He backed her two steps until she hit the wall. His hips thrust and trapped her pelvis between him and the stones. He rubbed her pearl with his sword, and she tilted her hips in encouragement.

"Saoirse, we shouldnae."

"I ken."

"I dinna want to stop."

"Neither do I. Magnus, we've already agreed to handfast, and we're betrothed. Ye have the right."

"I'm never taking from ye, *mo ghaol*. It will never be aboot what ma rights are or arenae. If ye ever dinna want to, then ye tell me. I will always respect that. If ye do want to make love, then ye need only tell me that."

"I want to."

Magnus chuckled. There hadn't been a moment's hesitation. She might have even started talking before he finished. "Soon, wee one. But our first time together will nae be hurried and where anyone could find us. I will strip ye bare and worship every inch of ye. One day, I will take ye against a wall, and show ye how ye demolish ma self-control. But it willna be yer first time."

It was Saoirse's turn to chuckle. "Ye said ye'd never take from me, then ye say ye'll take me against a wall. What happens if *I* wish to take *ye* against a wall?"

Magnus's eyes twinkled with mischief. "Ye ken they dinna mean the same. And once we're truly handfasted, ye may take me wherever ye wish."

He covered her mouth with his as his hands held her hips in place. He thrusted faster, rubbing his rod along her mons until her nails bit into his shoulders. He flexed his hips, keeping hers against the wall. He felt her tremble as her release claimed her. A moment later, he gave into the need for his own release. He pulled back, letting his plaid drop over his cock. He fisted himself beneath it as he continued to devour her lips.

Their tryst left them breathless as they exchanged short, soft kisses. Saoirse realized she'd forgotten to watch the door. It was just short of a miracle that no one interrupted them. She prayed no one saw them as they passed by. The gossip would be far worse than when they returned from the cave.

"I canna linger here any longer. I ken ye have yer work, and I—" Lightheadedness swept over Magnus, and he had to take four deep breaths to clear the fuzziness.

"Magnus?"

"I'm all right."

"Mayhap ye should rest. We came in here because ye're nae well."

"I didna feel poorly a moment ago. Mayhap ye are the cure." He pressed a kiss to her mouth before moving away from her. She settled her skirts and smoothed back her hair. Magnus crossed the room and hurried to dress before they returned to the keep. They tried to remain circumspect during the evening meal, but they stole glances. The hunger in Magnus's eyes made Saoirse's core ache. Each deep breath she took as she responded to his knowing stare only fueled Magnus's desire. Her breasts strained against the fabric, and he longed to have them in his mouth once more. They'd opened Pandora's Box, and there was no shutting their need back into it.

Everyone was retiring when the riders returned from assessing the damages. They knew there would be no late-night tryst. They hadn't agreed to anything, but they knew implicitly that they'd planned to meet again. Magnus greeted the men, who were filthy and exhausted. He wished to ask Alex if they could hold the handfast the next day, but he could tell his soon-to-be father-by-marriage was too exhausted for Magnus to bother him. Morning would be soon enough.

CHAPTER 14

The headache Magnus awoke to threatened to send him back to the chamber pot. The last thing he wanted was to vomit again since his throat felt like he'd drunk molten steel. He shut his eyes as he laid back against his pillows. The moment he did, he sneezed. Not once, not thrice, but six times. It rattled his head, making him groan, which made him wince. He sucked in a deep breath before forcing himself out of his bed. His hand went to his chest when he felt like he couldn't catch his breath. A tickle at the base of his throat caused him to cough. He flinched as pain radiated from his chest to his head and down to his toes. Before he could draw another breath, a coughing fit began. He struggled to inhale deeply, but he forced himself to the table with the ewer. He cared not that the water wasn't fresh. He lifted the carafe to his mouth and drank. It soothed his throat momentarily, but then he spluttered as a new round of coughing began.

"Óg?" Siùsan stood in the doorway, knocking after she opened it.

"Aye," Magnus rasped.

"Are ye ill? I heard ye coughing."

"I think I've caught something. I havenae been ill in

ages. Nae since the sickness first started going around the clan. Do others have the ague too?"

Siùsan shook her head as she approached. Her brother's sallow complexion alarmed her. There was a yellow tinge to his skin, and deep shadows had appeared under his eyes, making him look like a racoon. She reached out her hand and rested the back of it against his forehead. He wasn't feverish.

"We need Saoirse."

Magnus nodded, then grunted in pain. He shuffled back to his bed, grateful he'd worn a leine that night. He'd put the salve on before climbing into bed, and he hadn't wanted to smear it on the sheets. Now he appreciated the modesty in front of his sister. She drew back the covers and then pulled them over it, like she had countless times when he was a child.

"I'll be back in a moment."

"Thank ye, Sìu—" Magnus couldn't finish because his cough began again. He adjusted the pillows as another round of sneezes took hold.

What the bluidy hell is wrong with me? I canna remember simple things. I canna think straight. I feel like a bull's run over me. Ma skin itches as though I have a rash. This is bluidy miserable.

He laid with his eyes closed, alternating coughing and sneezing. He knew when Saoirse arrived because he recognized her lavender and heather scent. He reached out his hand as he opened his eyes.

"Magnus? Siùsan said ye've caught the ague."

"Aye." Magnus moved the pillow a third time, unable to get comfortable. He barely turned his head before sneezing on Saoirse. "Every time I try to get comfortable, I sneeze and cough."

Saoirse wondered if there was something on the pillow irritating him. She didn't think the laundresses had changed anything about their soap, and it hadn't affected him before. "Let me have yer pillow, please?"

He handed it to her, and she shook it. A fine dust came loose. She clapped her hands with the pillow between them, and more floated off. She stuck her finger in it and caught what appeared like powder. She brought it to the tip of her tongue.

"Saoirse, nay!" Magnus forced himself from bed. "If that's making me ill, then dinna do that."

"Wheest. I dinna have a better way to test ma suspicions." She touched the tip of her tongue to her finger. She could taste what she hadn't been able to on the mint. She hurried to the door and flung it open, ignoring Siùsan and Magnus's shock. Her aunt had stood quietly by the wall when the two women arrived. "Grandda! Grandda!"

"What's the matter, Saoirse?" Magnus held a hand over his chest as he lumbered toward her.

"Dinna get back in bed. Go behind the screen and put on a fresh leine. Put that one in the chamber pot. Stay away from the bed." Saoirse looked at Magnus long enough to give her instructions before she turned back to the passageway. "Da! Uncle Callum!"

Where were the men in her family? It was still too early for them to be in the lists.

It was Thormud and Blake who arrived first, recognizing their cousin's voice. Liam, Callum, Alex, Tavish, and Mòr appeared next. Her mother and aunts were right behind them.

"Grandda, it's arsenic. Someone's been poisoning Magnus with arsenic. The doses must have been ever so slight on the leaves to slow the reaction and make it appear like he was withering away. Impatience probably led them to put more on the last mint he chewed. But whoever it is has been powdering it on his bed linens. He sneezed whenever he moved the pillow, so I took it and shook it. A powder came off. It tasted ever so slightly like garlic. I'm certain it's arsenic."

"Wouldnae that have killed him immediately?" Siùsan leaned against Callum as she stared at Magnus, who appeared from behind the screen.

"It could have. It takes the size of a pea to kill someone, but I think that whoever did this was careful nae to give him too much at once. Óg, this explains yer skin problems. If this has been on yer bedding nightly for a while, it's irritated it. And ye've been inhaling it. That's why yer memory hasnae been good, and ye've felt confused. Prolonged exposure causes that and ague type symptoms."

"We ken how they've done it, but why? And who?" Mòr walked to Óg and didn't hesitate to embrace the younger of the same name. He was careful not to squeeze, but he loathed the thought of losing a man who was another brother to him.

"I dinna ken. None of the men seem to hold a grudge that Saoirse chose me. I dinna think anyone is angry that I didna choose another lass. I canna imagine why any Sinclair wishes me ill." Magnus shook his head, then groaned. The water helped marginally, but he still felt poorly.

"Ye canna stay in here," Thormud spoke up. "Come to ma chamber. Ye can stay with Torquil and me."

"Saoirse, will this kill me?" The question hung in the air, but it was one everyone thought. She walked to her betrothed and took his hands in hers.

"I dinna ken, Magnus. I pray we discovered this soon enough that it willna. Ye're a large and healthy mon. I think whoever this is underestimates yer constitution. But if they grow any more impatient, it will only take a small dose in yer food or drink to kill ye."

Saoirse's dark eyes met Magnus's lighter ones, a wealth of emotion flashing through them. He saw her fear, her uncertainty, her regret, but he also saw her love. He wasn't ready to leave his betrothed. He had too many plans for their life together.

"What can we do to get rid of whatever is left in ma body?"

Saoirse shrugged. "Aileen never taught me aught aboot curing it, only how it kills. It usually succeeds without a chance for recovery. Mayhap there is something aboot it in one of the books in Grandda's library. Mayhap stories from the ancients?" Saoirse twisted to see Liam, who nodded. "Bathe and rest in Thor's chamber. I'll see what I can find. But the best I can advise for now is drink as much water as ye can, and let's feed ye simple things like kale, carrots, peas, and beans. I dinna think they'd do aught to make ye worse. Auntie Siùsan, can ye see to that? I dinna want any of the maids to touch the food. Can ye watch Cook, please?"

"Ye think—" Brighde's shock voiced everyone else's.

"I dinna ken what to think, Mama. But whomever this is, is vera sneaky. Bessy didna ken who left the mint the other day, and Auntie Siùsan, ye never discovered who it was, either."

"I'll make them maself," Deirdre offered.

"I'll arrange for a bath," Ceit offered. "Tavish, fetch him some of yer clothes. Ye're the closest to his build."

Tavish had inherited Liam's barrel-chested build. Magnus Óg's build was similar and didn't taper the way the other men's did. Magnus Mòr and Blake's build was thicker across the upper back, so their leines would drown a man even as broad shouldered as the other Sinclair men.

Tavish, Ceit, and Deirdre didn't linger, each off to their separate task. Blake left, presumably to find Cerys or to go to the lists. Thormud left to prepare the room for Óg and to let Torquil know they would have a roommate.

"Óg, we will learn who's doing this." Liam spoke with the authority of being not only Laird Sinclair but the Earl of Sinclair and the Earl of Orkney, governing as the Earl of Caithness. "I pray it isnae one of our people, but if it is, justice will be swift. Ye are as much a member of this clan as ye are the Mackenzies. This is a threat against the laird's family, and I willna go lightly on the perpetrator. As Siùsan's brother and our fosterling, ye are as much ma son as Tristan is as ma son-by-marriage. An attack on ye is an attack on all of us."

Óg listened to Liam. If he didn't feel like he was about to keel over, he might have felt bad for whomever was ill advised enough to threaten him under Laird Liam Sinclair's roof. He shifted his attention to Saoirse, who gazed up at him.

"Can I have a moment with Saoirse?"

"Aye," Alex answered. Everyone filed out of the chamber, but they kept the door open.

"*Mo ghaol*, I swear I am nae leaving ye yet. Ye are stuck with me for at least three score years."

Saoirse nodded, but the lump in her throat made it impossible to speak. Tears burned her eyes as she fought to maintain her composure.

"Dinna feel like ye failed because ye didna figure this out sooner. There's a reason arsenic is such a preferred poison. With nay real taste or smell, most wouldnae recognize it. I canna even smell what ye did. The strong scent of mint must have disguised the garlic ye said ye smell now. This isnae yer fault."

Saoirse shook her head. He understood how she felt, but his reassurance did nothing to ease her guilt. "If I were a better healer, then it never would have gotten to this. Ye've suffered for days, sleeping in a bed with a deadly powder covering it."

"And I didna notice it. How could ye have kenned there was a problem when I didna ken? I am alive and marrying ye because ye are the best healer. Ye willna convince me otherwise." Magnus placed his hands around her waist but didn't draw her closer. He wore a fresh leine, but he wouldn't feel comfortable until he bathed. "I love ye, and I place all ma faith in ye."

"I love ye. I'm scared I didna figure this out soon enough. I'm scared this person will just find another way to harm ye. It's obvious they're patient if they're willing to wait for the arsenic to kill ye gradually."

"I'm nae dead yet. I might need a couple more days to regain ma strength, then I shall chase ma bride around our chamber. Once I catch her, I will make love to her for days." Magnus didn't want to worry Saoirse further, but he suspected it would be more than a couple of days. He fought throughout the conversation with their family not to show how much pain he felt. He'd swallowed his cough and been grateful for not sneezing anymore. But he needed more sleep.

"Ye need to bathe and go back to bed. Yer body has been through much lately. Ye need more rest."

"I ken." Magnus sighed, which caused him to cough again. Saoirse's eyes widened in alarm before she shook her head. She walked with Magnus to Thor and Tor's chamber, where a bath already awaited him. "I love ye."

"I love ye, too." Saoirse waited until Magnus closed the door before running to her chamber. She collapsed onto her bed as she sobbed. She knew he'd seen her fear, but she'd fought valiantly so he wouldn't know the depth of it. She was unconvinced she could cure Magnus, and that fear broke her heart. Frustration that they didn't know the culprit and the constant delay to their handfast only compounded her consuming emotions. She cried herself to sleep, remaining there until Magnus asked if she would dine with him in his newly shared chamber. As always, they left the door open. They spent the evening talking, but Magnus grew tired quickly. They spent the next four evenings the same way until Magnus convinced her he was finally well enough to leave the chamber for longer than a half-an-hour constitutional three times a day.

As much as they needed to discover the would-be assassin, there was something else more pressing.

CHAPTER 15

"Do ye wish to handfast alone?" Brighde asked. Saoirse stood beside Magnus in the bailey, five days after she'd discovered the arsenic. He'd recovered faster than she expected, but the bland food that she, her mother, and her aunts personally cooked seemed to encourage his rapid recovery. Beside those women, Saoirse made it clear that she only trusted Rose, Mirren, and Nessa to bring him anything to eat or drink. She spent any time not tending to other clan members with Magnus. They shared more stories about their lives since Magnus finished his fostering. She read to him and sang. They enjoyed long stretches of companionable silence as she sewed.

Now they looked at one another and nodded to Brighde and Alex. They'd sought the older couple that morning, unwilling to wait any longer. They didn't need to discuss their answer. They looked toward the postern gate, sharing the same idea.

"The tide is out. We could go right now," Saoirse suggested.

"If that's what ye wish. I'd like naught better." Magnus kissed the back of her hand before he turned his head toward Alex and Brighde. "Are ye all right with this?"

Saoirse's parents nodded. The younger couple left the older couple holding each other as they watched their daughter cleave to her husband. It was a bitter-sweet moment for them, but they'd known it would come one day. And as much as they'd contested Magnus's suit in the beginning, they'd always known he was the best choice for their oldest daughter.

Once outside the gate, Magnus linked hands with Saoirse. His impending handfast tore his emotions between being bright with excitement, and the serious-ness of knowing Saoirse now relied on him to provide for her and to protect her. He wouldn't take the duty and privilege lightly. He had no hesitations committing to his bride, but he realized that his days of thinking only about what was best for him, even when consid-ering his duty to his clan, were over. He prayed he never disappointed her.

Saoirse didn't want to let go of Magnus's hand when they reached the entrance to the cave, but they had to remove their shoes and stockings. Neither dal-lied, and soon Saoirse held Magnus's hand again as he guided her into the cave. The sun shone through the hole in the rocks above them, making the pool glow as though lit from below. While the pool was tidal, a warm spring fed it. It was one of the few places where the North Sea wasn't frigid year-round.

The narrow ledge caused them to stand close to one another. Magnus unpinned the length of plaid from his shoulder, and together they bound their wrists. They both savored a moment of marvel at the sight. It was the first step in joining their lives.

"Saoirse, I dinna have a ring for ye, nae even at home."

"That doesnae matter to me. We will figure something out."

"I would have ye pick out whatever ye want at the market."

"Thank ye. We have time before the kirking to sort that out."

"Are ye ready to marry me, lass?"

"Aye. So vera ready. I kenned we would one day, but I feared ma patience wouldnae last long enough."

"Mine neither, *mo ghaol*." Magnus gazed into the dark eyes he now knew so well. He'd memorized the tiny flecks of amber smattered within the whisky-brown irises. He knew the stories from the various Sinclair handfastings and weddings. He knew the vows they shared over the years. He would honor his time among them as a fosterling and now as a new member of the laird's family. He recalled Liam and Kyla's story and the vows they shared during their handfasting.

"I take ye, ma heart, at the rising of the moon, and the setting of the stars. To love and to honor through all that may come. Through all our lives together, in all our lives, may we be reborn that we may meet and ken and love again and remember."

Saoirse's eyes widened as she recognized them. Her soft smile confirmed he'd made the right choice. Kyla died long before Saoirse or any of her cousins were born, but she was alive in everyone's memory.

"I swear by peace and love to stand, heart to heart and hand to hand. Mark, O Spirit. And hear me now, confirming this ma Sacred vow." Saoirse spoke the same words Kyla had nearly fifty years ago. They finished their vows together.

"Ye are blood of ma blood, and bone of ma bone. I give ye ma body, that we two might be one. I give ye ma spirit, 'til our life shall be done. To thee, I plight ma troth."

Neither moved as they soaked in the weight of their pledges, the significance of melding their hearts and souls. But it wasn't long before the need to meld their bodies consumed them. With the privacy of the cave, they shared their first kiss as husband and wife. A kiss that would never be appropriate on a kirk's steps or in front of their clan and family. They pulled at the length of plaid still wrapped around their wrists. They continued their kiss as they fumbled with each other's clothes until frustration and amusement forced them apart.

"Yer hair is as light as the purest pearl, and yer eyes are the brightest topaz. Yer lips are richer than any ruby, and yer heart is gold. Ye are a jewel, precious but strong. Yer smile brightens ma day and lifts ma spirits. I will never take for granted that ye are invaluable. I will treasure ye and protect ye until ma last breath. I love ye."

Saoirse recalled how her father compared her to a jewel the day they spoke with Brighde in her healing room. But it felt entirely different as Magnus spoke his reverent words.

"Ye are as sturdy and enduring as the Cairngorms. Like them, I ken ye'll be there when I rise, just as ye will be when I'm abed. I ken ye are as unbendable as a mighty oak, yet ye will shade me from any danger. Ye have the strength of ten men, but I never fear ye. I trust ye just as I trust the sun will rise in the east and set in the west. I will stand beside ye and honor ye until ma last breath. I love ye."

"Those may as well have been our vows. I will never forget them, Saoirse."

"Nor will I forget what ye said."

They finished undressing each other, and when they stood bare in front of one another, they reveled in what they discovered. Saoirse's fingertips traveled over Magnus's chest in a way they hadn't as a healer. She had a privilege as his wife that she hadn't only minutes ago. They traveled lower than she'd dared with her father in the chamber or when she examined him in her workroom. She marveled at the peaks and valleys that formed his abdomen. Muscles that flexed under her fingers, with each held breath. She sensed Magnus's eagerness, but he didn't rush her.

She looked between them and spied his rod for the first time as a woman lusting for a man. She'd known he was endowed, but she'd not imagined such a sight once someone—she—fully aroused him. Even in the garden and her workroom, she hadn't appreciated its girth because it remained covered by his plaid.

"Do ye fear me hurting ye?"

Saoirse's eyes leaped to Magnus's. "Never, *mo chridhe*." My heart. "I ken it likely will, but I dinna fear it. Why? Do I look afeared?"

"This is something ye've never done. I ken yer family is open aboot relationships between men and women, but I dinna ken what stories ye've heard from other women. I loathe the idea that I will cause ye any pain."

"Magnus, I ken ye will never hurt me on purpose. I almost pity anyone foolish enough to try. I think yer guilt pains ye more than breaching ma maidenhead will pain me. I ken it will only hurt the one time. And I dinna doubt ye will make every time wonderful."

Magnus nodded, and Saoirse noticed his relief. She wrapped her hand around his rod and stroked, like she had before. Magnus's hands went to her backside and pressed her closer until his right hand slid between her thighs. His fingers traced her seam, tantalizing her as she grew damper. His left hand raised one supple breast to his mouth as he leaned forward. His tongue circled her nipple just as his thumb circled her pearl.

He nipped and drew upon it until her nipple tightened. He wrapped his mouth around her breast and suckled, his tongue flicking the turgid nub. Her head fell back as her spine arched. Her free hand gripped his shoulder to keep her balance, but she knew he would never let her fall.

"Saoirse, everything aboot ye is perfect. Ma eagerness scares me. I dinna want this to end before I pleasure ye, and I still worry that I will hurt ye."

"And if ma eagerness embarrasses me as a maiden?"

"I dinna ever want ye to feel embarrassed aboot what we share."

"Then dinna ever be scared." Saoirse's mouth snagged his, and her tongue darted into his mouth, luring his back into hers. When it slid past her teeth, she sucked gently. He squeezed the breast he was kneading as a groan rumbled within his chest. It sent a spike of excitement through Saoirse to know she satisfied him. "Magnus, I'm close."

She felt the throb in her pearl, then the tightening in her core as her sheath ached. He redoubled his efforts, and she cried out, unconcerned that anyone might hear her.

"I want to hear ye each time, Saoirse. I want to ken ye want me as much as I want ye."

"I do. Magnus!"

He lifted her and guided her legs around his waist. They trapped his rod between them, and every step he took toward the pool, rubbed it against her bundle of sensitive nerves. She squeezed her thighs and slid along him as the tension built once more.

"Ye shall make me come, and then I will surely need a moment to recover. I dinna want to climax until I'm in ye, Wife."

"Say that again, Husband." Saoirse was breathless, but she panted her request.

"I will. Every day for forever, Wife."

"I will gladly listen every day for forever, Husband."

Magnus growled as he nipped her earlobe. He repeated it over and over in a hoarse whisper as he waded into the far end of the tidal pool. It was warmest there, the outlet for the spring directly below. The water wore away a natural outcropping, leaving the stones smooth to stand upon. He lowered them until their shoulders were beneath the surface. He guided her hips to take the tip of his cock into her entrance.

"Are ye ready, Saoirse?"

"Aye. Please."

"We go at yer pace, *mo ghaol*."

Saoirse felt the head of his cock press forward as she lowered herself onto him. But it wasn't long before she felt resistance, and she knew he'd met her maidenhead. She drew back before dropping onto him. Magnus thrust at the same time, sheathing himself to the bollocks. He hadn't meant to enter her so far, but their movements drove him into her. He watched her expression, witnessing the surprise, but none of the pain he feared.

Saoirse forced her mien to remain neutral. The surge of pain was brief but intense. However, she wouldn't let that discomfort register on her face because she knew it would ruin the moment for Magnus. The tenderness in his gaze melted her heart, and she wanted nothing to mar this moment. With a deep breath, the sting eased, and she was curious about the sensations her husband created within her.

"What do I do?" Saoirse kept her voice low, not wanting her naïve question to echo in the cavernous expanse.

"Wait." The word came out strangled as Saoirse shifted, and Magnus tried to keep from climaxing. He'd never been with a virgin, and he was unprepared for how tight her sheath would be around his sword. He no longer feared hurting her since no pain registered with her, but he feared finishing before she began. When she chuckled, her core contracted around him, eliciting a groan.

He guided her hips to ride his length as he thrust into her. With a moment to collect himself, he relaxed and focused on pleasuring his bride. They kissed along each other's jaw, cheeks, and nuzzled the crook of one another's neck. Saoirse's hands roamed Magnus's shoulders and back as his squeezed her ample backside. She was petite in stature, but her body was curvaceous. He preferred her physique to the thinner women he'd known over the years. Everything about her was perfection in his eyes—and his hands.

"*Mo ghràidh, gràdh agam ort.*" My darling, I love ye. Magnus's heart swelled as Saoirse spoke when he did. They froze, and their gazes locked.

"I wondered if we'd be like Mama and Da one day and think so much alike that we said the same thing. Do ye think we might be like that already?"

"I think so. Ye're *mo chompanach anam.*" My soulmate.

"And ye are mine. I feel complete with ye. I feel like a better and stronger version of maself."

"I feel the same."

Their kiss signaled the end of their conversation as their movements increased. The lapping water around their bodies increased the eroticism of their coupling, heightening their desire and pleasure. Magnus felt Saoirse's stiffen as her climax washed over her. He thrust twice more before he joined her. As his seed filled her, he wondered if they were already building a family together.

Saoirse's mind wandered beyond the immediate as the euphoria waned. The prospect that they might have created a new life excited her, but a wave of selfishness crashed over her as she realized she wasn't ready to share Magnus any more than their duties would already require.

"It'll happen when it's supposed to. Until then, I will cherish every moment that is ours." Magnus knew her mind wandered to the same thing as his. She nodded, and they exchanged a brief kiss. The crashing waves reminded them they couldn't linger much longer. They used Magnus's plaid to dry themselves before dressing. He helped her back onto the sand, and they walked away from the lapping waves.

"I'm happy we came down here alone. I couldn't imagine a better way to share our first time together." Saoirse stood on her toes and kissed his cheek.

"It was incredible, wee one. I would lock us away for a sennight, only allowing anyone in with food and a constant supply of warm water, so we never have to get out of the tub."

Saoirse giggled. "Can ye imagine how wrinkled we'd be?"

"I can think of something ye'd keep straight." Magnus waggled his eyebrows as they put their stockings and shoes back on. They climbed the path to the top of the cliffs and turned toward the keep. Magnus's brow furrowed as he noticed a flash of reflected light coming from the trees near to the keep. He reached back and withdrew his sword. "Saoirse, if I tell ye to run, ye dinna stop until ye're through the gate. Ye find yer da or one of yer uncles or yer grandda. Then ye go to our chamber, and bar the door."

While Magnus shared a room with Thormud and Torquil, maids had scrubbed the chamber from top to bottom with every piece of fabric changed. Once it was clean, Siùsan had locked the door with her chatelaine's key. Saoirse would have to find her aunt to unlock it, but she wouldn't argue.

"What's happening?" She tried to look around him, but Magnus switched his sword to his left hand, just as comfortable with it there as when it was in his right. He shielded her at his side, away from the trees. He hurried them along the path, his eyes darting as he swept their surroundings.

"I dinna ken, but I'm certain I saw sunlight on metal. It was the reflection ye get when the light hits a sword." Magnus didn't stop scouting the area as he hurried Saoirse closer to the keep. When they reached the postern gate, he sent Saoirse inside to their chamber. Without discussion, they both knew she would move into the chamber Magnus had occupied when he wasn't ailing.

He watched her enter the keep before he jogged to the steps up to the battlements. He looked around until he spied a member of the laird's family. "Mòr!" He weaved his way past guardsman manning their stations.

"Aye?"

"Someone is in the woods. I saw sunlight on metal. Did anyone go out to hunt?"

"Nae that I ken. Where'd ye see them?"

Magnus pointed. "Saoirse and I were coming back from the beach. I saw the glint, but I didna see any movement."

"Let's ride out."

The two Magnuses hurried down to the stables, passing Mòr's sons. "Blake, Tor, ride out with us."

"What's happened?" Blake looked between the two men.

"Óg saw someone's sword in the woods. If we canna catch them, I want to ken where they were."

The four men hurried to saddle their mounts. None

believed they would catch anyone. The moment they left the walls, whoever it was would scarper off, but they hoped for a trail. The two older men led the charge as they crossed the grassy expanse and arrived at the forest. They dismounted and fanned out as they looked for any disturbance. Mòr was the best tracker in the clan, with an uncanny sense for the smallest clues.

"Here." It was only moments before the elder Magnus gestured the others to come closer. He pointed to crumbled leaves and an indentation in the dirt. It was too deep for anything lighter than a person. He looked around and noticed twigs hanging askew and snapped at chest height. He handed his horse to Torquil and led the way. He didn't want his mount to disturb anything before he looked. He wanted the others to follow, avoiding trampling clues he was yet to spy.

When the clues ceased, he looked into the trees. But there was nothing to see. He looked back at the younger Magnus and shook his head. "I dinna see aught else. There was someone here, but the trail ends at this spot."

"They didna just disappear." Blake looked around, his brow furrowed.

"They didna, but chances are they realized we were following and tried harder to cover their tracks. We can move apart and search further, but I dinna think we will find aught." Despite his pessimism, Mòr pointed where each man should start. They combed through the trees for another half-an-hour before they accepted they would find nothing more. They turned back to the keep.

"Other than the Gunns, have ye had trouble with anyone else?" Óg asked the others.

"Nay. We've had a few disagreements with the Ogilvies, but naught serious. It's been eight moons since the last time any of them crossed our border.

They tried to raid a few times, but it didna take long for their new laird to understand why his father and grandfather didna make the same mistake." Mòr shrugged.

It was a rare fool, and an even rarer clan, who thought to take from the Sinclairs. They patrolled their borders vigilantly, and their justice was swift toward anyone who thought to pilfer their livestock or harass their tenant farmers. Consequently, they hadn't clashed with any clan, except for the Gunns, in decades. Not since before Liam became laird. During his father's lairdship, only the Sutherlands challenged Domnall Sinclair. Their feud ended with Liam and Kyla's marriage, and now their alliance was indestructible.

"What's going on?" Liam greeted them as they rode through the gates.

"Óg spotted someone in the woods, but he was too far to see any details. The lads came with us when we went to look. We found hints that someone was there, but we lost the trail aboot two miles into the forest." Mòr handed his reins to Torquil before he patted both sons on the back, proud of their diligence.

"Any idea who, Óg?" Liam's brow furrowed. He disliked knowing anyone crept close enough to the keep that someone saw them. He wanted to know how they got onto Sinclair land and reached the keep without a patrol spotting them. He knew it wasn't a clan member. They had no reason to lurk or disappear.

"Nay. I saw a reflection on a sword, but I couldnae see who it was."

"Where's Saoirse?" Liam glanced toward the keep.

"I told her to go to our chamber until I came back. I need to let her ken it's safe." Magnus believed it was, but he would be vigilant now that Saoirse depended on him. He knew her family would always guard her, but he wouldn't use that as an excuse to be lax in his duties.

"Go up to her. Alex and Brighde told me the good news. If ye wish for a tray tonight, Siùsan will see to it."

"Good news?" Mòr narrowed his eyes before he grinned. "If ye bluidy well handfasted with the lass and didna tell me, I willna forgive ye."

"I handfasted with Saoirse. There. I've told ye." Óg's grin matched Mòr's. He oomph'd as the older man embraced him and thumped him on the back. He exchanged embraces with Liam, then Blake and Torquil. "I will ask Saoirse what she prefers. Thank ye, Liam."

"Go see yer bonnie bride. I expect to see ye in the lists, bright and early next sennight." Mòr's white teeth flashed as he teased Óg. It relieved him that the tensions between Óg and Alex eased. He enjoyed not being the youngest, even in his forties. His older brothers still teased him incessantly. And while he gave as good as he got, he enjoyed not feeling like the baby of the family's older male generation.

"A fortnight." Óg winked before turning toward the keep.

CHAPTER 16

"Who was in the woods?" Saoirse asked after unbarring and opening the chamber door. She'd followed Magnus's instructions, easily finding her aunt, and telling her that Magnus sent her. Siùsan saw her niece's expression, glanced in the bailey's direction, then hurried upstairs. Once in the chamber, Saoirse locked and barred the portal. She paced for what felt like hours until she settled for sitting on the cushions in the window embrasure and watching for Magnus's return. She'd seen him enter the bailey, then heard his pounding footfalls as he ran toward their door. She opened it as his fist hit the wood.

"We didna find aught to tell us who was in the woods. There were markings, but they faded, then disappeared, aboot two miles into the forest. But we ken someone was there recently."

"Do ye think they're watching the keep or us specifically?"

"I canna guess because I just dinna ken. I canna imagine anyone scouting Dunbeath to prepare an attack. Nay one has done that since yer Kerr grandfather arrived with De Soules and the Gunns to take yer mama from yer da. Nae a Kerr nor a Gunn rode home that day. Since then, nay one has dared."

"We're a powerful clan on our own, but with the Sutherlands and Mackays at our side, nay one dares. But mayhap they're counting on it being more than a day's ride to our families on either side of our borders."

"Saoirse, nay one is moving an army large enough to defeat this clan without the Sutherlands or Mackays noticing. Only the Gunns might allow someone to cross their land to reach here. Except for the Gunns, everyone west of Dunbeath is family. The Mackays, the MacLeods of Assynt, and us Mackenzies arenae threats, and we wouldnae allow any who are to draw this close. It makes me think this isnae aboot the Sinclairs or Dunbeath. This is aboot me."

"But who wishes ye that much harm? Is it the Mathesons?"

"That's ma best guess. Word could have spread aboot why Seamus and I ended the betrothal. We didna announce it, but people arenae fools. People kenned aboot what happened that night. That isnae a piece of gossip most people would keep to themselves." Magnus's jaw clenched.

"Magnus, I ken ye regret things aboot that night, but I wouldnae have done aught different from what ye did. She deserved it."

"And if that's the reason someone's trying to kill me?" Magnus shook his head. "I dinna regret nae marrying her. I wouldnae be here with ye if I had. But I dinna want to die before I get to be a husband to ye."

Saoirse slid her hands up his chest, then wrapped her arms around his neck and stood on her toes. "I'd say ye were vera much ma husband a little while ago. Mayhap ye'd like that chance again right now."

Magnus peered into Saoirse's dark chocolate eyes,

her eagerness contagious. He slid his hands over her backside and drew her closer. "Are ye sore, *mo chridhe*?"

Saoirse shook her head. "I thought I might be. I'm just—achy." She didn't know how better to describe the yearning she felt physically for her husband. Their passionate and erotic coupling played in her mind on a loop. The memory left her wishing to explore what else they could share. Her body longed for the still strange but oh so satisfying feel of Magnus buried within her.

"I canna leave ma wife in such a state."

Magnus squeezed her backside before yanking at the laces along her back while Saoirse unfastened the brooch at his shoulder. She dropped the piece of jewelry into his sporran before attacking his belt. She whipped it from his waist, letting it drop to the floor as they both toed off their shoes. She caught his Mackenzie plaid as it unraveled. She glanced at it as she tossed it onto the foot of the bed; the pattern registering for the first time.

"Saoirse?"

"I'm nae a Sinclair anymore. I'm a Mackenzie. I willna wear ma plaid anymore." Saoirse looked up at Magnus, the gravity of the bittersweet moment settling over her. "But I dinna have a new one either."

Magnus drew her over to a chair before the fireplace and sat down. He settled her onto his lap. "Ye will always be a Sinclair. That willna ever end. Everything aboot ye—yer compassion, yer morals, yer hard work, yer sense of family and duty—makes ye a Sinclair, and marriage canna end that. But I welcome ye into Clan Mackenzie. I'd like ye to wear ma plaid, but if ye arenae ready, I willna ask it of ye."

"I want to, but I dinna have one. I canna wear yers. I'll drown, and I ken Auntie Siùsan doesnae have one."

"Nay, she doesnae. And even if she did, I wouldnae wish ye to wear it. It would be a remnant of days better left in the past, better left forgotten. I ken mine are too big for ye, but I have more than one with me. If ye wish to wear our clan's pattern, then we can surely have someone cut it down to fit ye as an arisaid."

"Our clan." Saoirse let that idea roll around in her head. She'd considered her duties once she returned with Magnus, but she hadn't considered that she would no longer claim Sinclair as her name or her clan. When her gaze met Magnus's, she realized she made him nervous. "I like that idea. I'm proud to be a Mackenzie now. I just have to get used to it."

"I'm proud ye're ma wife, *mo chridhe*. It's warm these days, so ye dinna need an arisaid. If ye wish to wait until we arrive home, ye could have one made for yer size."

"Home." That was another jarring notion. She'd imagined the Mackenzie keep being her home, but now that her move was imminent and certain, she had a bout of nerves. She'd traveled many places with her family, visiting their extended relatives. But she'd always known she would return to Dunbeath, her chamber she shared with her sisters, and the comfort of home. "Will yer clan welcome me into yer home? Will Caroline?"

"Of course. Saoirse, ye've been to Eilean Donan before, and ye ken Caroline."

"I was a guest. It'll be different when I arrive and dinna intend to leave."

"I think it will thrill them that ye're ma wife. They couldnae ask for anyone better to join the clan."

Magnus pulled down Saoirse's right sleeve and kissed along her shoulder and over her collarbone. His hand slid beneath the neckline to cup her breast. She leaned forward, snaring his mouth in a kiss that made him fear leaking. Saoirse yanked her arms free from her gown and pushed it and her chemise to her waist once she untied the ribbons at her shoulders. Magnus lifted her breasts to his mouth, alternating suckling them. His tongue flicked her nipples as they puckered. She slipped her hands beneath his leine and over his shoulders. She relished the heat he emanated, especially knowing it wasn't from illness. He was a like the blazing sun during a summer day's zenith. Everything about him warmed her.

"Magnus, I admit I'm nervous aboot leaving here and joining a new clan. But I ken I want to be by yer side for the rest of ma life. Ma want is stronger than ma fear."

"I will help ye adjust. I willna abandon ye to Caroline and assume ye will be the best of friends immediately. I willna leave Caroline to introduce ye to our clan." Magnus grinned and nipped at her earlobe. "Mayhap I wish to show off that I have the bonniest bride in all the lands."

Magnus stood from the chair, then carried Saoirse to the bed. He placed her on her feet, so she could push her chemise and kirtle to the floor while he removed his leine. Their hands roamed over one another as they pressed their bodies together. Saoirse gripped his shoulders as she eased back onto the bed, drawing him with her. She settled against the pillows and opened her arms and legs to welcome his body against hers again, but Magnus shifted and crawled down the bed until he could rest his shoulders between her thighs.

He kissed along the inside of each leg before sliding a finger into her sheath. Her hips came off the bed of their own accord, but it brought her mons to his mouth. He kissed each fold where her leg met her hip. Then he flattened his tongue and pressed it against her pearl. He brought his lips around it and sucked. He watched Saoirse's eyes drift closed as she clenched her hands around the bedding. His tongue and fingers soon alternated working her sheath and button until she writhed. He chuckled when she grabbed a fistful of hair and pressed his face to her just before she climaxed. She stifled her moan, not allowing herself to cry out like she had in the cave. But he saw the flush climb up her neck and into her cheeks. He watched her labored breathing. And he tasted her.

"Magnus, hold me." Saoirse's request was so soft he nearly didn't hear. But he would oblige his bride with whatever she wished, especially if it meant he could be close to her. He shifted until she could wrap her arms and legs around him. He slid his arms beneath her shoulders and embraced her. "Ye willna crush me. Please dinna hold back."

"I weigh at least nine stone more than ye. I will crush ye." In these intimate moments, Magnus realized just how much larger he was than Saoirse. She was always precious to him, but he never considered her fragile. He simply didn't want to ruin the moment. At her earnest expression and nod, he settled more of his weight onto her. She pulled until he relented, but only for a moment.

"All, Magnus."

He exhaled and relaxed. At least his body. But the moment he did, she sighed. He watched her and realized she was content. Her fingers trailed lazy paths along his back, the light touch arousing him further. Somehow, she tilted her hips toward his rod, despite the weight bearing down on her. He rocked his hips, the tip of his cock sliding between her netherlips.

"I want to be inside ye like I want ma next breath."

"Dinna wait. I want to feel ye." She bent her legs and used her heels to leverage upward. His cock slid into her. She grasped his buttocks and pressed hard, encouraging him to sheath himself completely.

"This is where I belong. Inside ye. One with ye. I love ye, Saoirse."

"The feel of ye is pure pleasure. But kenning there is naught between us satisfies something I dinna understand, but I feel it in ma bones. I love ye, Magnus."

They moved together, their pace alternating between languid and frantic. Each time they drew close to the precipice, they slowed, drawing out their time united. What felt like mere minutes soon passed into an hour. Magnus shocked himself with his endurance, but he didn't want any of it to end. And the slower pace reassured him he wasn't hurting Saoirse. But when they finally could wait no longer, when their bodies demanded satisfaction, they clung to one another as Magnus's seed filled her. He remained buried inside her until his body no longer cooperated.

They climbed under the covers, pressing their bodies back together as they shared tender kisses and talked more about Eilean Donan, and what Saoirse could expect. The sun moved outside their window; the shadows growing longer. Hunger for one another led them to couple over and over. They ignored the summons for the evening meal, and they refused the offer of a tray. They dozed, chatted, and made love throughout the night. In true Sinclair fashion, they didn't emerge for four days. Magnus swore they would have the full week after their church wedding. He insisted the older generation of Sinclair men wouldn't outdo him when they welcomed their brides. Saoirse happily agreed, unwilling to be shortchanged what her mother and aunts enjoyed. When they finally emerged on the fifth day after their handfast, they wished they'd remained hidden.

"Óg!"

Magnus turned as Alex approached him in the lists. He'd missed breaking his fast because neither he nor Saoirse rushed to leave their bed. He shifted nervously since he hadn't seen Alex since he'd returned to the keep after seeking the mystery figure in the forest. Alex was now his father-by-marriage, and no one could misunderstand what Magnus had been locked away and doing with the man's daughter for half a sennight.

"I just returned from patrol," Alex said, as he caught up with Magnus at the entrance to the lists.

He ran away from home rather than be here and ken I was bedding his daughter. Wise mon.

"Aye?"

"We came across fresh ashes yesterday morning on our way back, so we fanned out to search the area. I found the trail, and it led back here. There's someone ye should see in the dungeon. He willna say aught, but we caught him only a league from the keep. He didna hear us coming, but he was watching the road to the keep."

Magnus didn't appreciate learning a stranger lurked only three miles from the keep. Whoever this man was, he was an enemy if Alex took him directly to the dungeon. Who was it? And why did this man refuse to say anything?

"I ken ye just said he wouldnae talk, but do ye have any idea why he was so close? Which clan is he?"

"Dinna ken any of it. He wasna wearing a plaid."

"Breeks? A Lowlander?"

"I dinna think so, even though he was wearing them. Naught aboot him makes me think he's from the Lowlands. If he isnae a Highlander, then he's a Hebridean. But ma guess is the former."

Magnus and Alex entered the keep. Both men swept their gazes over the Great Hall, but neither spied his wife. Alex glanced at Magnus and smirked as he shook his head.

"Mayhap ye were made to be a husband, after all."

"Because I'm wondering where ma wife is?"

"Aye. But ye're also ensuring it's safe in here. We both ken there's nay reason to suspect a threat, but we both canna keep from reassuring ourselves."

"True. Alex, I love Saoirse. I hope ye ken I dinna exaggerate."

"I ken. I may nae enjoy thinking aboot ma lass being any mon's wife, but since she is, I count ma blessings that it's ye."

"Thank ye." Magnus felt better for the brief exchange. They reached the door to the dungeons, and a guard stepped aside. They didn't have regular tenants, so there was only a guard posted when they locked someone away. They made their way down the stairs to the keep's dank bowels. The sound of skin hitting skin rang in the air.

"I am nae a forgiving mon with those who roam ma land and willna tell me why." Liam's voice floated toward the two new arrivals. Magnus knew it was Liam's fist that meted out whatever damage was being done to the prisoner. They arrived at an open cell and found Liam stripped to the waist with his hand wrapped around the stranger's throat. He squeezed enough to make the man splutter, then released him. He did it twice more while Tavish, Callum, and Mòr stood behind their father. He could have easily been mistaken for the brothers, despite being in his sixth decade. He was as fit as any man a third of his age. Magnus didn't want to imagine the pain Liam's fists delivered.

"Who's this?" Óg asked.

"He's forgotten his name," Liam responded. "I'm helping him remember something so important." The older man drove his fist into the prisoner's left pectoral. The man grunted and sagged forward.

"Ye ken, he will last longer than ye," Mòr noted. "He's being gentle and patient, but he willna remain that way."

Gentle and patient. I've seen Liam be both. The mon is gentle as a lamb and patient as a saint with bairns and weans. The fact the mon is still breathing, and Liam isnae beating him senseless, surprises me. I suppose, considering the circumstances, Mòr isnae exaggerating.

Óg drew closer and tilted his head to see the man's face. There was minimal bruising because it was obvious they wanted to leave him recognizable. But Óg wasn't sure anyone would know this stranger from Adam.

"Ye came onto ma land and have watched ma people. Ye werenae merely passing through, were ye?" Liam paused, as if he expected an answer, but none believed one would come. "Since ye've been living off ma land and hunting without ma permission, I convict ye of poaching. I could sentence ye to death right now. But we both ken what I want from ye. I'd say I'm in a far better position to hold out than ye are. The beating will only get worse, and either way ye will die rather than leave here. It's yer choice what ye must endure. It could be minutes, or it could be years."

The prisoner smirked. His gaze shifted from Liam to Óg, and a look of satisfaction entered his gaze, as though he cared not that they chained him in a dungeon cell. "Stubborn bastard, arenae ye? Ye just canna politely die, so I can go home."

"Ye are home," Alex snarled as he stepped forward. Now that Óg saw the man's face, Alex had nò reason not to pummel it while the man was uncooperative. His right fist swung an upper cut that knocked the unknown man's head against the wall. His left fist plowed into the prisoner's nose. "Ye dinna threaten ma son and go without punishment."

Everyone froze for a heartbeat as Alex's warning rang in the air. But he didn't think twice about his declaration. The next punch landed in the man's sternum, making him double over. But his restrained arms didn't allow for much movement. Just enough to strain his shoulders. He groaned, the first admittance of pain.

"Yer son? So I named him a bastard and was right. Everyone kens yer wife birthed ye useless daughters."

It was Óg's turn. His fist whipped out and boxed the man's ear. He grabbed a handful of hair and yanked backward.

"Ma father-by-marriage learned his patience from his father. I missed that lesson. Ye dinna speak aboot ma wife that way and nae feel ma wrath." Óg slammed the prisoner's head into the bricks behind it with more force than Liam or Alex had used. He drew a dirk from his waist. He put the point to the man's sternum and pressed enough to break the skin. "Mayhap I have patience after all. This shall be slow."

He increased the force, the tip cutting the skin. He added more of his weight to his effort, and the dirk punctured the skin. He would make it sheer agony if he didn't get what he wanted.

"Who are ye?" Óg stared into the man's eyes. There was something vaguely familiar about them. They weren't remarkable, but they nagged at a memory Óg couldn't pull forth. He wondered if he still suffered the ill effects of the arsenic.

"Wouldnae ye like to ken?"

Magnus pressed again, and the man howled. He knew it was only a matter of time before the man capitulated or died. He'd prefer the former. He noticed Mòr reach for one of the man's hands. He had the handle of a *sgian dubh* between his teeth. Once the prisoner's hand was free, Mòr grabbed his wrist in one hand and held the dirk in the other. He put the tip beneath the man's fingernail. The prisoner finally registered true fear. Mòr's form of coercion would be even more excruciating. Óg approved.

"Tell us who ye are, and he will cease," Liam offered.

The prisoner squeezed his eyes shut and shook his head. His legs shook as his discomfort grew. His breath whistled through his nose, and he tried to stomp a foot, but they'd shackled it too. He roared with pain as the first nail came off. Mòr didn't relent, setting to work on the next nail immediately. The man pished himself. That only made the others laugh, and Mòr worked faster.

"I relent. Stop!"

Mòr didn't, but he merely kept the dirk beneath the third nail. He no longer worked to pry it off.

"Did ye remember something?" Óg taunted.

"Ye made more than one enemy when ye broke the betrothal."

"Did Louisa send ye?" Óg wouldn't put it past the manipulative woman. The man fell silent again. "If ye dinna say otherwise, I will take that as an aye."

"I willna say who sent me. Just ken that it could be any of the enemies ye made."

"If ye dinna want to cause half the Highlands set ablaze, ye'd do well to speak. I will summon all ma allies and descend upon the Mathesons and their allies like the vengeful Almighty. Ye'd best hope the righteous mark their doors." Liam's voice wasn't loud, but his tone screamed the promise he made. "We do nae ride alone. Ye will find the Mackays, the MacLeods of Assynt and of Lewis, the Camerons, the Mackenzies, and the Sutherlands riding together. Do ye believe any clan could survive us?"

"Yers is nae the only alliance."

Six baritones laughed.

"Ours is the only one that matters." It was Liam's turn to smirk.

"It will take days to rally yer family. Just because ye caught me doesnae mean the threat is over. He'll be dead before anyone is off yer land."

"And since ye'll be dead too, ye dinna care what happens to the other clans," Alex surmised. The prisoner shrugged.

"Toss him from the cliffs," Liam decreed. "Let him consider his choices on the way down. If the rocks dinna kill him, the current and temperature will." He turned away and walked to the door, waving a dismissive hand over his shoulder.

"Da didna say when," Alex noted. "We can have a wee more fun before that. Among the five of us, we should be able to throw him clear of the rocks. Let the sharks eat him."

Alex drew his blade and swept it across the prisoner's chest from his left shoulder to his right hip. It was deep enough to bleed profusely, but it wasn't mortal. Callum, Tavish, Mòr, and Óg took their turns.

"Cease! I relent! I'm Caleb Matheson, the laird's nephew. The captain of the guard sent me. I dinna ken who gave the order, but I dinna think it was the laird."

"Ye left yer land to kill a tánaiste of one of the largest clans in all of Scotland, and ye did it without yer laird's directive. The bollocks ye must have," Callum scoffed.

"How much money were ye paid or who were ye allowed to fuck?" Óg cocked an eyebrow. The man's quick glance toward Óg answered his question. "Ah, both. Hope the tupping was good because ye willna live to spend the money."

The five men moved toward the door without giving the man chained to the wall another look.

"Wait. Ye're leaving me here?"

Callum looked over his shoulder. "Mòr told ye Da was being gentle and patient. Tossing ye would be too gentle for our taste. Ye can bleed and starve to death. Dinna bother screaming. Nay one is coming. Since we arenae keeping ye alive, nay one needs to guard ye."

The men left the cell, taking the two torches that illuminated it. They all knew Liam waited around the corner. They left the dungeon in complete blackness. They heard the prisoner's cries, but no one cared.

CHAPTER 17

"We send word to Hamish and Lachlan, and to Tristan. I dinna think we need everyone else." Liam stood behind his desk in his solar. He pulled pieces of parchment from a drawer and set a quill and ink pot on the right side. "Can Seamus spare men?"

"Aye. I canna ride on the Mathesons or anyone else without Seamus's permission. He willna hesitate to give it, but I dinna want to make things any worse than the shite heap we have."

"We can send messengers today. It'll take a day and a half to reach Uncle Hamish, and three and a half days to Tristan's." Callum looked at Óg. "It'll take a sennight for Tristan to get to Eilean Donan, and the same for us. We dinna need to leave before the messenger arrives at Castle Varrich. But we can meet them on the road. We can go to Dunrobin and wait with Uncle Hamish. It gets ye away from here."

Óg was slow to agree. He didn't like the idea of leaving Saoirse here. Now that they'd handfasted, she might be a target too. Then he considered it might be safest if he was well away from her until the threat ended. He was torn.

"Lad," Liam said as he walked to where Óg stood. "Tavish and I will stay here. Ride with Callum and yer da. She's safe with us staying back."

Óg nodded. It felt strange to think of Alex so easily as his father, but it flooded him with a sense of assurance. Callum had always felt most like a father to him since Siùsan raised him, and they were married. The greater age difference and the laird's wisdom always made Magnus wish Liam were his father or even grandfather. Any of the Sinclair men were far better than his own father had ever been.

Liam returned to his desk and scrawled quick missives to his brother-by-marriage and son-by-marriage before sealing them and handing them to Callum.

"I'll dispatch riders on ma way to find Siùsan. She'll arrange all the stores we need to travel that far." Callum, Mòr, and Tavish left, each knowing his tasks as they prepared men to ride out to a potential battle. Liam and Alex remained behind. As soon as the door closed, Magnus looked at Alex.

"Do I still call ye Alex?" Magnus blurted.

"I'd like ye to call me Da, but I ken I am nae that."

"I'd prefer it," Magnus confessed. He suddenly felt like the lost child he'd been when he arrived. "Liam always felt like a father of sorts, and Mòr was ma mentor. Ye, Callum, and Tavish were like aulder brothers, and I've looked up to all of ye since I met ye. I loathed ma father since ma first memories. There wasna a day during ma fostering that I didna wish at least one of ye was ma real da. Ye dinna think it odd that a mon auld enough to be yer younger brother would call ye that?"

"Nay. I thought it would be when I realized yer interest in Saoirse wasna fleeting. But ye're ma son, and I dinna think of ye any other way now. Aye, once ye were more like a little brother, but ye married ma daughter. I welcome ye as a son."

Alex extended his arm for a warrior handshake, and Magnus grasped his forearm. Instead of shaking it, Alex drew him into an embrace. "I'm sorry I didna get ma head out of ma arse sooner. I'm proud to call ye son."

Magnus nodded, needing a moment to collect himself. He'd never heard those six words strung together *and* directed at him. As he drew back, Liam rested his hand on Magnus's shoulder. He hadn't heard the laird approach.

"I suppose I shall have to move over then. I couldnae ask ye to call me Da when ye were a lad, nae while yer father was alive. Once he died, I thought ye might be too auld to want to, and I didna wish to overstep. But I have always looked upon ye as a son. If ma aching bones are any sign—" he shook the hand that landed the most punches "—I should go by Grandda, anyway."

"I—" Magnus could only nod. It was bittersweet to have this official recognition after so many years of yearning, and even envy, only to know he would leave once the threat was gone. As he looked at Alex, his dark locks showing flecks of gray and lines bracketing his eyes and mouth, the age difference that had once faded came back. But rather than feeling inadequate, he finally felt like he belonged, that he had the final piece to his family.

Alex grinned and ruffled Magnus's hair before playfully elbowing him in the ribs. Magnus swatted his arm away.

"Ye're but skin and bones, Da. Ye have the knobbly elbows of an auld mon." Magnus returned Alex's grin.

"Ye're nae too big for me to skelp." Alex clapped his hand on Magnus's shoulder and squeezed before embracing him once more. "If we dinna find our wives and warn them we're leaving, they'll skelp our arses."

Liam, Alex, and Magnus left the laird's solar. The two younger men went in search of their wives while Liam sought Callum to continue planning.

Saoirse listened to Magnus as he explained what happened in the dungeon and in Liam's solar. She knew she received an abridged version of the dungeon. She was grateful for that. As happy as hearing about her father and grandfather accepting Magnus as their own, she struggled to think about anything but his imminent departure.

"*Mo ghràidh*, ye're nae listening, are ye?"

"Hmm? Nay, I'm nae. I'm nae ready for ye to ride out yet, Magnus. What if—"

Magnus wrapped his arms around Saoirse, tucking her head against his chest. She wound her arms around his waist and closed her eyes. They stood together in their chamber, away from prying eyes and ears. He'd been uncertain how she would receive the news, so he wished for privacy. She appeared stoic, but he felt the tremors as she leaned against him.

"I canna tell ye naught will go wrong or make promises that guarantee ma return. But I can promise ye that I will do everything I can to *always* return to ye. I'm doing this to make sure that can happen. I need to ken that whoever this is canna make ye their next target."

Saoirse nodded. She understood and could accept what Magnus told her. It made sense—to her head. But her heart screamed at her to stop him, to not leave the safety of their chamber. Then she reminded herself that it was in this very chamber that Magnus nearly died. That memory left her feeling adrift, as though there was nowhere safe for him.

"Why'd they have to come all the way here? Why does anyone wish to harm ye that badly?" Saoirse thought aloud.

"If it is the Mathesons, then they didna accept the end of the betrothal like they said they did. Mayhap Laird Matheson blames me, or mayhap his vengeance is to save face. I dinna ken. But the Mackenzies are still recovering in numbers. We lost many warriors, along with villagers. We arenae weak, but we arenae as strong as we once were. I dinna want to bring ye to Eilean Donan when I ken there are more warriors to protect ye here. I trust Seamus and ken he wouldnae think twice aboot saving ye over saving himself. But I dinna want to bring a battle to our home when we dinna have the men to withstand an attack by more than the Mathesons."

"Is his pride so fragile?"

"Most men's is. He likely thinks bringing the Mackenzies low by killing me will make him appear more powerful than he is. I think he sent someone here, so it wouldnae be so obvious. If I died at home with nay explanation, it would look suspicious. But while I'm far from home and after traveling, it might be reasoned away, especially since poison would have killed me from a distance. Whoever set this in motion wishes nae only to punish me but to punish the Mackenzies."

"What happens if the Matheson doesn't take responsibility for this? Since yer prisoner said it wasna the Matheson who ordered this, why would he accept fault if ye kill the mon he supposedly didna send? Ye should ransom the mon back to get more information or for the laird to claim what he's done. If he willna, then kill the prisoner and let Matheson watch from the battlements."

Magnus listened to how simple Saoirse made it

sound, and to an extent, he agreed. It surprised him that someone committed to keeping others alive would speak so blithely about someone dying. He released her and walked to the door. He could hear men's voices belowstairs.

"Let's suggest that to yer da and Grandda." He was still growing accustomed to calling the men by their new-to-him monikers. Saoirse took his hand as they walked downstairs to the Great Hall. "Da?"

Plenty of people froze, but Alex grinned. "Aye."

Saoirse and Magnus joined Alex, Callum, and Liam. Those around them returned to their work and conversations, but Saoirse sensed their curiosity after so many weeks of Magnus being at odds with her parents. She even sensed some relief among her clansmen and women.

"Saoirse had a sound suggestion." Magnus peered down at Saoirse, who looked unprepared for Magnus to mention her role in their conversation. He gave her an encouraging smile, but he said nothing more.

"I asked Magnus what would happen if Laird Matheson refused to take responsibility for his clansman, even if he didna give the order. I suggested that ransoming the mon might make the Matheson talk, so instead of killing him here, take him with ye. If the Matheson willna admit aught, then let him see ye kill the prisoner. Then he might talk, or at least realize ye arenae there to jest."

Alex, Callum, and Liam stared at Saoirse long enough that she shrank against Magnus. Alex stepped forward and kissed her cheek. When he leaned back, pride shone from him.

"I ken ye wouldnae have shared that idea before Magnus arrived. I'm glad ye have the confidence to speak yer mind. I'm sorry that ye didna before. That's a good suggestion."

"Did ye…?" Saoirse glanced toward the passageway to the dungeon.

"Nay. He's still down there. We'll set off in the morn. I suppose, in the meantime, he should have some food and drink." Alex looked at Liam, who nodded. "Why dinna ye spend yer last evening together?"

"It's nae our last. I'm coming."

"Nay, ye arenae." Four male voices boomed, but Saoirse held her ground. She cocked one eyebrow, and all four men wondered if singing the praises of her newfound confidence had been a little premature.

"Saoirse, ye are nae riding into a battle. I canna concentrate if I think ma wife is aboot to be killed." Magnus glanced at Alex, Liam, and Callum, hoping they'd support him. They nodded, none of them liking the idea either. "None of us will focus."

"If there is a battle, then ye'll need a healer." Saoirse stepped away from Magnus's side, crossed her arms, and planted her feet hip-width apart.

"Nay." Magnus shook his head. "Saoirse, be reasonable." He wished to swallow the words as soon as he uttered them. The three Sinclair men looked everywhere but at the couple. All three men knew better than to mutter something so dangerous to a wife.

"Be reasonable? I'm supposed to stay here, like a wean ye've told what to do, and just wait to hear ye bled to death. Nay. I wouldnae be the first or the last healer to ride with her clan. I dinna need to be anywhere near the battle."

"Nay. There willna be a safe place for ye to hide. While I'm on the battlefield with all of our men, someone could sneak around and take ye. Kill ye. Nay." Saoirse's suggestion horrified Magnus. He thought he might be ill.

Saoirse picked up a lock of her hair and held it out to Magnus. "Other than ma mother and me, only Isabella Hartley and her son, Kirk, have hair like ours this far north in the Highlands. Everyone kens they're as much Sinclairs as I am. Someone may nae hesitate to kill the Mackenzie tánaiste, but nay one would kill a Sinclair woman. I dinna mean to be cruel, but Seamus has sons, even if they're wee lads. They can replace ye. There isnae a soul in Scotland who wouldnae ken I'm a Sinclair and would wish the torturous death touching me would guarantee. There are seven clans that would avenge ma death. Magnus, ma mother and aunts didna get their reputations for being fiercely protective without reason. It's a mad mon who crosses a Sinclair woman and thinks he'll survive."

"Nay. Ye dinna ken how to protect yerself." Magnus shook his head again.

The other three men took a step back. They knew what was coming. Saoirse held a blade at Magnus's throat and another under his plaid by his bollocks. Magnus stood like a statue, utterly unprepared for a knife-wielding bride to draw her blades on him.

"Tell me how I dinna ken how to protect maself." She pressed just enough to touch his skin without nicking it in either place. She withdrew them and stepped back. "If ma da and uncles didna teach all the lasses how to defend themselves, then ma mama and aunts would have. Auntie Mairghread may be the one who competes at the Highland Gatherings and is the *best-known* knife thrower, but Auntie Siùsan is just as good. I believe ye taught her, and she taught me."

"I'm nae—" Magnus stopped when Alex cleared his throat and shook his head.

"Saoirse, I agree with Magnus, but I ken we willna change yer mind. He'll worry the entire way there if he thinks ye willna forgive him for leaving ye behind, or worse, fears ye following. But he's right aboot nae being able to concentrate on the battlefield if he fears someone reaching ye. If Magnus agrees, ye come, but under these conditions."

"If he agrees?" Saoirse looked around. "Mayhap Mama would like to hear these conditions."

"Saoirse," Alex warned. The last thing he needed was his wife joining the conversation. If she and Saoirse joined forces, they'd be the ones leading the charge. "This isnae aboot ye. Ye wish to come to make sure if aught happens, Magnus can be tended to. If he canna concentrate for fear of ye being harmed, then he willna live long enough to have ye tend to him. This is aboot conditions he can live with and still keep himself alive."

Saoirse looked up at Magnus and found a pair of distraught blue-hazel eyes peering down at her. She nearly reconsidered, but something stronger pushed her not to relent. She wasn't blessed with the gift of second sight, but something told her they would need a healer. That meant her.

"What are yer conditions, Da?" Saoirse continued to look up at Magnus.

"Ye wear a pair of breeks and cover yer hair. Ye go into the tree branches with yer bow and arrow along with all yer dirks. Ye listen to Wiley and Tate, who will be livid aboot being left behind but who will guard ye."

Saoirse's lip thinned, and she shook her head. "Nay. Thormud and Tate always partner while Blake and Torquil always do. Wiley and Kirk can stay with me. I willna split up Thor and Tate."

"I'll stay with the lass, too." Everyone turned toward the English voice approaching. After more than a score of years in the Highlands, Dedric Hartley's voice still held an accent. A lad when the English stole him from his border clan and forced him to the English royal court, he'd remained a Scot in his heart. When his tenure as a knight to King Edward I ended, he returned to Scotland and the MacLellans. It wasn't long after that he met and married Isabella Dunbar. They moved north and joined the Sinclairs. He was one of the senior-most guards among the Sinclair warriors. He was also Kirk and Keira's father.

"Thank ye, Ric." Saoirse smiled at him. He was much like an uncle to all the Sinclair children, and Keira and Kirk were her cousins, as far as Saoirse was concerned.

"Yes, well, I have a soft spot for women with such blonde hair." Ric shrugged. He looked at Magnus and offered the new husband a sympathetic smile. "They're all cut from the same mold. Don't fight it. You'll still lose and just wind up exhausted. We're better with our women at our sides, anyway."

"Ye're better off leaving us to run the keep," Ceit said as she came to join them. She pinched Tavish's ribs as he walked beside her. "And ye can take this one when ye scarper off. I dinna need him under foot."

"Yer feet arenae what ye like to have me under." Tavish may have whispered, but everyone heard. "Wheest, *seillean beag*. Stop buzzing." Tavish had called his wife "little bee" since they met. He said her tongue could sting, but her love was sweeter than honey.

"Take him with ye." Ceit jested, but she leaned against her husband as he wrapped his arm around her shoulders. Her arms went around his waist as though she might keep him from ever leaving. None of the wives were excited at the prospect of watching their husbands ride away. Saoirse spied Blake holding Cerys against his chest as they whispered, near the fireplace. Cerys nodded at something Blake said, but they remained wrapped in each other's arms as she burrowed her face against her husband's chest.

As much truth as Saoirse spoke about the men needing a healer, she knew she insisted because she wanted to avoid the very scenes she saw with her aunt and uncle and with her cousin. But she wondered if she was jumping out of the pan and into the fire. Would she be able to say goodbye to Magnus when the battle began? Perhaps she should remain at Dunbeath. The decision tore at her, but the nagging sense that she needed to be there didn't dim.

"We'll take the tray this evening." Saoirse supposed the couples in her family would do the same. The Great Hall would be nearly empty since the married couples with men riding out in the morning would prefer their privacy too.

"Are ye taking this one, too?" Ceit's tone continued to jest, but her anxiousness was clear as she looked up at Tavish.

Liam mulled it over. He intended to send Callum as his representative since his oldest son was the clan's tánaiste and his heir. Mòr would want to be there since the threat was to his mentee, and Alex had a right as Óg's father-by-marriage. He'd intended to remain with Tavish as his second-in-command at home. He shifted his gaze to Óg and knew his decision.

"Aye. We all go, lads. Ceit, ye and yer sisters can run this clan with ease. Ye've done it before. Let there be nay confusion in anyone's mind that the Sinclairs are loyal to their allies, and nay one threatens our family without facing *all* of our wrath. *Familia prima.*"

"*Semper familiar.*" Liam spoke the first half of their family motto alone, but seven voices finished it. Just as Alex considered Magnus his son with no qualifiers, Liam saw his daughters-by-marriage the same way. They were his daughters and sisters to one another.

"Come, *seillean beag.* Help me pack," Tavish whispered. He rubbed his wife's back, and she hadn't lessened her hold. The couple bickered on purpose, as it had been their dynamic since the beginning, but no one doubted their devotion to one another. All of Liam's children loved their partners as much as they did the day they married, and their desire for one another never dimmed. If anything, it had only multiplied over the score of years they'd all been married.

Liam made his way to his chamber to prepare. He loathed riding away from home and separating his family. In the nearly forty years he'd been laird, it hadn't gotten any easier. He hated knowing he was taking his sons and grandsons into danger. He despised leaving the women behind to worry. And he feared the day he wouldn't return with all of his family. But it was the duty he'd been born into.

Kyla, mo ghràidh, *I need yer guidance again. Would that ye could be here to tell me in person. But I feel ye with me always. Watch over our family, ma love. Ye ken I canna do this without ye. I dinna think they're ready for me to join ye yet, but I long for the day we'll reunite. I promised ye this lifetime and the next.*

When he reached his chamber, he ran his hand over the carved doorjamb he'd created for Kyla as a wedding gift. It replicated the woodland scene she'd stitched on a leine she made for their wedding. On the left, there was a raven, a deerhound, a bear, and a boar with an "L" overlapping a "K". On the right was an eagle, a red stag, and a wildcat. The same initials appeared but in reverse, the "K" overlapping the "L." She'd worried about future generations disliking the letters, but it was their children who swore it was the most special part. Liam shook his head, clearing the wistfulness from his mind, but he would never let go of Kyla. They were the beginning of the Highland legacy that was the Clan Sinclair. He would ride out with three generations of Sinclair warriors to defend their family. He truly wondered whose death wish was so strong that they would take on his clan.

CHAPTER 18

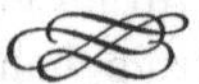

Saoirse and Magnus soaked in a massive wood and copper tub. Carpenters built the early tubs for the laird's family so large to accommodate the men's stature. The fact that their wives were so much more petite meant there was room for them to share. It hadn't taken Liam long to realize that he needed several tubs to accommodate his growing family once his four sons married. His sons were more like him than they realized since he and Kyla had often shared their baths.

"Saoirse, I still dinna agree that ye should come." Magnus's arms rested on the top of her thighs as she reclined against him, seated between his legs.

"I canna give ye a sound reason other than something in ma heart tells me I must be there. I dinna ken why, but every time I tell maself to stay here, this consuming need to go with ye'washes over me. It's nae even fear. Aye, I'm scared that ye might die. It terrifies me. But that isnae what this feeling is. It's more like a premonition."

"Do ye sense me dying?"

"I sense something is going to happen to one of ye, but I dinna ken if it's ye. I think it is since the feeling is so strong. I understand why ye dinna want me there,

Magnus. I've never suggested such a thing before. It never crossed ma mind when Da and the others rode out last year to defend King David against Balliol. Those battles Andrew Murray led were some of the most vicious Da and ma uncles have ever seen. They fought alongside the Guardian of Scotland, and they came home. Nae all Sinclairs did. But I never thought of going with them."

"If yer conviction is that strong, then I will heed it. But I need ye to do as we tell ye. Please promise me ye'll do everything ye can to follow Ric's, Kirk's, and Wiley's instructions. I ken I willna stop worrying, but I trust them. I trust ye."

"I will. I dinna want to distract ye, and I'm sorry that I will. I just feel like it will be worse if I dinna come, *mo chridhe*."

"I believe ye." Magnus kissed her temple before moving her wet locks to one shoulder. He kissed his way along the other as his cock came back to life. They'd already coupled when they entered the tub. He wished to lavish more attention on his bride. She gave him the vigor of a man half his age, her delectable body pressed against his. His hand slipped between her thighs, his fingers sliding into her sheath as the heel of his hand pressed against her pearl. Her head lolled back on his shoulder as her fingers gripped his thighs.

Saoirse could feel Magnus's cock pressing against her lower back. She knew what she wished to do, but it wasn't feasible in the bath. However, her body clamored for release. She pressed her breasts together, massaging them as Magnus alternated pinching and tweaking her nipples.

"Magnus, I'm almost there."

"I ken, Saoirse. Let me feel ye around ma fingers. I want to hear ye sigh ma name."

Saoirse closed her eyes, relishing every sensation

Magnus stirred. She focused on the increasing ache in her core before her muscles spasmed around his fingers. Her breasts rose and fell in the water as she arched her back.

"Magnus," she exhaled.

"The sweetest sound I've ever heard." Magnus withdrew his hands, unprepared for her to rise and swiftly grab a drying linen. She held one out to him as she ran the other over her body. He stood and accepted it, curious to discover what his bride planned. They were both soon dry, so Saoirse led Magnus to their bed, playfully poking him in the chest to press him onto the mattress. He sat, then eased himself back against the pillows. She crawled between his legs, her hands straddling his ribs as her breasts swung.

She kissed each peak and valley along his abdomen, drawing her tongue along the grooves beside his hips while she wrapped her hand around his length. She stroked his rod and watched him. She riveted his attention to her, as he suspected what she had in mind. She was yet to attempt it, and he hadn't suggested it. He was certain he would expire when she swirled her tongue over the tip of his cock but did nothing to take him into her mouth. She teased him with long swipes of her tongue from root to tip. When she wrapped her lips around its head and drew on it tightly, his hips bucked. He noticed her smile before she slid her mouth down the length of him. Then she set to work. He felt her hesitancy, but what she lacked in experience, she made up for in effort.

"Saoirse, lass—this is—Holy Mother—I—" Magnus gave up trying to speak. Watching his wife practically swallow him with a temptress's expression was the most erotic thing he'd ever experienced. It even trumped their first-time making love when they were in the cave pool. He clenched the sheets and forced himself not to thrust his hips, despite the near pathological need. "Saoirse, I dinna want to finish yet. I want to be inside ye, feel ye climax with me."

Saoirse lifted her head, leisurely dragging her tongue up his rod before nodding. His hands went around her waist. He lifted her and rolled to trap her beneath him. They'd discovered various positions they enjoyed together. Saoirse reveled in Magnus being on top, where she could appreciate his muscular build and his massive size. She felt precious knowing how much larger he was than her, yet he was always so careful not to hurt her. He appreciated the trust he always saw in her eyes when he hovered over her, ever aware of how tiny she was beneath him. He thrust into her, and they moved with synchronicity borne of a soul deep connection.

"Magnus, more."

"Whatever ye wish." Magnus drew back and thrust harder, pressing as deep as he could. Her core squeezed him, holding him in place until he withdrew to surge into her again and again. Her nails bit into his shoulder blades as euphoria crashed over her sooner than she expected.

"St. Columba's bones," Magnus groaned, fighting to maintain control. He wasn't ready for this to end. He knew they needed sleep, so they couldn't spend most of the night coupling like they wished. He would make this last them until they returned to Dunbeath. He didn't expect time alone with his wife while traveling with all the men in her family.

He rolled onto his back, bringing Saoirse with him. She leaned forward, her hands resting on his chest as her breasts swung with each rocking motion. His fingers pressed into her hips, but she controlled their pace. He thrust into her each time she bore down on his cock.

"I'm close again."

"Good." Magnus felt his imminent release, but the last thing he wanted was to leave his bride unsatisfied. They panted as they strained together to reach the mountain peak, then slid down into bliss as one.

Saoirse collapsed forward, sprawled across her husband. He shimmied until he could draw the covers over them. The movement, with him still buried within her, brought his cock back to life.

I couldnae go again this fast even when I was nine-and-ten.

"Magnus?"

"Aye." He rocked her hips as she rode him. This time, they moved slowly, drawing out each sensation. But it was only a matter of minutes before they once more reached ecstasy. Sated, they held one another. "We need to sleep."

"I ken," Saoirse said just before she yawned. "I dinna want to yet, but I look forward to waking with ye beside me."

"The only nights I will ever be away from ye are when I'm nae at the keep. Saoirse, there will be nay his or her chambers when we reach Eilean Donan. Seamus and Caroline werenae a love match, and I feel even worse for them now that I ken what it is to have a woman love me from the start. They dinna share a chamber. I dinna want that."

"I dinna want that either. Even after all these years, they havenae developed any tender feelings for one another?"

"They have. They love each other now, but they began with separate chambers, and I think it embarrasses them to consider sharing one now."

"I can understand that. Yer parents didna set an example for a loving couple who wished to share their time and chamber with each other. And he's laird. I suppose there must be pressure to appear lairdly."

"Aye. But Seamus wasna the one who wished for the separate chambers. He kenned couples could share without shame after living here as long as I did. It was Caroline who was too uncomfortable. She's the one too embarrassed, but I ken she wishes it was otherwise."

"Mayhap they will follow our example once we are there."

"I hope so. I think they would be happier since she spends most nights in the laird's chamber, but she sneaks back at sunrise with Seamus accompanying her. He leaves her door before coming belowstairs to start his day. I'm certain the servants ken what they're aboot."

Saoirse lifted onto her forearms, which rested on Magnus's chest. "Should I pack and bring everything with me? Will we stop at Eilean Donan?"

"Nay. We will return here with everyone else. When ye're ready, then we will depart for Eilean Donan. Ye arenae saying farewell to yer mama and family in the morning. Dinna fash."

"Isnae that inconvenient for ye? To come all the way back here?"

"Ye arenae riding into battle with me and nae coming back here after. Yer mama is already going to be beside herself."

"Thank ye. I didna want to suggest we come back in case ye need to remain at Eilean Donan after whatever happens. But I really didna want tomorrow morning to be the last time I see Mama before making ma home somewhere else."

"Saoirse, we still have our wedding coming up. We promised yer parents we'd be married in a kirk."

"I ken. I was afraid we'd do it at Eilean Donan as a formality. I really want ma family there."

"Aye. And I'd like Seamus, Caroline, and the weans to come back with us. I'd like them to be here too. It was going to be a surprise for ye. I sent a missive the day yer parents agreed."

Saoirse's face brightened. While she no longer thought of Magnus like an uncle, she still did Seamus. He was sixteen years her senior, but he'd been just as much fun as Magnus. He'd taken the weans fishing and on adventures to the beach. But just as quickly as she grew excited, it waned.

"Does he ken what's happened to ye since ye arrived?"

"Aye. I included it in the missive."

"What does he think? Does he fault us?"

Magnus stroked her back as he pecked her lips. "Of course nae. He trusts this clan as much as I do."

"We still dinna ken who slipped ye the mint and who powdered yer bed. I ken ye have that mon, and he probably brought the poison. But he couldnae have sneaked abovestairs to do it.. Someone—a maid—is the culprit."

Magnus grew quiet. He'd thought the same thing more than once since meeting the prisoner. The man orchestrated the murder attempts, but he couldn't be the one to carry it out. No man outside the laird's family came abovestairs unless it was to help with the tub or buckets of bathwater.

"I have faith Siùsan and the others will figure that out. I ken she hasnae stopped investigating."

"I nearly forgot that someone in our household must be involved since Da captured that mon. I'd hoped we'd solved it all."

Magnus hadn't forgotten. But whomever was responsible would be Liam's to punish. The man represented a different clan, which made it far larger than something Magnus could resolve.

"Morning will come all too soon. We should sleep. We willna solve all the problems tonight, wee one."

"I ken. I love ye."

"I love ye."

Saoirse slid to Magnus's side, but they remained wrapped in one another's arms as they dozed off.

Saoirse watched her mother approach as she stood with the men and horses. She knew Brighde disapproved of her leaving. But she also knew her mother wouldn't stop her. There was an undeniable benefit to having a healer travel with them. Brighde merely wished it wasn't her daughter.

"I wish ye were still a wean, and I could refuse to allow ye beyond the walls." Brighde squeezed Saoirse in her embrace. The younger woman rested against her mother, a sense of relief flowing through her that only her mother provided. She returned the embrace and absorbed all the love and strength her mother offered. When they drew apart, Brighde cupped Saoirse's face. "I am so vera proud of ye. Yer kind heart and yer iron will. I just wish I could keep ye with me always. There is nay one I love more than ye and yer sisters. Yer da feels the same way aboot ye lasses. Please be careful."

"I will Mama. I'm nae leaving for good. I will be back, and I will regale ye with ma stories of adventure." Saoirse tried to smile, but she felt her gorge rising with each word. Tears threatened, so she wrapped her arms around her mother again and squeezed her eyes shut.

"Wheest, *leannan*. Yer da and Óg will protect ye, as will the others. Just do as they say, and all will be well." Brighde spoke to convince herself as much as to convince her daughter. She'd repeated the idea over and over as the riders prepared to leave. It was barely dawn, but five score men prepared to ride out. It was a massive army by most clan's standards, but the Sinclairs were large and prosperous. They had the men to take with them while keeping Dunbeath well protected. "Give yer Auntie Amelia a warm hug for me. The same to Arabella."

"I will." Saoirse released Brighde, who turned to find Alex standing behind her. He wrapped his steely arms around Brighde and lifted her off her feet. They shared a kiss that was as heated as the ones when they first realized their feelings for one another.

Saoirse looked around and spied the other couples doing the same. Callum and Siùsan stood with Thormud, Rose, and Shona. But they may as well have been alone for how they kissed. Tavish and Ceit were in the shadows, since they were the most outrageous of the four couples. Theirs was practically obscene, but it was just as endearing as the others. Wiley, Tate, and Ailish cared not since they were too used to their parents' antics. Ailish embraced her brothers just as Rose and Shona embraced Thormud. Magnus Mòr and Deirdre clung to one another, her feet barely brushing his shins as he held her off the ground. Torquil embraced his sister, Ainsley, while Blake and Cerys shared a kiss that rivaled any of the older generation. Only Saoirse would ride out with her husband. She had a pang of guilt, especially as Mirren and Nessa came to say goodbye.

"I thought aboot falling out of a tree, so ye wouldnae be able to go," Nessa confessed. The three sisters clasped hands, just as they had since they were children. "Dinna go doing aught foolish. I wish to be an auntie one day."

Nessa's comment gave Saoirse pause. She and Magnus had coupled so frequently that she knew there was a strong chance she was already with child. She'd seen her mother glance at her belly as she approached, but Brighde had said nothing. Magnus had said nothing to Saoirse, but she suspected he hadn't thought of it.

"I wish to be a mama one day, so I willna do aught on purpose to risk that." Saoirse released her sisters' hands and wrapped her arm around each waist. They closed their circle and put their heads together. "I love ye."

"We love ye," Mirren and Nessa said in unison.

"Are ye ready, *mo ghaol?*" Magnus joined them, giving Mirren and Nessa brief hugs with a kiss on the cheek.

"Aye." Saoirse accepted Magnus's help to mount the gelding Liam insisted she ride. The mares she'd ridden in the past wouldn't be able to keep up with the much larger warhorses. With a sigh, she nudged her horse forward to follow her grandfather and uncles. Alex rode to her left, and Magnus on her right. She twisted to wave goodbye, as did all the riders. More mounted men and foot soldiers joined them outside the walls. Married warriors lived in crofts outside the walls, so there were scores of men saying their final goodbyes to their families. Liam, with Callum to his right and Thormud to his father's right, led the procession. Tavish and Mòr rode behind their father, with their sons beside them. The rest of the riders fell in behind Alex, Saoirse, and Óg, who brought up the rear of the laird's family. Once outside the village, they spurred their horses and rode south for the Sutherlands. Their army would double with the Sutherlands, then triple when the Mackays joined them. A tsunami was about to strike the Mathesons, and not one Sinclair cared if they all perished.

CHAPTER 19

The Sinclairs spent the night with the Sutherlands, their men camping outside the gates. Saoirse shared embraces with Amelia, Lady Sutherland. She was the older generation of Sinclair siblings' aunt, but everyone called her Auntie Amelia. Saoirse'd been happy to see her father's and uncles' cousin Lachlan and his wife, Arabella. But she'd been most excited to see her cousins Callen, Alasdair, and Gavin. At six-and-ten, Callen was joining them. It would be his first time riding out to a potential battle. At four-and-ten and two-and-ten, the other boys were far too young. She'd watched Arabella say goodbye to Callen, then walk away, only to burst into tears against Amelia's shoulder. It made Saoirse wonder how she would ever manage if her husband and sons rode off to battle. It was Lachlan who dried his wife's tears as they shared a kiss that rivaled any of the Sinclairs'. Hamish and Amelia were no more discreet, having stopped caring decades ago. They were a love match from the beginning, just like Lachlan and Arabella had been nearly twenty years later.

Once mounted, Liam and Hamish rode together, just as they had countless times. Liam's younger brother died when Callum was a baby, and Hamish's older and younger brothers died a few days before Liam and Kyla wed. They'd become each other's brother. Laird Liam Sinclair, Earl of Caithness, and Laird Hamish Sutherland, Earl of Sutherland, were enough to strike terror in anyone's hearts. Callum remained beside Liam, and Lachlan rode beside Hamish. That was enough to make most men pish themselves. Thormud and Callen sat proudly behind their fathers and grandfathers, with the rest of the Sinclair family and both armies following. Their combined army was unstoppable.

Three days into their ride southwest, the Mackays joined them. Tristan's dark hair made him resemble the Sinclair brothers so much that he could have been Liam's fifth son. They treated him as such. It was only his emerald eyes that differentiated him. His sons—Wee Liam, named for his grandfather, Hamish, named for his great-uncle, and Alec—were the spitting images of their father. By the time they reached Eilean Donan, their forces had amassed nearly three hundred men and one woman.

"Bluidy hell!" Seamus greeted them as he approached on horseback. His grin nearly swallowed his face. The leaders fanned out, and Magnus Óg dismounted at the same time as Seamus. The brothers embraced, squeezing and pounding one another on the back. After Siùsan left to marry Callum, for a few months it was only the two of them. They'd protected each other from their parents. Then they were the two outsiders when they arrived at Dunbeath to foster. They'd always been each other's closest friend and confidante. "I'd have killed ye if ye died."

"I would have only haunted ye. Ye canna be rid of me." Magnus walked to Saoirse and helped her from her horse. "Brother, I'd introduce ye to ma wife, Saoirse Mackenzie."

It was the first time anyone addressed her by her new name. Magnus noticed the surprise on many faces, then the acceptance. It was only Alex who appeared pained. He looked away for a moment to regain his composure before dismounting.

"Seamus, Alex's invited me to call him Da." Magnus noticed a moment of wistfulness in his brother's eyes. He didn't have that type of relationship with Caroline's father.

Alex shook Seamus's forearm before pulling him in for an embrace. When they separated, Alex spoke so others could hear. "Ye're Óg's brother, so can call me Da if ye wish. If nae, then I'm still Alex. But it would feel odd to have ye like a younger brother, then have yer own brother as ma son. Mayhap, it would be less confusing."

Seamus nodded, as eager for the acceptance as he had been when he first met the imposing Sinclair brothers. "I'd like that—Da." He looked to Liam. "Grandda?"

"Aye." Liam grinned. He saw Seamus no differently than he did Óg. They were his family, and they'd become such the moment Callum announced to the old Laird Mackenzie that the lads were going to Dunbeath to foster.

Everyone mounted and rode toward Eilean Donan. Saoirse examined the keep as they approached. It was now her home, even if they would return to Dunbeath before she officially moved in. She rode in the front, between Magnus and Seamus. It was an odd feeling to lead such an imposing force anywhere, but as the tánaiste's wife, it was her right and duty. She glanced at her husband, who beamed with pride at her.

When they arrived in the bailey, Saoirse spied Caroline, Henry, and Thomas. At five, Henry held Caroline's hand while she held two-year-old Thomas. Henry hid behind her legs as men poured into the bailey, over- whelmed by the number and size of the warriors ar- riving at his home. But he darted forward when Magnus crouched and pretended to creep forward. He ran into his uncle's arms, and Magnus swept him off his feet. He ruffled the child's hair before putting him down. He returned to Saoirse's side, once more helping her dismount. He wrapped his arm around her waist and guided her to Caroline and the children. Thomas reached for him. Saoirse thought she would melt in a puddle of gooey happiness as she watched her husband with his nephews.

"Lady Mackenzie, I'd like to introduce ye to ma wife, Lady Saoirse." Magnus erred on the side of cau- tion and offered a formal introduction. Caroline was a kind woman, with a generous heart, but she'd been raised in a far more rigid family than the Sinclairs. It was reminiscent of how Seamus and Magnus's parents raised them before the brothers left home.

"It's Caroline." Saoirse's new sister-by-marriage reached out her hands now that Magnus held Thomas. "Welcome to yer new home."

"Thank ye, Caroline. It's Saoirse." The women em- braced, and Saoirse immediately felt welcome. Greet- ings continued as they reintroduced Caroline to Tristan and Hamish, along with their families. She hadn't seen them since her wedding six years earlier.

"Come inside. Scouts told us ye approached, so we moved the evening meal forward. Ye must be ready to eat." Caroline ushered them toward the Great Hall.

Magnus looked around, knowing how he would feel returning to the keep. It was home because he'd lived there as a child and had returned as an adult. But most of the time, it felt merely like a place to rest his head.

When he peered down at Saoirse and observed her take in details she may have forgotten, he saw his keep through a new lens. It was now a home he shared with his wife, at least until they could choose a croft, if that's still what she wanted.

"We will share ma chamber, which is ours for as long as ye wish. If ye still want a croft of our own, I will arrange for it once we come back."

"Ye'd still consider a croft?" Saoirse turned to him in surprise.

"A place where I can chase ma bonnie bride around bare as the day she was born? I'd build it with ma own hands if it made it happen faster."

"I love ye." Saoirse grinned and nodded. Magnus wrapped her arm around his as he led her to the dais. Her Sinclair, Mackay, and Sutherland cousins found tables below the dais to take their meal. Saoirse joined the lairds, tánaistes, her uncles, and Caroline and the weans at the laird's table. The last time she'd been there, she'd sat amongst her cousins. Now she was sitting in a chair that would be hers until Henry was tánaiste and had a wife. Eventually, it would become Thomas's wife's. But for now, she sat beside Magnus and swept her gaze over her new clan. Before the priest could bless the food, Magnus stood and held out his hand. Saoirse rose and linked her fingers with his.

"Mackenzies, ye ken we've had ties to the Sinclairs since ma sister wed Callum. We strengthened our bond when Seamus and I fostered among them. Our connection is unbreakable now that I've married Lady Saoirse Mackenzie. I'd like ye to meet ma wife. Some of ye may recognize her. She's Alex's auldest daughter." Magnus gazed down at Saoirse, his love clear to everyone. "Lady Saoirse, I welcome ye to our clan."

He turned to Caroline, who handed him a folded plaid with a Cairngorm brooch on top. It was a deep hazel that nearly matched Saoirse's eyes. Her mother and aunts performed the kertch ceremony the night she and Magnus handfasted, so she wore one that day. Now Magnus presented her with her Mackenzie plaid. It was the laird's family pattern, making her status clear to anyone who looked. She accepted it and unfolded it. It was the right length for her. She'd refused to allow Magnus to ruin one of his plaids for her, and he'd understood her need to wear the Sinclair plaid for as long as she could. But now, she quickly wrapped it around herself as an arisaid and remained still as Magnus fastened the brooch to her left shoulder.

"I love ye, *mo sheud.*" My jewel. Magnus's earnest gaze left no doubt that he meant the phrase.

Saoirse ran her fingers over the brooch before stepping into Magnus's open arms. If the devotion radiating from them didn't assure everyone that they were a love match rather than one for an alliance, their kiss certainly did.

"I love ye, *mo chridhe.*" She turned toward the gathered clan and smiled. "I am proud to be a Mackenzie. I recognize some of ye, but nae others. I look forward to kenning ye all."

The clan cheered, but a few faces—several women's faces—looked less than enthusiastic. Saoirse noticed and looked up at Magnus, but he was still watching her. He kissed her cheek, then the back of her hand. He continued to hold it as they sat. Saoirse swept her gaze over the crowd, and there was still disapproval radiating from the women.

"Magnus, how many of yer clanswomen have ye bedded?" Saoirse whispered.

Magnus's eyes widened. "What?"

"There are at least half a score of women who look like they'd knife me in ma sleep. Are they women ye've bedded?"

Magnus's eyes darted to the crowd, recognizing the women who were most hostile. "Nay. I kept ma liaisons to wenches and widows. And it's been a long time, remember?" Saoirse nodded. "They're wary because of their experience with Louisa. I was never excited to introduce her to anyone, and I never kissed her beyond a quick peck at the betrothal ceremony. They're apprehensive."

"I have much to prove then."

"Nay. Ye dinna have to prove aught. They'll ken the difference before the end of the night. Even a blind mon can tell how different ye are from her."

Saoirse nodded as the priest began the blessing. The dais was crowded and noisy, with so many people seated together. She followed the conversations flowing around her, but she observed most of the time. Magnus sat so the servants couldn't serve his half of the trencher until after they served Saoirse, ensuring the deference went to her. Their joined hands rested on his thigh, but as the meal progressed, it became awkward. However, Magnus refused to let go. He didn't want to stop touching his wife, so they rested their hands on the table.

"Uncle Magnus?" Henry came to stand between his uncle and new aunt. "What do I call her?"

"Henry, that isnae polite. *Her* is sitting here. Turn to yer aunt and ask what Lady Saoirse prefers." Magnus smiled indulgently until Henry looked at Saoirse.

"I'd like it if ye'd call me Auntie Saoirse or just Auntie."

"Ye're already married to Uncle Magnus, arenae ye? That means ye're staying for good."

Saoirse knew what the child really wondered. "Uncle Magnus and I will be here for a day or two. Then we must travel again for a while. But soon this will be ma home for good. I havenae been here since ye were a wee bairn, much younger than Thomas. Would ye show me around, so I dinna get lost?"

Henry's eyes narrowed, but he nodded. Saoirse realized he'd seen and overhead Louisa manipulate the maid. She wondered how suspicious he would remain.

"Is that rope still tied to the third apple tree in the orchard?"

"Aye!" Henry's expression changed to excitement. It was his favorite place to play. "How'd ye ken?"

"It's one of the things I remember. Uncle Magnus tied it for ma cousins and me to play on."

"Ye played here?"

"Aye. I'm a wee younger than Uncle Magnus. I used to come here as a lass. Ma aunt Siùsan is Uncle Magnus's sister."

"She's ma da's sister too. How can she be yer auntie and mine too?"

Saoirse pushed back her chair and tapped her lap. Henry hesitated for a moment before he climbed on. She arranged him and leaned to speak conspiratorially with the child. "Do ye see the mon who's been the quietest all night? He's ma da. His name is Alexander, but everyone calls him Alex. Over there is his aulder brother, Callum. He's married to Auntie Siùsan, so he's yer uncle too. The loud one next to him is ma uncle Tavish. The really big mon is ma uncle Magnus. When ma uncle and yer uncle Magnus are together, we call him Mòr. Our Magnus is Óg."

"They're all really big men. Even bigger than Da and Uncle—" Henry twisted to see Magnus. "Uncle Óg?"

"Only when the aulder Magnus is there," he explained.

"Why didna Auntie Siùsan come or yer mama, Auntie Sersie?"

Saoirse smiled at the little boy, who couldn't say her name. She liked the nickname. "Mama and Auntie

Siùsan stayed at home because our clan needs them while the men are gone. And we arenae staying long before we must leave again. But I ken once I've been here a while, they will all come to visit. I have Mama and Auntie Siùsan, but I also have Auntie Ceit and Auntie Deirdre. I have two sisters."

"What're their names?"

"Mirren and Nessa. They're both younger than me."

"Ye have a vera big family, dinna ye?"

"Aye. See all those men down there?" Saoirse pointed to the tables filled with her family. "Those are all ma cousins. Some are ma uncles' sons. Three are ma Auntie Mairghread's and Uncle Tristan's sons." She pointed to Tristan, who looked over and smiled. "And some of them are ma da's cousin's sons. See that mon next to Tristan? That's ma da's cousin, Lachlan."

"Who're the two auld men?" Henry's hand thrust out and pointed to Liam and Hamish. They both playfully scowled at the boy.

"Did ye hear that? He thinks us auld, Hamish." Liam chuckled.

"Lad, do ye have a wooden sword yet?" Hamish asked.

Henry straightened with pride and nodded.

"Bring it with ye in the morning. Laird Hamish and I will show ye we arenae so auld. Mayhap we can even teach ye something that I didna teach yer da."

Henry's eyes widened as he looked at Liam, then Seamus. "Ye taught ma da?"

"Aye," Seamus answered. "All that I ken aboot being a laird, a warrior, and a mon, I learned from these men. I am who I am because I became a Sinclair when I fostered with them."

"Can I foster there too?" Henry's excitement made Saoirse feel bad as she glanced at Caroline, who appeared horrified.

"Henry, ye have a vera long time before ye can go anywhere. Yer mama needs ye too much. Grandda and Uncle Hamish will teach ye something tomorrow, but ye must stay and be a good helper for yer mama."

Henry slid off Saoirse's lap and darted to his mother's side. She lifted him onto her lap, and he wrapped his arms around her back. "I'm a good helper, arenae I, Mama?"

"The vera best." Caroline kissed his forehead and shot Saoirse's an appreciative smile. The child remained in his mother's lap until he drifted off.

"We'll have our turn one day, *mo ghaol*." Magnus whispered to Saoirse at the end of the meal. "I'd see if we can make that happen soon. And I wouldnae mind falling asleep against a certain pair of breasts."

Saoirse giggled before drawing her lips in between her teeth. She nodded before Magnus pulled her chair back. She squealed when he swept her into his arms. They cared not who stared. He carried her off the dais and up the stairs to what was now their chamber. They'd both noticed the glares had turned to giggles while she talked to Henry and returned when Magnus carried her off to have his way with her. Saoirse looked forward to calling Eilean Donan home. She just prayed Magnus returned from battle so it could happen.

CHAPTER 20

The Sinclairs, Sutherlands, and Mackays stayed with the Mackenzies for three days as they strategized. Their fervent hope was Laird Matheson would meet with Seamus and Magnus without having to involve the others. They would ride to the Mathesons' keep with a score of Mackenzie guards, but among them would also be Blake, Thormud, Torquil, and Tate. The four young men were to keep their heads down and be invisible lest someone recognize them. But if anything happened to Seamus or Magnus, two would ride back for help while the other two remained to watch over the Mackenzie brothers.

If Laird Matheson refused to take responsibility for his clansman, or if he did anything to threaten the brothers, the rest of the army would descend upon them, encouraging them to reconsider. Caleb Matheson, the prisoner, was a guest in the Mackenzies' dungeon while they remained at Eilean Donan. He'd ridden, tied to a horse, between Ric and Kirk Hartley, who'd led the Sinclairs' warriors. They would remand him to Alex and Callum's custody if they had to make an example of him before the Mathesons. At that point, a battle was almost inevitable. Wiley, Kirk, and Ric would remain at the campsite with Saoirse.

The older men worried it would insult Wiley and Kirk to not ride into battle alongside the others, especially when Callen would, and he was younger than both of them. But they'd pleased the older men when their chests puffed out with pride to be tasked with protecting Saoirse. She suspected it was partly pride but a lot of bravado. Their fathers and the other men terrified them, even though Kirk was one-and-twenty, and Wiley was eight-and-ten. They would keep her alive because they feared for their own if they failed.

True to their word, Hamish and Liam pretended to spar with Henry, who followed them like a devotee. Neither laird minded since they were both grandfathers several times over. But they were once more formidable warriors when they stepped into the lists. Both in their sixties, they knocked their sons and nephews on their arses repeatedly. If people didn't know better, not only would they think both men were at least half their age, but true enemies when they sparred against each other. The Mackenzie warriors stared, slack jawed, when Liam, Callum, Alex, Tavish, Mòr, Hamish, and Lachlan teamed together. None wanted to step forward to take on the hydra they appeared to form. They cheered when Seamus and Óg joined the mix. Saoirse convinced Caroline to watch from the entrance to the lists.

"How do they do that?" Caroline whispered the day before the army would depart.

"Practice. Da says they've practiced so many times that it's now just intuition. There's naught they dinna ken aboot each other's fighting styles because they're the same. They ken what their partners will do because it's what they would do. Seamus and Óg are that way because Mòr trained them, and they practiced with the others. Uncle Hamish and Lachlan are mirrors of each other. Uncle Hamish and Grandda have been fighting alongside each other since before the days when the Bruce fought for his throne. They've fought together within the last two years to return King David to his rightful place as our sovereign."

"They're incredible."

"Aye. Does it help ye to worry a little less?"

"It does. Seamus and Óg fought the Rosses and Roses for years before the floods and illness. I trusted they were as good as the men said, but I've never watched. I thought it would be too violent. But it's almost graceful."

"Aye. I doubt it's that pretty in battle, but it's like a dance they all ken by heart."

"Seamus hasnae ridden out to fight since before the floods. I'm scared, Saoirse." Caroline kept her gaze straight forward as she spoke.

"Scared that he willna come back?"

"Aye. Absolutely. We arenae as open with our affection as ye and Óg, but we love each other. But that's nae all I fear. What happens if the Rosses and Roses learn he and Óg are gone? What if they choose now to attack again?"

Saoirse nodded. She knew some of the contentiousness between the Mackenzies and Rosses because Magnus told her. She knew Magnus's father kidnapped a Ross woman, even though she was eventually returned to her clan. The trouble continued, even after Seamus became laird. There was land in dispute, and without a king who cared, there was no one to mediate. Edward Balliol, the pretender and usurper king, certainly didn't. Magnus had made inroads with Monty Ross, but they had resolved nothing with the Roses.

"Uncle Hamish! Grandda!" Saoirse called out to the two lairds as they donned their leines. The others continued to practice, but they wished to discuss the on-going troubles with Balliol. They hadn't the chance while they were at Dunrobin or on the road. They knew Andrew Murray, Guardian of Scotland, would summon them again soon.

"Aye, Saoirse." Liam raised his eyebrows.

"Actually, ma question is for ye, Uncle Hamish." Saoirse looked at Caroline, who didn't seem to know where to look. "Caroline's worried that Monty will launch an attack if he kens Seamus and Óg are both gone."

Hamish inhaled and released the breath slowly. He held the same concerns about his nephew. Amelia had been a Ross before she married Hamish. She'd been the Earl of Ross's daughter when they married, then a sister to the next Earl of Ross. She was the current earl's aunt.

"I sent a missive to Monty, informing him that his cousins and I would fight alongside Seamus and Óg if it came to battle. He kens we're riding out with them. I dinna think he will do aught while I'm with them. After we settle this, I would broker a truce between them. This has gone on long enough. Our family trees are too complicated to allow a feud between them. It draws too many people into the middle with nay way to choose sides."

"Aye. So far Brodie and Dominic havenae involved the Campbells, but if things escalate between the Rosses and Mackenzies, then it's inevitable," Liam explained. "Brodie will ride to his brother-by-marriage's aid. We'll ride alongside the Mackenzies. That'll put the Sutherlands in the middle."

"I only wish to be in the middle if it's as an arbitrator. I dinna need to be caught in the middle of their squabble with both sides expecting me to defend them." Hamish shook his head. His ties to Liam had always been far stronger than the ones to his wife's father or brother. But he was very fond of his nephew, Montgomery Ross. The younger man couldn't have children and hadn't married, so his nephew, Montgomery Campbell, was his heir and tánaiste. Thus far, the Campbells had remained uninvolved, just like the Sutherlands, but Hamish doubted their neutrality would last much longer.

"Riders approach! Rosses!"

Hamish and Liam glanced at one another. It was too uncanny that they'd just spoken of the clan and now members were arriving. The energy shifted in the lists, and Saoirse felt it. Her relatives and husband hurried toward her, while the Mackenzie warriors went on the defensive. Óg took her hand as everyone entered the bailey just before the riders.

"Monty, do ye have the second sight? I was just talking aboot ye," Hamish greeted the man.

"Och, that canna be good, Uncle." Monty swung down from his horse and looked around. He sobered as he spied Seamus and Óg staring at him. Mòr stood between the two brothers, and the other Sinclairs were nearby. Tristan and Ric were off to the right. "Seamus, I would speak to ye and Óg. There's something ye should ken."

Monty's gaze filled with regret as he sighed and shook his head. Whatever he would impart wouldn't be good.

"Caroline, Saoirse, come with us." Seamus held out his hand to his wife. She hesitated, unprepared for Seamus's instruction or his proffered hand. She couldn't recall the last time they'd held hands in public, but she smiled shyly as she accepted. She glanced at Saoirse and Óg, who walked arm in arm. She hoped her marriage would become more like the one Saoirse and Óg intended to have.

"Uncle Hamish, ye and Liam should come too." Monty sighed and shook his head again. The four lairds, along with Magnus and the two women, went inside to Seamus's solar. Caroline ordered food on the way. They didn't have to wait long for servants to bring bread, cheese, fruit, and mugs of ale. Once the group was alone, and they shut the door, Monty drummed his fingers on the oblong wood table around which they sat.

"This is bluidy complicated, but what aboot our families isnae." Monty clasped his hands and leaned forward onto the table. "One of ma clanswomen is involved in the attempts against Óg. Oona's—this woman's—mother was a Matheson. I didna ken that until a sennight ago. Her parents married before I was alive. Donan kenned, but somehow, I didna." It had shocked him that his second-in-command and partner had known. Donan assumed Monty had been aware of the connection his entire life like Donan had. "I recalled Oona married a Sutherland when we were all adolescents. But her husband died three years after they wed."

"I remember her. She was Amelia's friend. But she married a Sinclair aboot five years after her husband died."

"Oona? Morag and Ròs's mother?" Saoirse looked at her grandfather. The two young women were her age and close friends to her and Rose Kyla. They worked in the kitchens. Oona became the housekeeper when Hagatha passed away three years ago.

"Aye," Liam acknowledged.

"One of them did it, didna they?" Saoirse looked at Liam, then Hamish, then Monty, before settling her gaze on Magnus.

"They all did from what I learned." Monty ran a hand through his strawberry-blond hair.

"How'd ye find out?" Saoirse demanded. She sat back, her tone surprising her.

"By accident. Oona's husband is among yer men. She and her daughters left Dunbeath just after ye did. Sneaked away would be better. When they arrived, they claimed they were there to visit Oona's sister. She claimed her husband died recently, and she was considering returning to her clan of birth. That struck me as odd, since she's been a Sinclair for more than a score of years. Donan had her followed, but naught came up. It was Monty Óg who learned the truth. Apparently, Morag is a beauty and took an interest in ma unwed tánaiste."

"What did she tell him?" Magnus wondered.

"Plenty, but none that mattered. She flattered him too much, and he grew suspicious. He started asking questions once he learned her grandmother was a Matheson. We arenae on good terms with them these days since they're yer allies." Monty looked at Magnus and Seamus. "She let it slip that her mother's cousin is a merchant and travels. She claimed he sells the prettiest ribbons."

"That mon we talked to." Saoirse turned to Magnus. "That's how he kenned ye supposedly made a lot of enemies ending yer betrothal."

"Aye. And that's what Caleb meant when he said he wasna the only one there who could do the job." Magnus swept his gaze around the table, his stomach in knots.

"Ye've the right of it," Monty interjected. "The merchant is Oona's cousin, but he's also cousin-by-marriage to the mon ye captured. Once Monty Óg learned that, he detained the merchant. Tore his wagon apart and searched everything. He found naught, but he scared the mon within an inch of his life. He confessed everything. Yer captive supplied arsenic to Oona, who told tales to her daughters aboot Magnus Óg forcing Louisa and abusing her. The lasses thought they were righting a wrong."

"But why did Caleb get involved in the first place?" Saoirse asked.

"He claims Laird Matheson didna send him, but now we ken of two Mathesons and some of their extended family trying to kill me." Magnus was glad his mind was no longer fuzzy, or he wouldn't have been able to follow the convoluted tale.

"I wish to ken that too." Monty shifted to look at Liam. "The women are with me. I can return home with them and punish them. Or I can hand them over to ye to do as ye wish. Or we can take them back to the Mathesons. Which do ye want?"

"I want to see them." Saoirse rose. "I want ma friends to look at me and tell me how they could kill the mon they ken I love, how they could think I would choose a mon so reprehensible as they believe. They owe me an explanation."

"Dinna go in anger," Magnus said as he stood.

"I'm nae angry. Shocked, disgusted, and curious. But I'm nae angry. I reserve that for after they tell me why."

"They're with the rest of ma men aboot a half a league from here. I'll have them brought here," Monty offered. Saoirse nodded and took her seat again. Magnus did the same.

"What now?" Seamus asked. He'd listened silently, watching Monty for any signs of duplicity. He found none. For all their disagreements, he knew Monty to be honest, even if he was cunning.

"Ye can send me home with or without the women. Or I can ride to the Mathesons with ye and stand beside ye."

"Ye'd do that? We are feuding."

"Mayhap we were. But yer ally is now yer enemy,

and this has made them ma enemy twice over. That makes us more allies than adversaries. Besides, with Magnus Óg marrying into the Sinclairs, and the Sinclairs and Sutherlands practically being one, it's like ye're ma family now, too. Family doesnae harm family." It was a steadfast rule with Monty. There'd been too much time when his family had been at odds with his sister Laurel. It was in the past, but once Monty became laird and earl, he'd threatened to disown his other sisters in favor of Laurel if they continued to be cruel to her.

"And our borders?" Seamus asked.

"Remain as they are. Ma father wanted that land more than I ever did. Besides, we're at war again with the English. I dinna need to lose men fighting ye when I'm expected to send them to fight King Edward and Balliol."

"And the Roses?" Seamus pressed.

"I'll call them off. They willna harass ye without our support." Monty rose and thrust his arm out to Seamus, who stood and shook it.

"Who kenned trying to kill ye would make us friends." Seamus looked at Magnus before gesturing between Monty and him. Magnus scowled at his brother's poor humor before shaking Monty's forearm, too.

"And ye didna even have to be in the middle, Uncle Hamish," Saoirse whispered to the older man who sat beside her.

Magnus and Seamus exchanged a look before Magnus nodded. "Ride with us."

"May God guide the Matheson to the right choice," Tristan spoke up. He'd been silent too. "If he doesnae make the right choice…" He shrugged. "He canna be so stupid to think he can take on the Mackays, Sinclairs, Sutherlands, and Rosses along with the Mackenzies.

We're the five largest clans this far north. His clan is a mere fraction of ours."

"Hamish," Liam looked at his brother-by-marriage. "I ken ye chose yer alliance with us over the one ye have with the Mathesons. If ye wish to ride home, I—"

"I will thrash ye, auld mon, if ye finish that thought. Ye ken I dinna give a wit who else I'm allied with. *Everyone* kens ours is what unified the Highlands. The Bruce kenned it was us, nae him, even if everyone gave him the credit. Matheson has the chance to make this right. If he doesnae, our alliance is over. The Macraes, Mackintoshes, and Donalds canna protect them from our five clans. They canna get there in time, and they dinna have the numbers. Nae if we call upon the Mac-Leods of Lewis and of Assynt, along with the Camerons."

"Vera well. I was just offering." Liam shrugged. He knew Hamish would never choose another clan over his, but he'd felt compelled to offer since this caught his brother-by-marriage in yet another clan triangle.

"Are ye still riding out in the morning?" Caroline's voice was soft as she leaned toward Seamus. He covered her hand with his, where it rested on the arm of the chair in which she sat.

"Aye, *mo ghràidh.*"

"Then I have more to prepare if the Rosses are joining ye."

"Lady Mackenzie, we brought our own supplies. We dinna wish to inconvenience ye," Monty reassured her.

"Aye. But I still need to see to beds for ye and the evening meal for so many more men. Excuse me."

Once she left, Saoirse looked at Monty. "I want to see them."

"I'll bring them."

CHAPTER 21

Saoirse stood outside the keep's gates with Magnus, Alex, and Liam. She watched the Ross riders approach with three women among them. She could tell from a distance that the women's hands were bound around the waist of the warriors with whom they rode. They were prisoners. Liam stepped forward when the entourage stopped.

"Oona, stand before me and confess." Liam waited as the warrior lifted her arms over his head before he could dismount. He lifted Oona from the saddle, placed her on the ground, and gave her a none too subtle nudge forward. Her daughters soon stood with her. The woman's defiance oozed from her, and Liam was unprepared for it. She didn't resemble the woman he'd entrusted with his household after the woman he'd known from childhood passed away. Hagatha had been the Sinclairs' housekeeper for as long he could remember. He'd mourned her death almost as keenly as his mother's and Kyla's.

"I have naught to say." Oona glared at Liam, then looked away.

Saoirse walked to her two friends. "Explain." It wasn't a request.

The sisters kept their eyes on the ground. Saoirse stepped so close they could see her boots. Neither wanted to confront their friend in front of their mother. Saoirse looked toward Oona, then Liam. She canted her head toward the keep. Liam signaled one of his guards to take Oona inside.

"She's gone. Tell me how ye could try to kill the mon ye ken I love. Tell me how ye could betray me when we've been friends since we were weans. Tell me what yer mother said that made ye believe a mon ye'd kenned yer entire life is the monster she must have claimed. Tell me." Saoirse's voice remained quiet, but there was authority in it she now felt as a tánaiste's wife.

"Mama said he forced the woman betrothed to him before ye. We thought he would do the same to ye," Morag whispered.

"Did ye believe I didna ken what happened with his last betrothal?"

Both women nodded. Morag continued speaking. "We didna think ye would believe us."

"So, instead of taking yer fears to ma father or our laird, ye took it upon yerselves to try to murder him." Saoirse didn't temper her sarcasm. "Who did it?"

Ròs looked up. "We both did. Our mother said it had to be done. That nay one would believe us against Óg. She said we had to protect ye and defend our clanswoman's honor."

"Yer clanswoman? Ye're Sinclairs. Have ye ever met a Matheson other than that vendor?"

"Nay," Morag confessed. "But ye ken Mama. She makes a fine housekeeper because she doesnae take anyone's guff, and she can command an army of servants. She's nae someone ye can refuse."

Saoirse knew that truth, but it didn't diminish her disbelief that her friends could so betray her. "Ye didna think we would catch ye. How would ye have lived with kenning ye murdered a mon?"

"It would have been a righteous killing. At least, that's what Mama said." Ròs's eyes darted in Magnus's direction.

Saoirse felt sorry for the women. Even if Oona weren't so demanding, it would have been difficult for the young women to act against their own mother. To confess the plan to anyone would have been a death warrant for their mother.

"Morag! Ròs!" Everyone turned to watch a man in a Sinclair plaid running toward them. He stopped short when he reached Liam. His expression was distraught, and he appeared agitated. He looked at Liam, his mien clearly fearful. "I didna ken, ma laird. Will ma lasses hang?"

"I havenae decided, Darrell."

"And Oona?" Darrell twisted toward the keep before looking back at Liam.

"She wouldnae speak on her own behalf. If she continues to refuse, I will take her silence as an admission of guilt. She will die."

Darrell swallowed and nodded before looking back at his daughters. He grew more upset, his hands fisting and unfisting at his side. "Tell our laird all that ye ken."

"We did, Da." Morag burst into tears. Darrell took a step forward but stopped himself. He looked at Liam, who nodded. The guard hurried and engulfed his daughters in his embrace. He kissed the tops of their heads before resting his cheek on Morag's head. The young women clung to their father.

Magnus came to stand with Saoirse, who'd stepped aside for Darrell. He slid his arm around her waist, and she turned into his body. She encircled his waist and sagged against him. The situation felt overwhelmingly sad to her.

"Grandda?" Saoirse looked between her shoulder and Magnus's. The older man walked forward and placed his hand on her back. "Can ye do aught but hang them? Banish them?"

"To banish them would be worse than to execute them. There is only one means to provide for themselves, and it's more likely to kill them than give them the chance to start over." Liam looked at the young women. If he banished them, he would have to mark them. Anyone would know. Their best hope would be to become whores, but that life would prematurely age them. They were more likely to die from illness or at a drunkard's hand. "I will send them to Eynhallow Monastery as servants."

It was on a remote, uninhabited island in Orkney. The only thing there was the monastic house. As the Earl of Orkney, Liam had the authority to relegate them to servitude to the monks and nuns. It would keep them alive and away from harm, but not allow them a normal life after their role in their assassination attempt.

The women heard Liam, and both sobbed, but Darrell appeared grateful. Saoirse suspected he thought he would visit them, but she doubted Liam would grant him permission. Saoirse thought it was a benevolent decision, considering the other options. It pleased her that they would live, but it also satisfied her that they wouldn't go unpunished.

"They can remain here, but I will imprison them with their mother." Seamus said. Saoirse hadn't noticed him join them, but she suspected he had after Darrell ran through the gates. He would have investigated. Liam and Saoirse nodded, and Darrell's shoulders sank. It was more likely they would wind up in the dungeon than house arrest.

Monty arrived with the other riders, but he'd remained silent. It wasn't his place to be involved. He'd merely been the bearer of bad news. But as the group headed back to the keep, Seamus invited him to join them. The Ross men returned to their camp while Monty walked alongside Seamus. While they were hardly friends, their discord ended far more easily than anyone, including them, expected.

The massive army, one that rivaled those Andrew Murray could command, traveled southwest for a day to Loch Achaidh na h-Inich. At the northern end, lay Ach Dà Thearnaidh, or the Field of Two Descents. They aptly named it since there were two hills, making it a secluded spot. There were enough men to divide between the two sides. It was the traditional rallying point for Clan Matheson, and it would be the site of any battle. The Mathesons' keep, Crannog, sat on a small isle in the loch. It kept them well protected, but it wasn't entirely impervious to attack.

"I dinna want to approach in the dark, so Óg and I will venture to Crannog in the morning. I want plenty of daylight to see where they lurk. I'm certain the Matheson already kens we're on his land. His patrols will have alerted him." Seamus looked in the Matheson keep's direction. They'd been prepared for warriors to greet them, but thus far, they'd seen no one. They were at the field to survey the area and to prepare their warriors. They would make camp two miles away, a place much safer for Saoirse to wait.

Saoirse stood with Magnus as the leaders gathered to discuss what would happen next. They had a plan, but they'd known nothing was absolute until they saw the lay of the land. Saoirse's gaze swept the expansive field, and she couldn't understand how it was a strategic point for any clan to rally. She supposed it kept them hidden when they met before riding out. However, it appeared ill advised for the Mathesons to wage any battles there. If, somehow, they didn't know where the army lurked, and they rallied in the field before going to battle, the five-clan army would annihilate them.

"Saoirse, I still hope the Matheson will be reasonable, and it willna come to a fight." Magnus whispered to his wife. She nodded, but her eyes continued to roam across the field. They narrowed as she spotted something. She leaned forward and tilted her head.

"Is that the same metal reflection ye saw from the forest?" Saoirse nudged her chin toward the shiny object. She didn't want to point. She didn't know if it was a person, and if it was, if they could see her.

Magnus followed her gaze. "Aye." He turned to his brother. "They're watching."

"Where?" Alex asked.

"Straight ahead, but slightly to the left," Saoirse answered. "I'm certain I saw something shiny. It was like what Magnus spied from the forest at home."

Liam whistled and pointed. A dozen men mounted their nearby horses and rode to where Liam indicated. They didn't get far before a score of Matheson men rode forward. They were too far away to tell if the laird was among them until they rounded the left bank of the field. The Sinclairs turned their mounts and returned to the camp.

"Why are ye here?" A bass voice boomed.

"Why'd ye try to kill ma brother?" Seamus called back. "I think ye ken why we're here."

The Mathesons stopped a hundred feet from where the leaders gathered. It was clear the deep voice belonged to an older man. His plaid and brooch declared him the clan's laird. Magnus's eyes narrowed as he glowered at his would-have-been uncle-by-marriage. He signaled, and Thormud shoved Caleb forward when he was awkward.

"Tell us why ye sent this mon to poison ma brother," Seamus demanded. "Why did he tell Oona Sinclair that Magnus raped yer niece?"

"Caleb? I thought ye were dead." The disbelief in Murdoch Matheson's voice was genuine.

"Ye thought we killed him?" Liam stepped forward.

"Nay." Murdoch shook his head as he stared at his clansman. "Yer horse came back to the keep without a rider, blood splattered on yer saddle. We searched, but we couldnae find ye. Yer mother..." The laird dismounted and strode forward. His fist plowed into the prisoner's face. "Yer mother and father grieved for ye. Why?"

Caleb grunted at the impact, but he said nothing. The beating he'd taken and the cuts from the Sinclair brothers' knives left him nearly dead. The journey weakened him further. He barely stood on his own. But he could have answered. He chose not to.

"Why is he with ye? And who is the woman ye named?" Murdoch looked at Liam, then Seamus.

"He came onto ma land." Liam pointed at Caleb. "And dared to nae only trespass and hunt, but he thought he could send women to kill ma grandson."

"Grandson? Seamus, ye said it was yer brother who was the victim. I dinna understand."

"I married Lady Saoirse." Magnus continued to glower. He wouldn't believe anything Murdoch said until he had reason to believe him.

"He's ma son now." Alex stepped forward and crossed his arms. It signaled all the Sinclair men to do the same. Tristan, Wee Liam, Hamish Óg, and Alec did the same behind the Sinclairs. Hamish Mòr, Lachlan, and Callen raised their chins in defiance as they placed their hands on their hips. Monty stood off to the side and merely shook his head several times.

"Which makes him ma grandson." Liam leaned forward, his eyes narrowed. "Nay one comes near ma family."

"Ye married? That didna take ye long. Were ye already sniffing at her skirts, and that's why ye rejected Louisa?"

Alex lunged forward, but Magnus was quicker. He ran forward and slammed into Murdoch, tackling him to the ground. He wrapped his hand around the older man's throat and squeezed.

"Dinna speak of ma wife as though she were a whore. Dinna confuse Alex's daughter for yer niece. They ken what happened."

The Sutherlands and Mackays did, but no one shared the details of that fateful night with Monty. When Magnus said he didn't attack Louisa like Oona claimed, Monty believed him without question.

Magnus released Murdoch's throat and leaned back. The laird tried to throw Magnus from him, but the younger man's weight was too great. Magnus stood and grabbed Murdoch's leine, yanking him to his feet.

"If ye dinna want me to further humiliate ye in front of yer men, ye'll keep a civil tongue in yer head. I dinna doubt yer men all ken yer niece for what she is, but our men dinna. I have nay hesitation to destroy ye and her by announcing to everyone what she did."

"Ye wouldnae. It makes ye look weak."

"Weak?" Seamus's chuckle held no mirth. "Ma brother pulled a bed apart."

"Caleb rode to Sinclair land, convinced Oona to

poison me, and she had her daughters do it. Her mother was a Matheson, and she claims ties to yer clan. Yer nephew and yer clanswoman tried to murder me. With or without yer knowledge, it was yer clan who wronged me. Again." Magnus shoved Murdoch away from him. "Ye have a choice. Admit yer clan's fault or face us in the morning."

"I will do nay such thing. I didna sanction any of this." Murdoch grinned before he whistled. Out of the woods poured an army that initially appeared to rival the one that rode and marched to Ach Dà Thearnaidh. Macraes, Donalds, and Mackintoshes raced toward them, swords drawn and swinging at any Mackenzie, Sinclair, Mackay, Sutherland, or Ross they approached. More Mathesons joined the surprise attack.

However, Magnus cut Murdoch's gloating cut short when he drew his sword and ran the man through. He spun around, not waiting to watch Murdoch land on the ground. He hurtled forward, scooping Saoirse around the waist, and running toward the horses. "Ric! Wiley! Kirk!"

Magnus tossed Saoirse on her horse's back without a saddle and threw her the reins. He knew she could ride bareback, and even if she couldn't, there was no time to worry about it. His sword severed the rope hobbling the animal.

"We're here," Ric answered as he, Kirk, and Wiley swung onto their horses.

"I love ye, Saoirse." Magnus slapped the animal's rump. It leaped forward, and Saoirse had to clutch the reins and the horse's mane.

"I love ye," she called back, but she didn't dare turn to see Magnus lest she fall off.

The three men formed a horseshoe around her, all of them praying they weren't racing headlong for another enemy. She carried half of her dirks, but the other half was in her saddlebag, and her bow and quiver leaned against her saddle. She could feel the knife handles against her ankles, and the one strapped to her thigh felt heavy as she squeezed her legs to keep her atop of the steed.

"There's a copse of oak trees about a half a league from here. We ride to that," Ric instructed. Saoirse continued to cling to the reins and the horse's mane. She leaned low over the animal's withers, praying they made it to safety and that when she returned to the field, all of her family would be hale. They rode for fifteen minutes before the trees came into view. They'd slowed to a trot once they were out of sight of the battle. Their horses walked now, so they were unprepared when half a dozen men raced forward.

"What the bluidy hell?" Kirk uttered as the men drew their swords. Saoirse reached down to her left boot and pulled her dirk free. It was the longest blade she owned. The one strapped to her thigh was a *sgian dubh*. It would only do her any good if a man drew close. She didn't wish for that to happen. The three men closed in, keeping Saoirse in the center. Blessedly, her horse was trained not to move unless she commanded it. It hadn't the experience of a warhorse, but the sound of blades clashing didn't faze it.

Her head swiveled in every direction it could as she watched the attackers fight her clansmen. They all wielded claymores, the Highlanders' preferred double-handed broadswords, but only Ric, Kirk, and Wiley could do it one-handed. They each had a targe strapped to their left arm. It allowed them to fend off one attacker while engaging with another. The battle was over in a matter of minutes, but Saoirse felt time dragged with every ringing blow and groan of pain. Her protectors were victorious, but they each had wounds.

"Why were they here?"

"We saw ye."

Saoirse and the others watched fifteen more men ride out of the trees. She didn't recognize the man who spoke, but all of their attackers wore Matheson plaids, and so did this second wave of men.

"We kenned they'd send ye this way when the battle started. So bluidy predictable." The same man explained as riders fanned out and surrounded Saoirse, Ric, Wiley, and Kirk. It was one thing for three men to fight six. But to fight fifteen while winded and injured was too much.

"What do you want?" Ric asked.

"An Englishmon?" A warrior to Saoirse's right called out.

"A MacLellan by birth, a Sinclair by choice," Wiley responded. "Do ye ken who I am?"

"Nay and dinna care," the first man responded.

"Ye will when Tavish Sinclair learns ye breathed in ma direction."

"Hiding behind yer da's plaid? I dinna give a fuck if ye're the Lord God Almighty. Ma father is Murdoch Matheson, and ye're trespassing on our land." The man nudged his horse forward again. "With that hair, ye must be Brighde and Alex's daughter."

"If ye ken that, ye ken what ma father will do to ye."

"Bah," the man scoffed. "He's auld. And since I dinna see another woman with yer hair, I dinna fear ye mama slicing ma bollocks off." His horse took three more steps forward.

Saoirse hurled her knife between Ric and Kirk, and it flew close enough to the leader's ear for him to hear the whiz. It embedded in a man's throat who pointed his sword at Wiley and urged his horse forward, his intent clear.

"I am ma mother's daughter. Dinna think that's ma

only blade. If ye fear ma mama, ye should bluidy well fear me. I'm Saoirse Mackenzie." She cocked an eyebrow.

"Ye married Magnus?" Another man rode forward. He looked a great deal like Caleb, the prisoner.

"Are ye Caleb's son?" She answered with her own question.

"Nay. He was ma brother."

"It's only 'was' if he died during the battle. He's the cause of this."

"How?"

"What're yer names? Ye ken mine. To whom do I speak?" Saoirse planned to keep them talking. The longer they did that, the more time it bought Ric and the others to find a way out.

"I'm Stewart," the second man answered. "He's Harold."

"Stewart, yer brother came to Dunbeath to poison ma husband. He didna succeed. At least, nae at that. He succeeded in getting captured by ma da."

"But he—"

"We ken. Supposedly died and left blood on his horse, which returned to Crannog. Nay. He didna do that. He convinced a woman to do his dirty business for him."

"I dinna believe ye." Stewart spoke without conviction.

Harold grew tired listening, and he understood Saoirse's attempt at distraction. "Bind and gag them."

"Dinna fight," Ric whispered. "If they kill us, we canna protect our lady."

The Mathesons took Wiley's, Kirk's, and Ric's swords along with the dirks in their boots. They pulled knives from the men's belts, but none looked up their plaids. Everyone knew there would be knives strapped to the men's thighs, but none would be the one to search. They bound Saoirse's and the men's hands to their horses' reins. They looped rope through the bridles, making it impossible for any of them to break free. But they had nothing with which to gag them.

"We're going for a little jaunt," Harold taunted.

CHAPTER 22

Magnus swung his sword with a roar. He'd maneuvered himself to fight at his brother's back after sending Saoirse away. He forced his mind to focus on the enemies that swarmed toward him instead of worrying about his wife, but he nearly lost his head several times because his fear threatened to consume him. As much as the Sinclairs, Sutherlands, Mackays, Rosses, and Mackenzies tried to stay together to control the fight, their opponents forced them apart.

"Liam—to yer left, Seamus." Magnus noticed Liam fighting alone. Two men who tried to circle him had separated him from his sons. He'd felled both, but he couldn't make his way to his sons. Seamus and Magnus inched toward him until they could fight as a trio. Magnus had faith Callum and Alex partnered while Mòr and Tavish were a duo. He'd seen Thor and Tor fighting alongside Blake and Tate. But he didn't know where Hamish, Lachlan, or Callen were. He prayed the lad was with his father and grandfather.

When the battle began, he watched Tristan point toward a group of men. He, Wee Liam—who was as large as his grandfather and namesake—Alec, and Hamish Óg charged forth. Tristan and Wee Liam partnered while Alec and Hamish Óg fought back-to-back. The four heads of black hair with gleaming emerald eyes were enough to make their opponents fear demons stalking them.

"How the hell did they ken we were coming?" Seamus bellowed over the fracas.

"Ma guess is we shouldnae have left that merchant alive. He hied it here to tittle-tattle," Monty yelled. His second-in-command and lifelong partner, Donan, fought at his back. They were a couple feet from Magnus, Liam, and Seamus. Magnus hadn't realized until that morning that Donan was with the Ross men, but it didn't surprise him. As far as he knew, they were as close as brothers, since neither had their own by birth. Hamish and Lachlan were the only ones who knew for certain the relationship that existed between the men, and that was only because they were family who'd figured it out. The older Sinclairs and Liam all had their suspicions, but none cared. It was theirs not to reason why. During this battle, it was theirs but to do or die.

I need to get to Saoirse. If they saw her, then someone will have gone after her. What if they guessed where she was going? I bet Ric took her to the trees we passed. I canna stay here. Where's ma wife?

Magnus redoubled his efforts as he slayed one attacker after another. There were bodies strewn across the hilltop to the southeast of the Field of Two Descents, and the larger army—though not by much—forced the Mathesons and their allies into the lower position. The Mathesons and their comrades either ran from their pursuers or fought backwards as the Sinclairs and their allies pressed forward. By the time the fight reached the field, the numbers had thinned on the Mathesons' side.

"*Teàrnadh! Teàrnadh!*" Retreat! Retreat!

Magnus didn't know which enemy bellowed the

command, but the Mathesons, Macraes, Mackintoshes, and Donalds attempted to fall back. It was useless. The Sinclairs and their partners continued to widen their net until they surrounded their adversaries and trapped them on the field. The battle began with four-hundred-fifty men belonging to the Sinclairs, Sutherlands, Mackays, Mackenzies, and Rosses versus two hundred men from the Mathesons, Macraes, Mackintoshes, and Donalds. Inevitably, the Sinclairs' alliance would prevail.

"*Sguir!*" Cease! Seamus bellowed until his command drifted through the chaos. "Ye have lost! Lay down yer swords!"

No one hurried to obey, but they did when Seamus pushed Laird Donald forward with his sword tip pressing the back of the man's neck. Those who attacked capitulated when they watched Laird Macrae and Laird Mackintosh walk with Alex behind the former and Lachlan behind the latter. Laird Matheson laid dead where Magnus left him.

"Ye're too late." A man near Callum's age stepped forward. Two other men walked with him. "Ye killed our father and made me laird. But that doesnae bring yer wife back, Mackenzie."

Magnus stayed himself as he looked at one of the four Matheson sons. He'd gotten along with all of them until the incident with Louisa and the end of his betrothal to their cousin. Now his patience was frayed, and his fear for Saoirse soared.

"What did ye do to ma wife?"

"We didna do aught. But ye shouldnae have brought a woman to a battle. Who kens who might have gotten a hold of her?"

Alex spun Laird Macrae around. "Who has ma daughter?"

The man shrugged dismissively. Lachlan grabbed a

handful of Laird Mackintosh's hair and yanked so hard the man nearly toppled backwards. "Who has ma cousin's daughter?"

"Dinna ken," the man hissed.

"Dinna believe ye," Lachlan responded, as he brought his sword to the man's throat.

"Truly, I dinna ken. I received a missive from Murdoch that he suspected the Rosses would attack ye, and that ye couldnae get word to me. He said ye needed us."

Duncan Matheson's brow furrowed. "Nay, ye didna. Ma father received a missive from ye saying ye kenned the Rosses would ride to the Sutherlands to gather men before riding on the Mackenzies."

"Nay. I have the missive in ma chamber at Crannog." Laird Mackintosh tried to shake his head, but Lachlan still held too tightly.

"What of ye?" Magnus pointed his sword at Laird Macrae.

"Murdoch called upon us, same as he did the Mackintoshes and Donalds. He said the Rosses and Roses threatened to besiege ye."

Something about Laird John Macrae's claim rang false with Magnus, but he didn't know why. He turned toward Laird Donald, who stood with Seamus's sword tip now pressing below his left ribcage. "What say ye?"

"It was as Macrae said. The missive from Murdoch said the Rosses threatened ye."

"But ye all ken that I've been in talks with Monty to end the feud." Magnus glanced at Monty.

"But it hadnae progressed. We believed Murdoch because it sounded reasonable."

"Then why'd ye attack us?" Magnus demanded. "That makes nay sense."

"It still doesnae matter who sent which missive, Óg, or whether it makes sense. I doubt ye will find yer wife alive." Duncan Matheson smirked as he locked gazes with Magnus.

"If ye have done naught to her, then how do ye ken?"

"I saw her riding away with only three men. Mayhap others saw that too and decided she was an easy target."

"Where's yer other brother, Duncan?" Liam had accounted for every member of the four lairds' families, except for Murdoch's fourth son. Duncan grinned and shrugged.

"We search Crannog, then we burn it," Magnus declared. "If ma wife isnae there, I will kill every woman in yer clan until I get mine back."

Before that day, no one would have believed Magnus's threat. The Sinclairs had trained him, and they didn't harm women. They didn't use them as pawns or even in false threats. But the rage that radiated from Magnus left no one in doubt that he wasn't truly a Sinclair. He would wage his vendetta with whatever means he had, and that included taking from the Mathesons what he was certain they took from him. His woman.

Saoirse feared falling from her horse's back and breaking her neck as they rode with only the moon as their guide. They could do nothing more than a walk with four horses' bridles tied together, but they progressed east and away from where she believed Crannog lay. She didn't know to where they headed, but it was the middle of the night. Before they left the clearing near the trees, a rider arrived from the battlefield. He informed them all that the fight still raged. She didn't know how long a fight usually lasted until she whispered her question to Ric. His answer disheartened her.

Hours. It would be hours before Magnus realized she hadn't reached safety. Her captors knew that and used it to their advantage. They had a head start, but they refused to risk losing it, so they forced man and beast to continue traveling. It was summer, so it was late before the sun set despite them arriving at the Field of Two Descents during the early evening. It was likely well past midnight as they continued eastward.

"Lady Saoirse will break her neck if we don't stop." Ric voiced her fear as he called out to their chief captor. "At least let her ride with me. She won't do you any good as a prisoner or bait if she'd dead."

Harold grumbled, but he called a halt to their procession. He signaled for one of his men to unfasten Saoirse from her saddle. The warrior helped her down and walked her to Ric's horse. Ric leaned back and raised his arms as best he could. He watched Harold, who wasn't looking at them. The warrior lifted Saoirse up, and she ducked her head beneath Ric's arm as she came to sit in front of him. When they were underway again, Ric whispered to Saoirse.

"Your hands aren't bound to the saddle. Can you get your dirk?"

"How'd ye ken I still have one?" They'd taken the one from her other boot, and they had the one they pried out of the man she killed. It still hadn't registered with her how blithely she took the warrior's life. She'd known she sacrificed one of her blades, but she knew they would have eventually taken it from her, anyway. She'd wanted to ensure the men didn't think she was incapable of defending herself, and she couldn't ignore the threat to Wiley. She made certain they would think twice before attacking her personally.

She hadn't resisted when a warrior took the second

dirk, but when his hand wrapped around her calf, she kicked upward. Her boot connected with the underside of the man's chin and snapped his head back. She'd stomped her boot into his face. After that, none of the men tried to stick their hand under her skirts. She still had the one strapped to the outside of her thigh. She inched her skirts up. The dark shielded her from anyone seeing what she did. With no stirrup for her foot, she drew up her leg until she could reach under the material and pull the *sgian dubh* loose.

"Go slowly, but cut my hands free," Ric instructed. Saoirse hesitated, afraid she was more likely to slit his wrists than free him. But she knew they had few chances for freedom if they didn't escape before they reached their still unknown destination. She was cautious, but she worked steadily until Ric's wrists sprang loose. "Give it to me and hold the reins."

Ric worked with more surety, but just as much caution. Once he had her hands free, he appeared to shift in his saddle to get more comfortable, but he passed the blade to Kirk as his horse sidestepped at his movement. Saoirse watched from the corner of her eye as Kirk did the same thing, freeing his hands, then passing the blade to Wiley. Her cousin held onto the blade for at least an hour before they passed it along, and she returned it to her thigh sheath. All of them rode in the same position as they had before they cut their bindings. In the dark, no one could tell what they'd done. There remained one dire problem. They now had free use of their hands, but their captors kept their horses tied together. Saoirse didn't know how they would fix that.

"Ye would have us run the horses into the ground," Wiley mused. "Even if ye dinna care aboot ours, yers will fare the same. There's a loch up there. Let us water them."

"Nay." Harold didn't look back.

"Dinna say I didna warn ye when yer horse drops from beneath ye." Wiley looked at his compatriots and shrugged. Each of them suggested it at least twice, but the horses were moving at a walk now, so Harold refused to oblige each time. When he finally relented, it was still dark. He refused to allow any of them to dismount, which suited them because no one noticed the rope was missing from their wrists. The horses drank, and the men stretched, but Saoirse and the three Clan Sinclair warriors remained atop their horses for the entire night.

"We're nearing Dingwall," Wiley whispered. "That's Macrae territory."

"Ye sure?" Kirk asked.

"Aye. We traveled east and then north. We've skirted nearly all of Mackenzie land, staying on the Chisholms' and Frasers' of Lovat territories."

"Frasers? Are we still on their land now?" Saoirse asked.

"Aye. If we see even a hint of a Fraser patrol, we hail them. Auntie Deirdre's cousin is laird. The bad blood between our clans ended when Auntie Deirdre's father and uncle died. Alfred would help us."

Saoirse nodded. She prayed her cousin was right. So far none of the men had really done her any harm, and she doubted it was only because of her knife throwing skills. She knew being Alex and Brighde's daughter protected her, just as she'd claimed back at Dunbeath. But just because no one beat her or assaulted her didn't mean they couldn't still mistreat her. The sooner they could be free of their captors, the better.

But luck wasn't on their side. As they continued north, they passed no one they could signal. They rode for nearly ten hours, and she was in immeasurable pain by the time a keep took shape in the distance. She wondered how the men rode for so long without a single flinch or wince.

"I know you're uncomfortable, Saoirse, but you must keep still. We can't draw attention to ourselves right now. I need them to focus on my horse. Keep your sleeves over your wrists and prepare to hold on if we get free."

"What aboot Kirk and Wiley?"

"They'll know what to do." Ric reined in, then nudged his horse forward. It made the horse appear to stumble, and it neighed its displeasure. "Now you've done it. My horse has gone lame."

Ric brought his steed to a stop, forcing Wiley's and Kirk's horses to stop too. The gelding she'd ridden followed suit, but it looked around, confused.

"Keep going."

"No. I'm not killing my horse for you."

"Then we'll take care of it and you," Harold snarled.

"Let me look at his hooves," Ric countered. The sun was creeping toward the horizon, and the sky was lightening from onyx to sapphire. "If you won't let me do that, then at least let Lady Saoirse and me move to her horse. MacLellan can't carry both of us."

"MacLellan? Ye named yer horse after a clan?" Stewart turned around in surprise.

"Yes. My clan. I'm one by birth. This is my second horse of the same name. Now let me check on him."

"Let him, or we'll be at this for ages. We're too close to dawdle," Stewart insisted.

"Vera well." Harold rolled his eyes as he looked over his shoulder.

Ric pretended to lift his arms over Saoirse's head. While he still sounded English, Ric adopted wearing a *breacan feile*, or great plaid, not long after moving to the Highlands. He squatted beside his horse's hooves and reached beneath his plaid. He drew his own blade and stepped in front of MacLellan to hide his movements as he severed the rope. Once his horse was free, it made the rope sag from the other horses' bridles. He darted under MacLellan's neck and grasped the reins and mane of the horse Saoirse had ridden. He swung onto its back.

"Ride," Ric commanded. Saoirse was surprised, but she soon recovered as the three men swung their horses around. MacLellan followed its master's voice, so Saoirse had little to do but hold on. Their horses sensed the urgency and bolted, but they'd ridden the steeds for too long with too little rest. It wasn't long before all four flagged.

"Ye thought to escape, but all ye've done is make it worse." A voice that niggled at Saoirse's memory called out as Macrae men surrounded them.

With a scream, someone pulled her from MacLellan's back and yanked her in front of them onto another horse. She looked up and recognized Richmond Macrae, the laird's younger brother. "Make another sound, and I will throttle ye."

"Ye wouldnae dare."

"Wouldnae I? Ye were kidnapped and brought here. Do ye think I care enough aboot yer life to care if ye're dead?"

"Aye, ye do. If ye wanted me dead, ye wouldnae have had me kidnapped. Ye would have had me murdered. If ye wanted the satisfaction of being the one to kill me, ye would have done it the moment ye saw me. Ye need me alive to torment ma family. How much do ye plan to ransom me for?"

"Ye think awfully highly of yerself, Saoirse Sinclair."

Saoirse laughed. "Ye dinna ken?"

"Ken what?" Richmond looked around, his gaze latching onto Harold as they approached the men Saoirse thought they'd escaped.

"She married Magnus," Harold announced.

"Mackenzie?" Richmond squawked. "Mother-fucking piece of shite bastard."

"Dinna tell me ye wished to marry me?" Saoirse sniped.

"I suppose he's fucked ye like a cheap tavern whore."

"Don't speak—"

"Or what, Englishmon? Ye're in nay position to issue me threats."

"Ye shall regret this, Richmond," Saoirse warned. "I dinna ken how ye're involved or why ye arenae at Ach Dà Thearnaidh. Do ye ken who fights beside ma husband?"

"Aye, the Sinclairs."

"Bluidy hell," Wiley muttered before speaking up. "Do ye really think we came alone? Ma uncle Tristan and great-uncle Hamish came along with Monty Ross. Seamus rode with his brother. We number close to four-hundred-and-fifty men. I'd guess there were, mayhap, two hundred, two-hundred-and-fifty men against us. We will have won. Ye'll have five clans riding on ye before noon. Uncle Mòr is the best tracker I've ever seen. Óg will torture ye for touching ma cousin. Ye bluidy daft bastard."

They entered the bailey with a clatter of horses' hooves. Stable hands ran out to gather the horses. Richmond pushed Saoirse from the saddle. Her legs couldn't hold her, so she landed hard, knocking the wind from her. Wiley was at her side in an instant. Kirk and Ric pulled Richmond from the saddle and alternated landing punches. The sound of steel pulled free from sheaths made them stop. Richmond's face bled, and Ric landed a kick to his gut for good measure before backing up. Wiley had a dirk in each hand as he kept Saoirse between him and his horse, which didn't move, even when Saoirse bumped into it as she stood.

"Harold?"

Saoirse turned toward the woman's voice, her mouth dropping open as she stared. She had loathed all of the surprises this night brought. She hated this one the most.

CHAPTER 23

"I still want to ken why they attacked us. They must have seen us among our army." Magnus paced as their men regrouped and saw to their dead and wounded. They'd lost more than a hundred men, and nearly the same amount was injured. But they'd prevailed, and their surviving enemies were now bound prisoners. "It makes nay sense that they gathered to defend us, then they tried to kill us."

"It's us," Monty stepped forward. "I believe they did it because they saw us riding with ye, and they believed ye betrayed them."

"Ye told Siùsan that the Matheson insisted ye nay turn to Uncle Hamish for help after the floods." Callum glanced at his uncle. "He wanted ye dependent upon his allies and him. Seeing the Sutherlands probably didna help either."

"Mayhap, but something still feels off." Magnus stopped pacing and stared in the direction Saoirse rode. It was dark, but he peered into the blackness as if looking hard enough would make her materialize. He'd sent riders to fetch her and the others, but they'd returned fifteen minutes ago without his wife or her protectors. "They have Saoirse. I canna stay here while she's getting farther and farther away."

"Ye dinna ken where they're headed. I canna track them when it's this dark," Mòr reasoned.

"They headed east. I'm certain. They couldnae go to any of their territories without riding onto Mackenzie land. They must have head toward the Chisholms."

"Aye, but they could have turned south once they reached them. The only ones who live northeast are the Macraes." Seamus watched his brother, and it pained him to see the devastation on Magnus's face.

"Regardless, we can head east. It'll be daylight by the time we reach the end of our land. The path should be visible then. We'll ken at sunrise which way they turned."

"None of them have said aught." Tavish pointed to the three lairds sitting with rope around their chests, binding them together, with ten guards surrounding them. "Do we take them or send them with the other prisoners?"

"Take them," Liam decided. "We can exchange them."

"Then we ride," Hamish announced. There was never any dispute about riding through the night to chase Saoirse's kidnappers. It was merely a debate about their route. "Lachlan and Callen will remain to see to the men. Once the dead have been buried, they'll lead the army to Eilean Donan."

Lachlan nodded as he watched his son. He'd fought valiantly and impressed his father and grandfather. But the aftermath of his first battle was taking its toll. He'd checked on Callen twice, but the lad had wished to be alone while he vomited over and over. Now he rested with his head between his thighs. It was the same reaction they'd all had after their first few battles. Lachlan recalled the tremors that ran through him for hours and how Hamish had given him space to work through his thoughts and emotions. He worried for his son, but he would follow his father's example. They were three peas in a pod, so he trusted he did the right thing.

"Callen can see to the horses when he's ready." Lachlan intended to keep his son away from the massive burial plots they would use for the Sutherlands and their allies. Their enemies' clans could come to claim their slain if they wished. It wasn't their responsibility. "We'll be on the road at dawn."

He knew giving his son a few hours' rest and keeping him away from another potential battle was prudent, but he wished to support his family. However, as the Sutherlands' tánaiste, he knew guarding the prisoners and keeping his heir from another round of violence was what was best.

"Thank ye," Alex whispered. "I ken what ye wish isnae what ye must do. But I dinna want Callen to see more, and I dinna think ye do either."

Lachlan nodded, deciding he'd given his son enough space after all. He went to check on him.

"I'm saddling ma horse and riding out. If ye plan to join me, be ready when I am." Magnus announced. He fetched his saddle and hefted it onto his mount's back. But he needed a moment to compose himself. He rested his forehead against his steed's neck and stroked its head. They'd been a team for a decade, and it soothed his tension to lean against the stoic beast.

"We'll get her back," Alex said as he drew his horse beside Magnus's. "I ken it's yer right as her husband to slay whoever did this. But I willna hesitate if I get the chance first. She's still ma lassie, even if she's yer wife."

Magnus straightened and looked at Alex. In the moonlight, he could see the tears that brimmed in the man's eyes. They embraced, and it was the fatherly affection Magnus needed.

"I didna ken I could love someone as fiercely as I love Saoirse. Every breath hurts while we're apart. It feels like a part of me is withering every minute I dinna ken where she is." Magnus felt his own eyes growing misty. He hadn't cried since Siùsan left to marry when he was two-and-ten. He'd had one saint's day without her, and he'd sobbed in his chamber with only Seamus to console him. He inhaled a calming breath before releasing Alex.

They saddled their horses while the others gathered their belongings and readied their mounts, too. They were riding east within ten minutes. While those ten minutes had flown by, the next seven hours ticked by at a snail's pace. They cantered when they could, but in the dark, it was best that they remained at a trot. They had to water the horses every few hours, and Magnus knew it was wise, but he didn't want to stop.

At sunrise, Mòr dismounted and Óg went to stand beside him. The elder Magnus ran his eyes over the land, finding the trail easily. He counted the sets of hoofprints and glanced at his father before looking at Óg.

"There are at least fifteen of them, along with the four sets that must belong to Saoirse, Wiley, Kirk, and Ric. Whoever this is, is determined to reach their destination without losing Saoirse or the others. Four sets seem to shuffle while the others are clean prints. The depth of the indentations tells me they were walking. I think they tied Saoirse's horse with the other three."

"Then mayhap we can catch them if they're only at a walk."

"Mayhap, Óg. But they had a four-hour head start. Even if we galloped the entire way, it's unlikely we will." Mòr followed the trail with his horse beside him. He studied the evidence the riders left behind. "Óg!"

Mòr squatted and picked up the severed rope. He looked around, but he saw nothing else.

"What is it?" Óg came to stand beside Mòr again. He took the rope his mentor passed him. "This must have been someone's bindings. At least one of them got their hands free."

"That's ma guess." Mòr turned back to the others. "Keep yer eyes open for any more rope. It'll tell us which way they've gone without me having to get down to search the trail. And it'll tell us how many of them freed their hands."

"Do ye think they got away?" Óg asked hopefully.

"I dinna ken," Mòr answered honestly. He and Óg remounted their horses, and the group pressed on. They found three more pieces of rope, and they felt more assured that the quartet wasn't entirely defense-less. They continued until the trail veered north. Óg maneuvered his horse next to Laird Macrae's.

"They went to yer home. Why?" Óg met the man's gaze, his boring into the laird. He didn't blink while he challenged the older man. Laird Macrae tried to shrug, but he couldn't move enough to make it the dismissive gesture he'd attempted. Unlike Harold and Stewart's assumption that merely binding their captives wrists to their saddles would be enough, none of the more sea-soned warriors were so naïve.

Not only were Lairds Macrae, Donald, and Mackin-tosh's wrists bound and tied to their saddles, rope squeezed their arms to their ribs, and their captors tied their thighs to their stirrups' leather straps. They couldn't even pick their own noses if they wanted to. And unlike Harold and Stewart's disregard for dirks hidden beneath plaids, their captors made the lairds strip off their plaids and lift their leines to reveal an ar-senal of hidden weapons. Thormud strung together their boots and hung them from his saddlebags.

"Silence is nae an answer, Artair," Liam called. "I've kenned ye since ye were suckling at yer mama's teat. I can read ye like a monk reads the Bible. Ye ken why ma granddaughter, grandson, and the Hartleys are headed to yer keep. Yer mama would be beside herself to ken ye're a part of Kyla's grandchildren's abduction. Ye ken they were close. Ma wife was at yer mama's bedside when she died."

"That doesnae mean I give a shite aboot ye or yer family. Ye're getting what ye all deserve."

"What we deserve?" Seamus rode at the opposite end of the line of prisoners from Artair Macrae. He leaned forward to see past the Mackintosh and the Donald. "We're supposed to be allies."

"Nay, we arenae. We're the Mathesons' allies. We arenae yers. I dinna give a shite aboot ye, except to say, ye're getting what ye deserve."

"And just what is that?" Óg demanded.

"A lifetime of misery. It's just a shame ye didna have the good graces to die on that field."

Óg stared at Artair. He was getting a sense of what felt off. He was certain the man played a larger role in what transpired to cause the battle than he'd revealed. When they stopped to water the horses, Óg drew Liam and Alex aside.

"Artair didna just answer Matheson's request for help. Whatever is afoot involves him beyond being an ally."

"I get the same sense." Alex leaned back to look around his father to where the captives sat upon their horses while the animals drank. They could pish themselves for all he cared.

"What's made him want us to be miserable? None of us has disagreed with his clan in ages. They've only been at odds with the Rosses because they're allied with the Mathesons, and their trouble with the Rosses came from yer trouble with them." Liam had mulled over several scenarios as they rode, but none explained the Macrae's sudden animosity. Kyla and Margaret Macrae had become close friends over the years. When Margaret fell ill at a Highland Gathering, it was Kyla who'd tended to her until she died.

"Whatever his reason, it's obvious we need to head to his keep. And I dinna think the Mackintosh or the Donald ken what's going on. They appear like they wish to distance themselves from him." Magnus had observed both lairds' attempts to steer their horses away from Artair's. They wished to give him a wide berth rather than be made guiltier by association. "I dinna think we'll ken aught more until we find Saoirse and the others."

Liam ordered everyone back to their horses, and they were soon underway again. They had an hour's ride left. It couldn't go fast enough.

Saoirse watched Louisa Matheson cross the Macraes' bailey as she hid behind Wiley. She couldn't hear what the woman said to Harold, but neither of them appeared pleased as they looked in her direction. Louisa glowered at her, so Saoirse assumed Harold informed her she and Magnus married. Louisa stalked toward her and spat at her feet.

"He kept ma dowry, then married ye." Louisa waited for Saoirse to react, but the latter's expression remained impassive. "Ye're welcome to him. He abused me."

"And ye're a liar." Saoirse's voice was clear, even though it wasn't loud. Plenty of people froze, staring at the women in horror. Saoirse sensed Louisa wasn't a welcome guest, and people had already learned to tread lightly around her.

"What did ye say?"

"Ye're a liar. I ken what really happened. I *saw* the bed frame." She had. It surprised her that no one had broken the headboard into kindling, but they had merely moved it to a storage room. A new one replaced the splintered one. She'd also seen the deep scratches in the wood floor when Magnus brushed aside the rushes. When he'd dragged the wooden piece, it permanently marred the surface.

Louisa turned red and lashed out, swinging her hand toward Saoirse's face. Wiley grabbed her wrist and forced her arm down. He leaned in and whispered. "Touch ma cousin, and I will beat ye. Today, ma Comyn side is stronger than ma Sinclair. I dinna care if I kill ye."

He wouldn't, but Louisa didn't need to know that. The force with which he held her wrist made her believe he would follow through. There would undoubtedly be a bruise, but Wiley felt no remorse. He was exhausted, injured, hungry, and beyond livid.

"Ye—ye—wouldnae."

"Ye still have a free hand. Test me and find out." Wiley towered over Louisa, who was taller than Saoirse. She fought to free her wrist as she stepped away from Wiley.

"Enough. Louisa, go inside. We will talk later." Harold stomped toward the trio. He made to grab Saoirse, but Wiley, Ric, and Kirk surrounded her.

"Where are the Macraes?" Ric demanded.

"I'm the Macraes' tánaiste." A man Kirk's or Wiley's age hurried from the keep. "What's going on?"

"Coll?" Wiley crossed his arms. "Why did Harold Matheson bring us to *yer* keep?"

The new arrival looked around. "Why did ye come here, Harold? Where's ma father and our men?"

Wiley stalked forward, his barrel chest making him an even more impressive sight than the muscular Coll. He glanced down when Coll extended his arm. Disgust marred his striking visage.

"I'm nae shaking yer arm until I ken why a Matheson brought us here after abducting us from an attack his and yer clan led. I want to ken why yer father rode out to greet us instead of helping free us."

"Ma clan? The Mathesons summoned us to help the Mackenzies against the Rosses. I dinna ken how ye're involved or why ye and Lady Saoirse are here." Coll looked at Harold and scowled. "Why did ye come here?"

"We couldnae go to Crannog. It was too close. Besides, it's where we were told to come."

"Who told ye?" Coll swept his glance around the newly arrived riders, confused and growing anxious. Whatever brought them to his home could be nothing but trouble. He'd already learned it followed Louisa everywhere. He didn't know how she was involved, but she had to be.

"Give me ma wife!"

A baritone echoed through the bailey, the sound reverberating off every building as a horse charged forward. Ric and Kirk barely stepped aside in time as Magnus's horse barreled forward. He leaned over the side and snatched Saoirse as she reached for him. He pulled her onto his lap and spun his horse around. He was back out of the gate before anyone understood what had happened.

"Magnus," Saoirse breathed, as she wrapped her arms around his neck and rested her head against his shoulder. He kept riding past those who he arrived with until they were out of anyone's earshot. When he reined in, his hands ran over her body, reassuring him-self that she was as hale as she appeared. She smattered kisses on his cheeks and neck as she clung to him. He cupped her jaw and pressed the most tender kiss imag-inable to her lips. It continued until they were breath-less. Once more, they embraced.

"*Mo sheud, mo chridhe.*" My jewel, my heart. Magnus whispered it over and over between kisses.

"I'm safe, *mo ghaol.* I'm tired and hungry, and I'm sore from the hours in the saddle, but I'm all right. They didna do aught but nae allow us off the horses. We only just arrived."

"I ken. We spotted ye in the distance. I couldnae wait to get to ye, so I rode in without the others. What happened?"

Saoirse glanced back at her extended family, who watched them but kept their distance. "Can I tell ye when I tell them? Naught happened that only ye should ken."

Magnus nodded and nudged his horse forward. But he wasn't in a hurry to share his wife with anyone, even if it was family. When they reached the others, she no-ticed how weary her father appeared. She reached for Alex as Magnus brought his horse alongside her fa-ther's. He pulled her onto his lap and nearly smothered her. Magnus's arms felt painfully empty once more, but he couldn't imagine how Alex felt. The man had com-forted him like a father, but there'd been little Alex knew to say. Magnus saw Alex with Liam. He'd watched Liam embrace his son as Alex had embraced him. He'd seen Alex's shoulders shake, so he'd given them space. He was certain the others saw it, too. None of the Sinclair men were too proud to admit their heartache.

"Da." Saoirse tried to tap her father's chest, but she

couldn't move, her arms caught between them. "Canna breathe."

Alex eased his hold, but he didn't let go. His heart felt whole again. He'd despaired that he would have to tell Brighde that something happened to their daughter.

"Lass?" Liam had dismounted and walked to Alex's horse. Saoirse slid down and into her grandfather's arms. "Ma heart is whole again." He expressed the same sentiments Alex and Magnus felt. The rest of the Sinclair men felt similarly.

"I'm all right. Wiley, Kirk, and Ric are in the bailey." Saoirse looked around and realized neither Tavish nor Tate were there. She looked toward the gate and saw into the bailey. Tavish had both his sons held against his chest. Other than the Sutherlands and Mackays, she knew no other family who were so demonstrative.

She'd heard people mock them at the Highland Gatherings, but without fail, every year, her family trounced everyone else. Everyone knew the Sinclairs often threw races to allow other clans the chance to place. But for more than two decades, the only person who could defeat Callum at knife throwing was the sister who he'd taught to wield one. Mairghread only competed with the men on occasions, but it was enough to remind everyone that they should underestimate no one in the Sinclairs.

That's why everyone sat or stood in disbelief that they'd had to chase four members of the Clan Sinclair almost the breadth of Scotland. Liam mounted his horse and maneuvered between Tristan and Hamish. Seamus was on the other side of Tristan, and Monty was beside Hamish. Saoirse accepted Magnus's help back onto his horse, and the group rode forward, the five lairds leading the way. The three captive lairds rode amongst Thormud, Wee Liam, Alec, Hamish Óg,

Blake, and Torquil. They were barely visible within the circle the six young men made.

"Da, they're hale," Tavish called as he eased his hold on his sons. He glanced at Ric and Kirk before ruffling Wiley's hair.

A crowd had gathered in the bailey as the Macraes watched the unbelievable scene unfold before them. They knew not what to make of Saoirse's and Louisa's encounter or Wiley manhandling Louisa. It stunned them to watch Ric and Kirk beat Richmond into unconsciousness. Magnus storming in like a berserker terrified them. Tavish and Tate running toward Wiley, then swallowing him in their embrace confused them. Now they watched five lairds, three of whom were earls, ride into their bailey. Gasps went through the people as they witnessed Lairds Macrae, Donald, and Mackintosh being untied from their horses and thrust forward.

"Husband?"

CHAPTER 24

The single word brought all the new arrivals to a halt. Louisa glared at Artair Macrae as people moved aside to allow the laird to walk across his own bailey.

"Wife."

The chill between them could have frozen an icicle. It was beyond frigid. Magnus and Saoirse looked at one another, uncertain what was happening. Saoirse shrugged, since this was as much news to her as it was everyone else.

"Welcome home." Louisa swept her gaze over Artair. "In disgrace."

Artair swung around and pointed at Magnus. "It's yer fault I'm saddled with this hoyden. If ye'd just fucked and married the bitch, I wouldnae have had to. Ye couldnae even die, so I could have ma retribution. Ye ruined ma life by nae just accepting her. Ye both did." He pointed his accusatory finger at Seamus next.

"Ye were responsible for Caleb and Oona trying to poison me?" Magnus's brow furrowed.

"And I paid a king's ransom for their failure."

"That's what ye meant aboot making us miserable. Ye wished to make me miserable by taking ma brother.

When that didna work, ye wished to make Magnus and the Sinclairs, who sided with him, miserable by taking ma sister-by-marriage." Seamus walked into Artair, his chest pushing the man back enough steps that he stumbled and fell backward. Coll caught his father.

"How'd ye end up married to Lady Louisa?" Saoirse asked. She'd suspected someone in the Macrae laird's family had married her, but she expected it to be Coll.

"She's carrying ma bairn. Murdoch found out."

"Ye would have cuckolded me," Magnus accused. Louisa's lip curled in disgust as she shrugged one shoulder.

"He was drunk, and I thought I was in Coll's chamber."

"What?" Coll squawked before clearing his throat. "Why the devil me? I canna stand ye, and I havenae been able to since we were children."

"But I've seen yer cock." Louisa shrugged again. "We dinna have to like one another in the dark."

"Slut." Coll turned toward Magnus. "Ye lucky bastard."

"Ye wished to kill ma husband to punish him for yer rotten choices?" Saoirse demanded.

"*Solamen miseris socios habuisse doloris.*" To the unhappy, it is a comfort to have had company in misery. Artair appeared unremorseful as he spoke the Latin proverb.

"I want to ken how ye convinced the Mathesons to help ye," Monty spoke up.

"Enough money makes most men do what ye bid. Caleb disgraced himself by bedding his wife's sister. It was easy to convince him to fake his own death. It kept Murdoch from having to punish his own nephew. I suggested it to his sister-by-marriage's husband, who was the captain of the guard."

"Where is ma brother?" Stewart Matheson stepped forward.

"Dead. He tried to run when the battle started. I ran him through," Blake spoke from beside his father. Magnus Mòr nodded.

"And Oona?" Liam asked Artair.

"Convenience. She must have been greedy, too. I didna ken who she was. I only kenned there was a woman of Matheson descent living among the Sinclairs. I sent money for Caleb to pay her. I kenned a woman could poison the bastard, and it wouldnae be as obvious as a mon running him through. When we learned Mackenzie's whore was among the men, I ordered Harold to grab her and bring her here."

Harold remained mute as he stood next to his cousin. He watched the men who'd fought his clan, but he had no intention of revealing anything. He stood with his thumbs tucked in his belt, but he showed no emotion. He had none. Perhaps annoyance, but definitely no regret.

Magnus pressed Saoirse behind him. "Ye saw what I did to Murdoch for speaking so aboot ma wife. Ye're already going to die. I'll just make it happen sooner."

"Ye canna kill me in ma own bailey."

Magnus laughed. "Challenge accepted. Single combat to the death. Ye ordered ma murder. I have the right to defend maself. I will defeat ye, auld mon."

Saoirse watched Louisa rather than any of the men. Something sparked in the woman's eyes when Magnus threatened to kill her husband. She moved around Magnus and faced Louisa. "Why does the prospect of yer husband's demise excite ye so?"

Louisa's head whipped toward Saoirse. Her upper lip curled in disgust, but just like Harold, she refused to speak. That didn't dissuade Saoirse from continuing to question her.

"Ye're as angry that ye had to marry him as he is aboot marrying ye. Except ye want yer revenge against him. Ye want yer freedom." Saoirse's chin rose as she suspected she'd deduced what happened with the clans' battle. "Ye caused the confrontation, didna ye? Harold may have spotted me and brought me here, but ye're the reason there was a battle to start with."

"If only the men were as smart as us women." Louisa cackled. "However, imagine ma surprise when ma cousin rode into ma home when he had one vera clear task, and it wasna to kidnap a woman."

"Ye dinna pay as well as yer husband." Harold broke his silence.

"What?" Artair bellowed. He darted his gaze between the cousins.

"Louisa, ye forged the missives that went to the lairds. Ye summoned them." Saoirse cocked an eyebrow as she continued.

"How'd ye guess?"

"Because ye would have kenned yer uncle's script and his alliances. Because if I were ye, that's what I would do if I wanted ma husband dead."

"Dead?" Magnus questioned from behind her.

"Och, aye. She hoped Laird Macrae would die in battle, but she didna ken it would be against the Mackenzies instead of alongside. That was the Macrae's doing, wasna it, ma laird?"

"It wasna that hard to convince Murdoch that we owed the Mackenzies retribution for breaking an alliance that would have been profitable for us. Ye were already rebuilding and growing stronger. He was angry he had to forfeit the dowry, and I was just as angry since I was stuck with her and naught to show for it. I dinna need an heir. I have one. And I certainly dinna need a daughter as useless as her mother."

"I am nae with child anymore. I didna want aught

tying me to ye after ye were supposed to be dead. After all, Coll wouldnae marry his stepmother if she gave birth to his brother or sister. Harold didna do the job I paid for."

"Marry ye? I'd rather have the French pox. I'd probably get it from ye, too." Coll turned toward Harold. "Take yer cousin with ye when ye leave."

"She's still ma wife," Artair snapped.

"She'll be yer widow when this storytelling ends," Seamus decreed. "If ma brother doesnae kill ye in single combat, then I will for yer crimes against ma clan."

"Ye dinna have the authority," Artair smirked.

"But I do," Hamish stepped forth. "Yer land is within ma earldom. Sutherland is far more than just Dunrobin. What isnae the Sinclair earldom is mine this far north in the Highlands. With nay king to take this matter before, I am the law of this land. Ye kenned I'm already allied with the Mackenzies, and ye ken our familial ties. Ye are a daft bugger to think I wouldnae wind up involved. I will allow Magnus his single combat because that's what he wishes. But it isnae necessary. I have the power to declare yer death sentence."

Saoirse wrapped her arms around Magnus's waist and tilted her head back to whisper. "Dinna fight him. I dinna doubt ye'll win, but I've already lived through kenning ye were in one battle. Ma premonition is back. It tells me something will happen to ye if ye fight him. Please."

Magnus tucked hair behind her ear and kissed her temple. "Vera well. We've been through enough. I want us away from here."

"Laird Artair Macrae, I charge and convict ye of plotting to murder Magnus Mackenzie, Clan Mackenzie's tánaiste. Lady Louisa Macrae and Harold Matheson, I charge and convict ye of plotting to murder Laird

Artair Macrae. Ye will hang from the gallows until dead. Coll, see them erected."

"What?" Louisa stormed forward, but Harold wrapped his arm around her waist and lifted her off her feet. She flailed as she spewed curses at everyone in sight.

"What of Richmond?" Saoirse pointed to the man who staggered to his feet. "He insinuated that he ordered ma kidnapping."

"I didna. Ye assumed that. But I wouldnae have stopped anyone willing to do it. At least nae before I tupped ye."

Everyone gaped at the man. He was clearly concussed because no man in his right mind would say such a vile thing before the woman's husband and nearly every male member of her family.

"Vera well," Hamish nodded. "I sentence ye to death by hanging for abetting Lady Saoirse Mackenzie's kidnapping and admitting yer intention to rape her."

Seamus gritted his teeth and sighed before he walked over to Coll. "Ye will be laird tomorrow morning. It's clear ye werenae a party to this, so I dinna hold ye to blame. But this is yer clan's only chance for forgiveness. Wrong ma family, ma clan, or me, and I will tie ye to a stake, make ye watch me tear this heap apart stone by stone, then set ye ablaze. I may have fostered with the Sinclairs, but I am still ma father's son. I dinna forgive twice, nor do I ever forget." He was nothing like his father because the man had never held a sense of family. But none of the Macraes needed to know that.

"Thank ye." Coll ran a hand through his hair and shook his head. "I canna believe any of this. I'd…" He squeezed the bridge of his nose.

"Ye'd what?"

"Since we were already allies, I'd hoped to solidify it by asking for yer cousin once removed's hand. Lacey and I met at the last Highland Gathering, and I've developed an attachment to her."

"I ken." Seamus offered nothing more as he watched the man, who would soon be his equal.

"I still wish to ask, but I'm nae so convinced as I was an hour ago that ye might say aye."

"Give it six moons. If I have nay trouble with ye, I will consider it."

"Thank ye. Please excuse me, I have—" Coll waved to the open space at the end of the bailey, "—a task." With a heavy sigh and his head hanging, he walked away. His voice carried as he ordered carpenters to come forth.

"Do ye wish to stay and witness it?" Saoirse asked Magnus.

"Nay. I trust Hamish to see it done. I want us away from here. But I also ken ye arenae up to the ride back to Eilean Donan. Ye need a bed and sleep."

"Grandda and the others still need to deal with Laird Mackintosh and Laird Donald. I dinna think they'll settle that within the next few minutes. Wiley, Kirk, and Ric need tending to. I'd feel better checking on everyone else. I dinna see aught serious on ye. I suppose we'll spend the night here."

"Aye. I dinna think there's another choice because I dinna want ye sleeping on the ground. Ye have a healthy constitution, but ye arenae accustomed to this physical rigor. I worry aboot ye, *mo chridhe*."

"I'm nay the only one who needs rest. Ye fought a battle and rode for hours after. Let me see to everyone, then I just wish to retire with ye somewhere and shut the door. I dinna want to think aboot all that ma mind still needs to work out. Macrae wishing revenge against ye for him getting Louisa with child and having to marry her. Louisa's bitterness aboot being married to the Macrae, and her plot to marry Coll. She would have likely trapped him just as she tried to trap ye. Harold was supposed to see the Macrae dead and instead took me, Wiley, Kirk, and Ric. It's too much and making ma head ache."

"Let's have everyone go inside where ye can assess them. I'll arrange for a bath and a chamber."

"Thank ye."

An hour and a half later, Saoirse and Magnus retired to a chamber. There'd been cuts and scratches for her to clean and bandage, but blessedly, no one needed stitches. She couldn't fathom how it was possible, but then Magnus reminded her of how her family fights. They finished their bath and moved before the fire. Magnus ran a comb through Saoirse's wet hair before she spun to face him.

He set aside the comb as his hands caressed her shoulders and along her chest until he cupped her breasts. He kissed each nipple before she leaned forward to snare his lips in a passionate kiss that deepened as she moved to straddle him. She pressed against his chest until he laid back. His arm wrapped around her upper back as his other hand rested heavily on her buttocks. His fingers dipped between her thighs, her dew coating them.

Magnus rolled them until Saoirse was on her back, and he could suckle her breasts. She wrapped her hand around his cock and stroked until it may as well have been a piece of steel in her hand. His forefinger and middle finger rubbed her pearl until her hips moved of their own volition.

"I'm going to make love to ye until we canna keep our eyes open."

"I confess that may nae be vera long, but I look forward to every moment. I need ye inside me, Magnus. I dinna want it slow and gentle. I want to celebrate we're alive and well. They hurt neither of us, and we'll be free of this threat come morning. I want to revel in the feel of ye and ken that I dinna have to fear ye dying."

Saoirse opened her legs, and Magnus shifted between them. He guided the tip of his rod through her netherlips, coating the head before pressing it into her sheath. Her hips tilted to accept him as he thrust into his bride. Their moves were determined and forceful as they reveled in their physical and emotional delight that they reunited and were, as they should be, in love and making love.

"I want to watch ye climax, Saoirse. I want to feel yer bliss as ye hold me within ye."

"I want to bring ye the same pleasure ye bring me. I want to share everything with ye, Magnus, including ecstasy."

They relished the moment they both felt the euphoria wash over them, clinging to each other and crying out one another's name. They didn't stop until Saoirse crested once more. They rolled over again, settling on their sides, with Saoirse's leg draped over Magnus's hip. He rocked within her, his rod remaining erect for a few more moments. They moved to the bed, and it wasn't long after that they drifted to sleep in one another's embrace. It was a different type of bliss, but one they welcomed.

Morning arrived with thunderstorms, which matched Louisa, Harold, Richmond and Artair's expressions, but no one cared but them. Saoirse remained at Magnus's side as they watched the quartet ascend the gallows' stairs. She turned away as the four bodies dropped, dangled, and jerked. But it was over as quickly as it started. She felt bad for Coll, who was left to sort out the wake of destruction his father and stepmother created. The lairds from the five allied clans decided to bring Laird Mackintosh and Laird Donald back to Eilean Donan, where they would collect their surviving clansmen and return home. Before leaving Dingwall and the Macraes, both disgraced lairds signed a truce with the Mackenzies and Rosses. Liam, Tristan, and Hamish signed as witnesses.

The large party rode away before midmorning, leaving the foul weather behind them. They rode throughout the day, but they agreed to stop for the night rather than further exhaust themselves and their mounts. They were not in the same hurry as when they traveled the other direction. Eilean Donan, on its tidal island at the confluence of Loch Long, Loch Alsh, and Loch Duich, was a welcome sight to everyone. Caroline, Lachlan, and Callen greeted them as they arrived.

Caroline flew down the keep's steps and launched herself into Seamus's arms. He chuckled as he held his wife. She cupped his face and kissed him soundly. It appeared that a few days in Saoirse and Magnus's company helped ease her reservations about public displays of affection. None of the Mackenzies took note. Apparently, propriety had only mattered to the couple.

The extended family moved inside, grateful for the servants who buzzed about with food and drink. Unlike at the Dunbeath, there was no collection of bathtubs, so it forced the men to take turns. The younger generation opted to forego hot water and went to the lochs. Magnus and Saoirse removed themselves to the garden until it was their turn to bathe.

"This is lovely," Saoirse said as she leaned forward to sniff a patch of lavender.

"It is." Magnus wasn't looking at the flora. Saoirse sensed as much and wiggled her hips. He pounced. "Dinna tempt me, wee one."

"Or what? I think I should tempt ye as ye tempt me.

Why do ye think I had to walk away?" Saoirse giggled as he kissed her neck and walked her backwards to the shady corner where they wouldn't be easily spied by anyone walking by.

"Uncle Magnus! Auntie Sersie!"

They groaned but plastered smiles on their faces as their nephew bounced toward them. Magnus lifted him and tucked him against his hip. Henry leaned toward Saoirse and kissed her cheek.

"Ye're back. Did ye come out here to swing on the rope?"

"Nay. We're waiting for our turn with the bathtub," Saoirse answered.

"Turn? Nae turns?"

Bluidy hell.

From their matching expressions, Magnus and Saoirse knew they thought the same thing.

"Our turn to have it in our chamber," Magnus explained.

"Why dinna ye go to the loch like the others, Uncle Magnus? Then Auntie Sersie could have her turn sooner."

"Yer auntie will always have a turn before me, Henry. Ye dinna put yerself first and ahead of others. We may be the laird's family, but we must always think of others before we think of ourselves, and for the men, that includes putting the ladies in our family first."

"I'm sorry, Auntie Sersie."

"It's all right. Ye're still learning. Yer Uncle Magnus is right. As the laird's family, especially for ye as his heir, we must always consider what is best for our clan before we do as we wish. It's our duty and our privilege to provide for those who depend upon us."

"Yes, Auntie."

"Do ye want to play on the rope?" Magnus sounded

hopeful, making Saoirse smother her smile. She knew the boy's answer before he said.

"Aye! I canna wait to see how high ye push me this time."

Magnus's eyes widened as he glanced at Saoirse in horror. He thought the child would take himself off to play. She laughed and walked to the orchard, knowing her husband and nephew were close behind. The couple spent the next hour playing with Henry, and they both daydreamed about when they would play with their own child. By the time Caroline came to tell them their bath was ready, they were practically tearing the clothes from one another as they raced up the stairs. They remained secluded in their chamber until the next morning when everyone departed for Dunbeath, except the Rosses. Monty and Donan decided to make a detour and travel south to visit Laurel and her Campbell family.

As they approached Dunbeath after days on the road, Saoirse recognized two heads of white-blonde hair standing on the battlements. Brighde stood with Isabella as they awaited their family's return. Near them, she spied Deirdre's honey-colored spiral curls, Siùsan's strawberry-blonde waves, and Ceit's coppery-brown locks. Near Deirdre was a head of deep brown, almost black hair, and Saoirse realized it was Cerys. All the women awaited their husbands' arrival. She shifted her attention to Liam and watched her grandfather. She wondered if it saddened him to know he was not returning to a wife. Her grandmother had been dead nearly thirty years, but she knew Liam remembered her as though she were still at his side.

She maneuvered her horse next to grandfather's as the others raced forward, eager to return home and reunite with their family. Magnus's brow furrowed, but he let the others pass them too, until he realized what

Saoirse was doing. When she came alongside Liam, she heard him whispering.

"We're home, *mo ghràidh*. We're all here where we belong. Ye watched over us as I kenned ye would. Ma angel among the stars. Thank ye, Kyla. I couldnae have borne this without ye. I love ye, little one."

Saoirse regretted her intrusion, and it embarrassed her that she overheard such a private moment. But Liam reached out his hand to her and squeezed when she put hers in his.

"Ye are so much like yer grandmama. She had the silent strength ye do. She had the kindest heart and enjoyed healing others. But she was a formidable woman once she came into her own. I see all of that in ye. I'm so proud of ye, *leannan*."

"Do ye really think Grandmama is watching over us?"

"Without a doubt. She's been beside me since the day we met. Even if we canna see her, and I canna hold her anymore, she's guided this clan and protected us all. She's our angel." Liam glanced heavenward and smiled. He swallowed several times before he looked at Saoirse. She looked nothing like Kyla, instead a replica of her mother, except for her eyes. But she was Kyla's kindred spirit. He saw a bit of Kyla in every member of his family, especially Mairghread, who looked so much like her. It was these qualities that reminded him that his beloved was never far from them.

Saoirse thought it was a lovely sentiment as she turned to look at Magnus. He nodded and smiled. He'd heard the stories about Kyla while he'd fostered with the Sinclairs. He felt like he knew the woman even though she'd died years before he arrived.

"Saoirse!" Brighde flew down the stairs and into the bailey as the last three riders entered. Alex was behind her, having taken the steps two and three at a time, nearly knocking Tavish down them in his hurry to reach Brighde. All four of the brothers had raced to greet their wives, Blake appearing to straggle behind the older men as he tried to keep up with his father and uncles. Ric knew better and had run to a different set of steps that no one else used. He raced along the wall walk and reached Isabella the same time as the brothers did their wives after jostling and elbowing their way up.

Saoirse swung down from her horse and landed in her mother's arms. They clung to each other as more people filled the bailey. It was a time of joyous welcomes, mothers and daughters hugging their fathers, husbands, and brothers. Nessa and Mirren soon joined them, and Saoirse breathed easier. But as she pulled away and spotted Seamus, Caroline, and their children standing with Liam and Hamish, she remembered Dunbeath wasn't her home anymore.

"It'll always be here whenever ye wish to visit." Magnus whispered from behind her, having read the flash of sadness when she looked around. She nodded as she took his hand and walked inside.

The celebration continued for a fortnight. Amelia, Arabella, Gavin, and Alasdair arrived three days after they returned. A contingent of Sutherland guards rode to Dunrobin and brought them back. Maude, Hamish and Amelia's older daughter, arrived with her husband, Kieran, and their children Amy, Graham, and Mairi. Along their way from the Isle of Lewis, Mairghread and Wee Liam's wife, Elene, joined them. Blair, Hamish and Amelia's younger daughter, arrived with her husband, Hardi. Their children, Tira, Dougal, and Finnian, rode between their parents.

Saoirse had grown worried that Magnus would feel left out with only Seamus and Siùsan as his blood relatives. It relieved her to see the MacLeods of Assynt arrive with their distant relatives the MacLeods of Lewis. While Magnus and Seamus were still estranged from their mother and Gunn relatives, Catriona MacLeod of Assynt was their mother's cousin. She'd done much over the years to help repair the rift between the Mac-Leods and the Mackenzies. It wasn't a close relationship, except at family gatherings. Catriona and Torrian arrived with their sons Michail, Adan, and Edward, and their wives and children. Michail was married to Isabella's sister Blythe. It was as much an excuse for the sisters to visit as it was to celebrate Magnus and Saoirse's wedding. No one invited anyone from the Gunns, and they knew none would have shown up if they had.

Ten days into the fortnight long celebration that included the warriors' return and the families arriving, Saoirse and Magnus stood at the steps of Dunbeath's kirk. Sunset cast soft light on Saoirse's hair, making it glow like a halo. With Magnus's Mackenzie plaid wrapped around their wrists, they recited their official vows, binding them in the holy sacrament. The happy couple had eyes only for each other. Neither had a memory of the wedding Mass, only recalling exchanging their vows before their loved ones and the Clan Sinclair. They were fulfilling a legacy that Liam and Kyla began on those steps more than forty years earlier. It had only gotten stronger as each of the five Sinclair siblings married and built their families, following in their parents' footsteps of unconditional love and loyalty. Now the younger generation was taking up the mantle. While the sun grew weaker as they celebrated with a feast in the Great Hall, the brilliance of the clans' devotion to each other grew stronger.

EPILOGUE

"Could ye stop? I shall fall in." Magnus chuckled as Saoirse yanked his belt from his waist as they stood on the narrow ledge within the sea cave. They'd escaped the crowded keep as another of Liam's great-grandchildren prepared to marry the next day. They'd come with their family, just as they had for so many holidays and family events over the past thirty years.

"We dinna have that much time. Ye move as slowly as an auld mon. I ken ye arenae because ye wouldnae let me out of bed this morning. Ye're still as randy as a goat."

"And whose idea was it to slip down here for a tryst, wee one? I seem to recall someone saying that a wedding at Dunbeath wasna a real one unless we celebrated our handfast again."

"Wheest. Undress as ye talk." Saoirse whipped her kirtle over her head and squealed as Magnus's mouth latched onto one of her breasts before the gown hit the ground. Neither looked the same as they had all those years ago. Lines marked Saoirse's belly, a testimony to the five children they'd created and raised. Gray hair had taken the place of Magnus's dark locks. Both had lines around their mouths and eyes, but they were from a lifetime of laughter and love.

"Ye're as bonnie as the day I first made love to ye here." Magnus lifted Saoirse, and she wrapped her legs around his waist before he waded into the subterranean pool. They sighed as the warm water from the natural spring enveloped them, but they watched as the waves crashed against the rocks outside the cave's mouth. But it wasn't long before their attention centered on one another. Their kisses grew heated as their hands roamed one another's bodies. They'd memorized each inch, but they both still delighted in the feel of their partner.

Saoirse lifted her hips until Magnus's sword aligned with her sheath. She moved tantalizingly slowly as she slid down his length. He teased her by keeping his thrusts shallow. But as usually happened, their patience snapped, and their need consumed them. They moved together as the water swirled around them, still as erotic as the first time they joined in the pool.

"I love ye, *mo ghaol*," Magnus whispered. "As much as the day a woodland nymph greeted me at the gates and stole ma heart."

"I remember an Adonis riding toward me, who then carried a basket of flowers for me. I didna ken then that ye would be ma partner in this lifetime and the next, but it didna take me long to realize. I love ye, *mo ghràidh*."

They brought each other to the peak, paused while they savored the moment, then leaped into bliss together. They'd perfected their climb to their summit over the years, reaching the peak together. Once they recovered from the descent, they accepted they couldn't linger any longer. They dressed and returned to the beach. As they put their shoes back on, they noticed another couple straightening their clothes as they stepped around a boulder at the far end of the beach.

"Ye're as bad as we are, Rose Kyla!" Saoirse called out to her cousin, who looked unabashedly ravished. Her husband smoothed his hair as Magnus adjusted his plaid. The two couples made their way back to the keep, neither caring when their children spied them and rolled their eyes. Magnus swept Saoirse into his arms and carried her inside.

"I think ye need a bath to wash away all that saltwater, ma bonnie bride."

"Will ye scrub ma back, husband?"

"I'll do more than that. I promise ye that, wee one."

"I shall hold ye to it."

The couple's jesting innuendoes continued as they locked themselves behind their chamber door, not to be seen again until morning.

Celeste Barclay, a nom de plume, lives near the Southern California coast with her husband and sons. Growing up in the Midwest, Celeste enjoyed spending as much time in and on the water as she could. Now she lives near the beach. She's an avid swimmer, a hopeful future surfer, and a former rower. When she's not writing, she's working or being a mom.

Subscribe to Celeste's bimonthly newsletter to receive exclusive insider perks.
Subscribe Now

www.celestebarclay.com

Join the fun and get exclusive insider giveaways, sneak peeks, and new release announcements in
Celeste Barclay's Facebook Ladies of Yore Group

THE HIGHLAND LADIES

A Spinster at the Highland Court
BOOK 1 SNEAK PEEK

Elizabeth Fraser looked around the royal chapel within Stirling Castle. The ornate candlestick holders on the altar glistened and reflected the light from the ones in the wall sconces as the priest intoned the holy prayers of the Advent season. Elizabeth kept her head bowed as though in prayer, but her green eyes swept the congregation. She watched the other ladies-in-waiting, many of whom were doing the same thing. She caught the eye of Allyson Elliott. Elizabeth raised one eyebrow as Allyson's lips twitched. Both women had been there enough times to accept they'd be kneeling for at least the next hour as the Latin service carried on. Elizabeth understood the Mass thanks to her cousin Deirdre Fraser, or rather now Deirdre Sinclair. Elizabeth's mind flashed to the recent struggle her cousin faced as she reunited with her husband Magnus after a seven-year separation. Her aunt and uncle's choice to keep Deirdre hidden from her husband simply because they didn't think the Sinclairs were an advantageous enough match, and the resulting scandal, still humiliated the other Fraser clan members at court. She admired Deirdre's husband Magnus's pledge to remain faithful despite not knowing if he'd ever see Deirdre again.

Elizabeth suddenly snapped her attention; while everyone else intoned the twelfth—or was it thirteenth—amen of the Mass, the hairs on the back of her neck stood up. She had the strongest feeling that someone was watching her. Her eyes scanned to her right, where her parents sat further down the pew. Her mother and father had their heads bowed and eyes closed. While she was convinced her mother was in devout prayer, she wondered if her father had fallen asleep during the Mass. Again. With nothing seeming out of the ordinary and no one visibly paying attention to her, her eyes swung to the left. She took in the king and queen as they kneeled together at their prie-dieu. The queen's lips moved as she recited the liturgy in silence. The king was as still as a statue. Years of leading warriors showed, both in his stature and his ability to control his body into absolute stillness. Elizabeth peered past the royal couple and found herself looking into the astute hazel eyes of Edward Bruce, Lord of Badenoch and Lochaber. His gaze gave her the sense that he peered into her thoughts, as though he were assessing her. She tried to keep her face neutral as heat surged up her neck. She prayed her face didn't redden as much as her neck must have, but at a twenty-one, she still hadn't mastered how to control her blushing. Her nape burned like it was on fire. She canted her head slightly before looking up at the crucifix hanging over the altar. She closed her eyes and tried to invoke the image of the Lord that usually centered her when her mind wandered during Mass.

Elizabeth sensed Edward's gaze remained on her. She didn't understand how she was so sure that he was looking at her. She didn't have any special gifts of perception or sight, but her intuition screamed that he was still looking.

A Spy at the Highland Court **BOOK 2**

A Wallflower at the Highland Court **BOOK 3**

A Rogue at the Highland Court **BOOK 4**

A Rake at the Highland Court **BOOK 5**

An Enemy at the Highland Court **BOOK 6**

A Saint at the Highland Court **BOOK 7**

A Beauty at the Highland Court **BOOK 8**

A Sinner at the Highland Court **BOOK 9**

A Hellion at the Highland Court **BOOK 10**

An Angel at the Highland Court **BOOK 11**

A Harlot at the Highland Court **BOOK 12**

A Friend at the Highland Court **BOOK 13**

An Outsider at the Highland Court **BOOK 14**

A Devil at the Highland Court **BOOK 15**

THE CLAN SINCLAIR LEGACY

Highland Lion
Highland Bear
Highland Jewel

THE CLAN SINCLAIR

His Highland Lass **BOOK 1 SNEAK PEEK**

She entered the great hall like a strong spring storm in the northern most Highlands. Tristan Mackay felt like he had been blown hither and yon. As the storm settled, she left him with the sweet scents of heather and lavender wafting towards him as she approached. She was not a classic beauty, tall and willowy like the women at court. Her face and form were not what legends were made of. But she held a unique appeal unlike any he had seen before. He could not take his eyes off of her long chestnut hair that had strands of fire and burnt copper running through them. Unlike the waves or curls he was used to, her hair was unusually straight and fine. It looked like a waterfall cascading down her back. While she was not tall, neither was she short. She had a figure that was meant for a man to grasp and hold onto, whether from the front or from behind. She had an aura of confidence and charm, but not arrogance or conceit like many good looking women he had met. She did not seem to know her own appeal. He could tell that she was many things, but one thing she was not was his.

His Bonnie Highland Temptation **BOOK 2**

His Highland Prize **BOOK 3**

His Highland Pledge **BOOK 4**

His Highland Surprise **BOOK 5**

Their Highland Beginning **BOOK 6**

The Blond Devil of the Sea **BOOK 1 SNEAK PEEK**

Caragh lifted her torch into the air as she made her way down the precarious Cornish cliffside. She made out the hulking shape of a ship, but the dead of night made it impossible to see who was there. She and the fishermen of Bedruthan Steps weren't expecting any shipments that night. But her younger brother Eddie, who stood watch at the entrance to their hiding place, had spotted the ship and signaled up to the village watchman, who alerted Caragh.

As her boot slid along the dirt and sand, she cursed having to carry the torch and wished she could have sunlight to guide her. She knew these cliffs well, and it was for that reason it was better that she moved slowly than stop moving once and for all. Caragh feared the light from her torch would carry out to the boat. Despite her efforts to keep the flame small, the solitary light would be a beacon.

When Caragh came to the final twist in the path before the sand, she snuffed out her torch and started to run to the cave where the main source of the village's income lay in hiding. She heard movement along the trail above her head and knew the local fishermen would soon join her on the beach. These men, both young and old, were strong from days spent pulling in the full trawling nets and hoisting the larger catches onto their boats. However, these men weren't well-trained swordsmen, and the fear of pirate raids was ever-present. Caragh feared that was who the villagers would face that night.

The Dark Heart of the Sea **BOOK 2**
The Red Drifter of the Sea **BOOK3**
The Scarlet Blade of the Sea **BOOK 4**

VIKING GLORY

Leif **BOOK 1 SNEAK PEEK**

Leif looked around his chambers within his father's longhouse and breathed a sigh of relief. He noticed the large fur rugs spread throughout the chamber. His two favorites placed strategically before the fire and the bedside he preferred. He looked at his shield that hung on the wall near the door in a symbolic position but waiting at the ready. The chests that held his clothes and some of his finer acquisitions from voyages near and far sat beside his bed and along the far wall. And in the center was his most favorite possession. His oversized bed was one of the few that could accommodate his long and broad frame. He shook his head at his longing to climb under the pile of furs and on the stuffed mattress that beckoned him. He took in the chair placed before the fire where he longed to sit now with a cup of warm mead. It had been two months since he slept in his own bed, and he looked forward to nothing more than pulling the furs over his head and sleeping until he could no longer ignore his hunger. Alas, he would not be crawling into his bed again for several more hours. A feast awaited him to celebrate his and his crew's return from their latest expedition to explore the isle of Britannia. He bathed and wore fresh clothes, so he had no excuse for lingering other than a bone weariness that set in during the last storm at sea. He was eager to spend time at home no matter how much he loved sailing. Their last expedition had been profitable with several raids of monasteries that yielded jewels and both silver and gold, but he was ready for respite.

Leif left his chambers and knocked on the door next to his. He heard movement on the other side, but it was only moments before his sister, Freya, opened her door. She, too, looked tired but clean. A few pieces of jewelry she confiscated from the holy houses that allegedly swore to a life of poverty and deprivation adorned her trim frame.

"That armband suits you well. It compliments your muscles," Leif smirked and dodged a strike from one of those muscular arms.

Only a year younger than he, his sister was a well-known and feared shield maiden. Her lithe form was strong and agile making her a ferocious and competent opponent to any man. Freya's beauty was stunning, but Leif had taken every opportunity since they were children to tease her about her unusual strength even among the female warriors.

"At least one of us inherited our father's prowess. Such a shame it wasn't you."

Freya **BOOK 2**

Tyra & Bjorn **BOOK 3**

Strian **VIKING GLORY BOOK 4**

Lena & Ivar **VIKING GLORY BOOK 5**